THE FOUR STAGES OF CRUELTY

THE FOUR STAGES OF CRUELTY

KEITH HOLLIHAN

THOMAS DUNNE BOOKS
St. Martin's Press New York

This is a work of fiction. All of the characters, organizations, and events portrayed in this novel are either products of the author's imagination or are used fictitiously.

THOMAS DUNNE BOOKS.
An imprint of St. Martin's Press.

www.thomasdunnebooks.com
www.stmartins.com

Design by Kathryn Parise

ISBN 978-0-312-59247-9

First Edition: December 2010

10 9 8 7 6 5 4 3 2 1

This novel is dedicated to the memory of two good fathers,
P. G. Hollihan and Fred Williams.
Wish you could have seen it.

Die, dear, that I may love you;
Live, and be my foe.

—Nikos Kazantzakis

God has undertaken a plan: it is a daring and risky plan, involving God in so much ambiguity—one might almost say subterfuge—that he begins to look like a double agent, becoming compromised at many points in order to pull off the solution.

—N. T. Wright

THE FOUR STAGES OF CRUELTY

| | | | | | | | | | | | | |

Let's say your name is Joshua. You're eighteen years old, a quiet student who likes to draw and an otherwise normal person, but you're going out of your mind because your ex-girlfriend won't talk to you anymore and has been hooking up with another guy. You know her parents are out of town and you know she's with him in her living room right now, lying on the couch, shirt off, jeans unzipped, because that's exactly what you would have been doing with her on a Friday night a month or so before. You take your father's gun because you want her to know how painful it feels and how far you'd go to get her back. But when you're finally there, standing in the middle of the living room, nothing works out the way you'd planned. Not that you had any plans. The girlfriend, you realize, is no longer your girlfriend. She's screaming at you to get out, and there's a look in her eyes that doesn't fit with the way you feel. Meanwhile, her new boyfriend has decided to go all Rambo. It gets crazy. You're both fighting over the gun like it's a live snake, and it's pointing this way and that. You just want to get a firm hold on it, put it away, and go home. But Rambo won't let go.

And then he does, and you're both out of breath, and all the emotions have drained away, and you just leave. You drive home, numb and shaky, praying no one calls the cops or your parents. You're terrified for a month and ashamed for about a year. You bounce back a little in your second year of college and switch majors, dropping pre-medicine to work on a degree in psychology with as many fine art classes as you can squeeze in. Once in a while you think about that Friday night. You even gain some perspective on it. In one of your classes, you read some statistics about violent crimes and young males. It's practically an epidemic, except no one acknowledges it. At seventeen to twenty, the human brain isn't developed enough to fully distinguish right from wrong, reality from fantasy, but the young male has all this emotion and power and little ability to express it except through physical violence or acts of self-destruction. That's how soldiers and suicide bombers get recruited. Sitting there in the library, drawing pictures of her along the margins of your notebook, you think about that gun and what it felt like holding it, and how it slipped around in your hands when you were fighting, and how goddamn scary those few seconds of uncertainty were. And you put down your pen, cover up the drawing, and thank God that nothing bad really happened.

Now, let's say the gun went off.

STAGE I

1 ||||||||||||||

I can think of no gentle way to begin.

I need to explain why the biggest mystery for me was not how an inmate could go missing inside a maximum security penitentiary, nor what the drawings meant, or even who was involved in the murders. The thing that stays with me, like the memory of a limb now gone, is the mystery of human compassion. The twisted variations of it, the love and the hurt, the obsession and the neglect, the abuse and the need, all commingled and bound. Although I am as cynical and skeptical as can be expected, given my experience, I am not one to deny that genuine relationships can form between inmates and corrections officers. I do know, however, that those relationships are almost universally based on some form of trade, a commerce of getting by. You need them as much as they need you, and I will admit that debts accumulate and sometimes must be paid off in ways that compromise what you think is right. This can happen to any of us.

My name is Kali Williams. I doubt that my parents, when they changed a few letters in the more conventionally spelled Kaylee, knew they were naming me after the many-armed Hindu goddess of darkness and destruction. But out of that dull midwestern instinct to be safe but slightly different, I sprang: a personality of sharp edges and bruising elbows.

If this were just a story about Ditmarsh Penitentiary and my work within it, I would probably start by discussing the routine and even the incidentally interesting aspect of being a thirty-nine-year-old female—one of only 26 women on a corrections staff of 312—providing daily operational security over 950 (plus or minus) hard-core assholes, sex offenders, addicts, liars, serial felons, white-collar dick suckers, gangbangers, and relatively honest murderers. I enjoyed my job. I liked the bang and clang of the cellblocks, the armored ease you needed to show in getting by, the acute attention to psychology and mood. For the most part, the bullshit bounced off me, the rat-a-tat routine of jokes and looks, the subtle grind of male criticism disguised half-assedly as helpfulness. I never questioned the right and wrong of the work—it was pretty goddamn clear to me, and still is—but there were times when I got stuck wondering how I'd become this person who wore the belt and jangled the keys and relied on the way the quick decisions got backed up by the remorseless rules. Nothing good came of those moods, however, and I avoided them as much as possible. I have an irritable impatience for the overly steeped, self-pitying emotions of anyone with too much time on their hands, including, and perhaps especially, myself.

This is not about my job, though, or about me; it's about what happened, and all those mysteries I mentioned, and the mystery of compassion most of all. Even when I found the body dangling from a door in the abandoned cells beneath the prison, so terribly abused, it was the absence of compassion, the lack of pity in the place, that hit me hardest. Though surrounded by the dark output of violent lives, I had never before seen the ravages of such unrestrained brutality. I forced myself to edge past, pressing up against the cold wall where the scrawled drawings were most tangled, in order to see the face. In that dead gaze, was I the delayed rescuer or another tormenter? I'm not sure I can answer without sorting through the events that led up to it. As I said, I can think of no gentle way to begin.

2

I liked the in-between times, too. It was the illusion of control, the condensed privacy. The post-dinner lull was a favorite of mine, a period in which inmate frustrations seemed to ebb and alpha energy got transferred into focused tasks. Even in the winter I often crossed the yard when I moved from building to building, avoiding the tunnels just to take it in. The cell lights showed narrow slashes in the granite, like countless white crosses in a military cemetery. In the mess hall, you knew the born-agains were with group. In the gym, the squeak and snap of basketball. In the library, the amateur lawyers searched for precedents like paleontologists dusting off dirt-covered rocks. In their cells, the book readers flipped pages of dog-eared mysteries, hoping the endings hadn't been ripped out. At key-up, when we sealed the cells and locked the blocks, the inmates got restless and edgy again, but after midnight, those who weren't asleep wanted to be alone, and that suited us fine. All the innocence held until an hour before breakfast, when a sizable minority woke and did whatever exercises, prayers, or self-abuse rituals their OCD fixes demanded. By that time their brains were stirring and they had plans or worries or irritations to ponder, and for those of us who watched them, that was the beginning of another shit day.

Joshua Riff was an in-between kind of inmate. The first time I met him, I came in three hours prior to shift change, just after four in the morning, to wake him up in his cell. Most inmates jump long before you key, but Josh was still a puppy, a pale-skinned nineteen-year-old with wispy chin whiskers and sleepy eyes, sporting bed wood and mussed-up hair, a delinquent little brother late for school.

His cell was a dump. The typical inmate keeps a tight drum, even if it's overflowing with stuff, but Josh had scattered his belongings everywhere without organization—wet towel, dirty socks, one shoe flopped over, the other climbing the wall. He didn't have much, and he lacked the electronic amenities, visual distractions, and cardboard shelving units of a resourceful inmate, but if this were general population, someone would have rapped his head against the wall hard and forced him to tidy up his moldy shit.

Josh was not housed in a normal range, however, but in the Ditmarsh infirmary, or what we called the howler ward. It was a storage house for misfits—the injured, seriously ill, and not-all-there. I'd probably passed his cell a hundred times and never looked in. Like most COs, I didn't give the howlers and cripples and AIDS carriers much thought; it wasn't contempt so much as indifference to anyone who was too vulnerable to pose a threat or too weak to command attention. When Keeper Wallace told me where Riff was located, I made the quick assumption that my new friend was bugged up or self-injurious. He seemed utterly normal to me now, and that put another irritant into my brain, making me wonder why he wasn't shelved in gen pop like the other inmates. He was young and soft, but that shouldn't have made a difference—the cubs got tossed in with the wolves. So why the special treatment? Nothing pisses me off more sharply than unearned privilege, and I was already confused about the strange and unusual task I had been given.

It was not a good day for Josh either.

"Why?" he asked in a low, sleepy voice.

"Why do you think?" I answered just as quietly, and told him to suit up.

I could see the memory pass over him in the grim, stilted way he got dressed. His father's funeral, and me his reluctant escort. I'd delivered inmates to court or the hospital before, and once to a school, but never in the middle of the night without paperwork, assistance, or formal permission, and never with the strongly worded advice to remain discreet about what was going on. I should have asked why. I should have mentioned that a pile of rules were being violated and a stack of lies were being told. But I kept thinking, what good would that do me against Keeper Wallace? Whistleblowers never won out, they just got the hurt.

Josh avoided glancing at me as we walked. I figured he was probably rattled by the whole father funeral thing, and the less we said to each other over the course of the day, the better we'd both bear up. I brought him down the darkened stairwell of the infirmary and through the tunnel into the main hub. He looked up and around like a nervous tourist passing through. The hub was the focal point of the entire prison, the center space from which the four cellblocks, the education wing, and Keeper's Hall stretched out. When empty, it had a vacant stadium feel. At ground level, squatting in the exact middle was the bubble—the caged, bulletproof-glass central control space for guards, equipped with closed-circuit television monitors scanning every cellblock and most of the hallways and access points. Below the bubble was the armaments room—where wistful COs went to fondle the weapons they could not carry—and deeper still the old isolation range we called the City, our medieval dungeon, our prison within a prison, welded shut these past five years in accordance with the kinder, gentler approach of the current administration.

Six stories above, a full two stories beyond the four levels of cellblocks, was the glass dome. At night it reflected a muted glow that turned the entire hub into a dimly lit cathedral, while in the day, it was the world's strangest greenhouse, the sun grinding through hundreds of years of dirt. It must have cost a fortune when it was built, and it must have seen a hundred thousand inmates and COs wasting their lives below. And for what? Once upon a time, the architects and builders had believed that inspiration for reform would come from the contemplation of God, visible no doubt through that far aperture. The hub-and-spoke system, with its stacked tiers of narrow cells lit by high windows, was made purposely cramped and austere in order to restrict activity and encourage spiritual reflection, a miscalculation regarding the true nature of human psychology that only got more ridiculous as the years went on. Reform was a hopeless dream, I believed. You could restrict what inmates did, but you could never restrict what they thought—and what they thought about practically all the time was doing bad. Instead of dreams about the higher power, most people inside—COs and inmates alike—spent their mental energy calculating the power at hand, mixing it with thoughts about survival, making money, or getting some kind of sexual gratification or substance abuse in before the day was done. The rest was filler, the measly stuff of thwarted lives.

I avoided Keeper's Hall, where night shift COs might be doing paperwork, and we crossed the second yard outside. The cold air bit our skin. The ground was barren and snow free, but it crunched, the kind of early December morning that makes you long like a pagan for the summer sun to rise. Inside the front gate, Keeper Wallace stood behind the admittance counter all alone, waiting for us. He was flipping paper when we arrived, checking through old admittance reports, never a wasted moment for those thick, short-fingered hands. When he looked up, a tweak of guilt hit me, despite the righteousness that stiffened my spine.

I had admired him once, and that was the problem. There were four other keepers on staff—that's what we called our supervising COs—and all were of equal rank and similar seniority, but it was clear by the flow of decisions and the command he imposed that Wallace had the most authority at the field level. From the beginning I was drawn to his detailed knowledge and his understated character and above all his severe and never-wavering competence, a professional code surprisingly rare in an institution of vigilant discipline. In my way, without being obvious about it, I'd modeled my own conduct as a CO on his, disdaining the slackness and the easy corruption I saw around me on a routine basis. I'd assumed that a supervisor like Wallace would notice such adherence. But my first two years on the job warranted no special attention or approval apparently, and the respect I felt for him drained away when my application for URF duty got turned down with his signature.

The Urgent Response Force was a kind of SWAT team of elite COs called to task during prolonged or particularly dangerous emergency situations. I had wanted in for a number of reasons. The money appealed—an extra fifteen to twenty thousand a year. The toughness appealed—even the name sounded hard, the exhale made when baton met belly. And the bullet point on the résumé was the kicker. Maybe, just maybe, I could impress some federal law enforcement agency with a few years doing serious tactical work as a corrections officer. This late bloomer wanted to go places.

Despite my solid test scores, Wallace denied my application without any adequate explanation. Maybe I hadn't paid my dues. Maybe I wasn't connected to the right people. But I'd followed the rules and been turned down, so I filed a successful grievance, using gender to force my way into a club that didn't want me. To my paranoid eye, the assignment with Josh smacked of revenge, a trick to catch me out. Wallace had asked me to do it as a favor. He'd told me that because I'd lost my own father a few months before, I'd be suitable for the role, more sensitive in my handling of a social

situation. But I did not believe him. We did not think of inm
terms. When an incident of violence occurred somewhere inside th
one of the first questions we asked was, "Any humans involved?"—meaning any COs, even any civilians. The emotional well-being of an inmate was not our first, second, or third priority, and Wallace was no different in that regard from anyone else.

We exchanged good-mornings. Wallace didn't thank me or indicate through any shared glance or hurried movement that what we were doing was out of the ordinary. I'd been curious about who would be on shift at the gate, because I figured that would allow me to meet one of his cronies, someone else who did his bidding when the work was off-the-record. I wanted to see whether my fellow CO was sheepish or brazen about it and to get a little more insight into the way Wallace operated and what it cost and what it provided. Seeing the Keeper alone made my stomach twist a little bit more. Either this outing was so wrong he didn't want to involve anyone else, or no one else had been willing to attach themselves to the deed.

Instead, ever efficient and grim, Wallace told Josh to shackle up, and Josh held out his hands for his three-piece suit—the metal bracelets and taut chain looping his ankles, waist, and wrists.

When Wallace stood straight again, he grimaced, as though the bending over had bothered an already tight back. Then he spoke.

"You've got a day pass," he told Josh. "You've got a medical condition requiring a CT scan. You're getting the scan done at the veterans hospital. Officer Williams is your escort. There was another CO along for the ride, but you don't remember his name. I hope you'll remember that story without embellishments. It's for your own well-being as much as anything else."

I was rattled to hear the lie so openly blueprinted. Josh gave an inarticulate teenager nod, the kind you never quite trust, and Wallace turned to me and said thank you. This time I detected a flimsy gratitude in the sagging lines of his face. I gave my own inarticulate nod in return.

3

Josh was my property now, so I checked his bracelets and gave his chain a couple of quick jerks to make sure they were fastened, even though the Keeper had done the snapping himself. Then I directed Josh to the door with a little more force and spite than necessary. He almost tripped at the first few steps; then he remembered how to do it. You cup your hands near your groin, crouch so that your back is hunched and the vertical chain is slackened, and take high-speed baby steps to keep the ankle chain from striking taut. They call it the shackle shuffle, and it makes you move like a bitch.

A brown sedan was waiting at the curb edge. Wallace had lent me his car so I wouldn't have to pay for the miles. Josh sat in back on the right so I could keep an eye on him, like a child in a car seat, but he was so meek and glum I had to remind myself to keep a steady awareness. He turned rather suddenly as we pulled onto the old post road, and I realized he was looking back at Ditmarsh. The high walls were spotlighted but otherwise dim and hard to make out, but the dome was glowing like an orb. I bet he was thinking it should have been a lot longer before he saw the outside of that house, and I bet he was hoping without hope it would be a lot longer before he saw it again. Then it was all silence along the highway, my directions spread out beside me.

I typically tried not to converse at any length with inmates—it made the job easier when you saw through every attempt at banter or connection like it was one more grift or lie—but the holdout got harder as the day went on and on.

We hit the Super 8 motel first, and I parked next to the room door and walked Josh out. His mother opened the door and met us, hugged him, and thanked me. She was older than I expected.

"Please come in," she offered—as if there were any other way this was going to play out.

I showed appreciation for her kind hospitality, and we occupied the room like members of the same family, barely enough space in and around the twin beds to avoid one another's limbs. I unshackled Josh more gently than I had handled him before, and he looked at me for instructions.

Mrs. Riff took over. "Your suit's hanging on the bathroom door hook. I turned the shower on to steam the wrinkles out."

"Is that okay?" he asked me, and only moved after I gave my assent. I'm sure it was strange for his mother to see that.

Josh went into the bathroom. I wished the TV was on, a blast of Fox News to smother the uncomfortable hush. I could smell Mrs. Riff's perfume over the staleness of industrial carpet and bedspread fabric. Distracted by other thoughts, she put on a watch and some rings, and touched her hair awkwardly, like someone newly blind. There was a pinkness to her cheeks that did not look healthy. When she noticed me again, she seemed almost startled by my presence in the room, so I told her I was very sorry for her loss, but in such a stiff and trite way I probably came across more uniform than human. She nodded in acknowledgment and looked down at her lap, her mouth tight with irritation. The vibe I got was that at some level, below the politeness and the prim dignity, she nurtured a little spark of hate, and held me, and those like me, responsible for everything bad that had happened to her precious boy. While this pissed me off, it also settled my own anxiety and gave me a nice sense of distance from her concerns. I did not want to get personal, and the wretched scene was already too social worker by far.

When Josh came out wearing an off-the-rack black suit, his mother fussed with it until she was satisfied, and then they forgot about me and sat on the edge of the bed and talked. I removed myself to the deepest corner of the room and did a good job of keeping my ears shut, even though it was impossible not to absorb the long pauses and sniffs, the unspeakably hesitant touches of sleeves and shoulders, as though real contact was as forbidden as it would have been in the VnC room. Josh was hunched over and twisted away like someone hiding from a physical blow. Mrs. Riff looked at the tissue in her palm. Tough haul, I thought, but then again, those are the dividends you earn serving a major bit in a maximum security penitentiary. Lost birthdays, missed weddings, whole lives. Any sympathy I felt always curdled a little when I thought about the reasons they were inside in the first place. I did not know what Josh had done, but it had to be something nasty, horrific, or repeated to end up at Ditmarsh.

When it was time to go, I didn't put the shackles back on, but used the plastic zip cuffs instead, practically invisible if Josh kept his hands clasped and those overly long sleeves extended. Of course it was ridiculous to feel as though he were less an escape threat in his civilian suit than he had been in his orange smocks, but it seemed obscene to send him to the funeral in chains. Mrs. Riff took her own car, and we followed close behind. They walked into the funeral home together, me hovering in the near background. Casket open. A waxy, sharp-nosed face fixed in stern bewilderment. That cloistered, stuffy room. All kinds of memories for me, my own father's death so recent. I counted seven mourners total, and one of them might have been an employee of the funeral home. Part of me was relieved; the fewer who knew about this craziness, the better. I wondered if it had been arranged that way, in which case the paltry attendance seemed another sacrifice that might have made a prodigal son's shame even harder.

Once the service ended, mother and son hugged long and hard; then we parted so she could follow her husband's body to the cemetery and we could go back to the house on the hill. Spell broken, I became all business and made Josh change back into his orange jumpsuit right there in the reception room, then shackled him up again, walked him out, and slid him into the back of the sedan. He rested his head against the cold glass and barely looked up until we were on the highway and he announced that he needed to hurl.

I didn't understand the urgency at first, but then I saw him bucking, and I said, "Oh, no you're not," even as I took a shoulder check, launched the car across three lanes of traffic, slapped the hazards on with my palm, and watched the side mirror for oncoming. Before I could get out and open his door, he vomited on the vinyl seats.

His coughing and crying barked so violently it sounded as though he were being rent from within. I didn't care, or rather, I took all the caring I normally would have felt and zipped it up, knowing too well that inmates lie and fake and induce illness right before they ruin your career or take your life. So I dragged him across the vomit and out of the car and pressed him up against the door with a baton—what we in the business affectionately call a fuckstick—until I could get some zips free to secure his shackles to the doorframe.

"He hated me!" Josh said. "He hated everything about me!"

And he moaned and coughed, thick strands of spittle hanging over his mouth like tendrils of skin. Then softer, losing energy, shaking hard, so that I knew he was in physical shock, "I didn't know . . . I didn't even know. Oh, God, he hated me so much."

I'd jammed the fuckstick into his back so hard I'd probably bruised his kidney. Did I really think he'd try to escape—out there on the side of a highway, chained ankles to wrists, covered in puke and snot, wearing orange pants? And yet it's the astonishing unlikelihoods that generate the most hilarious ridicule in the CO room—those legendary fuckups dreaded by all.

He repeated "I didn't know" like it was a childish prayer, so often, so weakly that it became necessary, in that shriveled, suspicious part of me, to process what he was talking about.

"Didn't know what?" I asked, standing back, watching him carefully.

He hung his head and muttered that he hadn't known his father was going to die, hadn't known about the cancer, hadn't even known he was sick. His father had never forgiven him. And in dying without reaching out, his father had punished him in the cruelest possible way.

I've witnessed some Jerry Springer moments in my career, but this was a new twist in the ever-varied fucked-upedness of family.

"You didn't know your father was sick until Keeper Wallace told you he'd died?" At the funeral home I'd heard whisperings about brain cancer and the doctor visits, and out of that blur of detail I'd gathered that the progression from symptom to treatment to hospitalization and deathbed had been a quick seven-month tumble. But the boy hadn't been told?

He kept mentioning his mother's visits, and how she hadn't said anything, how she'd acted as though everything was all right, had excused his father's absence by claiming he was too busy, overwhelmed with work, unable to join them.

"He hated the goddamn sight of me. He always did," Josh said, and then he started throwing up again, this time on the outside of the car door. It was tough to watch, even for a softy like me. He hung on the zip wires as though his parachute had gotten tangled in a tree, and tried to wipe his face with his shoulder.

"I'm real sorry," he said for the fifteenth time, meaning the puke and the standing on the side of the road.

"Not as sorry as me." The pissed-off, hard-ass CO in me talking, the one who waded thigh high through the shit flow of lousy lives. I needed to reassemble some order. I popped the trunk, stared inside for a few seconds, came up with a gray flannel blanket and a bottle of blue windshield wiper fluid, cracked open the bottle, and proceeded to splash the fluid judiciously inside the car. The mess ran along the vinyl like an overflowed toilet, and I sopped it up as best I could with the blanket.

"You are not sitting in the front seat with me, you are not sitting in the front seat with me," I said to him, myself, and whoever else might have been listening in the cars streaming by.

But the backseat was soaked, so I ended up making him my wingman with three zip lines linking his chained right wrist to the handle above the passenger window. I even wiped his face with a tissue from my pocket.

We drove for another half hour, windows wide to clear any remnants of the smell, aching with the cold air, before I turned off suddenly at a highway McDonald's. Why did I do it? The weakest of weak moments. He was still crying, and there was revolt in my heart, and I decided suddenly and almost violently that if I didn't give that kid a moment to collect himself before going back inside, he might not make it, figuring if a few chicken nuggets cost me my job, they might just save my soul.

"Can your stomach handle some food?"

Meek and surprised, he just nodded, and then he told me he had twenty bucks that his mother had slipped him. It was a stupid thing to say, verboten to bring currency inside, but instead of punishing him or confiscating the bill, I told him the Happy Meal was on me.

I ordered food and a pop for him, coffee for me. At the service window the uniformed attendant looked shocked at the sight of us together in the front seat. I noticed the camera. Watch that show up on fucking YouTube, I thought. When the food got passed in, I pulled away and lodged the car in the empty lot close to the exit. I rearranged the zip cuffs so one of his hands was free enough to eat, then handed him the bag.

Though I was used to unpleasant messes, the faint smell of the vomit and the greedy way he slurped his food made me squeamish. They all did that, as though even the bite in their mouths could get taken away. I asked him if he felt any better. He told me it had settled his stomach and that it tasted really really good. Then he went to work on the extra-large fries.

I took a sip of coffee and watched the highway.

"Have you worked at Ditmarsh a long time?" he asked. Like he was new on the job and we were colleagues.

"About three years." I said nothing more. Watching him eat, I wondered if I should have gotten him two meals.

"I saw you once, in the infirmary," he said.

Great, I thought, my very own stalker, and added my own inanity to our conversation.

"Ditmarsh must be a big adjustment for a person like you."

I meant privileged, middle-class, so much better off than the average hard-timer as to seem like a different species.

"I'm starting to get used to it," he said. And then he began talking about his father again, and the shock of not knowing he'd been sick, and how he'd always thought they'd have the time to work something out between them.

I know what he wanted: unconditional love. He wanted to be told that it didn't matter what he'd done or how bad he'd been, that the love itself was limitless. But he didn't get any of it, and lacking the smallest proof, he wondered if there'd been any love at all. At some level, conscious or cancer-addled, dear old dad had chosen not to make peace with his son. Some fathers are like that, incapable of getting over shock, incapable of dealing with the jagged complexities of an imperfect relationship. I thought of my own father.

"In my experience," I said, "people die exactly as they live. You don't get that deathbed reconciliation."

He nodded, as though what I said actually resonated. Part of me wished I'd sugared it up a little. But maybe Josh appreciated the hard truths for what they were—those rocks you get to stand on. Anyway, that was our moment of connection, the link that led to everything else.

We drove the last stretch of highway, then took the old post road, and when he saw it, I could almost feel the tightness come over him again. Ditmarsh loomed on the hill above the river like a fortress, the dome radiating a gentle light above the walls. There could have been a city below it. A planetarium. It was difficult to picture the inmates warehoused in the dark ranges.

The parking lot was mostly empty. We were ahead of schedule. I stopped the car, turned off the lights, and remained in the driver's seat. When I spoke next, the sternness was back. "You realize, of course, that none of this happened." I wanted to make it intensely clear for his sake as well as my own. "You mention it to anyone, and your life will be shit." Both of our lives might be shit. "I'm not warning you. I'm stating a fact. Because there are people in there, people you may even trust, who will hold this against you with a level of resentment you may not be able to imagine." He said that he understood, though it looked to me as though his comprehension was all murky and confused.

Then he twisted and torqued in the seat in order to reach down to his ankle with the hand that was not zipped. He lifted his left foot higher until his fingers could touch his white sock, pulled out a thin roll of stiff paper, and passed it to me with two fingers like crab claws. I received it, shocked and baffled.

"I was supposed to deliver this," he said.

I felt my heart thudding hard. I felt fucked over and fooled.

"Deliver?"

I kept my right hand on the fuckstick under my left thigh. With my left hand I flattened the roll. A booklet, about half the size of a regular piece of paper, the binding sewed carefully with black thread—thin, but maybe twenty pages long. A black circle was drawn on the cover, and within it were three white triangles or pyramids, a single triangle on the bottom balancing two above it. In an instant, with a different take, I saw the drawing as the face of a crude and menacing pumpkin with two broadly sliced eyes and a mouth. The book had a title in bold square letters—THE FOUR STAGES OF CRUELTY—and it was probably the word cruelty that evoked the subliminal Halloween menace. A subtitle read *The Beggar Restored to Life*.

I teased open the pages and began to glance through. On the first page was a drawing of a desert, empty except for a distant hooded figure walking along the horizon line. The text read *"God promised a prophet but sent a warrior instead."* On the next page the man walked a cobblestone road that led to an elaborate medieval city with castle walls and peaked towers. The road itself was lined gruesomely with decapitated heads propped on the tipped points of spears. In the next box the perspective came from over the edge of his cloaked shoulder, revealing the jut of his chin but nothing distinct about his face. *"The rulers of the city had long feared that the Beggar would return . . ."*

I felt no reaction other than a mild revulsion. Technically, it was impressive: a series of incredibly precise, almost photographic ink drawings, the kind inmates generate when they have the talent, too much time, and too little paper. But the chopped-off heads and the exaggerated physique of the "Beggar" had the flourish of brutality, the muscular pornography favored by teenage boys without girlfriends. I looked at Josh for some kind of explanation.

"They wanted me to give it to my mom." He was utterly flat now, beaten down, worn-out, and devoid of emotion.

"Your mom?" I thought of the woman in the hotel room, those pink cheeks.

"For safekeeping. A place no one would look. But I couldn't pull her into this. Not on the day my father got buried."

"So you want *me* to take it?" The tone in my voice questioned not only his reasoning, it questioned his intelligence.

He shrugged. I don't think it mattered to him whether I kept it or threw it away. I think he was beyond the mattering. He just wanted the weight off his shoulders. There was no malice or manipulation in him, only resignation. I'd bought him some french fries, so he figured he could give up in my presence. A part of me jumped into a new line of thought: well, well, well, what have I stumbled onto here. I wondered whether his weakness represented any opportunity for career advancement.

"Who?" I asked. "Who's they?"

"Jon Crowley," he answered.

I knew Crowley, though not well. He was hard-core but a loner. As a CO, I treated him decently because he never hassled with trivial shit and seemed straight-up and composed, characteristics that could be confused with intelligence. He lived in the howler ward now, and had for about a year, because of a broken arm that kept getting rebroken. I had not thought deeply on Crowley's proclivity for unfortunate falls, but it didn't take much imagination to see it as a message from some dissatisfied customer or upset business partner.

"Why did Crowley ask you to put this somewhere for safekeeping?"

A long pause while he seemed to test the logic of his own argument. "He didn't. I borrowed it from him."

Now he'd stolen it. "Do you know what a box thief is?"

His face changed, a ripple passing through it.

"Yes."

"You don't want to steal something from another inmate's cell."

"I didn't steal it."

"Because if you take something from someone else's cell, they will figure it out and fuck you up."

"Crowley wouldn't do anything bad to me."

"And if they don't, someone else will, just out of principle."

"Crowley's my friend."

Crowley was his friend. I could not help but shake my head. "You don't want friends. Don't trust anyone who says he's your friend." And then I stopped myself. He was a nineteen-year-old kid in a fragile mental state. You learn, as a CO, that some arguments can not be won by force of reason.

I tried next to avoid the downward spiral. "How long have you been in the infirmary?"

"About four months," he answered. "Ever since I got to Ditmarsh."

"Why?" My curiosity was unwarranted. It wasn't my business what arrangements had been made and why, but I also felt I was owed something, an acknowledgment of a favor.

He shrugged. "I don't know. I wish I was in gen pop. I want to start my real time, get it over with. I keep asking Keeper Wallace to give me a regular cell, but he won't let me leave."

I felt the pitter-patter of my heart to hear him cop so openly to the special treatment. "You don't want to start your real time, Josh," I said. "You don't."

He nodded as if he understood, but then he began to talk about the pluses of his situation. "Crowley's drum is next door. It's been great getting to know him. I don't think I would have survived my first week otherwise. We talk a lot. I help him get his shirt on once in a while. He gives me advice about inside. And we got a lot in common."

My arched eyebrow. "What kind of friends are you, Josh?"

"He draws," Josh explained. "I draw, too. He got me into the art therapy class, way ahead of other people. Everyone wants to get in there."

Art therapy. I bet they were breaking down the doors for that one.

Josh sighed. "I'm just trying to help him. I'm worried he's going to get into trouble."

"Why would he get in trouble? What has he done?" I wanted an answer. I wanted it spelled out. But Josh gave me nothing to work with.

"It's not him, it's the drawings. Drawings can be misinterpreted," he said.

How was a kid like Josh Riff supposed to survive inside Ditmarsh? He didn't have the sense for it. Other inmates, with IQs a third as high, had better instincts for minding their own business, keeping their mouths shut. I looked through the pages of the book again. The Beggar wandered the city, unrecognized. His face in the hooded cloak was always hidden by shadow. In scene after scene he encountered people who lived in the city, barkeeps, prostitutes, merchants, temple priests. Some were old friends who looked shocked when they recognized him. Others seemed to have known him only by reputation but genuflected with respect and fear when his identity was understood. No one used any other name for him than Beggar—even the group of brigands who surrounded him in a dark alley and attacked. Pushed to fight, the Beggar threw off his cloak, revealing a muscular but scarred body, and he whirled among them, swinging a wooden staff, caving in their teeth, cracking their heads. "Brothers!" he cried out to the fleeing survivors. "We all suffer under the same cruel masters!"

"Who's the tough guy?" I asked. It was rhetorical, I suppose, because I wasn't expecting any kind of answer.

But Josh said, "That's the Beggar."

I counted four, five, six seconds.

"Is that supposed to mean something to me?"

"Crowley said he's a prophet."

Good grief. I flipped toward the end. The Beggar had been captured by soldiers, men wearing bird's masks and feathered helmets. He was brought to a central keep and then led down steep stone stairs to a cavern below the city. The door was marked by a jack-o'-lantern stamped into the page with raised outlines. I'd seen the circle and triangles before. I tried to remember where. When I turned the page, I saw the Beggar shackled to a wall, guards torturing him with poles and knives.

So this is what prison looked like through an inmate's eyes. I'd seen enough. I had no desire to entangle myself further. It was not my business if Crowley had offended someone or otherwise gotten himself into trouble, and I felt foolish even contemplating handing over such meaningless nonsense to the Keeper. I spoke slowly to Josh, wanting him to understand me on every level.

"I'm going to pretend you never showed this to me, and I'm going to forget we had this conversation. This comic book is not your property, it's Crowley's, and I think you overestimate the depth of your friendship with him. Inmates don't want other inmates to fuck with their stuff. If you want to drop this in the snow before we get back inside, that's your choice. If you want to rip it into shreds and burn it in your toilet, you can do that, too. But do not ask me to get involved in your problems. I've had enough of them today."

Josh started to argue but then recognized that whatever opening I'd offered to him before was closed now. And with my decision he was suddenly no longer human to me. He was cargo—walking, talking, bullshitting cargo—that needed to be watched over, knocked about, and told what to do, mechanically, without feeling, and definitely with a well-founded sense of superiority.

I took my cell phone out and dialed Wallace's desk number, and when he answered, I told him we'd arrived. I'd expected his personal escort again, some cover for the illicit trip, but Wallace seemed too tired and distracted to give a damn. I told him Josh had gotten sick in the car. He told me not to worry and to return inmate Riff to his cell. I didn't want to do it alone and asked, "Are you sure, sir?" But Wallace was sure. I didn't argue. To put up any kind of fuss risked scrutiny over other things—the fact that Josh had required attending to on the highway, that we'd stopped at McDonald's, that we'd sat in the parking lot for fifteen minutes while we talked about a comic book. Instead, I hung up, swore, and went around the car. The kid stank, and he didn't want to go inside again. I gave him a push. Forced to move or trip, he obeyed.

No one was in the waiting room, thank God. We got buzzed in, the heavy doors releasing and then slamming behind us with that sound of all life being sucked out of the universe. Bruno, an old hack who probably knew Wallace well, was minding the control deck. I unshackled Riff and put him through the metal detector doorframe; then I walked around it, as COs always did. I could understand Wallace's indifference better now. Bruno would do what he was told without question. "You smell like you've been in the bathroom of a nightclub," Bruno said through the cage. My female presence was the best thing that had happened to him in three shifts. "Bruno, you wouldn't believe me if I told you," I answered. And Bruno said, "I don't know. I've got a teenage daughter." And for some reason we both thought that was funny.

I unshackled Josh and left the bracelets and chains with Bruno. Then I walked Josh home. He was silent all the way to the infirmary. After I keyed his door, he sat on the edge of the bed without looking up, his face slack and dour, as though the intensity of emotion had drained out of him and left his features formless. I did not say goodbye.

Instead, I stepped over to the cell next door. It required deliberate effort to see inside. The cells in the infirmary had private doors with slots at eye level, an inconceivable luxury to anyone used to the cavelike lifestyle of gen pop, all bars and cold stone. I shone my flashlight inside and saw Crowley sitting on the steel shitter with his pants around his ankles. He smirked into the glare. He had that emaciated, bony, grayish-tattooed look of an ex-junkie, his eyes dark smudges, his hair wet and long, his chin unshaven. His right arm was in a cast, one of those half-body sheaths that wraps around the torso, the broken limb propped up like a gnarled tree branch, fingers dangling over the unit sink. His good hand braced the wall as if the room could tilt like a ship at sea.

"Right on," he said. "I've been waiting for someone to wipe my ass."

I said nothing and stepped away and walked back down the hallway, past Josh again, lighting up each cell in turn as if doing a count. Most of the drum rats were asleep and curled over or flat on their backs and staring skyward, flabby, old, weak. But in the third cell past Josh's, I saw the inhuman mess. His name was Donald Lorrey, but we called him Occupant. A bloated, obese body, an awkward imbalance in the way he sat in a corner of the bed, propped against the wall, stunned by medication. Most of his fingers and toes were gone, soft nubs left over on the ends of swollen diabetic appendages, and his face was gone, too. The goneness started at the lower right chin, where a jaw had once been, and it cleaved upward to clear out the palate and much of the nose and separate the forehead into two unevenly furrowed portions. The head was tilted up in the way the blind seem to sniff the air. A failed suicide, a big-time loser, a bullet doing the trick but not the job, the sight a source of occasional wonder and glee for the COs, who sometimes dared new colleagues to enjoy their lunch and then walk over and take a look.

You forget sometimes. In the outside world, there are accidents and oddities and strange events, but nothing like here. Inside Ditmarsh, there be monsters.

For a long time he sat in silence on the edge of the mattress, almost physically sore from the many blows of the day. Then he slid Crowley's small graphic novel back into the slot in the bedpost and started to take off his clothes. When the night deepened and all rustling stopped, he heard a whisper. It was Crowley from the next cell, asking how everything had gone down. Getting no answer, Crowley asked louder how he was doing. There was care in his voice. Guilty, worn-out, and frustrated, he told Crowley to leave him the fuck alone.

He got silence in return and hoped, wavering between anxiety and exhaustion, that Crowley was the understanding type. A half hour later he heard a tap and saw a flickering shape in the cut in his door, hovering for an instant like a moth batting against a window. It disappeared and then reappeared. Standing at the cut with his fingers extended, it took him three tries to catch the book of matches on a string.

Tucked behind the matches was a sliver of paper rolled tight, a dusting of hash inside. A gift. A peace offering. A gesture of friendship. "Thanks," he said into the silence, but heard nothing. He sat back on the bed wondering what to do. Could you light up in a drum? Smoking was against the rules. You had to be in a specific area of the yard, no more than twenty men maximum at one time, and he'd seen fights break out when someone got sick of waiting and dragged a tardy inhaler out of the circle to beat him senseless. He still smelled of puke, his clothes were in a pile on the floor, and he was sniffling with a cold, aching with the usual hard-on, and brutalized by grief and loneliness. A little toke of hash was the right medicine. Two hits and it was gone, a spark in his fingertips, and the world was spinning in a tighter groove.

Still unable to sleep, he got out his notebook and started to draw, a flashlight crooked on his shoulder. He'd discovered in the library a book he'd owned as a child, *D'Aulaire's Book of Trolls*. The story reminded him of his life inside, and he drew some of the inmates and COs that way now. There were trolls everywhere. Gnarled and gruff, unwashed and violent, huge and ugly. Some had twelve heads. Some had long noses, broken teeth, and tails. Some carried their heads under their arms. Some shared an eye. They had no souls. They ate humans in their stew and counted their treasure in caves. They came out only at night and burst into fragments at the mere sight of the sun.

4 |||||||||||||

After the delivery detail, routine resumed, and I was grateful for the discipline of the uniform. An inmate's way of seeing the world could seep into your brain like a virus if you let it. For a few days afterward I wondered if I should tell Wallace about Josh and Crowley and the comic book. But I didn't trust Wallace, and I didn't care to open my decision-making process to his scrutiny. It was his fault I'd been put into such an ambiguous situation. The consequences could fall to someone else. Crowley's friendship with Josh was a troubling aspect. It was difficult to imagine Crowley wasting any time with such a fresh and unlikely fish, but it was not unusual for an established con to use a newbie as a courier or errand runner or service provider. The reasons and the what-fors were never easy to follow, and there was nothing I could do about it anyway.

To be honest, I thought more about the mixed emotions I still had around Josh. I was bothered by the murky reasons he was allowed the pass and by the heavy shock he'd experienced not knowing his father was sick. I could still see him crumpled over and crippled by the revelation. I was not usually curious about an inmate, but a week later, one evening when I was home doing an online training class on inmate rights and three glasses of merlot to the wind, I broke away from the Q&A and googled Josh to find out what I could about him.

The Internet had distorted the value of information in prison. The code inside was not to talk about the particulars that led to your bit. This secrecy gave rise to rumors and innuendo that served as a kind of floating currency, measuring the ups and downs of an individual's status and reputation. As natural liars and unaccountable shiftless fucks, most inmates are inclined to bluff about their beef, accentuating the positive, downplaying the unsavory. If you're a skinner—a rapist—for instance, and nobody knows it, you put the hate on suspected skinners just to cover yourself from unwelcome speculation. If you're weak or disliked, you get labeled and tagged and sometimes bagged, based on whatever story gets spread, unless you throw down and take a stand. But now, if those inside wanted to learn more about a new neighbor, one sentenced in the last five to ten years, all they had to do was get a friend outside to do a search and dish the details during a visit. We dealt with the consequences of such trade all the time.

It didn't take long to draw my own picture of Josh from the news articles that popped up. He was in for first-degree manslaughter and had been sentenced to twenty-five years. It seemed a heavy bit, given the verdict and his age and the things that some hard men do to earn sentences half as long, but I'd also seen fourteen-year-olds walk in facing the fifty-year stretch. Sometimes the young perps get the harder hand so the courts can show the world, behold, here is justice, and this time we're not fucking around. The victim's name was Stephanie Patchet, a girlfriend, or ex-girlfriend in some accounts, shot by Riff with his father's handgun one evening after an argument in her family living room. I got sober scanning the pieces. An accident. A struggle. A slipped gun. An early version called it a tragedy, a later article described it as a malicious, well-planned homicide masquerading as juvenile distress. The verdict turned because of the notebook found in Josh's car, which was filled with drawings that proved, in explicit and occasionally pornographic detail, his murderous intentions. No examples were provided, but I saw her photo, the eager aliveness of a smiling face framed in mousy blond hair, the kind of shot always chosen by journalists when they want to canonize a victim.

It knocked me back to see that Josh was nothing more and nothing less than a girlfriend killer, and that his drawings had earned him the hard time. Given his milquetoast persona and the relative stability of his family life (minus those communication problems regarding his father's health), it was not surprising that his crime was unrelated to any of the thicker pursuits surrounding drugs or gangs, yet the revelation truly pissed me off. Wallace had sent me, without warning, on a secret road trip accompanying a lying, emotionally manipulative, murderous coward who'd killed a woman. I hate domestics. I hate passion murders. Why did thwarted love so often turn physically harsh? I was sick of young men and their fevered imaginations and the irreparable harm they caused through clumsy assertions of control.

Or did I just want the freedom to hate from a distance? The job usually allowed for that. Contempt was part of the gear you wore. The rote duty dulled your personal take on the world, and that suited me just fine. If Josh was an in-between inmate, then I was an in-between person. Thirty-nine years old, pretty in a conventional way, though one eye was slightly lower than the other and I wore my bang across it. I had combat experience in Iraq, but that was paper fake. I did yoga twice a week, liked bourbon, and knew how to rap the vulnerable point of an elbow with a baton. I had an ex-husband, but the marriage had left no dent on my life. I was all holding pattern and no hold. It took the rest of the bottle of wine to contemplate the details in full.

Such was my queasy and slightly disoriented state of mind the next morning when the violence began.

They had me working the tower. The task was to look down onto the yard and also to scan the slate rooftops with their fringes of barbed wire and even the absurd glass dome. I was there to catch odd breaks in the traffic flow, to spot what could not be spotted on the ground, to call warning if a fellow CO was under duress, to scatter perimeter shots if a clustered knot of violence ever unraveled and spread—in short, to simply be the watchful eye of a pissed-off and ever-vigilant God. Most COs counted it a lucky day to be assigned such duty—all that power with the luxury of being safe and bored, too—but the isolation up top emptied me out. I watched the inmates and COs and the civilians—or weak sisters—and thought, that's me down there, that's how small I am; and I got down on myself for thinking that way.

The office at the top of the tower was cramped with gray furniture and blue metal. Even with the chill I preferred the open air. Standing on the platform six stories above the yard kept me alert, or as alert as was possible overseeing such heavy routine. On a clear day you could see beyond the walls to the forest and the valley and the choked, twisted river, and beyond that to the crisp brown farmlands and the jut of the city. But on that day visibility was almost nonexistent. The sky was low-ceilinged. Time had thickened up, and every sound was muffled, as though the yard were contained within a lidded pot. Then the first snowflake appeared, and Ditmarsh became a fairy-tale castle.

It was easy to be distracted, and I let it happen. A million more snowflakes followed the first one, materializing out of the milky emptiness rather than falling from the sky, dancing in front of me, stirring whatever thin poetry I had inside. The snow landed heavy, piling up fast. The beauty was surprisingly insistent. I forgot about caution, movement, and status notifications for the moment and took it all in. The towers could have been turrets. The dip in the yard a grassed-over moat. The dome a crystal palace. What did that make me? Hardly a princess—too much uniform in my life for that—but still.

My reverie lasted long enough for me to be utterly startled when the siren blasted to mark midday. The buildings remained unaffected by the signal for two or three puffs of breath; then the doors burst open and the men hit the yard like schoolboys at recess. The change in weather slowed them up. Arms got outstretched, hands and mouths opened to receive the flakes. The exaggerated innocence made their brutality seem as random and regrettable as a car accident. You could get lulled like that sometimes. You could start to look on them like acquaintances.

I blinked to see through the blur. The men were not walking their usual defined routes at their usual regulated pace. No one else seemed to mind, but the disruption of flow across the yard bothered me because the situation was abnormal and called out for vigilance. Twelve minutes later, only two minutes longer than normal, the movement had trickled off and I willed myself to relax. A group of inmates entered the yard from the education center in the old wing, a class or counseling session having spit its dutiful attendants out late. I tracked them with less caution because their numbers were small. It was almost amusing when the scooping up began and the snowballs launched among them like a flurry of arrows from opposing ramparts. I picked up my binoculars for a closer look and was surprised to see Josh standing among the group. Despite the childish nature of the play, he looked more uncomfortable than the others, hands shoved into his pockets.

Then I saw Crowley in the larger scrum, chased by another man with a handful of snow. The horizontal cast, the strange slow-motion way he walked, twisting his body as if on a swivel. His pursuer moved awkwardly, too, and I recognized Roy Duckett, the one-legged kitchen chef called Wobbles. Funny to see the two of them together, as if competing in the Para Olympics. A snowball hit Crowley in the back, and he turned and waited for Wobbles to reach him. When they grappled, Wobbles slipped and fell hard on his back and lay there as if stunned, and Crowley fell on top of him and began to face wash him. I thought it was a bit rough, edging toward brutal, but two COs had gathered and seemed to feel there was no reason to intervene. Then a third inmate took the opportunity to launch himself into the tangle. I didn't like it, and I willed the COs to break it up. Even so, I was completely startled when the third inmate's arm began pumping up and down with the sped-up vigor of someone using a sharpened killing implement.

Three or four seconds later I scrambled inside the booth and came out with an AR-15 assault rifle. It was heavy but beautifully balanced and locked on, and I cradled it in my arms. A circle formed, but the COs did nothing to interrupt. Someone needed to take control, so I sounded the blare, hoping to clear the tight group and fire off a round, at least a skip shot to frighten them into stopping. At the sound, everyone in the yard looked up as though startled, then looked back to the scrum. Almost immediately Crowley managed to do something within the tangle, which evoked a howl of agony in his attacker, who scooted away on the seat of his pants, dragging his lower body. The fight had turned, as they sometimes did. With COs on hand, it should have ended there, Crowley could have been pulled off or restrained, but still no one moved in. Instead, Crowley knelt on his attacker's chest, his cast arm wedged into the guy's neck and his good hand stabbing down as though knocking chips off a block of ice.

I steadied the rifle and aimed for a spot on the snow next to Crowley, and everything resolved into a punctuation point.

I might have fired if not for the man who sprinted across the yard and tackled Crowley. Some civilian. Some weak sister. He appeared out of nowhere and did what no one in uniform had the inclination or the courage to do. Wrestling Crowley down, tying up his good arm from behind, he provided the COs with the excuse or the opportunity to rouse themselves, wade in with fucksticks, and pummel away.

Two COs dragged Crowley off, not gently. A half dozen more began the sorting-out process now that the event was over. I remained at the railing, staring down, watching the clumsy work going on, mesmerized by the falling snowflakes and the prediction of violence Josh had promised. What the hell had just happened? I'd interpreted the comic book as fantasy and little more, the melodrama of the story salty with the injured sentiments of some self-righteous con. It knocked me off balance to see Crowley attacked so soon after that conversation, as if I'd misheard everything. I thought about the possibilities and got nowhere. Then the hatch at my feet popped up and my replacement arrived a full fifteen minutes early. A short CO with a sleepy look on his face named Patrick Kim emerged from the staircase to join me on the tower. He muttered bitterly about the fucking cold and asked me about the excitement. I gave him my abbreviated version and offered a philosophical observation: "Who knew the kids hid shanks in snowballs these days?"

"Winter sucks," he said. "Go do your paperwork and get off my tower."

After I reached ground level and made my way through the tunnel to Keeper's Hall, however, I did not pour myself a coffee, find a desk, and get started, but drifted out into the yard to see the site of the happening first-hand.

The gathering had thinned of inmates and thickened with COs and weak sisters. I saw an assistant warden, a counselor, some medical staff. I did not see Josh; he must have been among the inmates led back to their cells. The sprinter who'd interrupted the fight was still there, a group of COs surrounding him, berating him hard. I knew him by sight as Brother Mike, an ex-missionary turned counselor who ran the art therapy program. I put it all together then. This was the class Josh had spoken about, the program they were all dying to get into.

Three orderlies and Keeper Wallace squatted before Crowley's attacker. The man's face was a mutilated mess, his barrel chest rising and falling in the suck for air. Through an overheard comment I learned that the plucked chicken was Lawrence Elgin, someone I knew to be of the Viking persuasion, which was a general categorization we had for gang-affiliated white supremacists. Looking for some way to make myself useful, I saw that Wobbles, the one-legged inmate Crowley had traded snowballs with, still sat on the ground unattended, his good leg and his peg leg scissored out from his girth. His nose and ears trickled blood, and I wondered if that injury happened when Crowley face scrubbed him. As I walked over, a smile spread across his mouth. "Hey!" he called, and pointed to the red snow between his legs. "Looks like I got my period, doesn't it?" It was the kind of shot I took all the time, as a woman inside a house for men, so I stopped short and decided to ignore him like everyone else.

There was nothing for me to do, no reason for me to be there, but still I lingered. I wandered around the site and noticed, in the center of the flattened snow, a toothbrush with flecks of gore and swirls of red around it. Kneeling, I poked it with a finger, delicately tipping it skyward. The bristle end was worn down from normal use, but the handle had been melted and twisted until sharpened to a deadly point. "Keeper Wallace," I called. I wanted him to see this, to know the weapon had been found by me. The orderlies rolled Elgin's heavy slackness onto a canvas stretcher and lifted him up. Wallace left them but, instead of walking my way, joined the circle around Brother Mike. The voices of the COs were heated, and although Wallace did not intercede directly, his presence toned things down for the moment.

Finally, as my legs began to stiffen and hurt from squatting, Wallace lumbered over. I showed him my discovery. "Leave it for the Pen Squad," he announced. The Pen Squad was the police unit working within the prison, in charge of all criminal investigations. Then he asked me if I'd been on hand when it happened.

"I saw it from the southeast tower," I said.

"And you came down to hang out after your shift?" he asked. "I don't remember URF being called in."

A sarcastic comment flung my way, but I knew it was bitter bullshit. There were other COs who'd joined the gathering. That in itself was an issue with Wallace, something he preached against. He believed that COs should not be distracted by incidents, because it was possible they'd been arranged, very deliberately, to cover planned happenings elsewhere, but it was in the nature of COs to cluster. We may have been curious bystanders, but we also had an instinct for self-defense. Whenever *they* threatened, we needed to be on hand in superior numbers.

"No sir," I answered. I would get no kudos for finding a shank, no thanks for preventing it from being stomped by orderlies or covered by snow.

He stood, gave a grim look around, eternally disappointed, and muttered, "Get Brother Mike out of here." A curt command to do something useful.

"Roger that," I said, which was my way of being funny. Keeper Wallace's first name was Roger.

I rose and walked off to join the lynch mob. Surrounded by so much uniform, Brother Mike looked small in his cardigan sweater. I did not side with weak sisters, but I did not always agree with my fellow COs when it came to matters of solidarity. The anger directed at Brother Mike was understandable from a jurisdictional perspective. He had inserted himself without welcome into a crisis situation, creating a new variable and an extra dose of confusion. But it was all embarrassment and bullshit, a collective act of CYA. Brother Mike had not disrupted some carefully planned containment strategy, but he'd showed them up, asserting a little masculinity in its obvious absence. Having seen enough, I announced, in a harsh voice, that I was taking Brother Mike to Keeper Wallace's office now. I implied, in the way I grabbed Brother Mike's elbow, that a shit storm of trouble waited. I marched him across the yard as though it were personal. Then I got him inside and stomped my feet to shake off the snow.

He had a trim gray beard and short hair, and the skin of his face and forehead was wrinkled and weathered. I'd thought he'd looked so vigorous racing across the yard to tackle Crowley, so lithe and purposeful, and now he looked old and cold.

"Are you all right?" I asked. "Any aches or pains?" I'd seen him torque Crowley's arm and wrestle him down. The effort had to have tweaked or torn something. But he dismissed my concerns.

"Only to my ears."

I have a soft spot for seniors who don't act their age. He'd already taken his share of abuse from my colleagues. I had no doubt they'd heap more on him later whenever they could, that he would be a marked man for a good long time. I wanted him away from me now, before anyone saw us talking like chums while the insult was still so fresh.

"Then you should go get warm. I've got paperwork to do and a shift to finish."

He did not move, surprised by the reprieve.

"You're not taking me to the Keeper's office?"

Did I need to spell it out for him? "I'm sure he'll find you later if he wants to."

"I see." He tried to smile, but the expression fluttered away in a tremble of post-adrenaline letdown. "I wonder, where do you think they will be taking him?"

"You mean Elgin? To the infirmary, I'd think." A good chance to the morgue.

"And my other student, Jon Crowley?"

"If he's injured, he'll go there, too. If he's not, he'll end up in the dissociation unit for fighting." It was already distasteful to me, this kind of concern, and I wanted to pry myself away from the good deed.

"I see," Brother Mike said, and he thanked me.

We parted at the juncture between Keeper's Hall and the education wing, each of us for our own separate worlds.

5

I did not know much about Brother Mike's world then, but I understood my own well enough, the daily pressure to be wary and cynical and to keep expectations low. That's my excuse for not doing more sooner. I could not stop thinking about my conversation with Josh, and his warning that Crowley was in danger because of the comic book, but while I wanted to approach him, to pull him off to the side and ask, Is this what you meant? I did not find the time. The default attitude among COs in inmate-related circumstances was to be dismissive of the reasons and the backstories, to shrug off the entanglements. What right did inmates have to ordinary human fears? You did not need to trouble yourself about where the violence came from, what politics, rage, or soap opera plots drove their impulses and sullen schemes. You job was to focus on the situation at hand.

I was still contemplating those limitations the next morning when I sat in the internal evidence room behind shatterproof Plexiglas and waited for inmate Cooper Lewis to relieve his bowels. I had been informed that Lewis had inserted something bodily while in the VnC for a family visit, and it was my job to find out what.

He lay on a rubber mattress in a larger than normal cell, a fair-complexioned man with a blazing red goatee. He had his arms behind his head, and he whistled as he stared up at the ceiling as though he were on some grassy field somewhere, alone and unobserved, watching oddly shaped clouds coasting by. He'd covered himself with a single white sheet that went from his waist to his ankles. The sheet was a mandated provision that mystified me. Though too small and thin to encourage sleep, it gave Lewis cover for anything he needed to do in secret below. I'd seen them do just about everything in my time, including excrete whatever foreign substance they'd suitcased and either re-ingest it or re-suitcase it in a wriggling, writhing wrestling match between object and anus. For whatever legal reason—and I would love to know the precedent for that particular decision in the storied history of search and seizure law—a corrections officer was not permitted to rush a cell when it became apparent that an inmate had discharged a foreign object. Instead, protocol was to wait until the inmate got up from the bed and willingly and voluntarily discharged said object by taking a crap in a glass toilet bowl. That almost never occurred in any timely fashion, but involved a shrewd cat and mouse game between the inmate, who had nothing better to do with his time, and the CO, who needed to wait and wait and wait until the bowel movement arrived.

At least—and here I suspected a truly sick mind at work—someone had mysteriously lodged a pleather recliner in the viewing portion of the room. Sitting in it, waiting for hours on end, it was impossible not to kick back so your feet were raised while you stared blankly at the inmate behind the glass wall with the foreign object up his ass. The parallels with watching television were far too obvious to overlook.

In the end, you waited until the inmate's boredom exceeded your own and they traipsed the divide between the slab of concrete and the glass toilet bowl and sat sideways to you and expelled. Then you inserted your hands into thick fireman's gloves that protruded into the glass toilet bowl basin and pretended you were a nuclear scientist handling radioactive material. Even though the heavy fabric made it impossible to come into direct physical contact with the waste, I always doubled up with my own latex rubber gloves when doing the awful deed.

People, even friends, sometimes ask me about my job with twitters of interest. They want to hear the sordid details, the glamour of it all. Except they don't want reality. They don't want to know what it's like to be a woman in such an environment. They don't want to hear about Cooper Lewis in the internal evidence room, or the other things I see or smell, or the things I do when I absolutely have no choice. They don't want me to go past the line of too much information and into the realm of the hard-core. That's why we call civilians weak sisters.

There we were, Cooper Lewis and I, playing our mind games—he ignoring me, me pretending that his existence actually mattered—when I noticed the mark from the cover of Crowley's comic book scratched into the Plexiglas.

The inside surface of the Plexiglas was a web of faint graffiti. I don't know why any CO would sit still and ignore an act of defacement while an inmate expressed his frustrations with some sharpened object, but plenty obviously had. There were drawings of lewd sexual acts and drawings of crude bodily functions. There were meaningless circles, random swoops, and lines of inappropriate poetry. I'd been blind to them before, the way you are blind to the white noise of an electronic appliance. But now the pumpkin with its triangle eyes and mouth glared at me from the upper right quadrant of the Plexiglas wall.

I unfolded myself from the recliner and stepped up to look more closely. Lewis glanced toward me warily, as if I were a feral cat getting too close.

There were no explanations to be gained, however, from the inspection. It was just a childish rendition scratched into the surface, but the sight of it teased my memory again. I'd seen that mark before. I just couldn't place where.

I was still standing there, lost in my investigative reverie, when the door opened and in walked senior CO Ray MacKay.

To be caught by a fellow CO in any pose but the most routine or confrontational was potentially embarrassing. And in this case I felt as if I'd been discovered in the bathtub with the shower nozzle. But MacKay did not seem to care. He stood next to me, as if at a barbeque, and asked what was cooking.

I snorted. "You got me," I answered, and retreated with rescued dignity to my recliner throne. MacKay followed and pulled up a foldout chair to sit next to me.

At least we'd ruined Lewis's good mood. Lewis scowled, as an inmate might at the sight of any CO, and went back to his whistling, but it was a more tense and hostile tune. It was easy to imagine that Lewis and MacKay had encountered each other in unfavorable circumstances before. MacKay was like that. He regarded rules as insignificant impediments. He knew every blind nook left in the institution and would steer an inmate into such a space for a brief talking-to without a moment's hesitation. He regularly and unapologetically fucked the pooch when others were scrambling to get tasks done. And yet, of all the old boys who might have earned my disdain, I dearly loved the man. He was the dirty uncle I'd never had, the tender-hearted thug of my dreams.

As they say in the movies, he also made me laugh. Impatient, he barked through the glass. "Jesus, Cooper, you baking a cake in there?"

Lewis responded with all the wit he could summon, a muffled suggestion that MacKay go fuck himself.

"Why me?" I asked MacKay. It was a rhetorical question, and I received a rhetorical answer.

"Because all shit follows gravity and flows downhill."

It could have been a workplace motto.

MacKay did not look like the type you could have a sensitive and intelligent conversation with, but I had found him to be surprisingly open-minded and quick. In appearance, he resembled an Irish cop from a vintage photograph: the speckled buzz cut and square head, one ear gone nubby and cauliflowered, as if banged hard with a pipe, a heavy fold of flesh at the back of his neck. Inside, he was sensitive, thoughtful, and quick to be offended, just another feminist with a quick temper.

"You sure he's packing?" I asked. The word packing never so physically accurate.

MacKay just leaned forward in the chair and stared at the glass.

"Got it on tape. He was in a private visiting room with his grandmother and his little girl. There's even a goddamn sign on the wall says cameras may be watching, but you don't read too good, do you, shit for brains?" he called out. "We seen it all. The whole sordid details."

I was quietly disgusted. The little girl in the room. A grandmother. I could tell you it doesn't get much lower, except it does, frequently, and always in surprising ways. "That's a new kind of sick," I noted, "getting your own grandmother to bring in your junk."

But MacKay turned to me. "Sweetheart, we're not talking about drugs. He upped one of those mobile phones. Didn't they tell you?" And when he saw they hadn't, he laughed. "The boys must have wanted to see the look on your face. Stupid bastards. You might have had a heart attack."

I remained utterly baffled until the understanding dawned. "He suitcased a cell phone?"

MacKay nodded. "Looked like a Samsung."

"Good grief," I muttered. The things a human being could shove up the ass. I felt awestruck, affirmed in my belief that there were no bounds to ingenuity when it met the curve of need.

"Yeah, Cooper didn't believe it either. He was downright skeptical when Grandma made the suggestion. He said, 'Granny, that's never going to fit up my ass,' and she said, 'It'll fit up no problem. You think I brung it here without trying first?' "

I could only blink in wonder. "She shoved it up her own ass before she got him to shove it up his ass?"

"As God is my witness. It must have taken him five minutes working it back there. We were cheering him on. He kept saying, 'No, Granny, it ain't going to go,' and she told him to keep pushing, and then the expression on old Cooper's face changed considerably, and he said his goodbyes and got out of there fast. We nabbed him as soon as he passed the control zone. And now look at him. Whistling like he's got nothing on his mind."

"And you couldn't resist coming in to watch."

MacKay nodded. "Yeah. I figure once in my life I got to see someone shit a phone."

A minute passed.

"If we knew the number, we could give it a ring," I suggested.

"Honest, Judge. We were just trying to answer the phone."

We laughed, pleased with ourselves, and waited some more.

I'm not sure why—an urge to think about something other than Cooper Lewis and his cell phone, I suppose—but I broke the silence and asked MacKay what he was up to these days, outside of work.

Right away I regretted it. I didn't know much about MacKay's private life, whether to suspect a Mrs. MacKay and a houseful of grandkids or, what was more likely, a shabby one-bedroom apartment with a divorce agreement buried in a stack of bills on the kitchen counter; and he didn't know much about me, though he sometimes teased me about boyfriends and wild weekends. It was a taboo conversation, especially in front of inmates. They sucked up information like parasites and found ingenious ways to use it against you. But MacKay didn't seem to mind, and Cooper Lewis gave no indication he could hear through the thick glass.

"You mean when I'm not waiting for someone to take a crap?" he asked.

It was probably the best answer I could expect.

"I've been bird-watching lots," he said.

I couldn't have been more surprised if inmate Cooper Lewis had shit a microwave. *Bird-watching*. Sometimes life hits you like that, the little astonishments that lead to major recalibrations.

"You're kidding?" I said. "I wouldn't have guessed."

MacKay looked at me as though I were making fun. "Yeah, bird-watching. You asked, so I told you. I'm treasurer of the Mourning Warbler Society."

A bit sour because of my surprise, but what did he expect? I'd pictured him in a camouflage jacket waiting for deer, or liquored up in an ice-fishing hut, or doubling down in some Indian casino. Not bird-watching.

The mood was wrong, and I wished I could rescue it.

"I'm reading *To Kill a Mockingbird* right now," I said. It wasn't about bird-watching, but there was a bird quality to it, one I figured a man of Ray MacKay's sensibilities could appreciate.

But MacKay looked at me in horror until I asked what was wrong.

"What the hell kind of a book is that?" he demanded.

Then I realized the title might alarm a bird lover in complete ignorance of it. So I began an embarrassed and awkward attempt to explain that *To Kill a Mockingbird* wasn't actually about killing mockingbirds. In fact, one of the best lines in the book even stated that to kill a mockingbird was a sin.

But MacKay said, "I'm just fucking with you, Kali. I like Gregory Peck, too."

I called him a bastard, and sat back, relieved yet embarrassed. I often felt superior to the men I worked with, and it was at a moment like this that I realized some of them knew it.

More minutes went by. Lewis had stopped listening and was starting to squirm on the slab, bringing his knees up to his chest. Nature taking its course, if ever there had been a more unnatural course taken.

"You don't have to sit this one out with me, Ray," I said as kindly as I could, trying not to sound patronizing again. "I'm all right. I know it's my job."

But MacKay said, "You kidding me? Wouldn't miss this for the world. Why don't you go powder your nose or beat up an inmate."

"You got this one?" I asked.

MacKay nodded. "Yeah, I'm serious."

"Well, that's a deal as far as I'm concerned."

Except I didn't move. I was paralyzed by suspicion and doubt. I couldn't help but wonder why MacKay wanted me out of the room. Most of the COs had something going on. The inmates wore you down that way, their passive and sometimes not so passive forms of resistance requiring a little give-and-take, a mutual back-scratching to pass a shift without incident. You started out doing something small for them in order to get a favor in return—a quickened response time at lockdown, a heads-up when something was going down—but then the favors kept getting traded, and you stopped knowing the difference, and you became colleagues in a way, and sometimes you even worked for them. MacKay despised inmates, but that didn't mean he didn't despise himself a little bit, too. So I took the opportunity to stall by asking MacKay about the other thing on my mind.

"You ever hear of an inmate referred to as the Beggar?"

I said it low, still conscious of Lewis. MacKay didn't flinch or redirect his gaze, but it was one of those moments when you realize a bell has been rung.

"Sure I know him," he answered. "He was here for ten years, wasn't he?"

Him? I knew of no Beggar. I had never heard the name before, and I wondered vaguely if it was a forgotten term in the ever-evolving and endlessly variant jailhouse jargon. I was not expecting such a routine answer. Another reminder: what I didn't know about corrections could fill a Chicago phone book.

"Are you kidding me? Who is he?"

MacKay leaned back, eyes on Lewis, and gave a reasonable shrug. "Name we had for a son of a bitch called Earl Hammond."

He stopped, and I figured that was it, but MacKay was just winding up, some pent-up bitterness working its way to the surface like slow lava.

"This was mid-eighties. He was in a gang, naturally. No big deal. Then he stabbed a fifteen-year veteran CO named Tony Bucker about fifty times. We buried Hammond same day we buried Bucker, put him in the City, cleared the other assholes out, and let him rot by himself in total fucking isolation for the next three years. Let's just say Hammond became a favorite object of frustration from that point forward. If you had a bad day, got a cup of urine splashed on you, got your ass chewed out by a keeper, no worries, you just headed downtown into the City and whooped some cop-killer ass for a while. We'd say he was begging for it. 'How was Hammond?' 'Begging for it!' Then some weak fucking sister took up his cause, and they transferred him in the middle of the night so none of us would make a fuss. But that was almost twenty years ago, so I have to ask, where in the hell did you hear mention of him?"

I was embarrassed to admit it.

"In a comic book."

MacKay looked at me as if I had confessed my love for Cooper Lewis.

"Something an inmate drew," I said. I saw it more clearly now. A piece of propaganda. *The Four Stages of Cruelty*. An account of the injustices incurred for the mere killing of a CO.

"Which fucking shitbird did that?"

And that's when I felt my first misgiving. Did I really know how someone like MacKay might react? I saw no way out.

"Jon Crowley."

MacKay nodded. "Mister Shank Fight in the Yard, huh? Well, it figures." And he went back to watching Cooper Lewis.

I let a moment go by, until the insistence of doubt nudged me on.

"Why does it figure?"

MacKay looked at me without understanding.

"Why does it figure the guy who made the comic book about Hammond would get shanked in the yard?"

"Jesus, Kali, how should I fucking know?"

His incredulity put me in my place. I'd heard MacKay's comment as acknowledgment of some logical connection when it was just the usual indifference.

Minutes later he was still amped up and pissed off.

"I'm sick of waiting for this fucker." But I felt like the anger was aimed in multiple directions at once—at Lewis, at Ditmarsh, at me.

"I'll wait," I said, ever the peacekeeper among violent men.

"No, you get going. I'm going to expedite this a little. There's more than one way to take a shit."

Pushing me around, taking advantage of our friendship to handle some personal business. Part of me felt sad for him. I had the awareness that it happens to all of us in time. We get permanently angry.

I couldn't stop myself. "Why does Lewis have a phone up his ass, Ray?"

"I don't know," he said, but more drily than before. "To talk to a lawyer?"

Cooper Lewis was a small-timer. If he'd achieved any status at all inside Ditmarsh, it was as a runner, someone who did favors or took falls. MacKay would know about that.

"Who's Lewis bringing the phone in for, do you think?"

MacKay's smile was cold, as if he were saying, look at you, gazing into the abyss.

"Sweetie, you don't want to take this job so seriously as all that," he said.

I pulled the rubber gloves out of my pocket.

"Well, I'll leave you these, then." And snapped them with all the indifference I could muster.

I had a suspicion that Ray MacKay wouldn't be needing them, and that inmate Cooper Lewis would be keeping his cell phone.

6

My shift ended at four, but instead of signing out, squealing from the parking lot at a resolute fifty miles per hour, and putting the walls of Ditmarsh into the rectangular frame of my rearview mirror, I did something well beyond the purview of my narrow responsibilities: I visited Brother Mike. On my way, I concocted the remotely plausible tale that I was following up to check on him. I'd been the one to extract him from the yard, so it made a certain amount of sense, though a CO under any ordinary circumstances would never have given a moment of concern to the fate of a civilian who'd thrown himself into a corrections matter. My real motive, pressing like a heavy weight on my chest, was a desire to atone for having ignored Josh's warnings in the Keeper's car. I wanted to assess my responsibility for the consequences I'd seen in the yard during that brutal fight. I wanted a better understanding of an event that was, in all likelihood, ultimately incomprehensible.

The studio that housed the art class was in the education or east wing, and that location enhanced all my misgivings and the sense that I was betraying my tribe. The east wing had been a two-floored unit until 1979, when the inmates housed within had risen up and taken control, killing four of our brothers in the initial siege. A full-scale riot resulted, during which only two inmates died, leaving the account books spectacularly unbalanced. To wreak as much destruction as possible, the walls between the isolation cells had been knocked down by the inmates involved, creating long, ragged passageways through the length of the wing. Afterward it was decided to go with the flow of that refurbishment work, knock down all the walls, plaster and paint over the unfortunate grim memories, and build classrooms and offices where cells had once stood. They housed the weak sisters within that new space, ceding them occupied territory for their anger management programs and therapy sessions, while turning the wing into an edifice for tolerance and a permanent monument to defeat.

The doors of Brother Mike's studio were open. I had never been inside, and I was surprised by the expansiveness of the space within, a workshop filled with broad tables and tall stools, lit by giant caged windows overlooking the yard. I called out but got no answer and so, finding myself alone, wandered around to look at the so-called art. The drawings and paintings on the walls were calmer than I would have expected. Bowls of fruit, the faces of loved ones. I stopped before an abstract piece and couldn't decide whether it was ludicrous or interesting. It was a large canvas divided into a dozen grids, with a single identical portrait of Elvis painted into each square. Fat Elvis, with the sideburn muttonchops. When I looked closely, I saw that each Elvis was different in the most trivial way—a shortened sideburn, a cigarette dangling from his mouth, a pirate's earring. I was drawn in by the irregularities and had begun to note each variation in turn when I was startled by a voice.

"I'm over here, I'm over here."

It sounded, to my ears, like a snarl of complaint. I turned around expecting accusation but got an impatient wave instead. Brother Mike appeared in the doorway of an office I hadn't noticed at the far end of the studio. He seemed a mixture of anger and energy as he moved toward me, pausing once to adjust a precarious arrangement of tools on one of the workbenches. Yet there was ease to him, too. He was at home in this room and in his own skin. In comparison, I felt as though I were masquerading as someone important.

I introduced myself by name, and we shook hands, his grip about as firm and commanding as I'd ever felt. He called me Officer Williams. I hesitated to call him Brother Mike. Using the term made it sound as though we were at a lodge meeting.

And then a smile came to his face. "If I'm in trouble, at least they sent you." A little flirtatious, the way old men can pour on the charm before much younger women.

I decided to go with the flirt. It's a cheap instinct, but too easy to pass up.

"I'm not sure why you should get in trouble for doing something the boys ought to have done themselves. I thought that was a decent takedown for a counselor."

"I used to box," he explained.

I smiled. "I'd say you used to wrestle."

"Only with sin."

It was a joke, I think.

"You look fine," I announced, as though my work here were done. "I just wanted to see if you were physically okay." The word physically sounded stupid to my ears.

He grimaced, but it wasn't pain. "I'm so sick about that," he said. "I know such things happen from time to time, but I'm still broadsided by it all. I think that's why I ran across the yard and got in the way. I couldn't quite believe the whole thing turned violent. I just wanted it to stop."

I saw my opening and put the question forward hesitantly. "Did it start because of something that happened in your class?"

I anticipated a gruff reply, a return to the bad temper, but he looked relieved. "I'm glad someone's finally asking me about it."

"You mean no one has been here to talk to you?"

I'd have expected the Pen Squad, Keeper Wallace, or some irate CO to have jumped all over Brother Mike by this point, a full day later.

"No one until now," he said, offering me the job. "Shall we sit down in my office?"

I nodded, reluctant now that my plan was actually working so well.

The office had a desk and a couch and another living-room chair with a coffee table between, and two walls lined with bookshelves and upright file cabinets, like a staggered canyon of skyscrapers. Papers and books seemed to have exploded from every drawer and shelf. He directed me to the couch, and I sank into its deep cushion. He took the chair opposite, and suddenly we were patient and therapist, or so it felt to me. This is where his ease comes from, I thought. He sees all the world through the prism of analysis.

"The class. Well, there was nothing really. Nothing unusual about the session. I wish I could understand it all better."

"It doesn't always make sense," I told him. "You had group?" The word session was therapeutic code. I pictured a circle of men explaining their inner rages, cheering one another's progress on, like addicts with a murdering problem.

"It was our monthly crit session, not counseling related. Anyone who's finished artwork that month can show it to the rest of the class for comment and feedback. Those discussions can grow heated sometimes."

"Inmates can get heated about anything."

He smiled. "You should see grad students."

I pushed further. "Did Jon Crowley show something?"

"He didn't. He was going to, but then he decided his piece wasn't ready, and we couldn't convince him to change his mind. He's a perfectionist. So a few others went instead. I have eight in that class, one of three groups I meet with every week. Horace Sunfish, Timothy Connors, Bradwyn Delinano, Roy Duckett, Josh Riff, and, of course, Jonathan Crowley and Lawrence Elgin. That afternoon, Timothy showed a very unfinished two-D collage, Bradwyn read a rather unfortunate love poem he'd also illustrated, and Josh showed some of his new drawings."

I knew everyone in that crew by sight, and I was surprised at how unlikely they were as a mix. Horace was an Indian. Timothy was an incomplete transsexual they called Screen Door, supposedly because he got banged so often. Bradwyn was half Chinese, half Puerto Rican. Roy was the old-timer with one leg who worked in the kitchen, Elgin a raging Viking, Josh an utter newbie, Crowley your average mid-thirties lifer.

"Did Crowley and Elgin have some animosity between them?"

Brother Mike sighed. "A general dislike. But nothing overwhelmingly hostile, or I wouldn't have had them in the same group. Lawrence can be unpredictable in his opinions—sometimes he's surprisingly thoughtful, in fact—but Jon can also be moody. If anything, the animosity that day was between Roy Duckett and Jon. Do you know Roy? Roy teased Jon quite hard about not wanting to show his work. But I didn't think much of it at the time. They're close friends, almost inseparable, and I find there's often less patience and everyday politeness in such relationships. But really, Jon's work was ready to show. I had glanced through it before class when Jon and I had our counseling session. He'd made a lot of progress over the last year on what was an ambitious project, but when the stakes are high for an artist, it can be difficult to open up."

"What was the project?" I asked.

He looked at me with amusement. "Are you interested in art?"

The sudden condescension made me bristle, and I responded badly.

"I just find it funny hearing the word art thrown around when we're talking about hard-core inmates."

He'd found me out, and he smiled now with a polite reserve. "You probably don't think much of what we do here."

"What is it that you do here?" I was relieved, at some level, to be talking honestly.

"Paint, draw, throw clay. Sometimes we expand into collage and poetry."

"I went to camp for that once. When I was in grade school."

"Exactly. You think it's camp."

We were grinning at each other. I don't know why I'd edged into mild hostility—perhaps an instinct to reestablish my bona fides as a CO. At some level I was bothered by the coddling that went on in this room, by the caring and nurturing of such unworthy beings. You had whole school systems out in the world where no one gave a shit.

"I thought it was supposed to be therapy. Art therapy," I said.

"The art isn't therapy," he said, and got engaged again. "Not the way you think of therapy. I don't believe art is therapeutic or even moral just because it's art. I don't believe it necessarily makes you a better person, whether you're the viewer or the creator. Art is too elusive for that. Work that's didactic or deliberately uplifting is usually crap."

"So why bother with it?" I didn't mean the dismissal to be voiced so harshly, but Brother Mike was undeterred.

"The art gives them confidence, a means of expressing themselves, sometimes for the first time. Most of the men here have low self-esteem, and what little they do have, the system grinds out of them through the daily humiliations and restrictions." He raised a hand. "I'm not criticizing. It is what it is. But as we refine punishment, we whittle away the human psyche. In my experience, that does nothing to encourage rehabilitation, let alone actual penance, the soul-saving stuff I'm supposed to be engaged in. Artistic creativity is a bit of salvation from that institutional degradation. It gives a sense of purpose, a sense of accomplishment, a platform to discuss moral and spiritual issues, occasionally personal insights." He laughed. "Maybe that's just ego speaking, but I swear, at conferences, my presentations go over very well."

I nodded. "Sounds challenging." Like I'd crashed some cocktail party and was agreeing with opinions I didn't quite understand.

"I build some trust, foster some self-expression, and channel the art making into the restorative justice work we do. Are you familiar with that concept?"

Restorative justice. I knew the term, and it had always seemed ridiculous to me. "A little. You let perpetrators and victims talk things through."

"It's my way of saving souls, Officer Williams. It takes years to prepare an inmate, and years for an inmate to successfully reach out to the people they've wronged. But when it happens, when those sides start to correspond or when they actually meet face-to-face, you'd be amazed at the emotions that surface and the humanity that gets revealed. And that's when people make a connection and move forward, sometimes with great positive impact on each other's lives."

"Why would any victim want to connect with a perp?"

"They're connected already. They'll never not be connected. This is just a way to handle the awesome psychic reality of that. Otherwise"—he shrugged—"the hate and the anger is like cancer killing us a little more every day."

His eyes were locked on mine, and I knew then he was a true believer. I, on the other hand, had never believed in anything deeply in my entire life—except for the importance of contingency plans, the likelihood of the most certain things fucking up, and, perhaps, on my worst days, the utter elusiveness of the human connection Brother Mike insisted on pushing.

"Well," I said, "I admire what you're doing." I didn't mean it, but I admired something about him, the true believer aspect, I suppose.

"We both have difficult jobs." It sounded like simple honesty, and a little chip of ice melted from my heart.

"Jon Crowley was working on a visual narrative," he said, "a story in pictures and words that delved into the themes of restorative justice quite heavily."

I was disoriented by his description of Crowley's comic book. Restorative justice was not the vibe I'd picked up glancing through the pages.

"The Four Stages of Cruelty," I said, the words slipping out.

"You've seen it?"

"No," I said. "Heard someone mention it." He knew I was lying.

"Since you're interested, perhaps you'd like to look at his source material. You can borrow this if you like."

He reached up to the shelf above him and retrieved a heavy, water-warped book and passed it to me.

"An eighteenth-century British artist named Hogarth developed a series of prints called, of course, *The Four Stages of Cruelty*. Hogarth believed art *could* change people. He was a reformer. Social injustice and the root causes of criminality were among his themes. You should look through. We can have a vigorous discussion afterward. And I make the most wonderful cookies."

I didn't know whether he was teasing me or getting rid of me, but I stood and prepared myself to leave, weary from my masquerade.

"One more thing," he said, as if it had been he who'd called us together. "I have something unfortunate to give you."

"What do you mean?"

I was slightly alarmed by the announcement. Brother Mike walked back to his desk and found a manila folder and brought it to me. I took it, cautiously, and looked inside.

A piece of white paper with an ink drawing on it. A woman holding a bejeweled sword, and that woman was me. An accurate likeness of my own face. My naked profile with long hair, an arched back, and pert, upturned breasts that could have been imagined only by someone who'd never seen a thirty-nine-year-old without a bra.

"I'm sorry to heave that on you," he said. "I removed it from a notebook. In this environment, there's obviously some taboo subjects. Gang symbols. Violent fantasies. Pornography. This crosses a couple of those lines. I have an arrangement, fully known to my students, whereby I forward anything I confiscate to Keeper Wallace. But I thought you might rather destroy it yourself."

"Did Josh do this?" I could not help but feel the flush of shame.

"You know him?" he asked.

"Somewhat." My day with the girlfriend killer had inspired a few fantasies. There was nothing surprising about that, but the thought disgusted me, and it was embarrassing to be sitting before Brother Mike with the drawing in my hand. I closed the folder. "I'll take care of it."

"Thanks," he said. "I'd rather you did."

I stood, the folder under my arm, and shook Brother Mike's hand like an insurance adjuster. Then I tossed out one last question.

"How did Jon Crowley finish his project with a broken arm?"

Brother Mike looked surprised, and there was something gratifying in the way I threw him off balance, however unintentionally.

"A good point, isn't it?" he said. "Lawrence Elgin asked Jon that in class. 'How did you do it?' " Brother Mike let out a ragged sigh. "I wonder, would you look in on them for me? I'd like to know their condition, and nobody has been willing to tell me a thing."

I promised I would do that, and felt the entanglements grow.

7 |||||||||||||

But I did not get the time to check in on Elgin or Crowley. Four hours after I got home that evening, I was summoned back for URF duty. Disturbances on one of the blocks, they told me, and the news felt like a delayed tremor following the fight in the yard. Sometimes it happened that way, a little thing leading to greater confusion, and you wondered if it was all connected or just random reactions or even the full moon.

I felt amped up driving back to the prison, a little overtired and adrenaline pushed, but excited to put on the battle rattle and do some actual emergency work. The gate camera was hooded over with snow when I got there, but they buzzed me in anyway. I stomped my boots off on the mat, adding to the dirty slush.

Tony Pinckney—Nosepicker to his closest friends—sat at the receiving counter in the cage behind the metal detector. Though five years my junior, we'd joined at the same time, so our work lives had often overlapped. We'd done rounds together many times, spent two weekends shooting guns, squirting chemical agent, and tasering each other at training courses. He'd once invited me to a minor-league baseball game—whether as a date or a guys' night out I never learned, because I turned him down. Now he was all business.

"I need a piss break and a coffee," he announced, as though my arrival were long overdue. He asked me to man the station for five while he relieved himself. That meant a further delay in my URF response time, but what could I do? I took off my parka but remained standing in the booth, all the video monitors in the world for my entertainment. I could see the blurry commotion on a stretch of D block, some inmates in their cells like good doggies, some sitting quietly on the floor grinning and chatting to show they were tough, a few shit disturbers pacing drunken angles and occasionally throwing up their arms at the camera to shout unheard rebukes about terrible injustices. I felt my heart tick up a notch, seeing the brutal undercurrent come to the surface, the rage that some felt was their God-given right to express. It was just for show, a make-believe fantasy of revolt, but it could easily go too far. I'd seen men commit violence and look bewildered about it later, as though they'd been forced to go through with something just to live up to the expectations of the situation at hand. The last thing I wanted was to be trapped inside some sick fuck's private delusion.

"Don't you wish you could have had a hot bath and stayed in bed?" Pinckney said behind me, calmer now, less burdened. He was the type of tall man whose striking height is apparent only when he's standing next to you.

I ignored the innuendo that came with his emphasis on the word bed. "Overtime suits me fine." With a reasonable number of emergencies to attend to, my salary promised to jump from fifty-two to sixty-five plus a year. That was all right by me.

We both caught sight of the fight that had erupted in D—one of the men inexplicably dragged out of his ground-level cell by two others, dropped into a huddled heap on the open floor, and subjected to a drawn-out performance of stomping and kicking in full view of the camera. Like fake wrestling, except these guys thought fake wrestling was real.

"Looks like Felix Rose," I said. Rose was gang affiliated though none too special, making it likely we were watching a little fringe-level payback.

"What I wouldn't give for some tear gas and high-powered rifles," Pinckney said.

"Just give me a fire hose," I added, sharing his frustration. The COs couldn't do a thing while the range was out of control. Rules were absurdly strict in handling crisis situations. You needed to negotiate for calm, practically beg the men to stop. You even had to keep providing their meals. Forgoing brute force or hunger as a deterrent, you were left only with boredom—eventually, having nothing better to do, the inmates allowed you to resume control of the situation. For the COs it was humiliating because it clarified the degree to which the inmates were truly running the asylum. Pinckney told me to have fun.

In the lockers behind Keeper's office, I got my gear on, a chest protector and fireman-type gloves, a helmet with a visor like some outer-space welder's, a spool of extra zips, a spare fuckstick, but no guns, no Tasers, no shield, nothing fun. All dress-up and no party.

In a full-scale riot I would have been on the front lines from the get-go, but this business was contained to one range, and there were plenty of URF COs on hand, so Keeper Pollack asked me to do normal rounds and check on the calm ranges. This was thankless shit. The inmates were on full lockdown, probably glad to be out of harm's way, though acting feistier than normal, especially when I was in the vicinity. I withstood more than the usual laughs and calls of abuse.

By midnight it was my turn to join the activity on D block and pretend to be in control of the situation behind the gates. An assistant warden stood halfway down the tunnel, talking on his cell phone. Of course, no one reminded him that he couldn't have a cell phone inside.

Three administrative cronies hovered near him. I didn't glance at them as I passed. Six COs huddled at the front line, including Keeper Wallace, the officer in charge. He looked plumper than normal in his vest, his eyes dark with the usual exhaustion. My arrival got Keon, another URF CO, a free pass to the lockers. He looked at me gratefully. "Hope nobody's sleeping on my bench."

Wallace asked me how things were in the other blocks. I had nothing outlandish to report. Everything was restless but under control.

Ray MacKay was there, too. He lifted his visor and grinned at me like a kid out for Halloween. We backed off the cellblock entry so he could brief me, meaning fill me in on all the fuckups and hilarious shit encountered thus far.

"D-one refused to comply when we ordered all ranges into lockdown. Or Hadley and Vargas refused, and the rest of their tier mates followed suit. Couple hours back, Hadley took a nap right in the middle of the floor and asked for a bedtime lullaby. Said it felt like he was camping outside and looking up at the stars."

From the range, Hadley yelled out, "Yo, Lieutenant Wallace, you got yourself an improved situation there. I wholeheartedly appreciate you bringing in cheerleader Williams."

Even in a helmet and body armor.

A few laughs from other inmates. "Send *her* in for negotiation. Promise we won't bite."

"Much!"

I'd once caught Hadley with Vargas's dick in his mouth. I wanted to remind him of that fact right now, but not in front of Wallace.

"How did those two ever end up on the same tier?" I asked. "Didn't they transfer in here together?" I spoke quietly. I did not want the assistant warden or any of his people to hear my complaining.

"For the same crap as this," MacKay said without any discretion. "We're just full of forgiveness."

Wallace shook his head. "They'll get tired eventually." He raised his voice. "You just let us know when we can get treatment for those men in there, Hadley. Every minute that goes by is making it worse for you."

"Fuck you, you fat fucking pig!" Vargas yelled out.

"That's a write-up, Vargas," Wallace said. "I'm taking note of everything."

Vargas and Hadley laughed like orangutans inside a cage at the idea of being written up for bad language.

"Don't think I won't," Wallace said, as much to himself as anyone else.

An hour and a half later, at two-twelve in the a.m., Hadley agreed to let Felix Rose be taken to the hospital. "I am *tired* of this sorry motherfucker whining and crying all the *goddamn time*," Hadley said. "You think it's so tough losing your precious kidney? That ain't the worst way you can piss blood, you hair-icle cocksucker."

I looked to MacKay. "What does hair-icle mean?"

"Don't ask me," MacKay said. "I thought Felix Rose was bald."

I tried not to laugh.

"He's saying heretical," Wallace explained, impatient with our joking. "He keeps calling him heretical."

"Jesus Christ," MacKay muttered. "Religious intolerance is at the root of all conflict these days, isn't it."

"You two quiet down and get ready," Wallace said.

Wallace informed the assistant warden and was told to proceed. He opened the gate and let me and MacKay go through. I was surprised that Wallace would ask me to step into a crisis situation, given his reluctance to have me on URF at all, but I was sure as hell not going to turn down the opportunity. I kept my riot mask up. I wanted full eye contact with everyone. I wanted Hadley, Vargas, and every other shitbag to know I was not afraid to be walking among them. There were syringes and homemade knives on the floor, tossed out from every cell in preparation for the inevitable shakedown after the reign of glory had passed. Hadley kept his distance, but he held a metal pipe in his hand with a duct-taped handle. A few of the inmates hooted and whooped to have two COs in their grasp, but nobody made a move forward. They're as worn-out as we are, I thought. When it came down to it, all inmates craved routine. It was their comfort blanket and their teddy bear. Mini-riots launched by sadistic assholes like Shawn Hadley were disruptions to the natural flow.

The range smelled sour and grim. Unwashed bodies. An acrid odor that reminded me of cat piss. I wondered if Felix Rose really was having kidney failure. He lay in his cell on the floor. He'd pulled a sheet off the cot to cover himself. The sheet was wet and sticking to his body. He wasn't moving. "Felix?" I called. He still didn't move. I stepped in closer and pulled back the sheet, fearing the worst. His face was drained white and drizzled with sweat. There were serious contusions on his forehead, purple mounds that stuck out like erupting volcanoes. Between and beneath the bruisings I saw something that startled me, a triangle deliberately burned into his skin like a brand, all welted and seeping. His eyes opened, a frightened rabbit staring. He started breathing rapidly, like a woman in labor, and muttered a few "please Gods."

"We're going to need a stretcher," I told MacKay. Felix groaned at my touch. "I'll stay with him."

MacKay backed out of the small space. I kept my fingers on Rose's neck, checking the weak pulse. "We'll get you out of here, Felix," I said. Back in the world, Felix was a drug-addicted break-and-enter lowlife who'd started a house fire to destroy the body of an old woman he'd clubbed to death. In here, he was just another sorry sack of shit. Despite it all, you care about the human life. Time on my hands, I looked up and around. Besides the usual amenities I noticed a postcard-size drawing taped to the single shelf above Rose's desk. The same pumpkin face, the same stack of pyramids.

Were they everywhere? I remembered that Rose was a friend of Crowley's. Did that put them together in some common cause? I thought of the Beggar walking across the desert toward the towered city, the many minions there who knew him.

"What a sweetheart you are," Hadley said behind me.

I whirled around, almost kneeing Rose in my haste.

"Couldn't have asked for a better Christmas present."

I was used to being in intimate contact with thugs and fuckheads, but I had never been trapped inside an enclosed space by one before. Hadley blocked the door, the pipe in his hand, his shirt wide-open, his free hand dipped into the top of his sweatpants. Of course I imagined the worst. The last time a female staff member had been raped—a nurse in the howler ward—the URF team, unwilling to break in and risk the nurse's life without negotiating a stand-down first, sat outside the door and listened for hours while the son of a bitch sodomized her. There was no way I would ever let that happen to me. I had my fuckstick at my belt and figured I could get it before he came down with the pipe, but then it would be hand-to-hand combat, and I had no illusions about any certainty of outcome there.

"You ready for a shit kicking, Hadley?" I asked.

He stared at me, the same stupid smile weakened ever so slightly.

"Go ahead, Ray, fuck him up," I said.

Hadley bit and looked around for Ray. I whipped out and down with the fuckstick as hard as I could, snapping the outside of his knee. He dropped like he'd been shot, rolled onto his side curling both hands over his kneecap, and called me every name I'd ever heard.

My breath heavy, I watched him for sudden movement, any sign that he was just waiting for me to step closer.

"You okay in there?" Wallace called out.

I didn't answer, and I couldn't will myself to walk past Hadley.

MacKay appeared, the stretcher under his arm.

"What the fuck?" he said.

"He made a move," I told him.

MacKay's face twisted into a sneer, and he pulled out a stun gun the size of a penlight from his waist belt and pointed it down at Hadley's groin.

"I'll cut your fucking balls off," he promised.

Don't, I thought, and turned my head away. The stun gun arced its electric jolt across the foot of space toward Hadley's crotch. Hadley's back arched for a frozen second, then released, and he lay on the stone floor moaning like a sick puppy, little spit bubbles specking the corners of his mouth. MacKay reached down and grabbed him by the sack, slowly but lazily, the way you'd pick up a bowling ball before a meaningless shot. "I bet you can't feel anything down there right now." And Hadley moaning no, no, no. "I bet it's all numb, like you sat on your foot for the last half hour, like you got a novocaine shot in your lip." Twisting hard, talking gentle. "You let me know later how it feels when it wakes up. I'm curious." The fat knuckles on his hand blotching white and pink.

Needing to get away, I stepped over Hadley and squeezed by MacKay, picked up the piece of pipe and walked over to the gate. Vargas watched me from the middle of the range, pissed off but not moving. "You fucking bitch," he said with as much hatred as I'd heard in a voice in some time. I passed the pipe through the bars to Wallace and kept my eyes on Vargas. MacKay released Hadley and let him crawl away from the cell. He twisted painfully along the floor, wishing us slow, horrible deaths. It would have been easy now to tag him and drag his ass out, but the order was not given, the protocol so extra-cautious it boggled the mind. A CO named Davidson came through the gate to help load Felix Rose onto the stretcher. I leaned against the bars, trying to get my breathing under control. Goddamn lucky, my racing heart told me. I avoided any glance back at Wallace, wondering how much he'd seen, whether they'd heard MacKay's Taser. Lucky, lucky, lucky. When Davidson and MacKay huffed back with the stretcher, Wallace told me to take Davidson's end and get out. "I can't look at you right now." So he had noticed. My first time with a little danger pay on URF, and already I'd been involved in a fuckup.

I exchanged with Davidson and grunted when the full weight became mine, surprised as usual at how heavy a human body could be. We shuffled along, passing the assistant warden who was striding fast the other way, calling out to Wallace for a situation report. The riot helmet was jiggling and slipping over my eyes, off kilter, as though I were suddenly a little kid wearing a fireman's costume for Halloween. Fuck fuck fuck, I thought, wishing that someone else was carrying Felix Rose's dying ass.

MacKay needed to rest three times along the way. I was thankful for each break. The stretcher was an old-fashioned canvas job from some *MASH* episode. There was no elevator to the infirmary. By the time we finally made it, Felix Rose had stopped moaning. The male nurses took him. I leaned against a table and felt my age, all thirty-nine years weighing on my lungs.

"Give me a minute?" I asked Ray. "Something I want to check on."

He nodded, just as beat. "Take your sweet fucking time."

I exited the triage room and headed down the main hallway where the full doors lined those private drums. At DI-2, I stopped and looked in.

Crowley's cell. Empty, so I knew he must be in the dissociation unit. Without opening the door, I scanned the walls for drawings, scratches, some of the circle and triangle marks I'd been seeing around, but I noticed nothing. I moved next door to DI-3 and peered inside. Josh lay on the mattress, his eyes closed. I hissed his name, and he looked up.

"It's me," I said, feeling like an idiot for entering into such Romeo and Juliet mode.

"Officer Williams?"

"Yes." I winced. I fished my keys and unlocked his door, stepped inside, and kept it propped open.

He looked terrified, as though his purest fantasy had suddenly turned real. Me in my body armor, all sweated up and ready.

"We've got two minutes, and you're going to explain some things to me."

He nodded. "What things?"

"The fight in the yard. Is that what you were expecting to happen to Crowley?"

A blank stare, then a nod. "I don't know. Maybe."

"Did Elgin jump Crowley because of that fucking comic book?"

Another careful nod. "I think so. A lot of people were really upset because they didn't know Crowley was still working on it."

"A lot of people?"

"Elgin. Roy. Others I heard about."

"Roy?"

"A little. He called Crowley crazy one time when he came to visit, and they were pretty mad at each other. Crowley wanted me to keep six for him."

Keep six. Watch his back.

"And where's the comic book now?"

Another shrug. "I don't have it."

"Crowley have it?"

"I don't know. Where is he?"

"Doing time," I said. I heard a noise on the infirmary range, some door opening and closing, and I felt panicked about getting caught in this impromptu moment of impropriety. I slipped out of Josh's open door and closed it behind me.

"Where's Crowley?" Josh asked again. But I ignored him and headed back for triage.

I peered into the caged beds in the intensive care unit, searching for Elgin. I could at least check on his status, but then I saw MacKay sitting on the edge of a desk in the triage area, looking bewildered and out of sorts. Something bad has happened, I thought, and hurried over.

"What's wrong?" I asked. "You all right?"

He didn't look good. He coughed, a hacking that grew worse until it sounded as though something loose were flapping inside his chest. He wiped the sweat off his forehead. "Bad time to catch a cold," he muttered.

I relaxed and found myself a chair and swung into it. We'd both take it easy, rest off the hard haul.

"You always got a cold," I said. "You caught it from cigarettes and rye."

I thanked him for helping me out back there, even though I was mildly horrified by what he'd done with the Taser. He must have picked up on my queasiness because he started in about the old days. How things used to be handled. If a prisoner fucked with a guard, there'd be time for payback at leisure. I understood the reasoning, but I was too tired to voice any nuances about more humane options. All I wanted was food. I had a can of tomato soup in my locker, a year old if a day. It never seemed so tantalizing as now. If I could only get there, take off my helmet, and spend fifteen minutes by myself, I might just be all right.

MacKay stopped talking. I watched his gaze fall, an odd look of dismay in his eyes. Before I could reach his shoulder, he slid deeper into the chair. Then his hands flew up, and he tipped out completely. I yelled for an orderly and started loosening his vest.

8

I'd been told once, by one of the COs who did summer work as a volunteer bush firefighter, that a forest could burn under the ground. Instead of a wall of flame eating its way across the woods in an organized front, there was another kind of battle in which wildfires burst out spontaneously at random spots. You could be walking through the trees in the dim smoke, feel the hollow heat of the ground below, and see a demon shoot out from the earth to consume a birch tree to your left, or a flame spiral in the air like a will-o'-the-wisp. You didn't understand the mechanism of the fire—where to intervene with it, how to anticipate or fight it—because it was actually going on below you, unseen. I felt that way about Ditmarsh during the double shifts that followed MacKay's coronary. C block burst out the next night, for reasons no one attempted to explain. It wasn't hard to douse those flames—the inmates gave themselves up like Iraqi soldiers, worn-out and thankful, biding their time for a later insurgency—but the preponderance of other isolated disturbances kept you wary and tense, dreading the next surprise. A hot shot on D-1, the needle still stuck in the dead inmate's arm. A CO nailed in the neck by a pin from a zip gun, attacked by some sniper with extraordinary aim, the pin probably tipped with contaminated blood or fecal matter. We all feared invisible arrows after that, listened for tings, slapped at the slightest itch.

I had no time to think of MacKay, yet I was sick over him and could hardly bear to ask for news. When the siren blasted an inmate escape two mornings after MacKay fell, the noise cracked the just brightening sky and obliterated all rational thought, as though the confusion had shrapneled and the fragments were whipping past our ears. An inmate escape? Why the fuck not? As good a time as any to jump the wall. Soon the word went around. By all counts, a single man down. Who've you got—who've you seen—when did you last see them? I knew the names of all the inmates I'd escorted and signed away at the dissociation unit with its hallways of isolated cells. But like everyone, I feared the kind of mistake you could make lockstepped into the forward march of turmoil.

Then the word came that inmate Jon Crowley was the wall hopper, and the information gave me a bad feeling all over. How had we missed him? A full three days following the yard incident, no one could account for where he'd been escorted, nor by whom, whether he'd been shuffled to the infirmary for treatment like the others involved in the fracas or whether he'd been sent straight to dis without delay. It baffled me that no CO put up his hand and claimed responsibility for having brought Crowley somewhere. Surely the trail would lead to that CO eventually. Wouldn't it be better to admit a mistake now rather than later? I kept thinking, he'll just show up. Someone has stashed him somewhere odd, lost him like a wallet or a watch or a set of keys, and then they'll remember. It had to be some bureaucratic oversight, some institutional fuckup—you did not escape from prison, not these days, not when your arm was in a half-body cast.

During my duty wanderings I kept an eye out for everyone who was part of Brother Mike's group. I located Screen Door and Horace and Bradwyn in gen pop, and although I saw no opportunity to talk to them, by sight each of the three seemed to share a timidity and wariness, or maybe it was just something I imagined. Josh was ensconced in his cell in the howler ward, and Roy Duckett was lodged in an open triage bed because of some head injury, while Lawrence Elgin lay in a similar bed within a cage, his wrists and ankles belted to the bed frame. More disturbing to me were the marks I began to notice on walls and floors and etched into doorframes and drains. Sometimes sentence fragments, with the occasional warped poem. "Shoot now." "Liquor up." "God Bless Ditmarsh." "Electricity is Zappy!" "Humpty Dumpty is the baddest of them all." But also curious scratches: lines and dots that looked deliberate but indecipherable, circles, loops, the outlines of unknown countries, other details that seemed randomly and fiercely scratched out. And finally, pictures everywhere, crudely drawn animals like cave paintings, huge penises, gashlike vaginas, melon-size breasts, contorted sexual acts of every deviant position and combination, swords and spears, hot-rod cars, the sun, the moon, the towers of a city.

Was I the first CO to pay them any attention? Through the filter of my overtired imagination, it seemed to me that the symbols were multiplying, that marks and drawings and depictions and scratches were growing thicker in hallways and walls the second or third time I came back to look. I longed to document the mess with my cell phone camera, though I knew that was crazy.

I was not the only one mentally taxed by the prolonged situation. Among the inmates and COs the usual rumors achieved an unusual frenzy. Someone had found an ingenious tunnel from the infirmary to the loading dock of the old furniture warehouse—that's how Crowley must have escaped. Other rumors focused on his current whereabouts. Crowley was on a Mexican beach having a last laugh, inmates claimed, and COs half believed. Crowley was in witness protection, whatever intelligence he'd offered up to the FBI so valuable they'd sneaked him out during a manufactured riot and made it look like an escape.

The four keepers were on hand almost all of the time, and I'd never seen that before. At various lulls I stoked myself to approach Keeper Wallace and inform him of the comic book that Josh Riff had shown me after the funeral outing. But each time, I let the opportunity go by and told myself that the knowledge I possessed was just more meaningless noise, that the graffiti and markings I noticed everywhere had always been there and were random and pointless. Then Wallace pulled me aside to give me shit about Shawn Hadley.

I couldn't believe, in the midst of everything else going on, that Wallace would even think to go back over the incident in D block, but he acted as though nothing had ever pinched his asshole tighter. "You jumped the force continuum," he informed me. I knew the speech, the hierarchy of physical engagement. Verbal warnings that went unheeded were followed by control holds, body blocks, and sanctioned takedown techniques. If the inmate did not stand down and submit, then the corrections officer applied chemical agent, or CA. Only if CA was deemed ineffective did the corrections officer resort to the fuckstick. Any head shots with fuckstick, fist, or boot needed to be reported and recorded in the head shot log. Of course the COs thought it was nonsense. We'd invented a head shot shooter to celebrate such occasions—tequila with a blood-red drip of Tabasco—but it still killed you to get singled out.

Wallace said, "I sent you and MacKay in there because I thought you could be nonthreatening, because I wanted to keep the situational dynamics steady, not explode them."

Implying, somehow, that the old joker and the new broad were too absurd a threat to inflame a disturbance and simultaneously that everything subsequent had been our fault. Should I have waited until I was raped? I wanted to ask. I knew he would counter that no officer (meaning no male officer) should act preemptively because of a rape threat. But I also knew that was bullshit. There were male COs who walked the blocks in constant fear that the big bend-over choke hold waited just around the next corner.

Wearily I insisted that my record of physical encounters with inmates was normal. That I'd never been reported before. Unlike MacKay, I wanted to add, I didn't tase Hadley in the balls and give them a squeeze for good measure. I am not the kind to stomp an inmate's guts out when they don't jump fast enough. I'd never dipped my finger in CA and jammed it under someone's eyelid when he was zip-cuffed. I'd never shoved a fuckstick up someone's ass in a blind dissociation cell.

Instead, I ate it all, every bit of pissed-off righteousness, and nodded.

I worked the next three days straight, through a haze of chaos and nerve-deadening exhaustion. The only sleep I got came a few hours at a time in the old barracks on the east field, behind what used to be the warden's house but now served as administration spillover. I slammed so many sliding steel doors I could feel the vibrations in the bones of my wrist. I yelled so many orders my throat went raw. I ran enough hallways in heavy gear to qualify for a marathon. We rousted inmates and dumped cells. We emptied tiers and filled them again. We delivered meals and meds and put up with the shouts of abuse. Just when you thought the calm had returned, something new happened and the shouting and the food throwing started all over again.

"It won't settle until after Christmas," Baumard, a veteran CO, told us. Baumard had the kind of bristly gray hair that was so accustomed to being buzzed short it probably didn't know how to grow long anymore. But he was also one of those COs of rare intelligence. He had made an ungodly amount of money in the stock market in the late 1990s, but had chosen—actually chosen—to keep working rather than powerboat his way off into the sunset. When it came to most matters, including financial, we listened to him like he was Warren Fucking Buffet. "All those family, spousal, and girlfriend visits lined up since Thanksgiving are fucked because of the lockdown, and it's our fault," Baumard continued. "They'll be pissed until January."

Too weary to be irate, we sat in the CO room the afternoon of Christmas Eve loosening vests and eating stale sandwiches from a lace-lined caterer's tray. I desperately needed to go to the bathroom, but Franklin walked out waving his hand and laughing about the toxic waste dump he'd left behind, courtesy of a week eating microwave burritos. The howls of offense from those closest to the escaping odor were enough to persuade me to hold my bladder.

At least our common misery reinforced our sometimes shaky solidarity. COs came in multiple shapes and forms. We had an ex-NFL football player and a surprising number of former schoolteachers. We had roofers and firefighters and retail security guards and ex-soldiers. We had men who loved ice fishing and men who voted Democrat. We had those who were always broke and others who were always flush. We had women who were single and on the dykey side, and women who were ripe and curvy from having kids. We could be as varied and unlikely, or as predictable and stereotypical, as the inmates themselves.

"Did you know Crowley was in art therapy?" a CO named Cutler asked, a nice enough fellow who was too out of shape and go-along-with-the-flow to get much respect from me. "All of this started just because someone didn't like someone else's drawing."

No one offered any explanations for why that would be so. I said nothing, though the guilt of my inaction around Josh's comic book was a constant throb in my temples. Others, with more energy, mumbled bitter feelings. Some touchy-feely program had contributed to our endangerment. As a CO, you just knew, on a moral level, that the softness was wrong.

A CO named Droune took up the common position. He cursed the weak sister who'd bolted across the yard and prevented a killing that might have solved many problems. The logic didn't hold, but that didn't seem to matter to Droune or anyone else. "That old son of a bitch, Brother Mike," he said, "ought to get his art licence revoked."

Baumard then gave Droune shit for letting a decrepit weak sister of the religious persuasion pull such a he-man boot stomping when Droune himself was such a floppy pussy. I didn't like Droune; his father and grandfather had been COs, and that made him a kind of third-generation idiot royalty. Baumard riding Droune was the only thing in a week to make me grin.

My good feeling lasted until I opened my locker. I dialed the combo and tugged. The lock snapped off. When I creaked open the door, I saw a drawing taped to the inside. The rush of embarrassment caught me hard—maybe my tiredness, maybe my sense that they never gave me a fucking break no matter how hard I worked to ignore it. But instead of reacting, I forced my voice into that tone of a teacher in a room full of grade school students, and said, "I suppose this delivered itself?"

Josh again. A similar drawing to the one Brother Mike had shown me. This time the female barbarian had a sword in one hand and decapitated head in the other, a snake tattoo winding around her wrist. She was sexy and saucy, hip thrust in exaggerated fashion to one side. She wore furs on her waist, high boots, and nothing on top, those well-endowed breasts with dark, lusty, and, once more, remarkably upward-pointed nipples. My distinguished colleagues gathered around.

"Amazing how those things get around," Cutler said.

"You mind if I make a few copies?" Droune asked, the twitters about to erupt.

I had no doubt they'd already xeroxed the shit out of it.

"Maybe blow it up, frame it, put it on the living-room wall," Franklin suggested.

Then: "Howdy, Radar," Baumard said in a loud voice. Everyone knew it was a warning, that Michael Ruddik had just walked into the room, meaning there was a rat on deck. Instantly I felt the dynamics of the school yard play out in predictable fashion. From being the target, I became another bystander. That didn't mean I sympathized with the new victim. Instead, I shared the group's disdain as much as I felt personal relief. On the surface, there was nothing about Ruddik to inspire any particular loathing. He was early forties, experienced, tall, athletic, even good-looking in a dark-haired, brooding kind of way. But he was widely suspected to be the resident Secret

Sam, a member of the corrections staff covertly assigned to investigate inmate complaints against COs. Every institution had one or more—sometimes FBI, sometimes DEA—someone watching the watchers. Coming off my recent meeting with Keeper Wallace about my actions involving Shawn Hadley, Ruddik was the last person in the world I wanted to run into. I shoved the drawing into my locker and got out my jacket.

"Check this out," Franklin said. Ruddik ignored him.

"Oh, come on, Radar," Droune said. "Don't be such a prude. That's a work of goddamn art."

Ruddik, who hadn't said anything, merely got a pair of rubber gloves from his locker and gave Droune a mock salute. Then he left.

I was about to do the same, given the freedom to go home for that most silent of nights, watch some taped talk show, and pass out in front of the TV, when Baumard asked me if I'd work his bubble shift for him so he could read his grandkids *The Night Before Christmas.*

9 ||||||||||||||

How could I say no? Single me. No children of my own. No brothers or sisters with cute nephews and nieces. No parent to look in on. No husband or boyfriend to fear offending. No presents to buy. I needed the cash. A bubble shift was as good as a night on the couch, except you got paid for it. With all the inmates snug in their cells and a complete lockdown enforced, there would be little need to pay attention. Safe, all-seeing, and powerful, requiring no physical exertion. If you kept one ear cocked for the radio and your partner kept his mouth shut, sweet dreams awaited.

So I said yes—before I learned that Cutler would be my shift partner, a man who couldn't keep his mouth shut for more than two minutes at a stretch.

Still, when we settled in for the duty after a dinner of pizza and chicken wings ordered in special by Baumard, even Cutler seemed subdued by the night and the long shifts leading up to it. The floor of the bubble was raised inside, and you felt like you were floating above the ground. The caged and glassed windows ran a complete circle around and above you, giving you full vision of the main hub. At night you kept the lights dim. On the console desk you had black-and-white cameras directed at fixed spots in the hub's major access points and the corridors of each wing. The grainy screens showed concrete, stone, and steel bars, like images of shipwrecks in deep water.

"Wish I was home," Cutler said, letting out a yawn. "Wish I was pretty much anywhere but here."

I rogered that and tried to keep my eyes from falling shut. The chicken wings, so tasty in the moment, had made me feel bloated and drugged. Soon Cutler was sleeping, his head thrown back, his bulbous neck doing something tubalike to the snores that bellowed forth.

Naturally, given such peace and quiet on such a blessed night, I succumbed to dark thoughts. My life at Ditmarsh had the taste if not the quality of failure. The job was a trap born of a momentous decision in my mid-thirties to enlist in the military before it was too late. But in my glorious 187 days of boots on ground in Iraq, all I did was live on a base, guard trucks, and feel grimy and sunstroked. The CO bit had not been in the plans. As soon I returned home, I looked into law enforcement, but there was nothing local going on. Then my father got sick. Despite feeling resentful about the situation that put me in, I took a job with the state corrections service to stay near at hand, and I ended up at the oldest penitentiary in the system, where none of the teachings and tactics I learned at the six-week corrections academy training course seemed to matter. The cliché of prison guard life was for real. I felt as if I too were doing time. My life outside was pared down, my belongings, my relationships, my routine all simplified. In Iraq I'd thought about friends and relatives all the time, wrote letters, sent intense feelings through e-mails, pictures, jokes. After my first year at Ditmarsh I stopped working so hard at keeping people near. And nobody seemed to notice.

I sat and counted the reasons I wished I had said no to Baumard's shift. Then I saw the sign.

In the middle of the bubble was a hatch where the floor opened up, and under it was a stone staircase going down to the armaments room below, and below that to the sealed-off dissociation holding cells we called the City. Above the door, on the wall, was an old fallout shelter sign: two yellow triangles on the bottom, one on the top within a circle. Except someone with a sense of humor had unriveted the sign from the wall and secured it upside down, like a distress signal, and scrawled the letters NOYFB beneath, like a Latin expression on some crest. NOYFB meant "none of your fucking business," and it was typical CO machismo. When I saw the mark in Crowley's comic book, I'd felt some vague recognition, but it was not until I was leaning back in my chair at the console deck and staring at the upside-down fallout shelter sign that I made the connection. Good God, I thought. How had that sign ended up in the drawing of an inmate?

It wasn't my job. None of my fucking business. And still I rose from the chair, gently, so as not to disturb Cutler, and walked over to the hatch.

Once, it had seemed like a juvenile prank, but the fallout shelter sign was ominous to me now, as though the menacing face were guarding the entrance to something wrong. The most common reason to descend the hatch stairs was to check the armaments or urinate in a corner, an unlikely act for me. We stored weapons down there along with assorted tools like fire hoses and canisters of chemical agent. Off the armaments room were four brick-sealed alcoves. Once upon a time, those alcoves were the beginnings of tunnels that led to other buildings within the complex, a means of escaping in case of dire emergency, but they were closed now, and anyone stuck in the bubble during a major disturbance would be holed up until the cavalry arrived.

Below the armaments room was the City. The old dissociation unit had cells so small and dark and inhumane that after a history of bad incidents and suicides and accidental slips, the door had been finally closed for good. I'd never been down there. The welding had taken place a few years before my time. The warden declared that sealing off the City was a gesture symbolizing the beginning of a new era. The old-timers were not happy about losing the best threat they'd ever possessed. The new dissociation range was like a stay at a Holiday Inn by comparison.

I felt gravity itself pulling me down. I would merely look, duck down quickly, and make sure the door to the City was still sealed shut. I gripped Cutler's damp shoulder until he blinked.

"Sorry," I said, guilty for stirring him. "I'm going down below. Something's not right."

He reached for his baton and rubbed his eyes to wake himself up.

"What do you mean?" he asked.

"Nothing," I said. "I'll be right back. I just want you to know where I've gone."

Before I descended the stairs of the hatch, I wanted someone to know where I was going.

The armaments room felt completely cut off from the world above, the bricked-up alcoves like four blinded eyes. The staircase to the City below was behind a heavy wooden door in the west wall, which was blocked by crates. A good sign, I thought as I heaved them to one side. There was a key hanging on a hook on the wall above it. Not so long ago, jailers had carried rings of such keys. The old padlock was as heavy as a cannonball. The lock opened, and I pulled the doors back.

"Everything okay?" Cutler called down. I could still see his shape in the entrance above me.

"Yes," I said. "I think it's all fine." Hoping it so.

The air that lifted up to me was mildewy and cold. I shone my flashlight on the wet walls and the narrow rounded steps. It was a steep walk down, and I had to lean back to avoid hitting my head. When I reached the bottom and came to the second door, I saw the propane canister on the ground. *They just left the goddamn blowtorch right there.* I felt my anxiety soar. A bar had been fitted back into place to keep the door locked from the outside.

The worst feeling in the world came over me.

"The lock's been cut," I shouted.

"What?" I heard.

Cutler did not come down. I should have turned back. This was all the evidence I needed to get the Keeper down here. But I felt laden with obligation and amped by the need to know, a desire to see what I had discovered. The door was thick and sodden. I could smell a thin odor of piss in the cold air behind it. The sounds changed and became less muffled as the world opened up into an expansive darkness. I heard something move, probably a rat, and stamped my foot and shouted to scare it off. The silence returned, but I could no longer believe it was an empty silence. "Crowley?" I called. My voice was deadened by the thickness of the stone. Before me was a pitch-black hallway. Shining my flashlight along the floor, I saw angled shapes like craggy rocks and realized that the entire hallway was cluttered with garbage. I made out broken computer terminals, upturned boxes of files, a weight-lifting bench, a metal bookshelf on its side. It was as though I'd stumbled on an abandoned warehouse or a flood-decimated building. The jutting rock created more shadows along the walls. The right wall was rough-hewn, while on the left I saw a row of doors with little space between them. My breath came rapidly, and I tried not to imagine larger shapes in the darkness flitting off whenever I moved my flashlight beam away. Some of the doors were shut; others were angled out of their rooms in disordered fashion like a series of unmade beds. I moved an inch forward and stopped. Anything could be down there. It would be better if I checked each cell in turn.

Opening the first door and looking in, I saw that the cell inside was barely long enough for a cot. Again, the room was filled with scattered garbage—a broken riot shield, an old cafeteria table. In the corner of the floor I saw a small, irregular hole with two raised stone rectangles straddling it. Rats came up through those sewer lines, I figured, probably had crept up even in the days when men slept inside. What a place to put someone. I shone my light on the walls within and saw graffiti scratched into the stone. I told myself it had been there for decades.

"Crowley?" I called again, irrationally, and part of me believed he might emerge from the darkness, blinded by the flashlight, babbling incoherently.

The second and third rooms were cluttered with garbage, too, their walls covered in more graffiti scrawls. By the time I got to the fifth room, I couldn't take my eyes off the shape ahead of me.

I wanted to run back to Cutler, to emerge from the darkness with a heavy gasp, as though I'd been underwater. But I also felt the need to see. There was nothing simple about that urge, however. It feathered into multiple threads—a desire to show myself strong and overcome the worst possible fright; an indecent, voyeuristic need that seemed almost pornographic in its insistence; and finally, a tender horror, a grief for human plight. Down here, in the clutter, the sour illness of cruelty. Nothing could be more awful.

His heaviness weighed the door down. I talked myself calm as I reached forward and pulled the door back gently, though my self-control was thin. Then my mouth was filled with saliva, my breath came in short, rapid intakes, and I struggled to see clearly.

The body was naked, suspended from the top of the door, jutted forward as if poised in mid-flight. There was a crusted paste all over his face and neck. The cast on his broken arm was gone, the unraveled chalky cloth strewn around him. He'd used some of that cloth to make the noose. It ate into his neck like an amputee's blood-soaked bandage. His knees were bent, and he had only to straighten his legs in order to rescue himself. His toes dangled. He was much smaller than he'd seemed in real life.

"Oh, Christ," I moaned, and realized that I'd been saying it over and over. I wanted to live my whole life without ever seeing such a thing. But it was too late, and I knew the smell and sight of Crowley would smother me forever.

I backed away, stumbling over a broken chair, the panic lifting me up. I struggled to grasp onto a single clear thought, and I shone my light around, paranoid again that there might be someone else inside one of the rooms I'd skipped. It occurred to me then, with all the horror I'd ever felt, that Cutler could slip the bar through the door as easily as an executioner slips a needle into an intravenous line, and I would be lost in here, too, disappeared forever, a joke among COs for years to come. I tried to calm myself, turn my back on poor Jon Crowley, and stride down the hallway, but then I was running, stumbling, teeth rattling in my mouth.

My light poured over the walls, the drawings different to me now. He must have used his cast, the chalk from the plaster, part of me realized—or did I figure that out later? Each cell room contained its own madness, a bewildering collage of images. At the top of the stairs I saw a last word, more hastily scrawled than the others and much larger, as if Crowley had stood there before the door and scraped the chalk up and down, losing hope: "DIG." Was it a command or a kind of pleading? I couldn't process what it meant, but I envisioned corpses, maggot-eaten bodies, flies swarming over an open grave. I slipped as I scrambled up the wet steps, fell so hard on my shins and elbow that my teeth clacked together, and crawled out of the hole and into the armaments room. Only then, when I was safely out, did I yell for Cutler.

Hours later, after the warden and the assistant wardens and all four of the keepers and half the senior COs and two Pen Squad lieutenants had been through, Wallace asked me whether I was all right. I didn't feel all right. My hands trembled slightly, and though I had moments where I considered myself extraordinarily sharp and lucid, there were dead spots, too, when my focus was utterly inert. The smell was in my nostrils, and I couldn't get the grip of the memory out of my brain. I saw the graffiti like some viral insanity infecting the stones, spreading outward, threatening to cover every brick and archway in the world above. Wallace mentioned the stain on my shin. I reached down and felt the pain, lifted my stuck pants, and saw the gouge out of my skin. He told me to go to the hospital ward and see to it, then go home, write my reports tomorrow.

I checked my watch. It was three in the morning. I did not want to walk through the tunnel to get to the hospital. I never wanted to walk through a tunnel again.

Outside, the sky was black. The air was sticky with cold. When I reached the hospital wing, I huddled to stop the shivering. It finally calmed down, and I proceeded around the corner and met eyes with the CO at the desk. He wanted to know what was going on, whether it was true they'd found Crowley. I muttered yes and pushed through the door. He asked me if I was all right, and I didn't answer.

The hallway was dim. I still had my flashlight on my belt. I pulled it out and shone it along the walls, intolerant of any pools of darkness. I could hear the breathing of those men in the utter silence. My steps echoed. I stopped before the infirmary cell where Jon Crowley had lived in endless purgatory while his busted arm healed. The steel sink and toilet. The empty cot with the single sheet. I remembered the smirk that had greeted me the last time I looked in, and the emptiness of expression in the dead face I'd seen an hour before.

I could sense Josh in the next cell, and I moved in front of his door. In that moment, all my anger toward him surged, my rage like a knife that ripped in a ragged line through the air, swinging out to hit something soft and vulnerable. His drawings of me pissed me off. What he'd done to his girlfriend ate at my stomach. And yet, in the lottery of life and death, he was protected from harm. I didn't know how to justify such random outcomes, that some men could be dragged down into the earth and torn apart while others got watched over by guardian keepers. I shone the light into his room and caught his face where he lay on the bunk, his eyes open, as if knowing with a preternatural instinct that someone outside the door was thinking about him, the expression pathetic, anxious, wary. He had said that he and Crowley were close. Well, let him hear the truth now.

"Your friend's a wind chime," I hissed through the grate, and stumbled on, seeking out a doc.

Josh lay on the bed and wondered if he'd heard right. He knew it was news about Crowley. He heard it as a tender kind of caring, a bit of human compassion, even an overture of mutual need. He missed his friend terribly. He'd been worried and anxious since the fight in the yard, frightened that he hadn't done enough to help. Now he had some news. Crowley was a wind chime, he thought, and let the words tap lightly through his brain, contemplating their poetic mystery, wondering what they meant. The answer, when it came, was simple. All rumors of escape or relocation had to be true. Crowley was gone, free somewhere. The wind blowing him about. He was a poem. A note hanging in the air. There was nothing more peaceful than sitting outside on a porch in the warm summer evening listening to the quiet tones of a wind chime.

When he woke up an hour or so later, heart knocking, he understood the real meaning of the dream. Not free. Not released. But dangling in a breeze. A hanging man.

STAGE II

10

When he woke, Josh was so flattened by the endless depths of unconsciousness that he was bewildered to find himself in Ditmarsh.

Then he remembered the news about Crowley and felt sick to his stomach, wondering what it had been like for him when it happened. Had he been very afraid? Had he known what was coming? Josh had hours to think about it.

During that long morning, despite the fact that it was Christmas, no one was allowed out of his cage. Nothing got delivered. At one point the hallway pounded with panic, army boots stomping by at a hard run, a door slamming against the wall, and a voice shouting for a doctor. In between there were long, empty oceans of indifferent silence. He wished the entire Christmas season to be over. He thought about his mom and ached with emptiness. He considered the peace that might have been possible if he'd never been born.

That afternoon, he was told to distribute meal trays in the ward. It was the first time the COs had asked him to do anything. The doors got unlocked. Able-bodied and compliant, Josh moved awkwardly and hesitantly down the hallway, unaccustomed to staring into so many homes. Most of the regular long-termers were docile on bug juice. They sat on the edge of their bunks, rocking back and forth, or paced their drums waving away unseen flies. A few were eager for chatter or news, though he had nothing to offer. The one with no face needed to be fed, so Josh set up a tray on the edge of the bunk and filled a spoon. When the spoon nudged the man's mouth, he ate mechanically. Josh fed him until the mouth stopped opening, and then he wiped the warped rivulets of healed flesh clean, afraid the nubbed hands might reach up and touch him.

By the time he got to the intensive care wing, he was tired of being free of his own cage and wanted to leave the trays on the chrome table outside, but a male nurse, overworked and weary, told him to finish the job. The room was a cavern with a dingy, antiseptic chill. The walls had been plastered until the edges were smooth and then painted a dull battleship gray. The ceiling shot twenty feet above to where the hanging fluorescent lights gave off a weak glow. The beds were in alcoves, the entrances arched. In the first alcove he saw a patient with some kind of vacuum machine parked beside the bed, rolling with a bad motor. Next over was an old bag of bones attached to an IV. Neither of them needed food, as far as he could tell, so he moved on, rattling the cart along the stone floor. He placed a tray on one man's stomach and put a spoon in his hand. He laid trays on med tables at the next two beds, where the men were sleeping. Then he came to a bed enclosed by a cage. Inside, he saw Elgin.

Even unconscious and strapped to the hospital bed railings, Elgin scared the shit out of him. In Brother Mike's studio he'd worn only an undershirt when working, showing off his tattoo colors, birds of prey on his broad shoulders, tangled spiderwebs spiraling from each elbow, naked angels with big tits peeking out from his own pectorals. According to Crowley, Elgin's artistic work was done in service of keeping his inking skills up, in the unlikely event he was ever released and could open his own parlor. Now half of Elgin's face was covered in a kind of cheesecloth, mottled with Chiclet squares of blood. There were uncovered stitches on his neck, a slashed line like a row of black flies drawn to the puckered gore. The sheet was tucked snugly below his armpits and then raised up in a tent around his waist, as if gently lifted from whatever horrifying injuries settled underneath. He was utterly helpless yet still fearsome. The cage door was closed, but there was no lock on the clasp. He could pull out of the straps, rise up, and swing the door out, and Josh would be too frightened to move.

Standing there, Josh heard a loud, reprimanding voice and looked to see who was so angry.

"What's your goddamn hurry? Some of us in here could actually eat that food."

He saw that it was Roy, sitting on a bed in the last alcove at the end of the room. The cot sagged below him. His peg leg stood against the wall, the halter at the top of the stick yellowed and stained. As Josh wheeled the cart over obediently, Roy grabbed a crutch from the floor and hauled himself off the cot.

"Just joshing you, Josh," he said. "I'm glad to see a pal at a time like this."

A pal. He'd never talked at any length with Roy before, only suffered his jokes and his relentless teasing, like the new kid in school. Roy limped toward him on the crutch. He seemed diminished now without his peg leg, breathing hard.

"You thinking about Crowley?" Roy asked.

Josh said he still couldn't believe it.

"I know, I know," Roy said, and then limped forward some more. "Help me get over to the big window. I need to warm my bones in some daylight, or I'm going to die in the dark like an old house cat."

He slid underneath Roy's wing and helped him maneuver his girth across the room. Passing Elgin's cage, Roy sneered. "You staring at that sack of beat-up shit made me miss Crowley more than I could stand. If God's got any spare time on his hands, he could send a nice chunky aneurysm up this fucker's leg."

Josh agreed. Together they moved on toward the caged window and stared out. The glass was greasy with decades of exhaled breath.

"Merry fucking Christmas," Roy said.

11

They gave me three days off after finding Crowley, and I was grateful for the break, even as I wished I had something other than the rattle and shock of the previous week to occupy my every waking thought. MacKay was still in intensive care and not seeing visitors yet, but at least his prognosis was good. I got the information by lying, telling the nurse I was his daughter calling from out of state. No one checked on me, no one called to congratulate me or tease me or hear the Crowley story firsthand, no one even called to wish me Merry Christmas, and my brain went to work on that silence, parsing it for meaning. I began to wonder if they blamed me, if they saw my industriousness as a betrayal, a finger pointing toward some other CO's guilt. When the phone finally rang on my third and final free evening, I reached for it with a high school nervousness. It took me a moment to recognize that the quiet voice on the other end belonged to Brother Mike.

"I'm sorry to bother you at home," he said.

It was no bother, I told him, though I was surprised and confused by the call.

"I wanted to see if you were all right," he said.

"What do you mean?" For a moment I didn't understand.

"Aren't you the one who found Jon Crowley?" he asked.

"Yes," I said.

"I'm very sorry," he said. "It must have been awful."

It was, and I realized then that I felt morally stained by the experience, that I feared it might never wash off.

"Thank you," I said.

"I wonder what happened," he said.

I didn't answer. I didn't want to go there with a weak sister. If I ever mused on the reasons, it would be with a fellow CO, and only then with caution and the worst possibilities left unspoken.

"Have you looked at the book I lent you, the one that Jon was inspired by?"

He meant *The Four Stages of Cruelty*, the drawings by Hogarth.

"To be honest," I said, "it wasn't my cup of tea."

Lying on the couch, with the phone up against my ear, I pulled the book over to my lap and turned the heavy pages again, though I had no stomach for it. Hogarth had drawn four distinct panels, and the rest of the book was commentary. At first glance the images seemed ordinary, street scenes of London in a vaguely Victorian era, but on closer inspection everything normal turned to murder. Boys who seemed to be playing with animals were actually torturing them. Men with maces and sticks beat horses. A child was crushed under a wagon wheel while four powder-wigged judges watched. A woman in an alley lay in an awkward pose, and then you noticed that her angled head was almost severed from her body, the slit throat gaping wide, and that she had been bound before death, her wrists notched by deep cuts. In a large room inside a brick-laden dome, a host of learned men in scholarly hats crowded around a slab on which the corpse of a hanged man was undergoing autopsy, the rope still around his neck. A dog chewed on the tossed-aside heart, and bones were being boiled in a cauldron. It was bestial cruelty, a mosaic of casual perversion, and I wanted none of it.

Brother Mike didn't seem to sense the vibe of my dismay.

"Hogarth followed the passage of a young man from his violent upbringing along his murderous path to his final end, hanged and gutted. He wanted to show that violence is contagious and has social origins, and that it follows a progression of cruelty. It's a crude theory, but have you ever doubted that upbringing and social environment contribute to the lives the men in Ditmarsh have led? Sometimes, learning about the juvenile records and the foster homes and the alcoholic fathers and prostitute mothers, I allow myself to wonder if we have the right people locked up."

"Was that what Crowley was trying to do? Make some kind of point about life in Ditmarsh?" I did not truck with the sentiments Brother Mike was describing, but I wanted to know more.

"I'm not sure," he answered. "I'm not sure we can ever grasp the full complexity of what violence does and where it comes from. I have this feeling that to truly understand the motives and the causes and the circular nature of it all, we need to hold some contradictory theories in place at the same time, and believe them to be equally valid. I don't think Hogarth ever gave enough credit to evil, for example. I don't think any social reformer knows how to comfortably tackle the problem of evil."

He didn't call it the mystery of evil, as I might have, but the problem, as though the existence of evil were a concrete issue with practical consequences, like a math question or a difficult repair job.

"And what is the problem of evil?" I asked, picking up the thread he'd placed before me, wondering what labyrinth I was being led into.

"Here, from my admittedly underschooled brain, are some of the essential questions: Is Satan responsible for evil? If so, why does the all-powerful God let Satan hold so much sway over the affairs of men? Is God responsible? Then what does that say about God as a loving being, or about man, created in God's image? Are God and Satan both irrelevant superstitions, and evil a material by-product of chemical, social, or psychological influences? Depending on your point of view, there are ramifications. What should we do with evil? Cut it out like a disease? Kill it like a monster? Put it away in a place where it cannot harm others? Hate the sin, forgive the sinner, and work on rehabilitation?"

"You're talking about matters beyond my job description," I said.

"And mine, too," he said.

A pause in our conversation. I stretched back and wondered what to say.

"So what's the answer?" I asked.

"Love," he replied, but the word was so curt, and the moment so awkward, I didn't know whether I'd heard him right, and I was too embarrassed to ask him to say it again.

I thanked him for calling, and we said our good-nights. Despite our differences, I was glad for the connection, the moment of human comfort.

I'd seen the faces of men who'd done what anyone would consider evil things, but their brains were usually so bewildered and pathetic, you wrote off their behavior as some sort of autism of violence. The spiritual counselors explained it with religion. The social counselors talked about case histories and abuse records. All of it was so much shit to those of us actually working the blocks, negotiating the moods, trying to keep the lies straight. People think we're thugs, a little thick and hard, none too smart or caring, but I honestly believe you need the disconnect—the brute confidence or the comfortable blitheness or even that little smirk of cruelty—to do the job well.

I fell asleep on the couch, my comfort spot when comfort won't come, and didn't wake up until the phone rang again. For a moment I expected Brother Mike, a continuance of our conversation, but the voice was different.

"So you've done it," the voice said, and then asked, "How does it feel?"

I knew the voice or thought I did.

"How does what feel? Who is this?"

"Do they know what kind of a cunt you are?"

That's when I understood the true nature of the call. I sat up and asked again who the hell was calling. The voice on the other end breathed steadily, without fear, for a dozen seconds, then hung up.

I checked the call record and saw the number listed as unknown. I checked the street through a gap in the curtain and saw nothing but darkened cars and trees heavy with snow. I lay on the bed and tried to close my eyes, but I kept seeing Crowley. Would I ever get his hanging shadow out of my mind? I had some pills in the bathroom cabinet for bad nights, but I didn't want to put myself under when there was a stalker out there, some drunk and bitter turnkey, some ex-inmate who'd finally made a house call. I tucked my prized armament of personal choice, a stainless steel .357 handgun, under a book on the night table because that's what you do when you're hearing footsteps on the stairs.

A few hours later, in the grimy light of morning, the phone rang a third time. I was eating raisin bran and staring at the counter TV, feeling unsteady and hungover from the lack of sleep. I checked the call display and saw the number of the local newspaper. They'd been hassling me to renew my subscription, but I hated having that waste of paper piling up unread, so I'd resisted their never-wavering siege for months. This time I was thankful to see a familiar irritation, and I almost answered. Then I stopped myself when I realized what was happening. Someone at the paper wanted to talk to me about Ditmarsh.

It had to be about Crowley. About finding him. The missing inmate. The one everyone thought had escaped. The one who showed up ugly dead inside the City. I did not want to talk to anyone in the media. I let the phone go to voice mail and checked the message fifty seconds later. Nothing.

I did the dishes and put in a load of laundry. I kept glancing at the local news station as I worked, and I stopped everything when a report came on about an inmate at Ditmarsh Penitentiary who'd gone missing during a recent disturbance and had since been found dead. The blood in my veins thickened as a reporter on scene described the events and then cued a recorded interview with the warden.

"If he'd escaped, as these erroneous rumors insist, we would have notified other law enforcement authorities, and I can assure you no such notification was made. Contrary to your misinformation, the inmate had been held in protective custody the entire time."

It shook me hard to hear the lie so blatantly spooled. Then came the kicker. While in protective custody, Crowley hanged himself, the warden said, and the matter would be investigated thoroughly, as was routine in all such cases, by the Pen Squad, an independent police unit inside Ditmarsh. "But I caution you," he said, the sternness of his voice utterly convincing, "this suicide was not an avoidable tragedy, but an act of violent defiance designed to inflame an already tense situation. Jonathan Crowley was that kind of inmate. This is difficult for the general public to understand. But that man went to his grave spitting in the face of authority."

It's not often you get to witness the truth shit-kicked so thoroughly. My phone rang again, a number I didn't recognize, so I picked up the receiver and thumbed end with enough firmness to choke a throat.

That's when I first started feeling paranoid.

12

My life never seemed particularly full when I was not working, but there were times when the thin cover of activities and interests got pulled back to reveal the great yawning emptiness. It was particularly depressing to go back to work when you had done nothing productive or fulfilling with a string of days off. Battered by the news report about Crowley, I felt incapable of rousing myself to any good purpose. I'd planned to go to yoga every morning once Christmas was over, but the willpower had strained out of me like water through a pressed tea bag. If it wasn't for MacKay getting transferred out of intensive care to a regular room, nothing would have moved me.

I parked in the hospital lot and recognized Baumard's decked-out truck. Other cars and trucks looked familiar, too. The boys were there in substantial numbers. When I got to the cardiac unit, Baumard was in the hall along with three other COs just off from the four-a.m.-to-noon shift. Their stamina amazed me. They worked, fought, complained, suffered, celebrated, ate, drank, and talked the job. I wanted to ask about the warden's comments on the news, whether anyone had heard them, but the vibe zipping through me made that entire subject seem like fissionable material, too radioactive to touch. Instead, I asked how MacKay was doing.

Baumard shrugged. "He's all right. All he has to do is cut out the drinking and smoking. In other words, he's a walking coffin." I was too upset to share the humor. So I looked around the doorway and saw Ray MacKay in his hospital gown, oxygen mask on his face, big hands resting at his sides, as cautious and immobile as a whale beached on the bed. Alton, a younger CO, stood at the foot, talking more to the TV hanging on the wall than to MacKay himself. Alton noticed me peek around and used my arrival as an excuse to say his goodbyes, thumping the mattress twice with his fingertips in a vigorous expression of best wishes. He nodded as he went by, grateful and relieved for me to take his place.

I wanted to cry. But a corner of Ray's mouth turned up when he saw me, the eyes brightening, and he gave a breathy "How you doing." Then he pulled the oxygen mask down to his chin. I was alarmed, but he said, "I put this on so I can watch TV in peace." His voice was stronger than I expected.

Same old bastard. Always smarter than he looked. I made a joke. "What'd you do, shit a phone?" It felt flat to me, but MacKay grinned and held up a hand for me to stop.

What do you say to an old man in his hospital bed sucking air? I planned to ask the usual questions, why he was dogging it, whether he liked Jell-O three times a day. Then I'd tell him how good he looked and other clichés of the strained and obligatory hospital visit. Instead, MacKay said he'd heard I'd found Crowley down there.

I nodded. I didn't want to talk about it. I wanted him to let it go. "Did you hear what they're saying?" I asked. "They're saying he killed himself in protective custody."

But MacKay didn't seem to hear me. "In the old days that was the spot." He nodded slowly between breaths. "Whenever we'd beat on a prisoner, it was a social gathering. A party with snacks. The right inmate, the right occasion, felt like the fucking Super Bowl."

I said nothing. He fiddled with the plastic bracelet on his thick left wrist, awkwardly, without much strength, pushing it away like an irritation.

"Inmates hated it down there. It terrified them. The aloneness was the worst. Drove them apeshit. You new jacks"—lifting his hand, the IV line lifting with it, to wag a finger slowly, mockingly—"don't always get it. The need. It's mutual, you know."

I tried to think of something to say, a way to squeeze the dread out. "I guess someone revived the tradition."

"Pretty sophisticated bunch, us jacks."

The words had gotten weaker. He felt for his mask. His hand fumbled so slowly I almost reached over to help. But he fitted the mask back on, and I watched its flimsy shape flex and steam up.

Who did it, Ray? I wanted to ask, and I didn't want to know. Were you there? Instead, I gripped the rail of the bed and watched him. His eyes looked small and far away. I didn't know what to do, whether to leave him or sit next to him. Then I remembered the book.

"Brought this for you." I pulled the paperback out of my purse. The copy of *To Kill a Mockingbird* I'd had since high school.

I placed it on the table beside the remote. A book so heavy with injustice and moral failure, it felt wrong passing it to him now, as though I were making an accusation.

"Jesus, thanks," he muttered, heavy on the sarcasm.

Time to leave, I figured. I resisted tapping the bed like Alton and just told MacKay to get better soon. I expected to see a glint of tears, because that's how I was feeling, but MacKay tilted his head in my direction and offered a lopsided turn of his mouth. It could have been a twist of despair, but I recognized it as a grin.

I'd hoped the others would be gone and I could walk down the hallway unnoticed, but they'd remained, and I was forced to stand with them, robotic. They talked about work with intense devotion. I listened to them parsing out the latest. They were laughing, in that morbid way we laughed at all the snafus and the sick things that happened, about the audacity of the warden's press conference announcement about Crowley. I felt gravity settle a little in my shoes. At least they didn't believe it. I had that going for me. But they did not hint at the other possibilities—the certainty, really, that some of us had done the awful deed. Then Stevens brought up "that fucking memo." I hadn't heard about any memo, so I felt free to ask what they were talking about, and Alton filled me in. "Basically the warden telling the COs straight out, he doesn't want to see so-called contradictory reports in the press anymore. Like the first thing we do when some shit happens inside is call our favorite reporter."

"Hell," Ringer said, "I don't even read the sports page anymore, it's so full of fucking lies."

I looked to Baumard, and he said, "They're plugging the leaks. It's their standard CYA strategy for dealing with their own fuckups." And then those fuckups got listed in familiar abbreviated versions of longer complaints. But nothing about Crowley, no explanation of whether that had been a fuckup or a coordinated exercise.

"Kali?" A voice behind me said, and I turned to see an older woman addressing me hopefully.

The men opened their little group and allowed the woman to approach. Baumard called her Rachel Honey. Alton called her Mrs. MacKay. She introduced herself to me as Ray's wife. I was only mildly surprised to realize that Ray had this pleasant-looking matron for a partner, a little glassy-eyed, tagged by forty years of marriage like a dead deer on a car roof. Rachel stated that she'd heard so much about me. Baumard announced it was time for him to sit with Ray. The other men dispersed to the vending machines and the restroom, leaving us gals alone.

"Do you smoke?" Rachel began. "I need a cigarette. Walk me out?"

I didn't smoke, hadn't even enjoyed it when I was in my twenties, but I very much wanted to leave the hospital. We said little to each other as we walked down the hallway, stood in the elevator, and then passed the check-in desk. Outside the automatic doors, near a pack of green pajama–wearing hospital workers, Rachel breathed through a Virginia Slim and scuffed at a spot on the sidewalk with her pink sneaker.

"Ray liked you," she said. The past tense hit us both.

"It sounds like he's going to be okay," I suggested. I didn't know shit. I just wanted it so.

Rachel nodded. "I hope." She was thin in the neck, her skin waxy. Looking at her, I could smell my grandparents' living room, reeking of cigarettes, a stand-up ashtray between recliner chair and love seat facing the TV.

"That place is what's killing him," she announced. "He just wants a second chance now. Funny how life—" And she stopped. I waited. Yeah, funny how life.

"Working at Ditmarsh has eaten him up," she continued. She shook her head and gazed at the parking lot. An ambulance arrived and did the loop. The cab doors opened and the paramedics got out. They were in no rush.

"Ray seemed all right most days," I offered. What was I trying to do, convince Rachel of something she would know better than anyone else in the world?

I had the sense my words did not penetrate.

"Ray never talked in any detail about the things he had to see and do," Rachel said, "but I knew when it was bad by the way he'd come home.

You're supposed to pretend the person you love doesn't hate his own life, but I don't care anymore. He was sick of it. He talked about you like a daughter, you know. He mentioned you lots, proud."

I let a moment go by. "I didn't know that." And started to well up. A sap. A weeper at sad movies. I would have flipped down my URF visor if it happened to be handy.

"It wasn't healthy," Rachel said again, and she gave me an uncomfortably direct stare, blue eyes drizzled with an acidic yellow.

Then it came.

"Ray wanted me to tell you that it wasn't him."

I waited for more, feeling sick to my stomach, the ingestion of corrosive information.

"He didn't put that inmate down there. But if it gets any hotter, he's going to say he did, that it was an accident, something stupid that happened before he got sick, maybe because he was sick." She looked disgusted and gazed at the blue sky. "If it comes to that, they'll suspend him. Then we wait until it all dies down and they let him retire and reinstate his pension. He wanted you to know. He had nothing to do with it."

"How can they do that?" I wanted to ask who's they? The warden? The Keeper?

Instead of answering, Rachel drew on the last of her cigarette with a controlled anger, stubbed it out more times than necessary on the concrete edge of the ash bin, and pressed it into the sand that lay on top like a fake tropical island.

"We'll probably move to Arizona if Ray's up for it. I have a sister there."

She looked up at me again.

"Ray didn't say this part, but I'm saying it now. You should find another life."

13

The lockdown ended in the infirmary, though Josh heard that gen pop was still under the the screw. Josh's limited freedom was a relief. Whenever he saw Roy in the hospital bed, he thought of his father. It made no rational sense. They were opposites in every way except age. Before everything changed, his father had been a composed and vigorous man who always wore a suit. He believed you could will yourself into success. He didn't trust Josh's interest in art, but even that seemed natural and normal, an indication of virtue rather than a parental failing.

Roy had none of his father's solid qualities. He was lazy and sneaky and unhygienic, and the charm of it was that he knew you knew and still tried shamelessly to get his way. When he was tired, he seemed like a great physical bulk collapsed into despair. But when he was energized by a good mood, possessed by some random opinion or desire, he talked with wild gestures and enthusiasm, shooting for more sophistication than his background or brain could manage. None of it was like his father, but the hospital bed made Josh think that way just the same.

One lunch, Roy insisted that Josh feed him. "Guy fed me this morning," Roy said, his plump, naked arms folded royally on his chest. "Do it or I'll tell the doctor you grabbed my crank while I was sleeping."

It was funny enough. Roy had a way of wearing you down and making you like him. He threw so much empty flattery Josh's way that some of it couldn't help but touch his pride.

"Oh, come on," Roy said, softening. "Just shovel a few spoonfuls in. It'll give us a chance to talk."

Josh wanted to talk, even if it was just to Roy. He pulled over a chair and sat down.

"There you go," Roy said, wriggling up on the bed until he was in a sitting position. "Don't worry, I smell pretty as a rose today. They give you a car wash with your oil change here."

Roy's ears were stuffed with wadded cotton, a faint pink, as though fluid still dripped. Josh lifted the spoon, and Roy opened his mouth to receive the bite. When Josh pulled the spoon away too quickly, the mess dribbled onto Roy's chin.

"You need a towel or something?" Josh asked, squeamish.

"Nah," Roy answered. "Hit me again, tarbender."

The chili smelled like wet dog. Josh slipped another spoonful past Roy's open lips and watched him chew. Odd to feel another person's bite on the end of a spoon.

"So you're a college boy, huh?" Roy said in and around the food.

It was not Josh's favorite thing to admit, a weak spot that might get him hurt.

"I was a college boy, too, a long time ago. Until my life sort of fell apart."

Josh nodded as if it were all true, as if it were the most natural thing in the world to talk about, but he didn't believe Roy for a second.

"Majored in psychology. They wanted me to do my Ph.D., but I was too fucking arrogant. Figured I could do what I want, go back anytime. Next thing you know, I'm selling cars, snorting coke, and fucking my boss's wife."

"Beats studying," Josh said. He didn't mean it.

"Cocaine is a bitch, man. Looks sexy enough from a distance. Makes you want her real fucking bad. Like an ache in your balls. Then it's all about her and nothing about you. Take every dime you have and still scream at you for more. Make you do things you can't believe you'd do. But I shouldn't be complaining. I wouldn't be half the man I am now without it."

Roy laughed at his own joke. Did he mean his missing leg? In spite of himself, Josh wanted to hear more of the life story stuff. You never asked another inmate what he'd done, what crimes or mistakes or bad luck had launched his bit. Crowley said you kept the truth to yourself and saved your bullshit stories for the counselors and lawyers, the ones who needed you to lie. Roy changed subjects, rolling onward, complaining about how dull it was in the ward, nothing but sick men dying and howlers howling. "How do you stand these fucking houseplants? No wonder you and Crowley got to be pals. He told me you were a stand-up guy."

From the grave a word of praise. Josh braced himself to ask about Crowley, but Roy didn't slow down.

"Tell you the truth, I was relieved to hear it," Roy said. "Been a rumor they had a rat holed up here, keeping him safe."

The shock hit him like a live wire.

"Oh, come on now," Roy protested at his surprise. "Jesus Christ, are you sensitive or what? Relax a little. I'm dying for conversation here."

Josh struggled to find the words, hurt this time and panicky, too. A mouth like Roy's could spread stories everywhere.

"I haven't been inside too long, but I know that isn't a good thing to say about someone."

Roy only stared, a bland look, as though disappointed. Josh felt there was nothing Roy didn't see out of those calm eyes and that Josh could be inside for a thousand years and not know a thing.

"I'll tell you something you won't believe, but you should," Roy explained patiently. "All that shit about how bad it is to be a rat is only true because every fucking guy in here *is* a rat. They get all upset about rats the way some married guy who smokes pole on the side talks about beating up fags. I'm including the fucking jacks, of course. Biggest rats of all. Ratting is just lube reducing the social friction. It's the way we all get by."

Josh could almost see it, could almost understand the inner workings Roy was hinting at, but the vision was too smeared with cynicism. He'd mull it over. He'd turn it around in his head with three or four other things Roy had told him, and the dozen or so things from Crowley, and even the bits he'd learned from Keeper Wallace and CO Williams. It didn't even matter if they were contradictory, he knew they were still true, because a shudder flowed up his spine when he heard them.

"Don't worry, though. I figured out why you picked up the rep," Roy said.

The fragment of a second stretched on, and Josh waited for the diagnosis.

"It's your personality," Roy announced cheerfully, and then went on to explain. "You show up here on a heavy beef, but you're the kind of dude who smells like he's got no priors whatsoever. So right off the bat the boys are suspicious. Strike two, despite the long bit, they're coddling you in the howler ward. Nobody appreciates that, and they want to know why. People start making shit up about you just because you're all mysterious. Some guy says, hey, I don't know about that fish. Another guy takes it a bit further and says, he's not really a fish, he's a hard-timer in witness protection, transferred here with soft digs and a new identity. Of course, one look at you and it's obvious how fucking laughable that idea is, but never mind. Almost in confirmation of the aforementioned idiotic reasoning, you get seen chatting up with that slutty jack, Officer Williams, trading little bedtime stories and night-night kisses. Now, I'm a flexible give-a-little-to-get-something-back kind of guy, but there are boys in here who'd eat their own cock before they'd chat up a cop, even a woman, and Elgin's one of them. He's got principles, you understand. Some guys seem to have a use for them. Me, I never seen any point, so why bother."

It was far too much to swallow at one time, a single indiscretion turned into a hundred broken laws. But the name that jumped out at him was Elgin.

"What about Elgin?" Josh asked.

"Yeah. That fucking guy has some vigorous opinions about you. I was talking to him this morning, trying to assess his attitude and condition, figured I'd find out how he felt about me while they still had him strapped down and sedated, and all he could talk about was you—"

"What about me?" Josh interrupted.

"Well, this is going to upset you a bit"—as though wanting to break the news gently—"but you're intelligent, so I'll lay it out there. Elgin thinks Crowley couldn't have finished that stupid fucking comic book without some kind of help. And he's got it in his head that you made yourself Crowley's right-hand man, so to speak."

This accusation, coming as it did on top of a pile of others, felt like the knockout blow.

"Is it true?" Roy asked. "Did our friend J.C. ever ask you to do him a favor, draw a thing or two?"

It didn't seem to matter how intently Crowley had implored him to keep the truth to himself. Crowley was dead now, and Josh could tell that Roy already knew.

"Yeah."

"Who's kidding who, right?" Roy asked. "Your secret's safe with me. But if Elgin gets any better, we're both in trouble. That cocksucker's got a nasty, vindictive attitude."

Josh sat in place, a little sick to his stomach and tingly in his limbs.

Roy lay back, gaze aimed at the ceiling, his hands folded on his chest. Then he said it was nap time. "Fucking shit food takes the good right out of me." And he closed his eyes.

Josh could do nothing except stand and leave, the cart rattling on.

That evening, he lay on his cot, shaken by thoughts of Elgin, the sense that even if he was careful, he'd still get swallowed. Then a face peered around the corner of his drum, and he was startled to see Roy standing there, his peg leg strapped on, a physical strength to him that had been utterly absent in the last week.

"I'm going to get you out of here," Roy announced. It was so ridiculous Josh didn't know if he'd heard him right.

Roy sat down on Josh's bed, the explanation needing that kind of physical proximity, and Josh sat up and squeezed to the side to make room.

"I'm talking about a transfer to another house. Solve all your problems. It came to me like a bolt from the sky. Crowley told me a lot about you, what you did, you know, to get in here, and well, it's pretty fucking obvious: you shouldn't be here. You know what I mean?"

Roy ran with it hard, building up the credibility of his argument, bolstering a thought Josh secretly entertained on a daily basis. He shouldn't be here. He was not like anyone else. It was self-evidently a mistake, a misdirection in justice, the one thing in this place that actually deserved to be corrected.

"I'm not dragging you around by the cock. I've got my bona fide successes in this territory. Got a bank robber named Ronny Vaughn out about three years ago. I obtained all his files, pored the fuck over them, and found a mistake they made in his sentencing hearing. Cops never turned over the bullets in his gun, which meant he didn't have any bullets in his gun, and they acted like he was armed to the teeth when they were assigning his corrections facility. We pounded at it and pounded at it until they had to reverse. Now he's chilling in a level two near his old lady, same duration but way smoother time, and a fuck of a lot easier on parole. It's obvious to any idiot you shouldn't be here—we just got to figure out a good reason why. We exert a little pressure, write a lot of letters, find the right judge, and make a little headway. I like the challenge of that. I'm a resourceful guy who, pardon the modesty, is smart as fuck. It's not like I want to lose you as a friend or anything, but if I can give a brother a better turn and piss off some cops and lawyers at the same time, man, that's the best kind of fun I can have these days, let me tell you."

It was ridiculous and pointless and a waste of time. Josh wanted it, but he couldn't imagine writing the letters, getting the files, seeking the information, going through the trials. Then Roy made a suggestion.

"Brother Mike's got all your files. He's got all the files of everyone in his program. I know because I used to clerk for that fart. Get him to give you your jacket. That way you skip the lawyers and red tape."

"What if he gets upset about it?" Josh said. "He's always talking about dealing with what you can change, not what you can't."

"Fuck that passive bullshit. That's for his benefit, not yours, keeping himself in business. You're his long-term customer, you know what I mean? He loses you, his market shrinks, so he wants you here, planted for a very long time. I'm not saying we'll succeed. But I am saying we should try. And he's got *your* fucking jacket. It's not his. And he needs to hand it over. Just insist. It's like getting your one free phone call. He legally can't say no."

Josh agreed to do it. It was impossible to stop the force of the argument even though he dreaded making the request.

"You got a session with him tomorrow, right? Ask him then. Don't tell him it's me you're working with, though. He'll get all fussy about that. Professional fucking jealousy."

"Okay," Josh said again. Anything to lessen the barrage.

"Hey. It means a lot to me that you trust me like that."

Roy reached over to shake his hand. The grip was firm, meaningful, and longer than comfortable.

14

Work should have been easy that night, with the gen pop inmates still under restricted movement, but I've never liked lockdowns. Caged up, they had too much time on their hands. They stewed and fretted. Their spite and anger got jacked up and became even more unpredictable. They plotted. Fantasized. Schemed ways to fuck someone up. Better when they had their regular routine and you had yours, distractions that kept everyone relatively honest. Of the many things inmates and COs had in common, a desire for the time to pass quietly had to be tops on the list.

I supervised meals and meds most of the evening. It was dull, thankless delivery work. The crazies and addicts were bouncing off the walls. The slightest goddamn delay in receiving their medication sent them into conniptions of desperation and anger. No wonder they were locked up in six-by-nine drawers. Addiction was the defining focus of their entire lives. It was the reason they were inside—whatever murder, robbery, rape, extortion, or drug violation they'd been sentenced for was spawned from a need that made them barely human. It was the reason they did what they did inside. Prostituting themselves. Begging for hits. Stomping each other's guts out. Conspiring to arrange deliveries and sales with the acumen of a payroll manager. Addiction distorted every word that came out of their mouths, made it all lies. What they wouldn't do for drugs, I didn't want to imagine.

In B-3 I saw the Pen Squad in full force around Crowley's old cell, not the one in the infirmary where he'd spent the previous nine months, but his permanent home in population. The officials crowded the entrance as if they were trying to get into a small nightclub. MacKay's joke: How many Pen Squad members does it take to solve a crime? A minimum of three. One to stand around where the evidence was before the inmates destroyed it. One to get told to fuck off by each witness in turn. And one to concoct a bullshit story so the case could be filed. Crowley's old cell was undergoing a total breakdown and disassembling. Rubber gloves on everyone. Belongings in boxes stacked up in the range. Mattress propped against the pillar. Crowley's block mates were watching from their bars, calling out the occasional insult, the occasional question or idiotic request. My helper, a semi-retarded thug named Martin, pushed the cart of meds and meals from cell to cell like we were a married couple at the grocery store. Martin delivered the meals; then I passed out whatever meds were lined up.

"About fucking time."

"Shit, Officer, that's the same piece'a ham as yesterday. You know I gone Muslim."

"Pigs serving pig."

"How come our buddy Crowley got a dirt sandwich?"

"I get four fucking pills. This is two fucking pills. I need four fucking pills."

"You tell that fucker next door to shut up. I'll be knocking him with a can'a soup in my sock soon as these doors open."

"This is already cold. You trying to bacteriate us?"

"When do we get out of lockdown? I got a scheduled visit tomorrow."

"This is some no call bullshit."

I answered some, ignored others, kept moving down the row. When I got to the Pen Squad outside Crowley's cell, I stopped, just as I normally would, even though I wanted nothing better than to scurry along like a flitty roach. It was a large mixed crew, and I only recognized a few officers. Melinda Reizner, who ran most of the in-house investigations, walked out of the cell with an evidence bin and gave me a nod.

We stood beside each other, a rare meeting of the "paramilitary without penises" support club. Melinda was five years older than me, give or take, but light-years ahead in terms of career. I just did a job—Melinda was going places. Once, during a break in a training session in which she instructed us about what not to do when we found evidence, I asked her how I could go places, too. The inquiry seemed to stimulate something mentorly in her mood, but it had not paid off in actual helpful advice. I figured she'd mulled me over but hesitated to relay the bad prognosis.

This time Melinda was the one eager to see me, a sparkle of enthusiasm in her eye, a respect almost.

"So you're the one who found him, huh?" She said it low-toned and casual, less an official question and more just something she was excited to talk about, like I'd done something remarkable. The ego stroking worked, even though Melinda had joked with me once that flattery was a tool. That's what investigators do. They make you feel special by playing on your vanity and lead you along like a sucker. With all the casual cool I could muster, I admitted that I had indeed been the one.

Melinda put the box down. "Lucky girl."

I didn't feel very lucky. "Are you expecting a shit storm?"

She shrugged and seemed to ignore my question. "Autopsy reports will get here in a couple weeks. Want to see them?"

"How can I resist?" I asked. Normally the voyeur in me would have been excited. Instead, I just felt queasy.

"We should talk next week about everything that happened."

"Officially?"

"You found him, you get your name in the file."

"Great."

"And you thought there was no glory in this business."

"That's the only reason why I'm here."

We wished each other a happy new year, and I moved on. Three cells later Marty pulled the cart up alongside Billy Fenton.

"If it isn't Officer Williams," Fenton said. "How nice to hear you strolling down my hall for a change." He took his allotment of pills from my tray. He had a rainbow assortment, which meant he was smart enough to complain of the right symptoms to the right doctors and psychologists to earn a nice fix, unless he really was a manic-depressive with high blood pressure, irritable bowel syndrome, and a chronic sleep disorder. He held a piece of paper in his hand, just obvious enough that I could read it through the bars without having to stop and stare.

"Pleasant dreams, Fenton," I said, and passed by without pause, forcing myself to keep trudging. The paper said, "Need a favor?"

Some inmates played with your mind. And if you weren't careful, they'd end up permanently occupying a part of your cerebral cortex.

My shift finally ended. I wanted to go home. I wanted to throw myself on my couch and sleep with the TV running. I wanted to obliterate every memory and enter the big nothingness, the hum of ancient reruns.

When I opened my locker, I found a note taped to the top shelf. A note where a drawing had been only a few days before. I needed a new lock. I needed a world without juvenile men.

I opened the note. Someone wanted to see me. Someone wanted to talk to me. Someone gave me a cell phone number and asked me to call them as soon as I got out into the world. Meaning as soon as I was sitting in my truck. It was urgent, the note said, in case I didn't read between lines. I saw the name at the bottom, Mike Ruddik. Our very own fink. The last man in the world I wanted to meet up with.

I had my parka on and was ready to slide on out when Wallace caught me just outside the locker room and gave me more bad news. I could tell it was bad by the way his puffy cheeks had pinked up.

"We've got some trouble. You're drawing press attention."

The words as somber as a creaking elevator cable. I waited for more.

"There's been some calls from a reporter about the encounter between you and Shawn Hadley."

Encounter? I was slow with surprise. The reporter's calls were about Hadley? Crowley was the one who had gone missing and turned up dead. Crowley was the big story. Not Hadley, a shit disturber who'd taken a crack to the knee and might miss a tennis game or two.

It had to be a mistake, right? I asked if he meant Crowley. I couldn't stop myself.

It was obvious I still didn't get it. I saw bottomless wells of experience in Wallace's weary eyes, and maybe a glitter of smug.

"Everything about Crowley is in-house. We're taking care of it our way, thoroughly and methodically and fully. And so far, Kali, no one has broken ranks." Meaning no one but me. Meaning if anyone did break ranks, it would be me. Meaning no one outside knew enough about where Crowley had been found and what condition he'd been in to even know there were questions worth asking.

Wallace went on. The institution would need to put Hadley through a disciplinary hearing sooner rather than later because of the attention. He left the rest unspoken, but I knew the way it worked. There were two ways disciplinary hearings got handled. The first was to hold a public hearing in the prison before a judge, with lawyers present. The second, for more minor offenses, was to hold a closed hearing with the Keeper as judge and no lawyers present. A good keeper made sure everything disciplinary stayed in-house. This often meant reducing the severity of the charges so that punishment could be more freely doled out. But if the inmate went Al Sharpton on you, all bets were off.

I could see the lines of separation being drawn. I tried to get analytical about it, put all my objections aside and dig for information.

"You said calls. You mean more than one caller?" I asked, remembering my late-night stalker.

Wallace's shrug was weary with indifference. "One reporter. A fellow named Bart Stone. He's been persistent. He's reached out to me, the warden's office, and a bunch of COs."

He left that detail hanging. Other COs. I knew what those calls would concern. What kind of CO was I? Was it actually easier for a woman to commit an abuse? Was I capable of handling the same pressures and strains as a man? Off the record, what in particular was wrong with me?

Then Wallace interrupted my interior rant with a tactical explosive device.

"Someone, apparently, has some kind of photographic evidence showing you standing over Hadley with your baton raised. I haven't seen it, so I don't know how serious a problem we have."

"How could someone take a picture of that?"

Wallace shrugged. "We had the incident camera rolling. Maybe it's video. Maybe someone snapped a cell phone shot. I have no idea. But pictures make everything hotter. A story with a picture can spread."

The idea of photograpic evidence shunted everything else aside and left me utterly silent.

Then Wallace suggested that I look into getting myself a union-appointed lawyer and start seeing a therapist.

He must have caught the look on my face because he offered some unexpected advice: "A good counselor can turn your life around, even your career." A pause. "I've seen therapy be of significant help to those who needed it. And I've seen those who should have gotten it fall into serious trouble very suddenly."

I was overcome by the suspicion that everyone around me, perhaps especially the Keeper, secretly wanted me to fail. I'd found Crowley when they couldn't. You'd think, in a reasonable world, such conduct would merit a free pass on other minor transgressions, a wiping clean of the dirty slate. Not here, not with me.

"Kali," Wallace added, using my first name with a touch of urgency, "make sure you think clearly about all this. Don't let your emotions push you around." Emotional wreck that I am. "You don't want to talk to those reporters. You'd do yourself more harm than good."

It felt like an accusation. But nothing could be further from my mind than talking to some reporter. I did not want to be at the center of any attention. That would only make my situation worse. My secret anxiety was that none of them saw me as one of the guys. Instead, in their eyes, I was an interloper, an affirmative-action occupant of someone else's job.

I drove home fast at one in the morning, my hands tight with anger, little sniffy sounds coming from me once or twice, watching the dashed white lines suck under my wheels. The offer of therapy was a setup. It would allow the administration to paint me as someone who didn't have the mental makeup to do the job. If Hadley's lawyers pressed for action, my employment would be the easy sacrifice and the institution could resume its normal routine without pause. Wallace knew I couldn't see a counselor under those circumstances. The administration encouraged it with vigor and enthusiasm whenever there was a trace of PTSD, but it was different for a woman. The men could talk macho about their sessions and joke about bullshit psychological terms because it showed them trying to be more sensitive, but if a woman opened a counselor's door, all her normal emotional reactions got labeled as softness or instability. I'd be forever marked.

On the way home I stopped for gas and picked up the newspaper. In the kitchen, with my uniform still on, I worked up the stomach to flip through the pages. A piece about Crowley took up a portion of the front of the city section.

It was appropriately hard-toned for a prison piece, and all lies, hewing to the warden's message that Crowley had killed himself in detention, a not particularly unusual occurrence in an institution for inmates. I looked for comments on the editorial page, anything to raise a question or call bullshit, but found nothing. I continued through the city section until the word INMATE in medium-size lettering below the fold drew me to an article about Shawn Hadley and me. It took a few moments with my head in my hands to summon the courage to read on. How bad was it? Short on details or information, a tone of pious neutrality in sentences that read a tad more literary than normal, the article covered the complaints of the lawyer and the legal actions being initiated against a number of corrections officers, in particular, Kali Williams and Raymond MacKay, as well as Warden Gavin Jensen and the Department of Corrections. I kept coming back to a particularly florid line about the canceled Christmas visits and the resulting disappointment of Hadley's three children and girlfriend. "*The eight-hour drive home that afternoon, in a beat-up Impala burning through gas, left the children exhausted and gave Cindy Harris the dreadful feeling she might never see Shawn Hadley again.*"

The writer was listed as one Bart Justin Stone. Angered, I googled him and found a page full of links. He'd done a few short pieces on the state primaries, a before-and-after job on the marathon last year, in which he'd apparently participated, and a series about a crystal meth lab in Kino Park. According to Stone, practically the whole town knew about the lab, yet it took the death of a teenage user to push the police into action.

I sat in stunned exhaustion, whatever good luck I had left draining from my limbs. I reached for the phone and listened to the messages. My union rep. My friend Gina. A hang-up. I checked the hang-up against the call record. The number looked familiar, and I remembered the crumpled note from Ruddik. A match.

15

In the morning at the appointed time Josh arrived at Brother Mike's office. All his nervousness clung to his skin like static electricity. He sank into the couch and waited for Brother Mike to look up from his desk. It was utterly quiet in the room, just the tick of the clock, and the waxy smudge of morning light leached through a window that overlooked the yard.

It was only their third private meeting, but the first two had touched on nothing in particular except Josh's art and his family life and the books he liked to read. Brother Mike had promised they'd start digging in soon. That promise or threat revealed itself now in the lack of friendly banter. Brother Mike left his paperwork, sat in the chair before him, and began speaking—the gray grizzled beard, the sparks of eyebrow.

"Do you know what grace means, Joshua?"

The word roused him, made him focus. He sensed the shit storm coming and braced himself.

"I know the bare bones of what you did. I don't know why yet. Maybe you don't either. If we're successful, in time, you might achieve a reconciliation, a personal forgiveness. But it's easy to see how much pain you're in, how uncomfortable you are in your own skin. Do you understand what I'm saying?"

Josh didn't bother to nod or shrug. You did not admit guilt or innocence. Your opinion was irrelevant.

"From our earlier talks, and your files, and the time I've spent with you in the studio, and yes, the times I've talked about you with others, I've come to some views about you. Do you want to hear them?"

"Yes," Josh croaked. As if he had any choice.

"You're profoundly out of touch with yourself and with God. It doesn't matter whether you believe in him, whether you pray fervently every night or only when you're frightened. You're weak. You're lazy. You're devastatingly narcissistic. You tell yourself lies to justify the things you do and the things you don't do, and you believe in those stories. That doesn't make you unusual. That's the human condition."

No better and no worse than anyone else. It was a conclusion he wanted to argue in both directions at once.

"Now, let me put forward an alternative path," Brother Mike continued. "It's through God's grace that we feel his will and his healing hand. You don't know what I mean yet. You're thinking, I need to please this man by agreeing to whatever he says. You're thinking, what does this have to do with therapy or restorative justice, let alone art? You don't have any idea what kind of journey you'll be taking. No matter what I say, you'll still sign on and tell me what I want to hear. But I'm telling you, your fundamental challenge is that you are disconnected from yourself and from God. What does that matter? Nothing and everything. No one else cares or will ever care. It's been my frequent experience in this place that the lost lamb is quickly forgotten by everyone except God. And sometimes I have to remind even him."

"Are we going to develop a program together?" Josh mumbled. He knew, or had learned like Pavlov's dog, that psychologists, counselors, and case officers liked structure. They liked to fill up a schedule, monitor progress, and write reports. They wanted you to sit, beg, and bark on cue. He wanted Brother Mike to stop being vague and set up those rules, give him a game to play.

But Brother Mike said, "I'm not interested in your correctional plan. I have no influence on your career as an inmate, unless you ask me to testify at your parole hearing, and I couldn't guarantee you'd like what I say. I warned a man about that once, but he asked me anyway. And when the parole board requested my opinion of his character for the record, I suggested that he was unrepentant, manipulative, deluded, and unsafe to release, though immensely eager to please.

"Since the early days of this country, there have been men with good intentions who thought the secret to reform was changing a man's behavior. If you can't change character, they felt, then why not change how a felon acts in the world? I don't think that's the answer. It's a kind of programming for reducing incidents of violence, with dubious results. The soul needs more attention than that. You might as well wait until a man is old and toothless if you want to solve the problem of violence. Let nature run its course, and a man gets too weary to take such instant and disproportionate offense at all the perceived slights of the world. But that doesn't mean he's a better man."

"But what if he's a better man before his time is up—isn't it unjust to forget about him for a couple decades or so?" Josh was roused to his own defense. He knew it was a trick. You weren't supposed to question the calculus of justice.

"I'm not concerned about whether your punishment is justified. Why should I be? You come from a good family. You were loved, not abused. They made sure you were healthy and educated. You are not noticeably deficient in your mental faculties. You probably went to church. In short, my philosophical friend, you had a lot going for you. More, I would bet, than any other inmate in this institution and many of the staff. If anyone is a poster child for the importance of deterring future wrongdoing through harsh punishment, I'd say you fit the bill. And maybe that's why they sent you here. Tell me why you did it. I'll know if you lie."

"You want to hear what happened?"

Brother Mike nodded.

Josh swallowed. He'd told the story before—done the jig of regret—but not for some time.

"We broke up in the summer before freshman year. I thought it was a mutual decision, but later on I started to wonder if she hadn't made plans to get me to agree to something I didn't fully understand." He stopped and slowed down, told himself to speak carefully. "Looking back, it seemed as though a lot of the reasoning behind the breakup had come from her. I felt duped. I was looking forward to being free. Then I realized I'd made a terrible mistake, and when I tried to correct that, to get back together, she didn't want to. It was like she'd never loved me. I couldn't understand how she could change so quickly in terms of her feelings. And then I found out she was already seeing someone else."

He'd spent the whole first semester in a daze. He couldn't concentrate in class. He felt fearful and panicked all the time. "She turned it all off like a switch. Something I couldn't do."

"How did you know she was seeing other people? Did you follow her?"

With every waking thought, and most of the sleeping ones. "It was a small world. You just knew what was going on."

"Did you have any contact with her, intimate contact where you could talk things through?"

"That was all I wanted," he said, "a chance to talk things through one more time. To understand why."

"Did she agree to see you?"

"No. So I went to her house when I knew she was alone. Or I thought she was alone. She turned out to be with this guy she was dating." He found the word boyfriend hard to say.

"Ah, but Joshua. Why did you bring your father's gun? It was your father's gun, wasn't it?"

He let the silence go by for a minute. He looked toward the window. Maybe he would never speak again. Then the words came, almost easily, floating on a strange sense of calm.

"I don't know."

"Oh, come on. You don't answer me like that."

He was back in the room. He wanted Brother Mike to understand.

"I wanted her to know how bad I felt. The gun was just a message."

"Communicating what?"

"Talk to me."

"And if she didn't talk with you. What were your plans for the gun?"

"I thought about using it on myself."

His throat was dry. Brother Mike seemed unmoved by the confession.

"You're saying you would have demonstrated your undying love by shooting yourself in front of her?"

Josh shrugged. "I didn't have any plans."

"Why not kill the other man, then? The male in her company. You must have hated him."

"I didn't go there to kill anyone."

One of the fundamental things Josh had no right to anymore was credibility. Why should anyone ever believe his story again? He waited for the exhalation of disappointment, the deep sigh of moral resignation.

But Brother Mike said nothing. The nothing went on until it achieved an uncomfortable tension. Josh moved on the couch to relieve the clench in his belly. There were diplomas on the wall, next to the shelves of pottery. Certificates. He nodded to them and asked Brother Mike what he studied in school. The narrowest line of smile formed on Brother Mike's lips, almost hidden in the beard.

"You want my story? I did a master's in social work and a Ph.D. in psychology before going to Vietnam for a year in the medical corps. After my service, I lived in Japan for a time studying pottery; then I returned to the U.S. and did a second Ph.D. at divinity school. I lived in a monastery in upstate New York for about a decade, then worked here for six years, left for missionary work in Central America and another monastery in California, then came back. My first doctorate was an analysis of cognition levels in criminal offenders. My second was an examination of whether the presence of evil in the world conflicted with the goodness or benevolence of an omnipotent God. And here I am, sitting with you, mixing it all together."

"Figure anything out yet?" Josh asked.

"More questions. A few answers. It's easy, in certain settings, to lose faith in the goodness of God because of all the suffering that occurs in the world. If you believe that every event is part of God's plan, for example, does that mean God allows evil to happen? Some believe that evil is in direct conflict with God's goodness, but that doesn't say much for God's omnipotence. So the general consensus, among those who care about such matters, is that evil is a consequence of God permitting us to have free will. We choose evil, or follow evil paths, because God allows us to be free. In that sense, returning to God means forgoing evil—in other words, choosing, with your free will, to give yourself to God. A complicated mystery."

Josh sat with it. "The thing I've never understood"—and it was something he'd thought about since coming inside—"is why God let's one person do what he wants even if it means making someone else suffer."

"Another mystery for you. A very complicated one. In theory, God could permit the evil act, done of free will, but prevent the evil consequence." He waited until Josh nodded. "But of course the questions come from there. Why then does he let the rapist brutalize the victim or the child molester destroy the child? The violation of innocence is appalling to contemplate. Why doesn't he stop the murderer's bullet?" Brother Mike shrugged. "What can I tell you, Josh? I'm sure you wish the thing could be undone, but if God stopped that bullet from firing or diverted it enough to give you a healthy shock and then sent you on your shaken way, what kind of freedom would he be offering you? Eliminating suffering from the consequences of evil choices would dissolve the meaning of free will. We would all be free to rampage in sin."

"But what about her?" he asked hoarsely.

"You cannot begin to understand God's plan. Submit at least to that. Maybe suffering exists to show us the way to forgiveness and atonement. Judas was an agent of Satan, and he caused great suffering for Jesus crucified on the cross, but his evil act, born of free will, revealed God's love for us and granted us the possibility of salvation. That's the mystery. And the most beguiling aspect of the plot is that Satan, in thwarting good, remains a servant of God, doing his ultimate bidding. You are the lamb that was lost, Joshua. God loves you even though you stray from his flock. He has plans for you, too."

"I want to get out of here," Josh said. I don't need to be here to learn to be good, he wanted to say. I need to leave, or I will die or do other horrible things. I won't have a choice. That's what you don't understand.

"You can't get out of here." A smugness to Brother Mike's smile. An endless benevolent love.

"Roy," Josh said, and then he remembered that he was not supposed to mention Roy by name. Fuck it, he thought, irritated by his own mistake and desperate. "Roy told me, based on what happened and the way my trial went, he thinks they put me in the wrong prison. Roy said he would help me try to get transferred. If you gave him access to my complete files and transcripts, he could look at them and see if there's some information we can use."

The request fell like a stone dropped into water. Brother Mike's smile disappeared. "Roy," he said with disappointment in the utterance. "Roy used to work in here, did he tell you that? My file clerk. He has an unhealthy curiosity for case histories." Josh wished he could have pulled the words back, but Brother Mike's anger continued to grow. "I think you should accept the fact that you're here. Using an inmate's legal counsel to get out of prison is pathetic. I've seen men waste their entire lives in that fool's quest. It's an avoidance of the very thing we've been talking about, the moral lessons of consequence."

"I know," Josh kept saying. "I know, I'm sorry. It wasn't my idea."

"Think of this prison as your own monastery. Free will is a limited and precious resource here. Moral consequence is in abundance. How you barter makes all the difference."

"You don't understand," Josh whispered. "I've got twenty-five years to serve. I don't think I can make it."

Brother Mike shrugged, his anger and his time depleted. "Take it from an old man, you'll have years left to live when you get out. Plotinus called time the life of the soul as it passes from one experience to another. Be grateful for those experiences. If you look hard enough, maybe you'll find something."

A long silence. Josh wanted to scream with frustration. He wanted to throw the old man down. Instead, he insisted, and didn't know where the strength came from. "Roy told me you needed to give me a copy of my file if I asked for it. I'm asking for it now."

Brother Mike stared at him, then rose and walked to one of the file cabinets along the wall. He pulled out a drawer, the long metal drone of a morgue, and fingered through.

"My catalogue of sin. I use a coded system for each file because I know how powerful this information can be."

He retrieved a thick manilla envelope from a hanging folder and brought it back to the coffee table, laying it before Josh.

"It's all in there, Josh, everything I have except my notes from our sessions, which you have no right to, but it also includes photocopies of the drawings you made. Be careful with it."

Josh nodded and stood awkwardly, the blood rushing to his legs.

"Someday I'm going to write a book," Brother Mike said. "A book that will blow the doors off corrections theory, and probably get me kicked out of the American Psychological Assocation, and probably rouse the Holy See as well. I'll tell you more about it someday, years from now."

We'll have plenty of time, he was saying. Josh said goodbye and closed the door. He walked, with that strange solitary freedom, through the education wing and into the main hub and down the tunnel to the infirmary, each gate and door opened for him by a CO as if he were someone important, as if he actually mattered. Every range in gen pop was in lockdown, only the infirmary open for business, so there was a grand emptiness to the prison, a sense of safety. When he got to his own cell at last, he opened the envelope and stared at the papers inside. Then he took the photocopies of his drawings and hid them the way Crowley had showed him.

16 ||||||||||||||

We kept the lockdown in place that New Year's Eve, another holiday spent in the concrete cave. The keepers decided to amend the annual New Year's Eve hot chocolate and doughnut social and distribute the goodies from cell to cell instead of opening up each block. Keeper Pollock sent me up to get Billy Fenton and bring him to the kitchen to help. Fenton did it every year. Getting out to walk around was a token of respect or an acknowledgment of special sway.

Only the dimmers were on in the main hub. I lifted a hand to the crew in the bubble, not even sure who was manning it tonight, unable to see into the dark space within. Then I walked the long tunnel to B block and greeted Ferris in the nest, a raised, protected room in the corner of the block where the CO kept watch. Ferris didn't bother to come down but activated the caged door for me to enter. TVs and stereos were on, but the noise within was subdued, the energy of the block powered down by some oppressive glumness. I climbed the metal staircase to the third floor. With each fourteen-foot rise in elevation, I felt an increased sense of solitude, a smallness in the world.

I walked the aisle at a slow pace, doing a mental count on each cell. When I got to Fenton's drum, I saw that he was already sitting up on his cot, waiting.

"Officer Williams," the voice in the dim interior said, "are those your catlike steps I hear?"

Don Juan in all his glory.

"Now, how'd you know it was me?" I asked, dry and sarcastic.

"Oh, you know how word gets around." A slow, relaxed tone, like he had all the time in the world. "The boys are jealous I caught a break. They always want my Christmas presents."

Christmas is over, asshole, I wanted to say. I tapped the green button on my shoulder radio twice and requested the open cell. It always took a few more seconds than expected. Then the click I'd been waiting for, and I stood back to allow Fenton space to step out.

Well-groomed hair, a little wet from some kind of product, an easy-going smile on a splendidly handsome face, like a movie star in some romantic comedy. He gave me a cheerful nod and slid by me gracefully, a scent of clean in the air behind him, so unlike the sour griminess of most of the inmates. Fenton was one of those occasional inmates in love with being a con. Early forties, but weathered well, wide shoulders, smooth skin with only a few tattoos. Self-assured and short-tempered. He had gotten into the pants of three females—three who had been found out, anyway—a secretary married to the head of maintenance, a nineteen-year-old volunteer religious counselor, and a CO named Julie Denly. I knew, without any understanding of the phenomenon, that plenty of women were irresistibly drawn to inmates. Even so, the sordid, awkward physicality of actually engaging in illicit sex inside a maximum security institution was utterly unfathomable to me. When Julie got caught—because someone on the cellblock jealous of Fenton had flown a kite to the Keeper—I had been astonished beyond belief. It was my first year on the job, and Julie seemed just like me, ex-military, hard-core, capable, so we got along, even spent some time together outside work, though I knew nothing of her relations with Fenton. I had no doubt Fenton could work his charms, but even then, before my jadedness got so keen, I knew that an inmate was a pathological liar, someone who told you relentlessly what you wanted to hear in order to get what he wanted and then threw all of those emotions away without remorse once you gave in. It didn't matter if it was an extra piece of toast or a career-ending affair—the level of emotional engagement was the same. After the scandal I met with Julie at a cheap restaurant off the highway. She wore a blue turtleneck sweater with plain hoop earrings, and she gripped her daiquiri like a vase of flowers that could tumble over. She told me about the letters and the secret messages and the words of love, and the level at which Fenton understood her, how he anticipated her moods and connected with her more completely than anyone she'd ever known. I could barely keep the running criticism out of my head. You poor, stupid, humiliated fool, you've ruined it for all of us. A few months later Julie moved away, and I never heard from her again. Fenton, on the other hand, was still serving eighteen to twenty for armed robbery and hostage taking.

From a dark cell near the front of the range an inmate mentioned that he had an erection to lend Fenton if needed. To his credit, Fenton ignored the comment. We clanked our way down to the ground floor, stood at the door, and waited for release into the hall, an endless, echo-filled corridor that was sloped, paint-chipped, and damp.

"You been double shifting?" Fenton asked. He seemed oddly unsure of himself when he spoke up, as though nervous about trying to make a connection.

"Almost every day. 'Tis the season."

We walked at a relaxed pace. Some inmates were always in a hurry, wired with ADD energy, but Fenton was all leisure.

"Between you and me—" he said.

Here it comes, I thought.

"Ninety-five percent of the boys aren't looking for this." He meant the disruptions and lockdowns—self-appointed emissary of the poor, misunderstood silent majority.

I said nothing at first, debated whether to ignore him, and finally spoke up.

"Fenton, why are you telling me this?" I asked.

And he laid it on thick.

"You, Officer Williams, are unusual in that you treat people with respect. That's a clean rep, no bullshit. The problem with the way things are run here is not enough communication. Most of the hard-ass COs just want to bust heads. But if you sat down and talked to us, there would be a lot less trouble."

"Give peace a chance, huh?" I said. Only part of me meant it ironically.

"Why not?" he asked. "I'm getting too old for this crap. You think I like twenty guys a day asking me what's going on and why? I'd rather be watching the soaps. Look at Elgin, not even a whole man anymore. That's where bullshit gets you."

I was tempted to stop talking with him altogether, just let the train run on down the tracks, but I couldn't resist. "What's Elgin got to do with anything? Are you claiming a CO had anything to do with his injury?"

"Shit, you think that one-armed painter messed up a hard-ass like Elgin that bad? No doubt he deserved whatever he got, but it's an insult seeing him hang on like a piece of meat. Tell your Keeper we give up. All we want is a fair shake, a normal routine, and a bit of tender loving respect. We'll be putty in your hands."

For whatever reason, some ease Fenton inspired in me, I made a confession.

"Wish I could help you, Fenton, but I don't exactly have the Keeper's ear."

"Really?" he asked, surprised. "That's not what I hear."

"Not so much."

"Ah," he said, and I regretted it instantly. They were data miners, collectors of random information. Somewhere, on a hospital bed with tubes up his nose, Ray MacKay was laughing his ass off.

We entered the hub, then took the hallway between the education wing and the gym. The lights were still dimmed.

Fenton stopped suddenly and turned, and my forward momentum actually pressed me into his shoulder. "Well, if there's ever any favor I can do for you," he said quietly, "you just have to ask."

Jesus fucking Christ, I thought, and pushed him forward with the heel of my hand. Oh, Julie, you stupid fool.

The lights were dim in the cafeteria, too, as though we were in a store after hours, and that surprised me. I was expecting a small crew of inmates and COs working together on the annual New Year's Eve hot chocolate run. I got nervous next to Fenton and kept one hand on the baton and the other at my shoulder radio. The eating area looked like a highway McDonald's, each table and chair unit growing by a single thick stem from the floor, like a field of bright pastel flowers.

Then we heard voices, a laugh, and a mop or broom handle hitting the ground. I decided to walk around the metallic counter and into the kitchen.

"Ahoy, Billy! About time you got here."

Roy Duckett stood before a steel counter wearing kitchen whites and an apron that started at his shoulders. He held the biggest wooden paddle I had ever seen, and he stirred a vat of hot chocolate like he was rowing a boat. Another inmate was sprawled across the counter—an easygoing lifer with muttonchop sideburns and a beer gut, named Eric Jackson, a.k.a. Jacko.

"And a happy New Year to you, Officer Williams," Roy added.

A small TV was set up on a counter, sports news recounting the football games. I saw an enormous punch bowl filled with cheese-covered nachos, a platter of buffalo wings, and another of baby back ribs dripping in sauce.

Roy and Jacko were without CO supervision. In my early days I would have assumed the worst—that the COs were hostaged, stuffed into the cabinets and meat lockers, a trap set for me—and reacted appropriately. But with experience I had come to understand that there were moments of laxness, moments of audacious inmate independence tacitly permitted under the contract of barters and deals I did not follow or condone. I had also learned that I should not interfere. It made me feel twice the fool—out of the loop and humiliated by my submission to those rotten unwritten rules.

I could see they wanted nothing more than to laugh at me. A voice within urged the crackdown, the negation of promises, and the cancellation of the hot chocolate run, throwing the entire institution into order and discipline, even as I knew that such heroic and reckless prudishness would be the end of me, or at least the end of my job, which felt about the same.

So I swallowed the bitter pride I could taste in my mouth and said nothing.

Then I noticed Josh Riff off to the side.

He looked caught out at something, seeing me there.

I met his eyes, but I did not want the other inmates to see the contact, so I kept it briefer than brief, the indifferent harshness glazing over me like a lizard's blink.

If he'd wanted out, he would have communicated something in that look other than deer in the headlights.

So I left, knowing I had an hour to go on my shift, three hours to go on the year, wanting nothing more than to be as far away from Ditmarsh as possible when the calendar flipped over another digit.

17

When she was gone, Roy introduced Josh to Fenton with a flourish, describing Fenton as "the finest hot chocolate pourer it's ever been my pleasure to know."

"He's the one, huh?" Fenton said.

"He is the one," Roy repeated.

Until then, Josh had felt lulled into a rare camaraderie. Roy had convinced the CO in the infirmary that strong-backed ever-eager Josh would be of assistance on the rounds, and so he'd been led along on this holiday excursion. Then came the surprise. The television and the food had been a revelation to him, a glimpse of some other kind of inmate life. They'd even passed around a thick spliff. After Fenton showed up, the illusion of easy pleasure got tugged roughly away, and Josh felt as though he'd been handed over by Roy as a kind of sacrifice. Fenton had a smooth and pleasing face, a relaxed manner, but that was the surface. Josh had heard things from Crowley about Fenton's activities, and the vibe of respect and even fear the others felt for him was obvious. All except Roy, who seemed more powerful than usual, some kind of change come over him, a different Roy, who told people what to do.

The party, just as quickly as it had been interrupted, resumed. Josh looked at Roy for some kind of understanding. Roy merely winked.

"Eat, eat," Jacko commanded, jowly in his baseball cap and his unshaven chin. They reapplied themselves to the ribs and chicken.

Jacko said, "Shit. Wait. Everyone get a mug of swill. Fuck a duck. We need a toast."

Josh received a mug of frothy, foul-smelling juice, like a rotten orange stuck in the moist toe end of an old sock.

"Here's wishing you a happy dick-sucking New Year."

The men, as if in chorus, lifted mugs and cheered.

Josh took a sip and coughed, the taste more effervescent and vile than expected.

Jacko looked wronged. "Hey, that's quality brew."

"Last week was a fine year," Roy noted. "Drink it down, Josh, or we'll feel fucking offended." So Josh took another, bigger sip and fought the sick feeling as it went down his throat.

"How many years you been working the hot chocolate, Fenton?" Roy asked.

Fenton, the least cheery and lubricated of them all, chewed the meat off a large, veiny rib. "That'd be nine, Wobbles. Same number of times I fucked your wife when she visited."

"Well, that's nine times I didn't have to," Roy said. "Thanks for being a sport."

Roy moved nimbly among the pots and the food, swinging almost like a monkey between counters, more light-footed and eager than Josh had ever seen him, scolding Fenton for leaving lumps in the hot chocolate, taking a rib from Jacko's hand before he could eat it. The drinking and the eating and the stirring continued. Josh wondered if the hot chocolate duty was ever going to begin. But it was all good. They didn't pay him undue attention, but they didn't ignore him either. As long as he kept his mouth more or less shut, drank from the mug when it got filled up, and laughed when the others laughed, they seemed to think he was one of the boys.

He felt warm in his bones. Whatever he'd drunk crystallized the room around him, so that he saw little details that much sharper. He noticed the cutting rack, for example, where all the knives were kept behind a long cage, the shape of each one drawn in marker. He wondered why and then noticed an outline in the space where the butcher knife had been, like an empty shadow.

"All right, party's over," Roy said. "Get on out there and start delivering, or we'll never get to bed."

Jacko poured hot chocolate from the pots into two red jugs and loaded the jugs on a wheel cart with boxes of doughnuts underneath. Then he passed Josh a smaller Tupperware pitcher. "This here's for dispensing on the upper tiers. Fill up the pitcher, then you don't need to carry the jugs up."

"That's a technological innovation we came up with about two years ago," Roy added.

"Me?" Josh asked, surprised to be sent out.

"Fenton will show you the ropes," Roy said. "He's an expert. A fucking doughnut artist."

"Fuck you, Wobbles."

And then they were beyond the doors of the cafeteria and in the hall.

"You push the cart," Fenton said. "I deal the doughnuts."

Josh was nervous about Fenton taking him around, but high or drunk, he felt a little thrilled, too, given their new and easy acquaintance. Josh pushed the gurney down the hall, and they left the cafeteria behind them, moving as fast as the misaligned wheels would allow.

The tunnel took forever. They passed through the octagonal space of the hub.

"So where do we start?" He could think of nothing better to say.

Fenton had gone internal, whistling to himself, looking about. He rapped the cage of the bubble as they passed by. "Hey, you boys want some hot chocolate and doughnuts?" he called out in a louder than necessary voice. Two COs were inside, sitting in chairs, hard to see in the dimness until you stood right before them. They gave Fenton an indifferent glance.

"Ha ha," he said to Josh as they pushed on. "Every year I love giving those fuckers the hot chocolate middle finger. They can't leave the bubble before the end of their shift any more than you and I can leave the prison. Imagine being stuck in that little room watching us yard apes walking by like we're on vacation. Armed to the fucking teeth, though. That's the one cool thing about that job. Other than being a sniper in the sentry tower, I can't see anything else worth doing here, unless you like telling grown men to bend over and hold their ass cheeks apart."

"Open Sesame!" Fenton yelled as he stood before the hall to C block and waved at the camera.

Five long seconds went by before the gate opened, the clunky automatic mechanics of it giving Josh the feeling that Ditmarsh itself was alive.

When they reached the gate at the end of the tunnel, a CO stood inside the block in front of the secure watch booth, what they called the jack nest. He must have been stretching his legs or doing rounds.

"Evening, Fenton. You fellows are a little late this year," the CO said through the bars, and buzzed them in, pulling back the cage.

"You can't rush quality," Fenton answered. "This is fine hot chocolate we're talking about."

"I bet it is."

As soon as they stepped into the block, Fenton howled skyward and tore up the quiet.

"Happy New Year, motherfuckers! Stick your dicks back in your pants and your mugs out your cages if you want to join the party. Your kids are tucked into their beds. Your wife's getting drilled up the ass by her new boyfriend. You might as well cut loose. Anyone slips me the good stuff gets two doughnuts, and his neighbor gets none. Pay up before your neighbor does, especially if you hate the rat fuck like you know he hates you."

"Easy, Fenton," the CO said. "I'd like to start the new year riot-free." But his voice was almost drowned out by the reaction from within. The inmates boomed and roared in response, cheering and cursing Fenton's presence. Josh had never heard such chaotic noise before, vibrating his bones like a single angry voice. His heart bounced off the walls of his chest, fright mixed with a kind of stadium excitement. It was his first time on a general population range. Two apartment-like complexes faced each other across space. Each level jutted out over the one below. The stacks of cells were smaller than he'd expected, but the number of cells was greater. They left the CO and started down the open hall, Fenton leading, Josh pushing the cart carefully behind him, nervous about the bumps that threatened to overturn it.

"We'll work bottom up," Fenton said. "Stick below the overhang or someone will douse you."

The drums had bars, not doors like in the howler range, and Josh could easily see into each man's crib. The lights were dimmed but not out. There were TVs on in every third or fourth drum, headphones muting the sound, little campfires flickering blue flame. Amazingly, the din of noise did not seem to come from any of the individual cells they passed, but from everywhere else at once. A few jokes, a few nods, but most of the men looked worn-out, without cheer, only half alive. To Josh's surprise, Fenton was intent on getting the work done. He filled the pitcher with hot chocolate and passed it to Josh, who poured it the into mugs that were thrust out through the narrow spaces between the bars.

"Where's Sonny?" one man asked.

"Sonny's taking the year off. Josh is twice the man Sonny is."

"You guys come around so late I was almost asleep."

"Fuck yourself and take a doughnut."

And to a weeping younger inmate: "Stop crying, buddy. You're dead to her."

As Fenton skipped a cell: "Where's mine?"

"You're a box thief and a bastard. I'd rather choke you to death with it than let you eat it."

"Hey, Fenton. The best wishes to you and your family."

"Give him an extra doughnut, Josh. No, not the jelly filled, that sugar one. It's not like he's letting me fuck his sister."

At the end of the row they abandoned the cart and took only the pitcher, climbing the metal stairs, walking back the way they came, doing switchbacks up and down the line. It became Josh's job to run back to the ground level and refill the pitcher every time it ran out. He hated being away from Fenton and on his own. He walked fast, trying not to make eye contact with anyone in a cell. Still, hands reached out. Mugs gestured for extra swill. Kisses got blown. Others hung back, indifferent to his existence, and he felt like a rodent scurrying by.

A new tier of cells around the other side of the block. It must have been a wing for sexual predators, because Fenton's disposition changed. He allowed Josh to pass out only a few doughnuts. "Fruit," he said. "That guy will blow you for a six-pack. This one's a sleazy fucking diddler." To accentuate the point, he pressed his lips to the doughnut and sucked out all the jelly, then let Josh give it to the man in the cell.

When they finished the block, Fenton sent Josh out into the hub on his own.

"D is next. You go ahead and be my reconnaissance," he said. "Let me know if there's any fun and games waiting."

Confused, Josh left Fenton behind and pushed the cart forward by himself, all the confidence drained out of him. He headed back into the hub and crossed it, then got buzzed into the next hallway. He steeled up as he approached the nest. There was a jack inside, watching Josh from on high through the Plexiglas. Josh nodded and asked for entrance into D block.

"Where the fuck is Fenton?" the jack asked him through the microphone on his console.

Josh pulled up on the cart with both hands and gave the jack his straightest answer.

"It's just me," he said. "Fenton's on C. We're running behind, so we split up."

The jack looked furious. He spoke into his radio and told whoever was listening that Fenton was no longer doing his appropriate rounds. Josh got nervous fast. A hitch in the static, then a voice said Fenton had been spotted and everything was fine.

This didn't please the jack. He told Josh there was no way he'd let a fish into D and to get the fuck out of his sight until Fenton showed up. Josh turned the cart around and walked back down the hall the way he'd come.

He found Fenton in the hub, just exiting the hallway from C.

"What you got?" he asked.

Josh was excited without knowing why. "The jack didn't like that I was by myself. He asked where you were and wouldn't let me in."

Fenton nodded. "That's what I was expecting. You play chess?"

Josh said he knew how.

"Then you'll understand my thinking. When the guy you're playing tempts you to take some halfway decent piece, you got to figure it's a trap. But sometimes the best way to look like you're falling for it is to make a sacrifice."

Josh didn't know how that applied to the current situation, exactly, but he asked Fenton what the plan was going forward.

"Deliver us some doughnuts," Fenton answered.

Josh put his faith in Fenton, but his nerves were bad as they traveled the long hall and approached the jack nest again. This time the jack waited outside the nest, standing on the floor before the cage.

"Hey, boss," Fenton called out cheerfully, as if nothing was up.

The jack asked Fenton why the fuck he wasn't doing his rounds properly. Fenton made up a story about a weeping con, the need to provide solace to a brother in pain.

The jack told Fenton to leave the social work to the weak sisters and get his ass in gear. Fenton rogered that and asked for permission to deliver doughnuts to D. The cage snapped open, and Fenton nudged Josh forward.

Josh pushed the cart into the block. Then something happened to his feet, and he fell forward, colliding with the cart and pulling it down on top of him. The large and small containers of hot chocolate tumbled off the cart and struck the ground, the contents rushing along the floor in a brown flood. With his hands and knees covered in the stuff, Josh looked up from his embarrassed brew-drunk sprawl, terrified of the consequences, then felt the world smack him back down as God's hammer, or the heel of Fenton's hand, hit him so hard on the top of his head that the pain spritzed out through his eyes. He huddled there, every muscle in his ribs and back tightening in expectation of Fenton's boots to commence shit kicking. Instead, he heard Fenton voicing his utter contempt for the stupid, clumsy fish who'd just spilled the whole fucking wagonload of hot chocolate.

"Jesus, boss, I am completely fucking sorry," Fenton said to the jack. "We will, and I mean will, clean this up right away. I am going to stick the mop up this fish's ass or he will lick the floor clean, and that's a promise." Then to Josh. "All right, get your shit-ass up and fucking move!"

Josh stood, the heat of the smack to his head still filling his face. He righted the cart, scooped up handfuls of soggy doughnuts, and chased after the empty containers. Fenton waited impatiently, as though his hand could strike again at any moment. Then they were walking down the hall back to the hub.

"You all right?" Fenton asked him.

Josh felt a hand on his shoulder.

"Had to make it look good."

And Josh realized he hadn't tripped on his own, but had been tripped up intentionally.

"That, my friend, was a head fake. A couple badasses on D want to take me down," Fenton explained. "Gave the jack a little New Year's bonus. We go inside, unsuspecting, then bam, suddenly a few extra cell doors would have opened."

"You mean he'd let them out?" Josh asked.

"Accidentally, of course," Fenton said. "You did good, though. That was a convincing fall."

"My head hurts like hell," Josh said.

Fenton laughed. "Sorry about the slap."

When they entered the hub, Fenton stopped suddenly. "Fuck if I want to go all the way back to the cafeteria. I got people I want to see."

"You want me to get the bucket and mop?" Josh asked.

"Let that fat pig do it himself."

One minute obsequious to the CO, next the spittle of disdain.

"So, according to Wobbles, you and Crowley got to know each other good, huh?"

This is it, Josh thought. This is how the hurt comes.

"We had drums beside each other."

"Crowley used to do a valuable service for me before he went a little free style. He wasn't all wrong, just a little confused, if you know what I mean."

Josh didn't know whether to nod or say nothing, the nervousness gnawing at him.

"All I want to know is how Crowley finished his annual report. Roy says you did it for him. Is that true?"

He had no choice but to admit it.

"Roy says you can draw just about anything, huh?"

"I suppose."

"You think you can remember what you drew for Crowley?"

Josh shrugged, afraid to death of offending, afraid of answering wrong.

Fenton didn't wait for any words to come out.

"You want a good home, Josh, a range where you feel safe, you come to B-three. I'm inviting you in as one of the boys. A fellow of your skills and intelligence should feel valued, not afraid. Look at this place"—one hand sweeping the air, taking in the open dome above them, as though transforming the prison into a kingdom with his gesture. "All of these monkeys locked in their cages. You on the outside walking around, looking in, passing them treats, a prince among thieves. I'd say it's pathetic what you can drag a man down to, except most of these mutts think they have a good thing going. You realize that? They all got their plans. The things they wake up every day thinking are important. But none of them know what they're sitting on. What they got right in reach."

Fenton rattled the empty jugs. "Now go get us some fucking refills. I'll hang out here until you're back."

Josh started to push the cart. Fenton called out to him.

"Here. Try these." Something placed in the palm of his hand. "Fuck the tunnel. Walk across the yard to get to the kitchen. You can look at those stars and feel like a free man."

18

At the end of the last day of the year I got pushed into an hour of overtime when an inmate in his cell experienced an epileptic fit. The doctor on call, a hack with smudged glasses who acted superior to everyone around him, was incredulous. Were the medications given on time? Was the right medication given to the right prisoner? More incriminations, a questioning of my basic intelligence. I'd given out 97 treatments in my round of 168 inmates. It was possible I'd made a mistake in the order. But wouldn't that have led to other inmates experiencing bad symptoms, a chain reaction of mistakes? The doctor grumbled. Fifteen minutes later he discovered a blood track on the inmate's inner thigh. "Injection," he announced. There wasn't the slightest note of apology in his tone, just pure pride at his forensic genius.

"So you're reporting that the inmate had a negative reaction to contraband drugs," I said, not even bothering to thin the sarcasm, "and that my conduct had no connection with his condition whatsoever."

The doctor grunted. "Looks that way."

Oh, fuck you, I thought. "Write it down that way, Doctor. I'm out of here."

There were two hours left in the year when I kicked open the front door of the penitentiary and saw the parking lot. Pitch-black and twinkly in the sky, the ground lit by the lights of the sentry towers like a sports arena at night. As I approached my truck, I saw a figure in a parka standing deeper in the parking lot, waiting. At first I thought it must be Wallace, but then I saw that the man was taller and more broad-shouldered than Wallace. A hand lifted, beckoning. I adjusted my direction to head his way. I didn't like walking toward him, but I didn't want to show any sign of nervousness either. Then I felt a twist in my gut, not fear but trouble. It was Ruddik.

"What do you want?" I asked, letting all of my exhaustion show on my face.

"Cold, isn't it," he said, as though we were waiting at a bus stop together. Then, "My car won't start. I've got cables. Could you give me a boost?"

It was the last thing in the world I wanted to do. "Of course," I said. One of the COs probably drained his battery for a laugh. "Wait here. I'll drive over."

"Can I drive with you? I'm half frozen from waiting in my car."

It seemed an unlikely request coming from such a dour and self-reliant loner.

We walked to my truck and got into the cab. I didn't want to spend any time with Ruddik. Then I wondered, what if my own engine didn't start? There were COs who didn't appreciate me much either. That's all I needed.

But my truck started. I let it idle with the vents opened and the heat cranked. Ruddik offered to scrape my windows, but I told him not to bother. I got out and did it myself. When I was back in the cab, we waited another few minutes, barely speaking, until I announced we might as well move. Ruddik directed me to his car. An old Duster. No wonder it didn't start. Had to be fifteen years of salt-eaten junk. "No one could accuse you of being on the take," I said. It was a stupid joke, but I was tired.

"If I was, I'd be smart enough not to spend it on a sixty-thousand-dollar truck, wouldn't I?"

I popped the hood and let him go out and attach the cables. Both hoods were raised. I was blind to what he was doing but could imagine the handles being clipped on. Then Ruddik appeared and motioned that he was going to start his own car. I heard the starter grind and then turn over. The Duster roared out noise, gunned three times—my own lights dimming with the drain—then catching and settling, the motor grumbling but steady.

The cables got released and folded up. The hoods got slammed shut. I wanted to wave and spin out of the lot, but I waited. Ruddik opened the passenger door and thanked me. "You mind if I sit a few minutes while my car warms up, and hold you here until I'm sure it runs?"

He climbed in, stomped his feet, pulled off his gloves, and warmed his hands. I thought about turning on the radio but didn't. Instead, we watched the prison wall like a drive-in movie screen, not speaking. I realized I should have some feeling for the place, some deeper or more poetic emotion, but I was numb. You shouldn't be numb about where you work. Not when it took so much out of you. Maybe I was in shock. Too much had happened lately. It wasn't all terrible. But it was thankless. And when the pressure came down, you wondered why you bothered. Just enough money to keep you locked in.

We both heard the sound of tires moving over snow and saw the headlights. A car arriving at the prison parking lot. Neither one of us spoke. I saw that the car was a taxicab. It stopped at the gate. Beeped twice. The door of the prison, closed so tightly, opened as if magic words had been spoken. A CO appeared. The taxicab's doors opened, and two men got out from the front seats. The man from the passenger side opened the back door and leaned in. When he stood up again, his arms were loaded with buckets of Kentucky Fried Chicken. The driver leaned in and got his own armful. The CO at the gate ushered them in.

"That's a lot of chicken," Ruddik said quietly. "Those COs must be hungry."

I didn't say anything. My mouth closed.

"Some nights I sit in my car just to amuse myself and I watch that taxicab make two or three trips up here. It's not always KFC, mind you.

Sometimes they've stopped at the liquor store. Sometimes I can't tell what's in the bags."

The prison gate opened again. The two men exited. They got back in their cab, which pulled away quickly, the headlights whipping by in the turn; then the cab made for the slope down to the county road.

"That's twice already tonight, but I bet they'll be back in an hour," he said. "What do you think that costs in taxi fares alone? Coming all that way. In the middle of the night. I bet you add up all those fares and the cost of the deliverables, and those COs are putting a lot of money in that cab-driver's hands. Boy, those profit margins must be awfully good."

"It's New Year's Eve, for God's sake," I said softly, though I knew it happened all the time. I thought of the cafeteria and their goddamn ribs. I hated the smell of food when it came into the COs' room. I turned a blind eye. I didn't want to know where it went. The others were in a good mood whenever a shipment arrived. They moved faster than normal, motivated, organized, like men around a barbeque. They made the delivery. I wanted nothing to do with it. I didn't want the taste in my mouth.

"Sure," Ruddik said. "And the COs eat it all, just like they say they do, and they don't deliver it to some murdering gangbanger's cell, and they don't get paid off for lots of other things either. I'm never there when it happens, of course. So who really knows? What happens on the other side of those walls stays on the other side of those walls. Funny, isn't it? A maximum security prison is the safest place in America to commit a crime. Nobody ever gets caught. Doesn't matter if you're smuggling in fried chicken or heroin. Doesn't matter if you're arranging for an inmate to get a quickie or letting him into someone else's cell to give them a hot shot. You'll never ever ever get caught. It's like it never happened."

"You waited for me, didn't you," I said.

"I knew one of these nights we'd run into each other, have a little talk."

"Why?"

He ignored my question. "Off the top of my head, here's a list of things I know go in there. Heroin. Crack. Cocaine. Marijuana. Alcohol. Pornography. Perfume. Aftershave. Stockings. Sunglasses. Kentucky Fried Chicken. Pizza. Doughnuts. Coffee. Coffee beans. Game Boys. Baby back ribs. Subway sandwiches. Tobacco. Cough syrup. Syringes. Needles. Panties. Lube. Condoms. Batteries. Valium. OxyContin. Crystal meth."

"Why are you telling me this?" My hands were on the steering wheel. It was warm in the cab, though the frost still lingered on the edges of the windshield, but I'd never felt so cold. I hated Ruddik, despised his morbid puritan morality. "You think this is a good idea sitting here? Inmates watch the cars out in this parking lot. I once drove a friend's car to work because mine was in the shop. You know that I had three inmates ask me about my new car that very day? They watch every goddamn thing we do. Inside and outside. They watch us more closely than we watch them. I'm going to get labeled a rat just for being with you."

"Is that what you think of me?" he asked. He turned to me for the first time. I was used to him looking away quickly, like a man uncomfortable with other people, but he seemed confident enough now.

"I think you have a job and you do it. I imagine it's not very easy. You're a CO and you watch the COs. I'm not sure how you handle the contradictions."

"Why? Because you're afraid of pointing the finger at a bad guy? I thought that's what you wanted to do. Become a law enforcement officer someday. Right?"

It cut, his mocking me. "I do my job. It's not easy for me either, you know. I rely on my colleagues. They look out for me."

"Do they?" Ruddik asked. "I'm here to save your neck, Kali. They're going to get you. You're on the enemies list. You think the pressure's bad now that Hadley has filed a notice of abuse, but you wait and see what they start disclosing about you. Complaints from all quarters. The inmate you beat. The inmate you screwed. The CO you blackmailed. I've seen it happen. You think you made anyone happy finding Crowley? You think they like whistle-blowers? They'll turn you into a joke. They'll let the press have bits and pieces. You'll be a sadistic inmate rapist by the time they've finished with you. And in the end, you'll move so far away from here you might need a passport."

"Thanks for the advice. Now could you get out of my truck so I can go home?"

He didn't move, of course. "Elgin getting hurt was the best thing to happen in a while. You wouldn't think a tough guy like that could get so scared. He's going to roll for us in exchange for a transfer. But I need help lining up some other informants. I know you've been poking around. I know you asked questions about Crowley and that you've got your suspicions. I think you have a knack for it. I want you to come on board."

"How do you know what I've been doing?" I asked.

"Most of the time I get my information from inmates," Ruddik answered.

"Figures," I said. "An inmate will say anything. An inmate lies like he breathes."

"Of course," Ruddik said. "I'm not stupid. But I'm also open to the possibility that a liar can have his motivations for telling the truth."

"An inmate's only motivation for snitching on a CO is revenge."

"Yes. But what inspires the need for revenge?"

I didn't answer. We might have been in an empty world. No sound but the truck engine and the vents and our breath.

"Justice," he said. "Some inmates, a surprising number of them, get pissed off when they see a CO getting away with something illegal. It offends their sense of justice."

"They play you."

"They play," he agreed. "Some of them love it. They play one side against the other like they're playing chess. Some of them think they're geniuses. I've met a couple who really were. Most of them are stupider than they realize. We have to get them out in a hurry when they make a mistake and go too far. Crowley did. Of course they say it's suicide. But I know it wasn't. You know it, too."

"Who's we?"

He didn't answer. "We've got warrants. We've got wiretaps. We're monitoring bank accounts. We're setting up relationships. We're starting to figure things out."

The words sank in. It made me queasy to think about an investigation of that scale going on. Who would go down? Then he turned on me.

"If any of this information gets out, I'll know you are the one who told it. If you tip anyone off, if you tell your best friend or your hairdresser, I'll know it was you. If a CO gets out of the country in a hurry, I'll know it was your fault."

I thought about Tony Pinckney and the three-week honeymoon he'd just taken to Australia. It was ridiculous. It was insane.

I said, "If there was something serious going on, Keeper Wallace would do something about it." It was a leading statement.

"Keeper Wallace is dirty," he answered. "A few months ago I got one of my guys to circulate five one-hundred-dollar bills inside to buy some particular services. I had my suspicions. When the money was in, we began to follow Wallace. We followed him for a weekend and saw nothing out of the ordinary. But then, a half hour before we were going to close it down on a Sunday afternoon, he walked into a jewelry store in the mall and came out with a small plastic bag. We went into the jewelry store and asked the clerk what he had bought and how he had paid for it. A necklace. In cash. We confiscated the cash. Two of the hundred-dollar bills turned up."

"It could have gotten to him a hundred different ways. It could have been money owed to him by another CO, someone who really is dirty." Who would have expected me to defend Wallace? But I felt threatened by the information, the applecart of my little world overturned by it. I'd admired Wallace once. Part of the reason why his actions had hurt me was because I admired him still.

"It wasn't proof," Ruddik said. "It just lined up some more arrows. They're pointing to places you wouldn't believe."

I could barely breathe. I cracked my window to let the air in. I wanted the cold to bring me back to life.

"I'm angry," he said. "I'm doing something here that I would never normally do. I've been watching you. I think I know where you stand, what kind of person you are. I've thought about this for a while. We've been inching along. It's not going fast enough. We need reinforcements."

"I don't know if I can do that," I said. "I'm not like that."

A rat was a rat.

"My best informant was very close to Jon Crowley. Through his information I came to believe that Crowley knew something important. I started working Crowley, bringing him along. I wanted him to know that we could stop the beatings, give him some protection if he helped us out. Imagine my surprise when he disappears and then hangs himself in the City. It's almost laughable."

I tried to swallow it down, sick to my stomach. I saw Crowley dangling forward, frozen in flight, the noose eating into his neck.

"You saw his body. What do you think? Ever been pepper sprayed in the eyes? In the old days, the boys would put you in a room, douse you with it, and block the vents and door cracks so the air couldn't clear and you couldn't get away. Ever been tasered so bad your skin burned? Ever gone days locked in darkness, thinking you might never see another person again? I don't think it matters if they made that noose and hung him with it or left him down there and told him they were coming back for more. Do you want to find out why?"

I did and I didn't. I thought of Ray MacKay, oxygen mask lowered to his chin, and couldn't get the hard lump out of my throat.

"I want you to do me one favor," Ruddik said.

He put a business card in my hands.

"There's an Internet address and a password on this," he said. "Go to the site and see for yourself."

"What is it?" I managed to ask.

"A video. Just watch it. Let me know if it reminds you of anything. If it does, and you want to do something about it, call me."

Then he opened the door and was gone.

19

If he thought Fenton wasn't watching, Josh would have snaked his way through the hallways back to the kitchen. Instead, he opened the door to the yard and stepped out. The air was cold. The night was dazzlingly bright, the cold air crystallizing into sparkles all around him. The noise of the cart crashing and banging across the uneven stones was louder than he expected. He stopped. No one else in the entire world existed except for him. He was the last man alive. Two pills in his hand. He had no idea what they were. He looked up into the sky, just like Fenton told him to. The sight of the stars piercing the empty blackness took his breath away. The thought of his own little life in the midst of so much dense space made him tremble. He took the pills, swallowed them hard. How good it was, despite everything, to be alive.

A hundred feet later he thought of the sentries in the guard towers. They'd be astonished to see him moving about. No doubt they had him in their sights. A sniper shot. A bullet in the back of his head as a final joke. Could Fenton arrange something like that? Checkmate. The paranoia was upon him. It happened no matter what drugs he took. The fear of total loss of control. The sense that he was under someone else's influence.

Reaching the cafeteria building, Josh expected to wait in the cold until the duty guard roused himself, but the gate was ajar and Josh simply pushed the cart in on his own. In through the cafeteria, marveling at his own sense of direction, he emerged into the kitchen. Roy was gone. Jacko sipped from a tin cup, smoking a cigarette.

"Where's Fenton?"

"He sent me to fill up," Josh said, lifting one of the large empty containers from the cart and placing it under the spigot of the cooking pot.

"I'll get that," Jacko said, and stumbled over.

He stirred the hot chocolate with the huge wooden paddle, peered in to examine the contents. "Needs more water," he said. He reached down and grabbed a plastic mop bucket, then poured the dirty water into the steaming cocoa.

"Oh, shit." Holding the empty mop bucket in his hand and looking down to the place where he had grabbed it from. Another bucket beside it, this one filled with clean water. He chucked the mop bucket across the room and picked up the wooden paddle again.

"Advice from the cook. Go easy on the hot chocolate."

"Roger that," Josh said.

He went back to D block through the hub. There were moments when he didn't know how many steps he had taken, how much time had passed. He kept remembering what he was doing, waking up to his present awareness, realizing that he was pushing a cart down a long hallway in a prison. His heart had never beat so rapidly. He felt as if his face were on fire. He knew his teeth were shedding. There was a finger inside his skull, scraping at the inner shell of his cranium with a nail, a hollow sound he realized mimicked the squeaky wheel of the cart.

He couldn't find Fenton. Not waiting in the hub, not waiting outside the nest in D. The mess was gone. The jack was nowhere to be seen. Josh didn't know what to do. "Hot chocolate and doughnuts!" he yelled, and behold, the gate opened and he was drawn inside, pushing the cart before him. He went from cell to cell on his own. The men said things to him, he spoke back. There was no communication to it, no connection.

Back in the hub, all the ranges finished, he crossed over to Keeper's Hall. He saw a roomful of guards. They called out to him, and he stopped and wished them a happy New Year, offering up his wares, the last box of doughnuts. They grabbed the box from him and chewed and stuffed their faces. Released, he pushed on down the hallway, more minutes gone by, and realized he was lost. Then he heard a strange sound, a faint animal growling, and pushed on farther, turning a bend. The noise was coming from behind a door, and for some reason, some unexpected bravery or curiosity in him, he pushed the door open and peered inside. A female CO, her shirt unbuttoned, her breasts free, stood in the middle of the room, bent over but facing him, her hands braced on a table, her long hair dangling, her blue uniform pants in a pile on the floor. Behind her, thrusting hard, was Fenton, the widest smile on his face Josh had ever seen, recognition mixed with pride even as he maintained his rhythmic dance.

"Connie! We've got an audience!"

The jack's face lifted and stared at Josh, her mouth rounding, her eyes widening, a pleading expression. "Oh Jesus Christ."

And Fenton laughing. And Josh fleeing down the hall, the cart rattling wildly until he abandoned it and ran into the hub. Somewhere the tick of a clock struck twelve, and a thousand voices roared in mock celebration, like a beast awakened. He walked as fast as he could, almost a run, sweat on his neck, voices in his ears, and broke for the tunnel to the infirmary and home.

It was only when he got to the infirmary that he allowed himself to slow down. The gate pushed open. It shouldn't have been open. Why was he able to walk right in? The cells were completely dark. Only a single row of fluorescent lights to show his way. There was no one at the CO desk, no one in the common room, no nurses. How would he get into his own cell? He desperately wanted to find his bed bunk, splash water on his face to steady his racing heart, and sleep. His cell door was open. It shouldn't have been open. But he didn't go inside. Instead, he walked to the end of the hallway as though compelled, turned the corner into the cavern of the intensive care wing, each bed in its alcove, and saw the cage surrounding Elgin's bed.

"If it isn't himself," Roy said.

The cage door was open, and Roy sat on the edge of Elgin's cot, weighing it down. Josh looked to his left and his right. There was no CO anywhere. Vague memories of a party somewhere. Fenton fucking someone. He couldn't put the pieces together.

"They took his leg off today, can you imagine, and still our friend promises us the hurt."

With horror he gazed down the torso. Amputated? The blanket on the bed was suspiciously flat on the left side, but Elgin was awake, his uncovered eye darting back and forth between them. His arms were bound by the Velcro restraints attached to each side of the bed. Josh imagined Roy slipping the restraints on while Elgin was sleeping, then sitting patiently and waiting for him to wake up.

"What a surprise to see Crowley's little bitch," Elgin said.

Roy shushed him.

"We've been talking, Lawrence and me. He's filled with bitterness. All the pain he's caused in this world and he wants to cause more. He hates you something awful, Josh. It's remarkable, really. He thinks you're going to finish Crowley's work and that means you need to be stopped. Do you want to tell Josh what you said you'd do to him a few minutes ago?"

"Fuck you, Wobbles, you cocksucking—"

Roy ripped the bandage off Elgin's face and shoved it deep into his mouth. The mottled spots of blood made Elgin look like a motorcycle crash victim, all road rash. His good eye bulged with anger. His body undulated against the restraints, working them.

"You needed to go through me," Roy was saying. "No one gets into the City without me."

Elgin bucked and lunged, thrusting upward. He struggled to open his mouth around the cloth.

"What are we going to do with you, Lawrence?" Roy asked. His face was the picture of reasonableness. And he put his big, meaty hand across Elgin's mouth.

Josh had never seen a hand so large. It filled the trench between Elgin's chin and the tunnels of his nostrils. It embraced Elgin's face and suctioned down on it. It became the center of stillness in a writhing, bucking, undulating mass.

"There, there," Roy said.

The calm voice distorted Josh's understanding of what was happening. The frantic, biting, lunging force on the bed, each thrust to the sky more violent, more hate-filled.

"Shhhh," Roy was saying. "Don't fight it. There ain't nothing you can do."

And Josh, without understanding whether he was commanded, bidden, or destined, threw himself over Elgin's body, weighing it down, knowing then and there that he was eternally damned, wanting it to be over as quickly as possible, wanting Elgin to die. The wind must have been howling outside, the snow pounding down like hail. The world was a cesspool of seething hate.

The body burst upward with a violent thrust for air. Roy whispered into Elgin's ear, calming him, telling him it was going to be all right. And for a second Josh thought it was true; the great muffled howls were gone, the rolling chest was becalmed, but the air was polluted with a stench, a foul mixture of piss and shit.

Josh fell back, still feeling how Elgin's heart had beat wildly, begging for release before stabbing upward with one last electric jolt. All of it over now, the calmness back. Roy undid the Velcro restraints and tsked about the raw welts on the forearms, rearranged the sheet, tucking it under Elgin's torso with a grimace. He replaced the bandage on the half of Elgin's face, like a badly fitted toupee.

"If I were you," Roy said, "I'd be in my crib an hour ago."

20

I didn't remember driving home. I wasn't aware of the world around me until I pulled into the driveway. I was awake but moving without thought. Inside the house, I pulled off my boots and parka. In the kitchen the cat's water bowl was filled with bloated pellets of food. The fridge was leaking again, and I stepped in the pool of water with my sock foot. I stripped in the bedroom, folding my uniform over the dresser, feeling sallow and flabby, and put on a shirt, sweatpants, and slippers.

I fired up my computer. It took a long time to start. I looked at the business card, blank except for a strange URL, one of those nonsensical number-letter strings that spam addresses sometimes use, and a password: NOYFB. I launched the browser and typed in the address.

A space came up for a password, and I typed that in, too. The screen flickered and changed, and a video screen popped up. I watched it load and I hit the play button. A home movie started up. Credits came on, "Midnight Walk" appearing in bold white font, like words on a computer screen. Then PowerPoint candy canes and mistletoe came fluttering down the screen like snowflakes. The screen blinked, and suddenly a subtitle appeared: "Produced by the Ditmarsh Social Club." A symbol below like a trademark. Three inverted triangles, encircled, the glaring pumpkin face. What the hell was the Ditmarsh Social Club?

I felt a pin-size hole in my stomach, the beginnings, no doubt, of some kind of terrible gut-eating cancer. The person holding the camera strolled the hallways of Ditmarsh. A row of covered cell doors with wide slots at waist and floor level. The dissociation unit. The camera stopped before a cell, and a hand knocked almost politely on the metal door. In response, other hands from within were thrust out and cuffed. The door opened, and a CO went inside, visible only from the chest down. A minute later an inmate emerged in shackles. Worse, I realized, he wore ski goggles with aluminum foil in the eyes. He had on heavy ear protectors, the kind airplane flagmen wore to block out all sound. Blind and deaf, he was led forward by the arm, a troop of six unidentified COs surrounding him. A voice called out hello, a muffled echo. A door opened. The camera was outside. It was nighttime. The camera panned up. The walls of Ditmarsh were revealed from inside the yard. There was no snow. Stars in the night sky above. I heard a voice. "Fuck, it's cold." I didn't recognize the person who spoke.

The scene cut. A door opened to a roomful of people, one of the meeting rooms in Keeper's Hall. Party whoops welcomed the camera. The camera swiveled back and forth as though greeting people on the left and the right. Then it was placed on a tripod. A face peered into the camera as if to set it properly. I recognized Droune. Then it was back to legs.

It was as though I were watching a frat party. Typical macho CO behavior. The alcohol was flowing, the voices were loud and raunchy. If Ruddik wanted to prove to me that the guards jerked off on company time, brought in liquor and music, well then he'd proved it, but that was hardly my business.

Then some of the behavior started to get outlandish. One of the COs had dropped his pants and was shuffling around the room. I saw what must have been a female CO doing a slow grinding dance to the music, like a stripper, and wondered if it was Connie Poltzoski, a gruff woman in her early forties. A hard drinker and smoker. Debasing herself in front of a roomful of ten or twelve men. None of it looked good on camera to someone like Ruddik. But I kept watching.

The video changed again. The party must have ended or become subdued. I could hear footsteps and voices with clarity. The camera was picked up this time and thrust into a hideously made-up face. Lipstick-smeared mouth. Dark mascara eyes. A scared look. When the camera pulled back, I recognized the inmate. What was his name? The transvestite called Screen Door, wearing a strapless cocktail dress. She was slender and timid but still looked gangly and manly, awkward on high heels. The camera tilted up and around, and I saw that every CO in the picture was now wearing a hood. I was so startled by the transformation that it took me a moment to understand. The hoods were gray flannel. They were loose. They slumped to the shoulders and needed to be adjusted and shifted often.

I watched helplessly as the hooded COs converged on Screen Door.

They forced him to stand on a chair in his high heels. The camera panned up, and I saw that Screen Door was wearing a bedsheet rope around his neck. His eyes bulged in terror. He was crying. The muffled voices told him to shut up. One hand held a Taser close to Screen Door's body, and Screen Door leaned away from its touch, as if he could imagine it going off at any moment. I heard someone spitting obscenities. Screen Door was guilty of numerous crimes. He was a pipe-sucking homo. He didn't do what he was told. He needed to be dealt with. The chair was kicked away. For one awful moment Screen Door was suspended in the air, and then he collapsed in a heap on the floor. The laughter overwhelmed the sound of the video.

Then they pulled him up and noosed him again, even as he begged for his life. The screams were horrible. The chair got kicked, and he fell the same way, and to the COs it was just as funny, even as Screen Door coughed and spit. After he was mock executed a third time, a CO lifted him up and embraced him with his arms. Then he spoke and told Screen Door that he'd been saved, that he was born anew. Someone laughed and told him to sin no more. I didn't recognize any of the voices.

The screen blackened. Somewhere in the darkness I heard a car honk hysterically, and I realized the new year had begun.

STAGE III

21

Ruddik wouldn't tell me what it was about. He wouldn't even tell me where we were going. He asked me to meet him at a McDonald's parking lot off Route 36 at eight-thirty in the morning, the second day of the new year.

I slept badly and woke early. Driving east, I watched the sun rising fast, changing from a dispersed haze to an intense but distant orb. The snow had receded from the road and become a grimy nothingness on the shoulder.

The McDonald's, just off the exit ramp, was adjacent to a strip mall that included a sport store, a tax attorney's office, and a Chinese restaurant. I was ten minutes early and feeling coffee-deprived, so I nudged into the drive-thru line. Naturally, as soon as I was locked into the decision, cars in front and cars behind, I noticed Ruddik sitting in a vehicle I didn't recognize, a silver Ford sedan, parked next to the Dumpster, staring forward, waiting. The sense of screwup came over me, like I was late for a job interview. I tried to catch his eye, wishing I hadn't committed to the drive-thru, but he didn't see me. I tapped the horn, but he still didn't look over, and I got an annoyed stare in the rearview mirror ahead of me.

When I had finally been handed a large coffee black, I was two minutes late. I rolled through the parking lot, saw an empty spot four over from Ruddik and an old couple in a car going for it, cut them off in a move that was half vindictiveness, half desperation, and suffered their glares as I locked up and walked over to Ruddik's car.

I sank deep into the seat. There were some food wrappers on the floor at my feet, but it was a clean car with a rental smell. "You got stuck in that lineup," he said. So he had seen me. "I thought we'd drive together the rest of the way." I nodded. He was dressed civilian. Jeans and a golf shirt under a fleece sweater. His hair looked good, like he'd just gotten it cut.

"Whose car is this?" I asked as we hit the on-ramp and cruised back on the highway.

"It's budgeted to the investigation," Ruddik answered. "We leave it at that parking lot for special occasions."

A car *budgeted* for special occasions. And who is *we*? I still didn't know, but Ruddik had an air I didn't recognize in him, a calm professionalism and confidence, a hint that the uptight righteousness he displayed in uniform was an act. I didn't ask him anything. I saw a briefcase on the backseat. Saw the gun in the shoulder holster inside his sweater. I wondered if that was special duty or just typical macho shit. Unlike most of the male corrections officers, I didn't carry a gun on civilian time. For some reason, we were entitled to carry, even though we had to check our weapons as soon as we stepped foot inside the prison. It always struck me as the height of lunacy—pack a gun while you're out with your family at Applebee's just because you can, store it in a gun locker when you get to work so the bad guys don't wrestle it away from you.

We got off the highway, headed north on a county road, then wound our way west again around White Wolf Lake before turning into a suburb marked by one of those tony stone gates. Large houses, spread duly apart, lots of trees, plenty of judicious speed bumps, the glimpse of a golf course.

Knowing exactly where he was going, Ruddik turned up a hill and into a new lane still lacking public works, a stump where a fire hydrant would go, multicolored wires splaying from a telephone box, the ground torn up, the curbs unfinished, and three houses in various states of construction. Ruddik parked the car across the street from the third house, a two-story McMansion. Two worker vans were parked in the unfinished drive. I glimpsed a few construction men in the open hallway, another one behind a window on the second floor.

"What are we doing here?" I was reaching for a joke, but nothing came.

"How much do you think a house like this runs?" Ruddik asked. The serious look had returned to his face, the grave disapproval of misdeeds.

I gave it my appraising homeowner's eye, the one on the lookout for defaulted subprime mortgage deals. The neighborhood, the size, the amount of land. I pegged it at three-quarters of a million.

"More," Ruddik said. "And last week they decided to go with brick on the exterior." He pointed at a pile of bricks under a tarp on the front yard. "And you know that's not cheap."

"Okay, what's the point?"

"The house is owned by Allison Marie Harris. She's a single mother of three boys, twice married, twice divorced, just moved from Sacramento, California."

The name did nothing for me, except I wondered why anyone would move from California to the Upper Midwest.

"One year ago Allison Harris was in a state prison for drug possession. An eighteen-month sentence. Her three boys were temporarily placed in foster homes. She got out quickly, after just five months, then went on social assistance. Didn't have a penny to her name. And now she's moving into a million-dollar house in the suburbs."

I tried to understand where he was going, what connection he was pointing out. "Is she family to one of the inmates?"

"Not quite," Ruddik said. He looked over and gave me that long, mournful glance, then put the car back into drive. "She's Roger Wallace's kid. Your Keeper's daughter."

Everything I'd known about Wallace and how he operated shifted in an instant.

Ruddik nodded. "Twenty-five-year veteran, Roger Wallace, still working because he can't retire, buying his daughter a million-dollar dream home. Go figure, huh?"

The car suddenly moving, pulling away from the curb, my brain slowly chasing after.

"I wanted you to see the house before we talked. You had to know it's real."

22

Ruddik brought his briefcase into the diner, and we sat at a booth. I was tired and grateful for the idea of cheap comfort and food. It already felt like a long day.

"Lawrence Elgin is dead. Did you know that?" he asked me.

I shook my head, another thin slice of shock.

"His condition kept getting worse until they had to take his leg off. I wanted him to talk to me before the operation, spill it all, but he wouldn't budge without a transfer. I tried to get him treated in a civilian hospital, but the paperwork didn't come through quickly enough. A blood clot got him on New Year's Eve, around the time you and I were sitting in the parking lot talking. I call that bad luck and worse timing."

The waitress came to take our order, and it took me a moment to bring my thoughts to her question and decide what I wanted. While I hesitated, Ruddik asked for eggs and bacon. I got it together and ordered yogurt and a fruit plate.

"I'm sorry about that," I said after she left. I meant Elgin. I meant the loss of his snitch.

He shrugged. "It always gets harder just before it breaks. At least that's what I tell myself."

He started to bring his briefcase up to the surface of the table, then stopped.

"Here's what you need to know about me," he said.

I waited with a certain amount of anxiety for the next pronouncement. I realized partway through that I was listening to a confession.

"I'm a drunk. The socially acceptable term is recovering alcoholic. I used to fall asleep at the kitchen table in front of my family with a drink in my hand and my gun still loaded in its holster. That's how bad it was. Not a drop for eight years now, but a daily urge as strong as you can imagine."

I nodded. I knew drunks like that.

"I lost my wife and daughter, but if I'm honest with myself, that doesn't bother me as much as the bad career turn. The job meant everything to me. Have you ever had that kind of frustration in your life?" Maybe not that, I thought, but I understood frustration. "I miss my girl, but I miss the job harder. That's not a pleasant admission to make, but I try not to fool myself."

He shifted the cutlery around and brought the sugar bowl in closer.

"This job I have now is a shit job. But I do it because it's a second or third or fourth chance at the kind of work I do well and because it is nasty and no one else wants it. I've never been in a place where illegality is so openly tolerated. We can argue from now until the end of time about what the rules should be in a self-contained world like Ditmarsh, but I think we can both agree that some actions are wrong no matter where they occur. Anyway, the main thing for you to know is I'm a drunk. And I work very hard to make up for that. You can ask my ex-wife if you can find her."

He stopped talking. Was he waiting for my answer? I acknowledged that I had been sufficiently forewarned. I didn't offer any of my own confessions in turn, nor did I think he expected it.

The waitress brought our coffee. Decaf for me. I needed nothing further to up my adrenaline.

"You saw the video. What did you think?" Ruddik asked as he stirred in cream.

Did he want me to express my outrage? I didn't feel any. No one was hurt, all of it theatrical, boys being boys. I was numb to the cruelties that might have shocked a weak sister. It was only what happened to Crowley that made the video matter.

"How did you find it?" I asked.

"On the kind of site where you find such things. It's already gone. Someone took it down."

"Who?"

He shrugged.

"The Ditmarsh Social Club," I said. "I want to know what that means." And I did. Intensely.

He nodded. "I agree. We need to figure that out somehow."

I hesitated. I didn't know how to have this kind of conversation. "Not just the name. There was a mark, an emblem, below the name. Did you notice it?"

"Three triangles," Ruddik said. His interest encouraged me, made me braver.

"Three triangles inside a circle," I said. "I'm sure it comes from a fall-out shelter sign." I took a pen from my pocket and drew the marks on a napkin, then turned it around. "You see? That sign is in the bubble, above the stairs where the hatch goes down into the armaments room and the old dissociation unit. That's how I found Crowley."

He looked impressed. "How did you make the connection?"

I wasn't ready for my own confession and felt my words curving away from the full truth. "I saw the sign first in a drawing, something Crowley had done for his art class. Then I noticed the same mark a number of places around the prison, mixed in with all the other graffiti. When I was working the bubble on Christmas Eve and saw the old fallout shelter sign turned upside down, it just clicked. I checked out the City because it seemed possible that the mark meant something. I didn't know Crowley would be down there."

He looked as if he had something to add, but he cut it off. "Good work. That's how an instinct can pay off. Now, is there anything else you want to ask me before we go further?"

I didn't know what going further meant, but I did want to ask a few more things.

"What's your official status? You're what? FBI?"

He nodded, and took a long second before answering. "In a way. When I think we're ready for that level of disclosure, I'll explain all the interde-partmental connections."

Fine. The reluctance peeved me. But I had another question, and I didn't want to erode my standing before asking it. I was surprised by how much it pained me to voice the words.

"You say Wallace is dirty. How do you know for sure?"

I suppose part of me still didn't want it to be true.

"The house is a bribe," Ruddik answered. "I can't prove it, because we haven't secured a warrant to trace the finances, but my belief—based on scrutiny of Wallace's unpromising long-term savings situation—is that the house was funded by a single transfer, a giant payoff for something that recently happened or is about to happen. But Wallace is only part of a larger picture."

Ruddik unsnapped his briefcase and carefully spread four sheets of paper on the table, arranging them so that a dense schematic of lines and bubbles became connected. It looked like a technical drawing of a nerve cluster or the layout of tunnels on a lunar station.

"Consider this a work in progress. I've been building a network map of Ditmarsh Penitentiary by mining a variety of data points. It's a hodge-podge, but an interesting one. Basically, think of it as a visual display of who spends time with who. I've included inmates, COs, and civilian staff in key positions like the mail room, the purchasing department, the infirmary, and other high-contact or heavy information flow areas. I've tried to analyze where shifts and meetings and work periods overlap, who knows who outside the institution and in social settings. Which staff goes on vacations or training courses together. I combine all that with financial information. I look for prisoners who have shown bumps in their inmate account balances. I look for the COs recording the most overtime pay. I follow promotions and watch who gets special-duty opportunities."

Our food arrived, and Ruddik slid the papers to the side, careful not to sully his map. I thought about URF and my struggle to join. Special duty.

"It's new stuff," Ruddik said. "Some people call it mosaic theory or network analysis. In the last few years it's become standard in CIA and Homeland Security work, tracking phone calls, account transfers, flights, hotels, bar bills, mining all that data to draw conclusions about otherwise residual contact between apparent strangers. The goal is to sift through the trash and surface the connections."

"I never knew that sort of thing was possible," I said.

"Take a Homeland Security example," he said, eating as he talked. "You've got three foreign students who have no apparent relationship with one another. But they pop up in your data because each one has attended a different flight school. Fine. We're all suspicious of Arabs at flight schools. So you start tracking phone calls, bank deposits, vacations, business trips. You look into what each one does in his free time. Since they're Muslim, you're particularly interested in mosques, community groups, and special groceries and bookstores. Maybe you can't see any conspiracy or connection. Just an innocent fascination with learning to fly an airplane. Then you realize that all three went to the same fitness club at least once within the last year. Now the gym becomes your next jump-off point. Does the gym itself arouse any suspicion, or is there anyone attached to the gym who could be a person of interest? Sure enough, you connect the gym to another person you've had your eye on for some time, a courier type. Two more connections, and you're linked to a banker in Switzerland who funnels cash for Al Qaeda. Bingo. There's no proof, and there's no crime, but you know there is a connection between those three students and a terrorist financier. Nothing random about it."

Ruddik drove his toast into his egg and took a hasty bite leaning over the table.

"It sounds like that Kevin Bacon game," I said. That's all I could think of: the idea that any person could be linked to Kevin Bacon through a minimum of six other people.

"You're talking about six degrees of separation. That's an old Zimbardo experiment and very fundamental to network theory, but his scope of interest was just about random connections. We're interested in the *intensity* of connections to show directional flow and draw conclusions about behavior patterns. The example I gave you about the three foreign students is a real one. That was three of the nineteen terrorists from September 11. When intelligence did a retro assessment of the trails the hijackers left behind before that day, we were able to discover connections between all nineteen hijackers. Rather than the mosques, like everyone expected, the gym was in fact the best nexus point for determining who knew who." He grimaced. "That gym was the key, and we never knew it. They were workout pigs. They liked lifting in front of mirrors, and they got to know each other that way. Incidentally, a tendency for narcissistic behavior got upped in terrorist profiles subsequently. When assessing the motivations of extreme ideologues, we'd seriously overlooked personal aggrandizement as a coping mechanism."

I stared at the map on the table. Some of the bubbles were densely connected with lines that led to other bubbles.

"So how does it work with Ditmarsh?"

"Basically I'm focused on the shadow hierarchy," he said.

"Shadow?"

"As opposed to the real or formal hierarchy. You know how it works. The warden is a political figurehead. The deputy wardens are more like functional executives, chief operating officer, chief finance officer, and so on, while the keepers, or lieutenants, are the line managers with supervisory control over the rank-and-file COs, who have the most contact with the customers—or inmates."

Customers? His corporate language threw me. I thought of the institution purely in the terms of a military organization.

"The shadow hierarchy explains what really happens inside—as opposed to the way we pretend things are supposed to happen. Why do some keepers have more clout than others? Why do some worthless COs have such easy shifts and other highly trained COs are always running into trouble? Why are there blocks that run smooth and others that don't? How come when you pull one or two inmates out of a tier that's running fine, you get a sudden surge in chaos and random violence? You know as well as I do there are inmates with more control over the daily routine than any CO. If you want to get something done, you've got to work through them; otherwise the whole system grinds to a halt and the other COs start ignoring you in the staff room because you've poked a stick into the wheel."

"I'm not blind," I said, a touch bitter. "I work there, too."

"So you look for connections," he said. "And sometimes you observe some interesting patterns." He put his thick finger on one of the nodes. "I'm looking for my gym, and I've got a couple candidates."

"Like where?" I asked.

"B-three is a node for sure. But that's Billy Fenton's ground, so no big surprise."

I nodded. Although I had no evidence to back up my suspicions, I'd sensed power emanating from his surroundings, like waves of heat.

"The infirmary spiked slightly in the last six months, though I can't tell whether that's a distortion in the data or something meaningful."

"Okay," I said.

"Another really dense node is the art therapy group."

In spite of everything, I wouldn't have guessed. "What's going on there?"

"Maybe it's Crowley," he said. "Crowley was in the infirmary. Crowley was on B-three. Crowley was in the art therapy group. Crowley ended up dead. If we can find out why, we'll learn more about what he was involved in and who else was part of it."

The plates had been cleared away, the coffee refilled.

"I want you to help," he said.

"What do you mean by help?" I asked, nervous as hell.

"I think you have a knack for this stuff. And I want to see what you can come up with when you get your feet wet. Nothing crazy. Just a toe dip. You're able to talk to some people I can't, ask different questions. Let's start with the Ditmarsh Social Club, for example. You want to know more. I want to know more. I want you to ask around about it. There must be some old-timer you can trust. I want you to get a sense of how they react when you bring it up, maybe learn something valuable."

I didn't answer right away. I kept my face straight despite the misgivings. I suppose there's a point when you join the other side, whether you commit to it or not. Just by listening to Ruddik's overtures, by not walking out on him, I'd cut myself loose from any trust any CO might have owed me. I wasn't sure I wanted that trust anymore. I was sick of the lies.

Ruddik kept working on me.

"I've shown you a lot of stuff here this morning, Kali. I've made myself very vulnerable to you. This is not a game. I'm asking for a little help. Another set of boots on the ground. No one has to know but you and me."

In a snap I made my decision, my fateful affiliation. "I can do that." I nodded. "I've got some ideas who to try."

Ruddik nodded and looked pleased. "I knew you would."

I try not to get too jacked up emotionally. My great plans have generally been followed by setbacks and downward spirals, so I've developed a philosophy for emotional survival: modulate the lows, suspect the highs. But I was excited driving home. I got stimulated by the idea of exposing connections, uncovering truths. And I liked the way Ruddik talked. I wanted to impress him, perhaps for no more complicated a reason than the attention he was paying to me. He thought I was important. Maybe that's all it took. It helped that he was easier to be around than I ever would have expected.

And then came the low. When I got home, I checked my messages and heard Keeper Wallace's voice. He told me I had to be present for a hearing the next afternoon, on my day off, to deal with the next stage of the Shawn Hadley deal. I would have felt a tinge of bitterness no matter what, but that the news came from Wallace, after what I'd learned that day, just notched up the spite.

23

I called MacKay early the next morning, amazed at how quickly they'd shipped him out of the hospital. It showed you how little our insurance covered.

"They got you off the oxygen yet?"

"Doesn't matter," he answered. He sounded pissed off, a feistiness that was reassuring. "I'm moving to Arizona. You can wheel your oxygen tanks right onto the fucking plane. I hear they sell extra canisters at the airport in Phoenix. Think of me getting a tan while I soak Medicaid fucking dry."

"Can I see you?" I asked. He hesitated. As the silence went on, I figured he was closed for business. No more good times with his favorite substitute daughter.

When he told me yes, I thanked him in relief and said goodbye. Then I had to call him back and ask where he lived. He called me a sweet little idiot.

I drove to the east side of town. Once Irish, now heavy on Somali and Hmong. The clapboard house reminded me of the one my parents raised me in. I knew there were cubbyholes under the stairs where bowling balls and vacuum cleaners were stored and where kids could hide. I knew there was a dirt-floor basement loaded with old furniture and rolls of moldy carpet that couldn't be parted with. MacKay and his wife lived like typical working-class families with exactly no residual income. It made me ashamed of all my various suspicions over the years.

Shuffling in slippers like a grandfather, he showed me in. The living room had a matching plaid couch and recliner, and a rickety coffee table in between. Ray haunched down slowly into the recliner, so I took the couch. His color was bad, his hands prominently veined. Mrs. MacKay was out, and I wondered if he'd arranged it so. The TV was on, volume muted. I was surprised to see a church service on the screen. It wasn't even Sunday.

Ray killed the TV by pressing his big thumb on the power button.

"In the kitchen, in the cupboard over the stove, there's a bottle of Kentucky. Get us a couple glasses."

"Jesus, Ray," I protested.

"Piss on it," he said. "I gave up cigarettes. If you won't get it for me, I'll get it myself."

He started to haul himself forward, so of course I summoned the dependable enabler of my childhood and walked into the kitchen on orders.

The tile floor was torn neat the fridge. A collection of miniature porcelain cats lined the windowsill over the sink. A pair of binoculars hung from a tea towel knob next to a calendar of different birds. I found the bourbon and the glasses and poured. I did not dare to water it down.

"Do you miss it?" I asked when I sat across from him again. I felt guilty showing up in uniform.

A grin, a shake of the head, a whoosh of breath. "Yes. I miss the goddamn place. I should have been a tour guide. All day yesterday I sat here looking at a photo album. How are things in there?"

I did not know how to answer him. "Kind of fucking weird, Ray, actually," I said. "I'm not sure what's what anymore."

His eyes squinted. "Like what? You in trouble?"

And with the question, a barrier fell and I could not help but think of my father. Sitting before MacKay, the room devoid of life like an airless museum, I wondered why it had been so hard for my father and me to connect. I remembered the year my mother left him—left us, I suppose, to live with her sister—and how little we had to say to each other while she was gone. Had it been depression that kept him from really connecting with me, even when it was just the two of us together? That possibility seemed obvious suddenly, and something else became clear: the urgency I felt inside to remain busy at all times, under pressure, involved, vigorous, pissed off, resistant, and ambitious in futile and self-defeating ways—and the vacuum in my life when I had none of that—was a kind of shadow illness. Was depression my problem, too, dealt with in different ways?

"Maybe I'm about to get in trouble," I acknowledged. I was more nervous than I wanted to admit.

"What kind of shit are they throwing at you?" he asked.

The fatherly concern I never got.

"I have a sentencing hearing this afternoon," I said. "They're saying I whacked Shawn Hadley a little too hard."

MacKay shook his head. "Sorry about that. Ask him if he wants his balls back."

"It's not really that," I said. "I'm trying to find something else out."

"Like what?" And when I hesitated, he said, "Jesus, Kali, you interrupt my busy fucking morning and can't spit it out? What's on your mind?" I took his impatience as a good sign.

"I want you to tell me what you know about the Ditmarsh Social Club."

He didn't look at me, but there was a thin smile on his face, and he sat back in the recliner and stared at the dead TV screen for a full minute.

"I'm not even going to ask you why you're asking," he finally said.

"Okay," I said, and didn't move.

"I'm wondering if there's a way we can not have this conversation."

"That's up to you," I said. "But I'd like to know what you know."

"You think it will help you somehow? You think it will alleviate whatever shit storm you're facing?"

"I do," I said, though I didn't believe it. I believed I was walking into the shit storm face-first.

"You're a big girl. You can make your own choices."

I waited. He shrugged, started rolling the bottom edge of his glass on the armrest fabric.

"The Ditmarsh Social Club was a choir," he said. "About a hundred years ago. Turn of the century."

"A choir?" It was the last thing in the world I expected.

"Like one of those barbershop quartets. You know. A bunch of well-groomed men singing in harmony, deep voices and high voices all mixed together. They showed up at the state fair. They did some ball games. Sang at the Governor's Mansion, that kind of thing. Swell bunch of choirboys."

"COs?" I asked. "Men who worked at Ditmarsh, not inmates?"

He glared at me. "Of course they weren't fucking inmates. Yes. Hacks. Turnkeys. Us. The choir was a noted feature of Ditmarsh Penitentiary until World War One. Then I guess people stopped enjoying that kind of singing. Probably because of the fucking radio."

He stopped talking. I realized he was trying to catch up on his breathing, get it steady. Too many words coming out in a single flow. I felt like shit for pushing him.

"So then it went away?"

"Went away. No more social club until the 1950s, except when it came back. When it got revived, let's say, it was different. Kind of an inner circle. A club for the COs who were trusted, who were on the inside of things. There was the Ditmarsh Social Club, and there was everyone else, all the working stiffs."

"How come I never heard of it?"

"Because it went away again. For good reason."

"What reason?"

"I started working at Ditmarsh in 1977. Never knew anything about the social club until the early eighties. I got pledged, you could say, in 1985. Seemed like a good thing to me. You got extra duty. You got your back covered if you fucked up. Kind of what the union was supposed to do but never actually fucking did. Then I saw it wasn't all gravy."

The glass empty now, in his lap. He scratched at the Band-Aid on the back of his hand and recrossed his varicosed ankles.

"I think we were watching too many Charles Bronson and *Dirty Harry* movies. You have to understand, the courts were ridiculous. They loved bad guys, hated cops. They gave us a hard time if an inmate fell down. Consequently, the inmates had a lot of sway, and officially we couldn't do shit about it.They had all kinds of mandated luxuries. They worked the system to their extreme advantage. So the social club took it on itself to restore a little justice to the place. I probably don't know half the shit that went on. But sometimes, when some correction was needed, we made it happen. We made sure the inmates got the message. Unofficially we ran the City. No one went down in the hole without passing through us. Everything that happened down there happened because of us. You remember when we were talking a few weeks back about that cocksucker Earl Hammond?"

I nodded, a little dry-mouthed. Of course I remembered.

"Well, everything with the social club turned to shit after that fucker iced Bucker."

"Why?" I asked. "How?"

"Jesus, that's hard to explain." He let out a heavy breath. "Not exactly pleasant memories. Hammond was fucking evil, and he deserved everything we could lay on him, so we decided to make him the supreme example, demonstrate what justice really meant. We cleared out the whole City for him, and he was the one and only living soul down there for three years."

"Three years," I said.

"Long time," MacKay agreed. "I stopped thinking that was a good thing around year two." He grunted, a shortened laugh, and gave me a strange look, as if still puzzled. "I started feeling sorry for the fucking guy. Me. Of course, you couldn't admit that to anyone else. In fact, you're the first living soul I've ever told. But I've never seen anything more cruel than keeping a man down in an isolation pit day and night for year after year. It just got to me."

"What happened?" I did and didn't want to know.

"Hammond started going nuts. But in an ugly way. You could see his mind kind of folding in on itself. He'd been mentally healthy before. Down there, he started changing, turning into something not really human. Some of it could really set you off. You showed up, and he was covered in shit, shit everywhere, and he'd been left that way for a week, and you just hated him for it. Or you'd pass him his food and he'd throw it at you as soon as he could, so we started shackling him up for meals, and then in general pretty much all the time, to minimize the hassle and the danger. That's why we called him the Beggar. He had sores all over his body. He had these long nails. And the worst part, I swear, was that when he talked to you, you realized he had no fucking clue where he really was. I mean, seriously, he thought he was in another world. Sometimes it was a world full of demons and he was a hero sent to save everyone who was good. I remember as though it was yesterday him telling me that the God we all called God was actually evil, and the real God was trapped in another universe behind a barrier, and it was his job, the Beggar's job, to overthrow the evil God's rule over this world and free us all and right the wrongs. And incidentally, he might have to kill every one of us to make it happen.

"It was crazy as shit, but he believed it. Sometimes he told me the walls had turned to liquid fire, and other times he said the demons had been with him for hours, mocking and torturing him, and once he told me the chief fucking demon was sitting with us in the corner of his cell that very moment, waiting for me to leave."

And then, to my astonishment and eternal guilt, Ray MacKay started to cry.

"It was heavy, Kali, I have to tell you. I started sitting down there with him my whole shift, just to help him keep it together. I'd tell him to hang on. Get through another eight hours. That the next eight would be better. And with the human company he came around a little bit. He was a smart son of a bitch. He'd crack a joke when you weren't expecting it, and then I'd wonder for a week if he wasn't playing me, but I'd see the look in his eyes the next time down there, and I'd stay again and just sit with him, and sometimes point my flashlight at the part of the wall he said the demons used as a gate to come get him."

Ray put his face in his hands and disappeared for a while. I felt less than human for not easing over and putting my arms around him. I was shocked, I suppose. I didn't have any room in my brain to imagine Ray MacKay talking in that way.

"I quit the club," he said, looking up, wiping everything off, the tears and the soft grief. "I didn't want to be part of it anymore. And the club didn't last much longer after Hammond was gone. I wasn't the only one keeping Hammond company. Half of us felt like shit about it. Other half went harder the other way. Push and pull. They shipped Hammond out, sent him to California for some technical reason related to his original charges. About a year after he was gone, a few of the top guys in the social club got in trouble for a little criminal activity. No big surprise. During the investigation one of them erased himself with a revolver. Another drove his pickup truck onto the ice on Long Lake to get to his fishing hut, even though it was late March and sixty degrees. A third guy did go to prison, and that, of course, was probably worse than death for a jack who'd been a hard-ass when he lived on the other side of the bars."

He drank from the glass and noticed it was empty, then gave me a funny look.

"So there you have it. That's the fucking story. Whatever reason you wanted to know, keep it to yourself. I'm paying for my sins twenty years later."

I thanked him, and he told me to go, and then he told me to bring over the bottle of Kentucky before I left. So I did.

24

I tried Ruddik from the car as I drove to Ditmarsh for my hearing. Ruddik didn't answer, and that left me lost. I was at the stage with him when I wanted more talk. I wanted some answers, too. I tried to focus on driving, but the information I'd picked up churned inside me, wreaking havoc on my poor stomach.

Then the cell phone rang, a number I didn't recognize. I was still leery of unexpected calls, given the press interest in Hadley, but I couldn't stand not answering and got relief and release when I heard Ruddik's voice on the other end.

"I found out about the Ditmarsh Social Club," I told him. It sounded ridiculous when I started explaining the history—that it had been a kind of glee club a century ago, that it re-formed in the '50s, not to sing, but as a kind of vigilante group. And when I mentioned Earl Hammond and the City, he interrupted and asked me who I was talking about.

"Hammond was an inmate here about twenty years ago. The social club kept him in the hole for three years after he killed a CO. Then he got transferred, and the social club broke up after that."

He told me he didn't understand. "Slow down. Get me into your head. What does this inmate have to do with Crowley? Am I missing something?"

My chickens had come home to roost. I could come up with no quick and reasonable way to divert the need to explain why I'd failed to mention the comic book and the Beggar before. So I told him about Josh and Keeper Wallace and the special trip, and I told him about the Beggar and that the fallout shelter mark I'd seen had been in the comic book, and I told him I thought the fight in the yard between Elgin and Crowley had something to do with the comic book, too.

"Like you said, the art therapy group could be your gym. Maybe Hammond fits into it somehow."

I stopped myself from talking. I wanted to let him catch up, think it through, ask me something. Maybe I expected more praise, an instant promotion, but I was surprised at Ruddik's reluctance to grab hold of my vague theories.

"All right. Where's the comic book now?"

I told him I didn't know, feeling stupid for once having had it in my possession and letting it go.

"Then we probably ought to approach the man who runs the art therapy group," he said. "Find out if he knows."

"Brother Mike," I said. "I can do that. I've met him."

And so I had my next step. When I hung up, I realized how fast I was going and eased my foot off the accelerator. I saw a brown trooper's car only a few seconds later and felt lucky. The smokies didn't always dish out tickets to us law enforcement cousins, but they were a little arbitrary about our exact degree of kinship. They didn't take us quite as seriously as we would have liked.

When I got to Ditmarsh, the delayed anxiety of the trial hit me again. It seemed so ridiculous and small compared with the monstrosity of the place and the things that had happened inside. It felt as though another me, in another life, were rushing through the halls to make it to the hearing on time. Wallace met me outside the small courtroom in Keeper's Hall and asked me where my union lawyer was. I realized then, with a sudden numbness, that I'd never actually taken him seriously when he'd suggested it before. It still stunned me that my conduct was under scrutiny, that a corrections officer could be called into question for forcibly restraining an inmate. It was like arresting a surgeon for making a patient bleed, or court-martialing a soldier for shooting at an enemy combatant.

"Do you really think it's necessary?" I asked Wallace.

"I wouldn't mention it twice now if I didn't," he said.

He walked away, pissed at me, and I felt my own bile rising. A million-dollar house, and this asshole was giving me a hard time.

My presence was pro forma only. I sat in the back row and watched Hadley's lawyer berate, cajole, and fellate his way into a continuance. Of the five or ten reasons he gave, one crawled under my skin. The institution had failed to produce requested evidence, namely the videotapes of the event in question, required in law (though rarely in practice) to be recorded whenever the Urgent Response Force was engaged.

"The terrible things that happened in that cell are being hidden from us, Your Honor," his lawyer intoned. "Officer Kali Williams and Lieutenant Raymond MacKay engaged in sadistic practices knowing full well this administration would cover up their misdeeds. I demand that the evidence be produced."

Keeper Wallace promised to deliver the tapes as soon as possible. The judge asked Wallace not to waste the court's time. The delay pissed me off, too. If Wallace passed over the tapes, everyone would see I had done nothing wrong, or nothing overtly brutal. They might watch a little scuffle in the cell, catch a glimpse of Hadley flopping and twisting for a second or two, but that was in MacKay's presence, not just mine. Release them, I thought, and get this over with. The reluctance to give anything over to the lawyers and the courts was counterproductive. It made everyone think there was something we were hiding, that the clichés were true.

Walking out, Hadley gave me a smirk. My only satisfaction was seeing him limp. Wallace and the Ditmarsh lawyer rose out of their chairs and gathered around the judge for a good laugh and a "how ya been" conversation. The judge, evidently, had been a parole hearing superintendent many years previously. I watched Wallace nodding and smiling, displaying a casual ease you didn't see on his face when he was working. I waited half a minute for some over-the-shoulder glance of sympathy and finally left the room ignored or unnoticed.

25

I called Brother Mike that night, using the number he'd reached me from on Christmas Day. He sounded unsure of himself at first, as though preoccupied and hazy. It seemed impossible at that moment to bring up Hammond or the comic book, so I asked to see him in person, away from Ditmarsh. He hesitated before saying yes and invited me to visit him at his home. I didn't quite know what to make of the reluctance. I just knew I had a few hours that Saturday before my afternoon shift.

I drove out early, well beyond the city, to what had once been farmland edging up on the river and now was being gobbled up by suburban developments. The turnoff to Brother Mike's property was a narrow, unplowed road into the forest, just two gutters of dirt funneling through the hard snow. The Land Rover had the clearance and bumped along fine, though it would be hell to back out if I couldn't turn around. Then I came to an old house, a chimney puffing smoke, a wedge of front yard, and a deer fence surrounding the back.

He met me at the front door, and his smile was so broad and effusive I knew I must have misinterpreted him on the phone. He ushered me in, took my parka, and hung it up, and after I took my boots off he beckoned me down the hallway into the kitchen. He'd just made tea and cookies, the dear aunt I'd never had.

We sat on high stools next to a kitchen counter. A large window overlooked the expansive backyard, and there was some kind of structure back there, a sagging house covered in old sacks, too big to be a sweat lodge. I wondered what it was for. A plate before me. The cookie looked like a pile of horse manure, hairy with fiber, something a hippie might sell in a coffee shop. The tea was strong, the way Irish grandparents like it, mixed with much milk.

"How are you?" he asked.

It seemed easy, in that moment, to admit the truth.

"A little overwhelmed."

He nodded with understanding. "There's been an epidemic of that lately. They have me under investigation now, did you know that?"

I did not know that.

From the kitchen counter he found a sheet of paper and passed it over. A memo, marked disdainfully with a mug ring.

I read the official notice. Envelopes bearing Brother Mike's home address had been discovered in deceased inmate Jon Crowley's personal effects. This demonstrated an inappropriate and unprofessional degree of intimate contact, and a decision of suspension from employment was being deliberated.

"It's complete rubbish, of course. I don't deny that the correspondence occurred, but such things are overlooked," he said, "except when they are not." He sipped his tea. "They're putting a great deal of pressure on me. I can't enter the institution without getting searched. My art classes, when I'm allowed to hold them, are constantly interrupted. Even my private counseling sessions are cut short. Worse, my colleagues are experiencing similar problems, clearly because of my transgressions. They're being supportive, so far. I heard you were under investigation for inmate assault."

I raised my mug in a toast to that. "No wonder you didn't want to see me."

He smiled, a little sadly. "It wasn't that. I apologize if it sounded that way. But what is it that you're here for?"

I hesitated for only a second, and he grabbed my arm to interrupt.

"Hold that thought. I have something I want to show you."

We went out the back door. In the mudroom, he found me a pair of galoshes and a heavy sweater to wear, and I felt like a child traipsing behind him through the path worn into the snow. We approached the strange hut I'd seen from the kitchen window, and I sensed great warmth coming from it and an unusual but pleasant smell, like hay in a barn or recently harvested wheat baking in the sun.

"This is my kiln," he said. "I'm a potter by calling. The rest of it, the restorative justice work and the art classes are duties I perform in service of my own conscience. If I were free from all that, here's where I would be. I'm firing right now. I only do it twice a year. Do you want to look?"

He lifted a tarp, and I heard a hushed roar from within, like the sound of the ocean in a seaside cave or a gurgling volcano. The air was hot in my nostrils, but I smelled charcoal and metal. When I could stand the heat blowing out, I saw a patch of darkness only a foot square and a show of shooting stars inside. It was beautiful, but I stepped out to get relief from the heat, and Brother Mike let the tarp fall back into place.

"My style is derivative of the Japanese masters who come from the region of Bizen. Most Japanese pottery making is extremely precise, involving many tests and carefully controlled temperatures. In *Bizen-yaki*, however, the kiln is a primitive space fueled by kindling and logs, even branches, leaves, straw. In the heat and flame the contaminant materials disintegrate into fine particles and blow about in a maelstrom of sparks that collide with the fresh pottery and stick to it, burning into the clay like fossilized lines. It's a largely unpredictable process, and it brings out colors only God could come up with."

The energy radiated from him, his face glowing with excitement.

"It's comforting to me," he added, "that beauty can come from violence, if only in metaphor."

I huddled in the thick sweater he'd given me, cold now that the tarp was down, feeling a slightly feverish heat linger in my cheeks.

"I want to know more about Crowley's comic book," I said. "What was in it. What it meant."

No change in his face, nothing altered in his smile, but everything different nevertheless.

He began to walk slowly around the kiln, checking the tarps, feeling the heat with his hand a few inches away. I followed him. There was a pile of pottery shards in the back, where the woods edged up to his property.

"All sorts of animals are attracted to the warmth," he said. "Once, I unintentionally baked a cat or a muskrat in a large pot. It must have crawled in while my back was turned."

"Tell me about the character in the comic book," I insisted. "The Beggar."

He picked half of a vase up from the snow and swung it down casually to smash it further. There was nothing angry in the gesture, only preoccupation.

"The Beggar," he replied. " I thought, for Jon's purposes, the name Beggar was quite apt. It has a fine historical and literary lineage."

I asked what he meant.

"I mean that historically, most inmates were debtors, or beggars. Ordinary people who'd committed no crime but being poor, not unlike today's minor drug offenders. As late as the early 1900s, if you walked by a prison in a city such as New York or Philadelphia, you would see hands outstretched, the prisoners inside begging for alms, sometimes dangling a shoe from an upper cell grate to the street below—the beggar's grate, as it was called. They could earn their freedom, you see, if they bribed the keepers. Another, more literary reference, perhaps, was John Gay's *The Beggar's Opera*. Have you seen it? You really must, as a corrections worker. It was inspired by Newgate Prison and featured a keeper who secretly runs a criminal organization from within the prison, using helpless inmates as lackeys. A brilliant lampoon of class structure and a call for reform. If you believe that our institution of prisons today is in part a tool of the capitalist system, whereby the underclasses are ruthlessly punished and only the rich have access to justice . . ."

I couldn't take it anymore.

"I know the Beggar's name is Earl Hammond."

"You know about Hammond?" No pause in him, no stunned surprise.

"You do, also, apparently."

"I've heard of him. Most of us in the restorative justice field have followed his work. Hammond was another inspiration for Crowley."

His work. All those sources of inspiration. The pretension took me back, roused my irritation for the skewed sensibilities of weak sisters.

"Hammond killed a CO, a man working a dangerous job to keep the rest of you safe. Hammond was so violent even within a maxium security prison that they kept him in extreme isolation."

"Yes," Brother Mike acknowledged. "For years. But that was before my time, and I can't pretend to understand it all. And there was nothing about Hammond then that would have moved someone like Jon. It was what happened afterward, when Hammond was released from extreme isolation, that transformed him into someone worthy of admiration."

"What did happen?"

"Why, he changed."

He said it matter-of-factly, as if I should simply understand.

"Changed how?"

"He'd been a gang leader, drug dealer, and murderer. Through whatever miracle was visited upon him, years of isolation didn't destroy his mind but freed it. He became an antigang leader, a fearless and outspoken advocate for institutional reform and restorative justice. Hammond was one of the first significant inmates to go public with such support. And that, as you can imagine, was no easy road. He tried to make amends for his own transgressions, even reconcile with the family of the CO he'd slain, but the COs lobbied for him to be isolated again. The gangs hated him, too, because he'd betrayed them, turned over all he knew about them to destroy their way of life, in exchange for more access to other inmates. He was fearless about being a model for personal responsibility and the power of forgiveness."

"You told Crowley about Hammond."

"I did. I used his example in the context of our conversations about restorative justice, and I saw how Hammond's spirit and example changed Jon's heart. Jon became a disciple of sorts. Hammond's voice had been silenced for so many years, and Jon wanted to tell the world Hammond's story, show the path that is possible. Jon's comic book was a way of chronicling Hammond's redemption. As an artwork, it was daring and bound to be controversial."

I did not want to argue about what Crowley's book had accomplished. Instead, I wanted to know more about Hammond.

"How was Hammond silenced? What happened to him?"

Brother Mike shrugged. "I have no idea. It was rumored that he'd been given a new identity, for his own protection, and hidden somewhere in the federal detention system. But that's not a story I trust, since I doubt the Hammond I read about would have agreed to it. The worst side of me believes he was eliminated, if that's not too sinister a phrase. Perhaps I communicated that suspicion unintentionally to Jon, because it pervaded his work."

I was put off by the idea that Hammond might have been "eliminated," even though it seemed like a coherent and reasonable explanation. It jabbed against my own misgivings, the suspicion not of conspiracies, but of delusional fantasies. The comic book reeked of that.

"Why did he draw such a strange world? Why didn't he just show Hammond as he was? In Ditmarsh, in the City, in other institutions, speaking to inmates."

"You're asking an artistic question, and a political one, and perhaps a practical question as well. There was no support for Hammond as a person. You saw Jon's fight with Lawrence in the yard. An inmate with gang associations and any knowledge of Hammond's history would have loathed Hammond and hated anyone who wanted to glorify him. Same with the COs. It was too contentious. So Crowley's decision was to depict a figure like Hammond."

"So he made up this character of the Beggar?"

"Well, not exactly made up. I believe he modeled the Beggar after Cain, the firstborn son of Adam."

"Cain?" The surprises continued to accrue. "You mean Cain from the Bible?"

"Who slew his brother Abel with the jawbone of an ass because he was jealous that Abel's sacrifice to God had been looked on more favorably. Who then hid his brother's body and fled."

I wondered where the hell he was going now.

"Why Cain? Isn't Cain despised?"

"By us, yes. But think of it from an inmate's perspective. Cain is the first criminal in history. And like Job and Isaac and Jonah, he's the victim of a cosmic injustice. The God of the Old Testament was involved in some questionable episodes. Asking a father to sacrifice his son. Destroying innocent lives in the flood. Giving Adam and Eve the temptation for knowledge and banishing them from paradise for choosing it. Why? Even the story of Judas has appeal to an inmate. Judas was blamed for Jesus' trial and crucifixion, but Jesus needed to be betrayed in order to reveal his divinity. Isn't it possible that Judas sacrificed himself in full knowledge of the role God needed him to play? If so, why scorn Judas for all history? It's the kind of sentiment an inmate can relate to."

The litany of arguments offended me, but I also suspected they were a deliberate attempt to divert my attention. It seemed pointless, now, to leave anything unsaid.

"I need the comic book," I told him.

"I don't have it," he answered.

"It is evidence in a very serious crime."

It was a bullshit claim, the last resort of a scoundrel, and he called my bluff.

"You're confused, Kali. Crowley's work concerned a spiritual mystery, not a criminal one. One of the biggest theological questions is *unde malum*. Where does evil come from? Crowley was interested in the opposite of that query. How do *evil* people find the strength to do good? That's why Crowley depicted Hammond. That's the answer to your mystery. Nothing less, but nothing more."

That got my back up. Lie to me, I thought. Tell me what you need to in order to get your way, but don't patronize me.

"You're not going to give it to me?" I bit the phrase off.

"As I said, I don't have it."

"Then who does?"

He shrugged. "You do."

I waited, intensely irritated. "What do you mean?"

"Keeper Wallace asked for it. I assumed you knew that."

Wallace had beaten me to it. Why did that surprise me? My anger and helplessness threatened the little composure I still held on to. I thanked Brother Mike for his time and left him standing by the kiln. I saw my own way through his house, changed back into my own damn jacket and boots, and strode out the front door.

26

My shift was an exercise in frustration and delay. The lockdown was over. The inmates were sullen, vindictive, and wired. I wanted quite desperately to talk to Ruddik, but our paths didn't cross, and he was already gone when I was done. I did not like the way I was feeling so quickly hooked by that man, but I told myself that any emotional resonance was being amped up by the circumstances. Life at Ditmarsh was a daily labyrinth that left me isolated by each bewildering turn. Now I was exploring caverns and staircases and secret doors, and I wanted to share that news with the one person who could understand.

Instead, I found myself alone in the records room at Keeper's Hall, and I decided to poke around the files for information about Earl Hammond. The ancient file cabinets screeched when I opened them, but I found nothing about Hammond inside. So I sat down in front of a clunky coffee-stained desktop computer and googled his name.

There were no Ditmarsh-related hits, but in a general search, there he was, an article in *Time* magazine from June 7, 1994. I leaned in. The article was from northern California, Pelican Bay. There was a picture of a white man who had thick, Afro-like hair rising from a high forehead, and earrings in both ears. His eyes, however, were blocked out by a black bar across the page, the way some gossip magazines hide bystanders. The caption read, "Could this convicted killer and crime leader bring an end to prison gangs as we know them?" You looked at the picture and answered the question for yourself: no fucking way. And then you read on. In the interview, Hammond related with intriguing frankness his gang past, the murders he'd committed or ordered, and the criminal activities he'd orchestrated. There was a sense of typical inmate boasting to the confession. "I led one of the most successful criminal organizations in the United States, from inside a maximum security institution, while under constant supervision. No one was more ruthless or strategic. I know I can bring those same capabilities to destroy what I helped build." And the article then detailed his virtuous activities, the small groups of inmates he spoke to all the time, his cooperation with the FBI in breaking gangs down, the talks and courses he led that had been taped and distributed to other institutions across the country. He was, the reporter noted, quite moving in his speeches. He talked about his remorse for all the wasted lives, those of victims and perpetrators, and he insisted the only real power one person had over another came from the heart. You needed to be lost to be found.

From the way he talked and the way he manipulated those who listened to him, including the writer of the article, you could tell that Hammond had charisma. I'd met my share of psychopathic egotists, but few were as sophisticated. It was easy to find him chilling and intriguing, and it was just as easy to dismiss the article for falling for such horseshit. I was sensitive to the way outsiders could romanticize even brutal criminals—they got a brief glimpse, overdosed on the inmate's composed moments of charm, and didn't have to experience the other moments, the sudden rage, the horrifying viciousness, the sadistic cruelty, and the undercurrent of extreme narcissism.

In the truck after work, I called Ruddik's number. I didn't care how late it had become. He answered this time, a quiet voice, as if he were trying not to wake someone. I hoped, even though it was ridiculous, that there was no one else living with him. Plowing on, I told him about Hammond and the comic book and Brother Mike's explanations. He asked me where the comic book was now, and I told him Wallace had retrieved it already. I heard the disappointment in his silence.

"Have we been outmaneuvered?" I asked, fearing the answer.

But he surprised me. "I don't think so. I think the comic book's a dead end."

I started to protest and then stopped. He was the professional.

"Think about it," Ruddik continued. "What could Hammond have to do with what's happening at Ditmarsh now? Wallace is real. The Ditmarsh Social Club is real. We have to focus on what's in front of us, not get lost in the details of something that happened years ago."

I let my silence go on. I didn't want to sound naive by arguing.

"Okay," I said.

"I've been thinking a lot about next steps, and I want you to hear me out on this."

"On what?" I asked.

His voice was calm, but I had a feeling he was being very careful with me, and that made me wonder where he was going.

"What we've learned so far has been helpful, but it's not helping us track the real economy of the prison."

"The real economy," I said. "You mean contraband. Deals."

"Exactly. In a perfect world, I'd have full access to the Pen Squad. I'd know what they know about intercepted shipments and I'd get reports on what their informants have been telling them. But this is far from a perfect world."

I could hardly disagree.

"So what I'd like to do is set up our own experiment."

"Meaning what?"

"I want to see what happens when you approach an inmate and offer a trade."

"What kind of trade?"

"The kind of trade that goes on all the time. In exchange for money or some other valued service, you offer to supply some information, bring in some contraband, arrange to have one inmate housed near another. You know what I mean."

"Jesus, Ruddik. Are you serious?"

"Of course I'm serious." That grave and muted tone again, the lone lawman vibe. "This is the kind of thing we do in undercover operations all the time. It's only unusual because you're not officially part of the team. I'm getting creative because I don't have the budget or the resources to bring in another professional, and I can't do it myself right now, because I'm currently very much on their radar. That's why I'm asking you."

"But what if I get caught?"

He laughed. "You won't get caught."

I didn't like being laughed at. "In the event that I did get caught, what would happen to me, legally speaking?"

"First of all, I wouldn't be asking you if I thought you'd be caught. This happens all the time, illegally, and no one's getting caught. What's more, no one's even looking. That's my job, remember, and I'm giving you the green light." The laugh again, a chuckle that was a little easier to take. "But in the unlikely scenario that something unforeseeable did go that wrong, you'd be up shit creek for a while. I'm not going to bullshit you. You'd be arrested and charged. I'm almost one hundred percent sure that I'd be able to disclose proof of your participation to the prosecutor's office before any trial and get those charges dismissed, even though that might put this investigation and all my time here at risk. But I can't be one hundred percent sure you'd get your job back. So there you go. That's the parameter of worst-case scenario, as best as I can configure it. I'd put the odds of catastrophic failure at five percent."

"Thank you for not bullshitting me," I said.

"You're right. I'm sorry I didn't lay it out there from the beginning."

And it might have been because of that apology that I agreed to do it. There's a self-destructive part of me, a vortex of negative attraction I find difficult to dampen, no matter my better instincts.

"I'll do it," I said. "I'll try it."

"It has to be someone that matters, though, someone whose connections and influence will lead us to others."

"And who would that be?" I asked.

"You tell me," he said.

It was as obvious to me as it was to him.

"Billy Fenton," I answered.

"You see?" he said. "I told you you had a knack."

I didn't like that paternalistic tweak, and right then and there had my first serious goddamn misgiving.

27

Crowley had said that time crawled slowest when your head was crowded with bad thoughts, and it dragged now. Five days went by, and Roy kept Josh's files. He wouldn't allow Josh to see them, but whenever they talked, Roy mentioned some of the legal details he was pondering. He seemed enlivened by his efforts, cheerful.

Josh didn't like to visit Roy in the intensive care unit because the continued emptiness of Elgin's bed was an indictment, a finger pointed his way. The lack of any questions about what had happened, the lack of any CO poking around made Josh wonder if what happened had been a dream. Instead, Roy visited Josh a few times every day, his arrival always announced in advance by the tap tap tap of his peg leg on the hallway floor. It got so Josh didn't even look up when Roy appeared in his cell doorway, just lay there staring at the ceiling trying to pretend Roy wasn't even there.

"Who died?" Roy asked.

It wasn't funny, but Roy snorted at his own joke anyway. He hobbled in to sit on the edge of Josh's cot, and Josh rose up and squirmed aside to make room for the heavy man and avoid touching him.

"You still don't trust me, do you, Joshy?" Roy said. "The best fucking friend you got."

Josh asked what he meant, suspicious of all overtures for more intimacy.

"I'm doing all this work for you, digging through your case files. They're pretty fucking boring, I have to say. Who the hell did you piss off so bad to get thrown in here? I seen this reference to something you drew, but I ain't seen no drawings. You offend someone's artistic sensibilities?"

Josh shrugged. He didn't want to talk about the drawings. He didn't want to talk about any drawings. He tried not to even think of where he'd hidden them. He knew that Roy could read his mind.

"I need some quid for my quo, Josh. I need some inspiration. Tell me about the things you drew with Crowley. Bore the shit out of me. I want to know more."

"I've told you everything," Josh said. He'd told Roy about the Beggar and the city and the tower and the demons, and Roy had asked him every possible detail. How many horses were there? What did the tower look like? How many windows did it have? What did the Beggar say to the demons when they tortured him?

"Every time you tell me, you seem to remember a little bit extra."

"Maybe I'd remember a lot extra if I knew why it was important."

That shut Roy up, and Josh feared he'd crossed a line. If you tell me more, I'll tell you more was a proposal, and an implication that he was holding back. It wasn't true. He just felt pushed into lashing out.

"What do you want to know?" Roy asked. He said it so seriously, so drily, that Josh wished he'd never asked. He just wanted it all to go away.

"What does the story mean?" Josh said, needing to say something.

A long wait while Roy leaned back against the wall and stared at the other side of Josh's cell, as if looking out at distant places.

"You ever read *Treasure Island* when you were a kid?" Roy asked.

Josh nodded. "I remember it."

"Well, Crowley's story is about another pirate, sailing a different kind of high seas. And this pirate had a crew, and the crew worked hard for him, partly because he was a scary son of a bitch and partly because he promised to make all of them rich. And that's what happened right here in Ditmarsh. There was this pirate, we'll call him the Beggar, and he sailed the high seas and collected a lot of treasure over the years."

"What do you mean treasure? How do you collect treasure in prison?"

A belly laugh.

"How? Everything you want to do in here costs gold. You want to get high? You pay. You want to survive? You pay. You want to visit some sister, take out a brother, or get a jack off your back? You pay. Little bits of that, call them transaction fees, go here and there. But if an organized bunch of pirates happens to control all that buying, selling, and servicing, the gold accumulates. The Beggar got rich, Joshy, inside a fucking prison, and other people got jealous, so he hid that treasure good, buried it deep before he went away, and all the rest of us are dying to find out where."

"How can you hide a treasure in prison?" The story was ridiculous to Josh, another bundle of Roy's lies.

Roy rapped his peg leg on the floor. "There's tunnels here, Joshy. Caverns. We got demons down below us and elder gods and a lost civilization. Every bit of it mapped out in Crowley's comic book. You help me find the treasure, I'll give you a little taste. Polly want a cracker?"

He laughed hard, and maybe that's why neither of them heard the footsteps in the hall until an inmate stood in the doorway of Josh's drum. Josh had never seen him before. A bald man in his forties, a spike of orange goatee below his mouth, no mustache. He cradled his left hand in his right, and there was blood soaked into a dirty cloth.

Roy looked pissed off.

"What the fuck you doing here, Cooper?"

"I cut my hand, Roy," the man said, "doing your kitchen work. We're all wondering when you're going to come home."

"I bet you are," Roy said. "You did that to yourself to check in on my friend here, didn't you. Well, you can't, so get the fuck out, and tell Fenton he wants any more of our time, he talks to me first."

Lewis unfolded his middle finger on his good hand and let it remain extended for ten seconds before slowly walking away.

Josh's heart went all pitter-patter to hear himself talked about. Roy met his eyes.

"A good reminder, Josh, of the kind of rogue I protect you from, with or without your gratitude."

Then another figure appeared in the doorframe, this time a pissed-off jack.

"What the fuck are you doing in that fish's drum, Wobbles?"

Promptly Roy rolled to one side and the other, built up momentum, and heaved himself off the cot.

"Nothing, sir, just taking a breather while I do my rehabilitation walk. Can't wait to get back to population, boss. This place makes me sick."

"I fucking bet," the jack said as he stepped away to allow Roy room to exit. Neither man gave Josh a glance.

28

I didn't know how to approach Fenton, didn't want to approach Fenton, but I understood why Ruddik wanted me to. Fenton had his fingers in every pie. Fenton was a big node on Ruddik's map.

It took me three days to work up the nerve. I told myself the delay was about timing and opportunity, and the importance of not getting caught. But it was also about lacking the right plan, something I could believe and Fenton might believe. Otherwise any overtures of mine would smell like a setup. Ruddik called me each day to check and see whether I'd gone through with it yet, and when I confessed I still hadn't, I either got another speech of encouragement or the silence of disappointment. The very thought left me exhausted, spiritually and physically. It was never easy to shake Ditmarsh off at the end of a day, but even the most elusive sense of ease became impossible. When I wasn't thinking about Fenton, I was thinking about Shawn Hadley. I got an update in my memo box each day about the status of the complaint against me, more paperwork being filed as the dates and duties got ticked off. The union had promised me a lawyer, but so far no one had been in touch.

I called Ray MacKay up one morning to see if he was getting memos, too.

"Memos?" MacKay scoffed. "Any memos I get from Ditmarsh go straight into my 'I could give a fuck' file. You worry too much."

"How come?" I asked. I honestly wanted to know.

"Because you got scruples."

He made the word sound dirty. I laughed.

"I just wish they'd release those goddamn tapes."

It was a stupid thing to say. Releasing those tapes might implicate MacKay as much as they might ease the scrutiny on me. The words sounded like the kind of whiny protest that comes out when you're trying to grab onto others during your downward spiral.

But MacKay didn't take offense. "Kali, you are one naive little girl."

I waited for another detailed explication of my gender- and experience-related inadequacies.

"Why would they release those tapes if they didn't have to?" MacKay continued, a teacher in the classroom.

"Jesus, Ray, I don't know. Maybe because I work at Ditmarsh and Hadley's complaints about me have made the newspaper."

"What fucking newspaper, that shit rag? Nobody is worried about a female CO stomping an inmate. That's practically porn site material. But as long as they hang on to those tapes, and as long as you give a shit, they've got a bit of sway over you. Who knows what's really in them, right? Could be you ass fucking Hadley with your CO dildo. Let the imagination run wild. You're at their mercy for a while, Kali. Face it."

Fuck that, I thought. MacKay gave me the courage to kill two birds with one stone. If I hadn't been on my way to Ditmarsh, rocked by my persecution complex and those little revenge fantasies, I might not have followed through. By the time my half-hour shift break came around, I was still angry. The Keeper's Hall was light of COs. One at the counter. Another at the desk below the board. "Paperwork," I said when I arrived at the file cabinets. "Incident report," I clarified. Neither of them gave a shit.

I found the right forms and glanced at the movement board. Fenton was on rec time in the gym. Scraden was the senior CO watching the gym. I knew Scraden through MacKay and figured I could chat him up about what MacKay was doing with his life, what a drag it was to not have him around. I set out through the main hub, past the bubble, and down the tunnel, like I was on a mission.

I saw Scraden in the corner nest, paying no attention to the scrum on the gym floor. I didn't see Fenton on the floor and knew he must be in the weight pit doing the clank and clunk. But when I stuck my head inside the weight pit, I saw only two inmates within, both heaving hard, bare-chested, covered in tattoos and sweat and wearing fingerless gloves. Their swollen biceps, skinny little legs, feathered hair, and headbands made it look like 1980 all over again.

I went back to Scraden and stood outside his cage.

"MacKay says hey."

Scraden looked unimpressed. "I'm touched. Did he mention he owes me forty bucks?"

"He did not."

"Must have slipped his so-called mind."

"Heart attacks will do that to you." Ever amazed by the soft caring of an old-school CO.

I decided to go for broke, pretend I was there to collect Fenton for a visit, and not even bother to explain myself, because I'd never explain myself normally.

"Where's Fenton?"

"Tummy ache," Scraden answered. "You need him or something?"

"Yeah." I didn't elaborate.

"Fenton's clunk buddy Mendero told me he went to the infirmary in the a.m. all sick and moaning. But unless he's got cancer or a burst appendix, I imagine he's back in his cell taking a pharmaceutical nap. That fucker gets more candy than a kid on Halloween."

I knew it. I'd passed it over to him. All those red, blue, and green pills in a little Dixie cup.

"Thanks," I said, and raised a hand in farewell.

Walking there, I wondered, did I still have the guts? It would be easy to let it go. Try again on another opportunity. But everything was flowing so easily and freely—so inevitably—that I felt invisible. I couldn't be sure I'd get that feeling back again real soon if I passed it up now. I went for B block.

My luck was back. The nest was unoccupied. I didn't even have to explain myself. I just called in for entry, popped the cage, and walked inside.

Up the stairs to the third tier. The cell doors were closed, and all the cells were empty. I counted the cells leading up to Fenton's and glanced in as I passed by, saw him lying on the cot, arm thrown over his eyes. It was the most privacy I was ever going to get. I forced myself to walk all the way to the end of the tier, as if doing a normal round, then made my way back. By the time I got to Fenton's cell again, he was sitting up on the cot, a grin on his face, looking pleased to see me. He mentioned my catlike steps. He mentioned my good smell. I ignored him, but in a different way. I wanted him to think I liked it, or at least didn't mind.

"I heard you had a bad stomach," I said.

"Nothing a nap and a surprise visit couldn't cure."

I stood at the bars to his cell. I could have opened them up, probably should have to avoid being seen, but I didn't. Partly I feared being in an enclosed space with Fenton. Partly I didn't want the block supervisor or another inmate to come back and spot me walking out of Fenton's cell. Oh, the stories they'd share. But Fenton knew I was out of sorts. It was nine, ten, eleven seconds of silence.

"I need some help," I said. My face wouldn't contort the way I wanted. My lips had drawn down into a quivering line, all my confidence drained away. Fenton would see through my act like an audience watching a high school play.

But he thought I was distraught and reached up to touch my hand through the bars. I let the touch stay.

"What's wrong, baby?" he asked.

You didn't call a CO baby. But a CO didn't stand in front of your cell and tremble.

"I'm going through some heavy shit with Shawn Hadley." The words barely made it out of my tight throat. In my moment of untruth I was crumbling.

Fenton looked surprised. A wariness came over his face, and maybe a twitch of opportunity. He was all business. But he kept his charm on the uptick. He knew how to progress a deal.

"Hadley's got a lawyer," I said, as if Fenton didn't know. "I'm in big trouble if the trial goes bad for me. I didn't do anything wrong, but it doesn't look good."

He wouldn't give a shit if it wasn't coming from me, a reasonably attractive cougar on a cellblock for men. Just the same, I did my best, the lie spooling out like a badly cast line.

"Officer Williams. You have my deepest sympathies. Nothing hits me harder than you being distressed. But what can a guy like me do about that?"

Here it goes, I thought.

"I was hoping you might talk to Hadley and convince him to drop the complaint."

He didn't say anything for a long minute. I expected laughter, a guffaw, maybe a punch in the face through the bars.

"And why would I do that?" he said, all caution now.

He wanted me to spell it out.

"You must need an item or a bit of info once in a while. I could do something for you. And don't get any wrong fucking ideas. I'm not talking about anything disgusting. I'm talking about getting you something you need. Maybe bringing you in something from the outside. I don't know how this works. I just need some help."

I didn't need to sell it any more. We were dealing straight up in lies, and for some reason, that made our communication more direct and honest.

"I'm not a dealer," he said. "I'm just a stand-up cat doing too much time who enjoys a taste once in a while."

Bullshit. "Yes, but you must know people who are. I'm sorry. I don't know what I'm doing here. I've got to go." Act or not, I wanted away and would have scooted off, but he stopped me with pressure on my hand.

"Hey, you're a little desperate. I know how that is." I remembered Julie in the turtleneck gripping the daiquiri. "You give me your number. I'll get someone to call you. One of these cage monkeys must want something. Maybe I can trade a favor for a favor, discreetly, of course."

My number? It was the last thing in the world I expected. You never, ever let an inmate latch onto your outside life. You didn't tell them where you lived. What you ate. Where your kids went to school. Your hobbies. But I gave him my cell phone number. I could throw the phone away afterward. Get a new number. Move to another state.

The bell signaled movement. I pulled away as if a Taser had touched the bar.

"Thanks," I said.

And I was gone, fleeing like a little girl, face flushed, dirty all over. I forced myself to slow down, lift my head, and walk out like nothing had happened. Like I was bored as hell.

29

Two days later my shift ended at 10:30 p.m., and at 10:55 I pried open the Land Rover door, the metal screeching in complaint about the cold. The men had been docile, juiced out, end-of-day solemn, but I was still bone tired and heavy-limbed afterward. The lack of sunlight, I told myself, the way the days started dark and darkened early. The truck started—every day I expected it not to—and I dropped the glove compartment and fished for my cell phone while I waited. When I clipped up the cover, I saw the message light flash.

A woman's voice. A number to call back. I keyed the number into the pad. Three rings. A man's voice answered. I didn't know what to say.

"You called this number?"

A shuffle, and a light laugh. A TV turned down. I pictured a motel room for some reason.

"Where are you?" the voice asked.

"Driving back," I answered. He'd either know or he wouldn't. We were speaking the code of familiar conversation. Intimate strangers.

"There's a BP off thirty-six with an all-night truck stop kind of diner. Get a booth, and someone will be there in thirty or forty."

I heard a woman in the background: "Yes, you. I'm not fucking moving. What? Shut up." A lover's bitching.

Another sound. It could have been goodbye. Or maybe they'd forgotten about me and closed the phone. I shut my own and pulled back onto the road. My breath was tight, and my hands were doing a little dance.

A booth next to the long window. My parka shrugged off my shoulders. My fingers wrapped around the porcelain mug of decaf coffee. I should have been in bed, reading a book or watching Jon Stewart from between the sheets. What the fuck was I doing here? A surprising number of cars stopped in to fill up. I thought highway gas stations this close to the city were for emergencies only. But there was another population, from another planet entirely, coursing along the dark lanes. I was riding in the grooves of some other life.

I saw a large green Chevrolet pull up alongside the windows, some hunched-over winter hat wearer inside peering out, and wondered if that was my rendezvous. But the car disappeared around the corner of the building, and another ten minutes went by. I looked at my watch and wondered if I should order something, just to stay put. Then a young woman in a jean jacket with scruffy wool trim and a winter hat with a pom-pom and chin strings slid in before me. The girl smiled and shrugged off her jacket, showing a brightly colored tattoo on her bicep. Her fingernails were lacquered blue with little stars, some of them chipped down to nothing. I sat up, feeling fifteen years older and infinitely less wise.

The girl asked for two coffees and a water. I already had coffee, I started to say. Then I realized the second coffee wasn't for me.

"I have to pee," she said, and she was gone.

I waited. I needed to go to the restroom, too, but had been too afraid to leave the table for the last half hour.

The door chime clanked, and another customer walked in. A man in a plaid coat. Tall, six and a half feet easy, and long strides. I knew his walk, a cellblock roll. He looked around the room at the three other occupied tables and, without looking down at me, slid into the booth, pushing the girl's coat to the wall.

"She's in the bathroom," I volunteered, feeling stupid for saying anything.

The man had blond eyebrows over a sharp forehead ridge. He sipped his coffee, then tore open four packs of Equal and let it collect on the surface like an industrial powder spill, dipping it down with the corner of the packs of paper. Small green squares tattooed on each of his knuckles—prison marks.

"Nasty toilet," the girl said. She slid in tight to the man.

The man leaned forward, fixing a bootlace or pulling up a sock below the table.

"The stuff's out back. The guy in the library will take it from you tomorrow night between eight and key-up. Don't keep nobody waiting."

The library? He must mean the library in Ditmarsh, but I didn't have time to parse that confusion. "Out back?"

"Go outside in the parking lot," the girl said, "and around the back. Behind the Dumpster is a clear space except for this tree stump. Kick it over. It's all hollow. Inside is the stuff. Take it out. Put the stump back."

I waited. "You're kidding me."

"Not bad, huh," the man said, smiling for the first time, proud of himself. "Saw it on the History Channel."

I found the stump in the hazy diner light and kicked it over, then felt around underneath. A Baggie. In the truck, I looked more closely. At least five hundred pills. I pulled out of the parking lot, my bathroom need painful, but I was too scared to go back inside where the girl and the tall man were both eating western omelets. At home, I opened the bag and looked more closely. A collection of red, yellow, and green pebbles, some round, some numbered, some oblong and time-capsuled. Way more pills than I'd expected.

The girl had told me, stick the condom in your vagina, tied tight with the string hanging out. Nobody will pull on that string but you. It was kindly advice. They knew I was a first-timer. They expected to see me again. For the relationship to grow.

I put the Baggie into my underwear drawer, where I kept my jewelry, and put on sweatpants. I brushed my teeth, thinking, do you brush your teeth at the end of such a day? I lay on the bed and flipped channels, too tired to read. Hours later I was still awake because my heart wouldn't slow down. I had this urge to call Brother Mike or even Ray MacKay and talk to someone who understood how ambiguous the world could be. In the end, I soothed myself the chemical way, with two sleeping pills downed with water. I slept like the dead.

30

He had a dream about his father. They were at a restaurant filled with men, and they shared a kiss. The other men were gay, but Josh was able to explain quickly with only the mildest embarrassment that it was different for him, he and his father were father and son. It was only natural, in other words, and the feeling between them had been tender, intimate, welcomed. Everyone understood.

When he woke up, he spent most of the morning baffled and upset by what had happened in his dream, the textured rasp of his father's grizzled chin. His approving smile. Then, around ten o'clock, as he mopped the area around the nurses' room, Josh came to a hard-fought conclusion. He'd wanted love from his dad. The dream had been about the desire for love, not any kind of homosexual urge. He was surrounded by men, fearful of them, dependent on them, younger. What's more, he hadn't kissed a girl in a year and a half, ever since he and Stephanie broke up. He could list pages and pages of things denied to him now, but kissing a girl was near the top, except it wasn't even about sex, it was about affection and love. He longed for that kind of touch, and he longed for understanding from his father. All those feelings had gotten churned together in his dreams.

Roy came to his cell just after lunch but remained standing in the door.

"It's deal time," he announced. "No more beating around the bush."

Josh waited for the word.

"I want you to draw for me," Roy continued. "Crowley did. We made a lot of money. I was his middleman. You probably don't know how valuable a middleman can be. You can do some smooth time that way. You won't have to worry about trouble. Your middleman got your back."

It occurred to Josh that Roy didn't do a very good job watching Crowley's back. But that wasn't why Josh said no.

"I don't want to draw for you. I don't want to draw for anyone."

There were times when he never wanted to draw again. Talent might have been a gift from God, as Brother Mike insisted, but Josh feared it was another kind of gift, a wormhole into the rotten part of his brain, a path for viruses.

He figured Roy would throw out a snide joke and come back later, try him again and again. He wasn't prepared for the hurt that showed in Roy's expression. The jaw slackened ever so slightly. The old man was genuinely stunned.

"I can't believe it," Roy said. "All the support I've given you. The things I've done to keep you safe. I saved you from Elgin. I saved you from Cooper Lewis. I've gone through your files for six fucking days like Perry Mason. And that's what I get in return?"

Roy spun on his peg leg and left.

Josh was still thinking about Roy's reaction an hour or so later, when he was startled by a voice above his head.

"You have a visitor."

A jack stood in the door. There was nothing to do but comply. He rose up, baffled, and slipped his feet into the sneakers without laces.

His mother was in Florida. She'd gone after the new year and was staying for a month. Had she come back early? If so, what was wrong? The jack told him he could escort himself to the VnC, and Josh went out hesitantly, used to the hand-holding. It was a cold afternoon. A group of hard cons were outside, some doing circles around the snow-covered field, others in the smoking ring.

There were three areas to meet with visitors. An old-fashioned row of desks behind Plexiglas was saved for cons who had zero physical contact; then there were private rooms for lawyer and family visits, and a large common area, filled with scattered tables, some round, some rectangular, and fold-up chairs. He stood at the entrance and looked nervously for his mother. The two largest tables were taken up by families, children slumped or slouched, husbands and wives trying to steal some time. At a small table an old man with white hair was playing cards with an inmate who must have been his middle-aged son. At the back of the room, a couple sat side by side, as close as they could get without the woman sitting on the man's lap. Josh took in the noises, hushed voices, long pauses, sniffs, and laughs, the rustle of potato chip bags.

He couldn't see his mother, and he wondered if she was in one of the family rooms waiting for him. The anxiety was building, a lightness in his hands. He knew something was wrong. He saw a young woman waving to someone and looked beyond her. The jack at the desk hadn't even looked up from his newspaper. Josh strode toward him, then was bumped and knocked off stride, a hand on his chest. The girl who'd been waving stood in his way. He tried to get around her, but her hand pressed harder on his chest. She smiled up at him, told him it was great to see him, and gave him a hug around the waist. It was only when he smelled the oily perfume in her hair that he woke up to the fact she was there to be with him, not someone behind him, and he was there to meet her. Not his mother. Her. This girl he'd never seen before in his life.

As if he were playing a part in a movie, he allowed his hand to be held and followed her to a table by the bricked-in window next to the magazine rack. They sat across from each other like an eager young couple. She clenched his fingers in hers. Then she used his name.

"So what's it like, Josh? Am I the first girl you've touched in a while?"

She had big, dark glittering eyes, dark hair parted dead center, and naturally tan skin. She was short, five feet and an inch at most. She wore an unzipped winter parka, all paisley on the inside lining and a mane of gray fur around the hood. She had a frilly low-cut purple blouse on under that. She clenched his hands even tighter and squirmed in her seat.

"I heard a lot about you," she said, "from Billy."

His heart was in his throat, and his belly was all warm. Fenton? He wondered if she knew what he'd done to his girlfriend. If she was okay with that, because some people just were.

She smiled up at him and took off her jacket.

"What's your name?" he asked. He worried the question would break the spell and change everything. But she was just as cheerful.

"Deanna. Call me D."

"Have you been here before?"

She grinned as though it were the most thrilling and insightful question she'd ever been asked, but the answer never came.

"Want to play cards?"

He muttered sure, and she pulled her hands away and walked over to the bookshelf where the games were stacked. She knew exactly where to go. He saw the dragon tattoo on the top of her ass when she crouched down, the jeans riding low. She had gleaming white sneakers with the laces loose. He saw the jack at the desk eyeing her over his newspaper. Then D was dealing the cards.

They played hearts for twenty minutes. She told him the rules. They laughed when he lost and then laughed when he started to win. He felt her sneaker toe against his shin and kept his own leg stiff, the pressure from her foot sometimes intentional, sometimes drifting away. Then her foot was resting on his. They talked about her sister and her car troubles and the mall near her house. Then she asked him for a hot chocolate.

The vending machines were in the hall past the jack's desk, on the way to the restrooms. You needed a key for the restrooms. He was embarrassed. His mother always paid for everything. He told D he didn't have any money for the machines. She fished into her front jeans pocket and pulled out a crumpled dollar bill. Every hot beverage cost fifty cents. She knew it. He scooped up the bill and walked through the maze of tables past the jack's desk and into the hall. He fed the dollar into the machine. It whirred but didn't take. He took it out, rubbed it up against the edge of the metal, and fed it through again. Then she was beside him, the restroom key in her hand.

He turned to her. Part of him wanted to ask her whether he was ordering her the right choice. Her smile was gone, replaced by a dreamy seriousness. She reached up to touch his cheek, her thumb along the line of his jaw, then ran her hand up to his ear and cupped the back of his head. She pulled his face down and gave him a wet peck on his lips, a hot breath of tongue. She stroked his chin, her eyes fixed on his, then reached into her mouth and pulled out a wad of gum. He expected more kisses, and she leaned into him, but her hand was down the front of his drawstring pants. He felt her hand touch his cock, as hard and vertical as it had ever been, and reach down for his balls and then pull him in closer. He felt her finger between his legs, pushing up, forcing in, a piercing pain in the center of his being. The finger stayed there, pushed up a little higher, the pain thickening then easing off, her hand snaking out and away, gripping his balls, stroking once along his cock, and she leaned into his chest and slipped past him, disappearing into the bathroom.

He leaned against the vending machine, weak, tears in his eyes. He looked around and saw no one. In the haze, he remembered what he was meant to do, and he pressed the button, waited for the first hot chocolate to fill, pulled it out, and pressed the button again. Like a good boy, he brought both hot chocolates to the table. It should have been funny—a golf ball up his ass—but his heart was pounding.

He sipped his drink while he waited. He was halfway done, and figured she was never coming back, when she appeared before him. She was quieter. Her smile was sweet but less full of the energy that had passed between them before. He picked up the deck and started shuffling.

"It's time for me to go," she said after they'd played another hand. "Billy likes you. He wants you to know there's a lot of good things waiting for you. I'd like to see you again, maybe a room next time."

"I'd like that, too," he said, all chalky-mouthed.

"Tomorrow night at the library," she told him, "you can bring Billy his little package."

She rubbed the back of her hand where they put the stamp with invisible ink. After she pulled on her jacket, she gave him a deep, lingering hug until the jack told them to refrain from physical contact. The sweet smell of her made him drunk. He walked out the other way, past the jack at the desk. The two jacks at the checkthrough metal detector gave him a patdown. One said, "I seen that hot little bitch before," but Josh was already walking away. He was off balance and flushed as he crossed the yard. It was dark outside, the evening may as well have been midnight, and he felt free and alone and trembling with hope. When he reached the infirmary, he barely glanced at the jack and waited for the door to click open. Then he was down the hall. It was almost time for dinner. He could sit in his drum for ten minutes and compose himself, then grab chow.

When he got to his drum, everything inside his chest flew up into his throat. Roy was sitting on his cot, the photocopies of Josh's drawings in his hand. Roy was amused, all pleasure in the smile spread across his face.

"Where do you think Crowley learned how to hide his work, Josh?" Roy asked him. "You should have invented a different spot."

"That's my property, Roy." Breathing hard.

Roy didn't give a shit.

"Now I see why they sent you here."

The drawings in Roy's hands, his fingers folded around the pages—Josh wanted to jump for them. Tear them away. But he did nothing, just waited.

"Here's you fucking the shit out of her. Here's you stabbing her with a knife. Here's her sucking your knob while you've got a gun to her head. My, what a big cock you have. I never thought I'd say this, Josh, but you're disgusting."

"That's got nothing to do with reality."

Roy laughed. "Ever do a Rorschach test, kid?"

Josh didn't bother to answer.

"I done more than my share, and I don't mind admitting, every single one of those ink splats look like pussy to me. Of course, you can't admit that, because you know somehow you're sick—about sex and everything else, too. So you end up telling the doctor you just see a plate of hot lasagna or an open-faced roast beef sandwich." He paused, grinned at Josh. "You got a whole lot of lasagna on the brain, don't you." Head shaking in a mocking disapproval.

He rose up and thrust the pages into his pocket.

"In any event," Roy said, "you've given me better leverage than being nice to you ever would, all the pleasure that was. I show these drawings to some of the more sensitive fellows out there, jack or con, and your life will be a living hell. I'm sure you understand. So, fresh start, new relationship. I've been happy enough to accommodate your surly bullshit so far because I like people in all their various moods and personalities. But there's business to be taken care of, and time ticking by. I need an extra helping of cooperation from you going forward. You know what I mean? Tomorrow we'll have a little talk about the work you did for Crowley and what you can start doing for me."

Then he was gone, and the call for dinner rang out. Josh didn't leave the drum, just lay there, his chest heaving. An hour went by. A cramp grew in his stomach, and he told himself it was all in his mind, not a ball of coke exploding into his intestine. Did you just reach up inside there and pull it out? The mechanics were beyond him, and then the overwhelming urge came and he rushed to the toilet, sat his ass on the cold metal, and practically fainted with the pain as it passed through him. It had come to this, he thought. All the good feelings were gone. Hope was like an adrenaline shot. It gave you a jolt of heart-thumping life and left you beat to shit afterward. Then he was on his knees, his fingers in his own muck, searching for it, whatever it was, knowing that something large had squeezed out—retching, the water streaming in his mouth and from his eyes. He couldn't let Fenton down. Every gift came with a price. Don't make friends, Officer Williams told him. You don't want any friends.

When he finally grabbed something, he thought it was too small, but he could find nothing else, and he washed it off in the sink. In his hand was a thin plastic case, an oblong ping-pong ball, a fake egg of some kind, and he an unlikely chicken. He could have cracked it, but he didn't dare and had never desired anything less. He put it on the shelf behind his stack of letters and washed his hands again and again.

His mind kept racing, and he thought about the drawings, the shame of them. By the time they came along for lockup, he couldn't stand it anymore. The doors slammed shut—bang, bang, bang, bang, down the line, one after another. He reached his own door just as the jack arrived to key him in, and he began screaming. The jack body-checked the door shut, slamming Josh's fingers. Josh stuck his hand out the slot, and the fuckstick crushed his knuckles. He stuck his face into the slot, and the fuckstick drove him back like a pool cue against the ridge of his eye socket, a black hole of pain, and he was lying on the ground unable to see, holding his face, blood in his hands. He stood up and stomped the world. He tore his shelves down, all the clothes and books and letters crashing low. He leaned into the desk and lifted, wrenching it from its bolts in the wall. He kicked the wall. He rammed the door with the chair until the chair disintegrated. He tore at his bunk. He howled and thrashed and scratched. And when they came at him, bursting in, surrounding him on all sides at once, pushing him down and taking the life out of his lungs, he gave them every last bit of fight he had.

31

I slept hard until the alarm woke me late in the morning. It was a struggle to find the clock. I fell across the other side of the bed, dry-mouthed, limbs hardly obeying my brain, and stretched about. Bizarre memories of the night before. At first I thought they were dreams. Then the shock of knowing it had happened.

Fifteen minutes later I was sitting on the toilet with my head in my hands, feet planted on the cold linoleum. I needed to go through with it. I got an old, forgotten condom out of the drawer, ripped the plastic, and pulled it out. Ribbed, thin, those hopeful compromises between protection and pleasure. Shaky hands, each pill going in. Packed like a sock filled with gravel and tied off. I stood and leaned over, lifting a leg like a dog, and worked it into my body.

Then I put on my uniform and drove to Ditmarsh. All I could think about was the library. I had to maneuver myself there somehow before nine o'clock to do the drop. Getting out of my truck took a lot. Entering the north gate, smiling at Jones, and walking around the metal detector took everything I had. Jones waited until I was inside, then told me I needed to report to the Keeper's office. Every muscle in my face stopped working. I was a small animal that had walked into a trap.

Keeper Pollock was in the office, and he made me close the door. Pollock was a white-haired buzz cut about six minutes from retirement. The kind of simple soldier who smoothed all nuance out of right and wrong and made rank, seniority, and loyalty the cardinal virtues of a well-served life. He told me Detective Melinda Reizner of the Pen Squad wanted to talk with me. I felt like a child moments from breaking down, confessing every wrong and begging for forgiveness. But instead I managed to ask why I was wanted.

"You got me. Maybe they want to ask you about your boyfriend, Hadley. We're all wondering where love went wrong."

I thought about the videotape evidence and MacKay's take on why it hadn't been turned over. I told myself the meeting with Melinda didn't have anything to do with the drugs inside me, and I headed off, stiff with a bravery I didn't feel.

The Pen Squad was officed in a closed-off hall inside the old warden's residence behind the infirmary. As a CO, I had never passed through the secure door before. I'd escorted inmates to the entrance but had always handed them off to one of the detectives or intelligence analysts within and then waited for the interrogation to be finished. In my experience, the inmates walked in full of bluster and walked out quiet and wary. Like everyone else, I assumed they were guilty or at least in possession of knowledge that made them complicit in whatever was being investigated. Like everyone else, I assumed they would quickly inform on one of their fellow inmates in return for some legal favor or break.

The young man who answered my buzz resembled a weak sister or a civilian visitor more than a plainclothes officer. He knew who I was. Detective Reizner wasn't ready to see me. Fast-talking and harried, he shrugged with an empathetic smile. "You know how it is. We're working late tonight."

He showed me to Melinda's office: a desk, a computer, and four filing cabinets. There were no frills. Zero personal touches. A long foldout table with an off-kilter stack of files, a video monitor, and a tangle of cables.

"Do you mind waiting a few minutes?" he asked.

I said I didn't mind. He closed the door, gently but firmly.

The fluorescent lights sucked away all hope. I looked around the room for something to distract me. Memos on the wall, official notes about this and that. A chart listing inmate personal and family visits over the last three months. A statement, copied from the plaque just inside the north gate, describing the offenses for which visitors could be arrested and charged. I saw an evidence box and peered inside. Filled with impressively creative homemade weapons. The long plastic tube with a brutal pointed end had probably been a plate stolen from the cafeteria, microwaved, melted, and folded repeatedly until it looked (almost laughably) like a death-dealing dildo. The short aluminum pipe and elastic band was a zip gun for shooting darts. What men will do with their free time. Jacked up on fear, greed, envy, and hate. Throw in a little mental illness, and stir.

I saw a file containing Jon Crowley's autopsy report.

It was impossible to resist picking it up. It even allowed me to hope, almost rationally, that Crowley was the reason Melinda had called me in. The pages were meager, only a half dozen pictures, the details rough. Highly compromised liver function owing to long-term untreated hep C. A duodenal ulcer. So much for our prison health-care system. More germane to the events in question, partial hypothermia and acute asphyxiation. Third-degree chemical burns to his chest and face. One hundred and thirty-seven separate contusions.

Ten minutes later the door opened and Melinda appeared with an older woman at her side. "Oh," she said. "They've got you in here." Surprised to see me, but instantly changing gears, she threw around introductions. "This is Cynthia. Been around the longest and knows more about the work than the rest of us put together." Cynthia, dressed in blue jeans and a plaid hunter's shirt, told Melinda she was full of shit. Melinda looked more like a businesswoman running a corporate division. She asked Cynthia if they could follow up later, and Cynthia left us.

Melinda closed the door, and the way she relaxed, a little downturn in her energy, gave me my second blast of hope. "Sorry. Busy day. You been in here before?"

"Deliveries only." Tense and ready for anything, I kept myself friendly and humorous, eager to please. I saw inmates do it every day.

"Well, thanks for coming in. Some COs wouldn't." Melinda continued: "I've been meaning to talk to you about the whole Crowley thing, but we haven't slowed down since."

Crowley. I could talk about Crowley. I'd thank God if I could talk about Crowley.

"But now I've got a new reason to chat."

I waited, and wondered if my hand would shake if I lifted it to my face.

"What about?"

"You have a fan in here."

"A fan?"

"Someone who wants to see you. Wants to see only you."

I asked who.

"An inmate named Joshua Riff."

"The kid from the infirmary?" The question sounded inauthentic in my own ears.

"Last night there was an incident." Melinda hesitated, and I could see her composing a story. "The COs heard screaming, ran to his cell, found him in an agitated and destructive state. He refused to restrain himself, so they moved in to prevent self-injury and temporarily housed him in a safe room."

Rubber walls, wrapped tight. Maybe even sedated. Probably softened up first.

"They searched his cell, standard procedure, and found something."

She showed me the clear bag. A white plastic ball broken open, a pouch of white powder poking out.

"He admitted to the drugs. Says he was supposed to bring them to the library. We can't get the details out of him, though. Who passed them on, how he got them, who he was going to give them to. He says he wants to talk to you."

"The library."

"A nice bit of intelligence to stumble on. We'd been keying in on the warehouse ever since we found a bag inside the southwest wall. We'll get a camera on the library tonight and see if we can figure out the drop-and-pick patterns."

A few hours later and it might have been me. I could picture the video of a blue-uniformed CO in the library, looking nervous, stumbling through a handoff.

"Will you talk with him? He's scared and doesn't want to say any more to us. But I want to find out what he knows, see what kind of trouble he's in. We might be able to turn him into a regular informant."

I didn't want the assignment. Not this way. I wanted to walk.

"I know it's not in your job description," Melinda said, "but I figured you wouldn't mind helping out. We won't record it, so you'll never have to worry about it showing up. Just a friendly chat, and maybe you can prime him to cooperate with us. He's insistent on you."

"Okay," I said. I didn't mean yes. I wanted time to think, but Melinda misinterpreted.

"Fantastic. I knew you'd be into it. Here's the two-second course on interrogation. Say little, listen a lot. It's difficult for people to stay quiet. It makes them uncomfortable. It's human nature to want to fill the gaps. Good interviewers use that. You know what I mean?"

Nod.

"Then let's get it over with. Do you need to pee?"

I said I did. I wanted the drugs out of my body, even if that was the worst idea in the world.

32

His face was puffy, a black eye and a thick lip you could put a steak on. Older than before, and younger, too. Our time in the car, so imprinted on my memory, seemed hazy to me now, different people in different times.

I needed to show him kindness. A mercy and decency I didn't feel. "How is your face?" I asked. "Are you all right?" My head tilted with caring. My heart was stone. I hoped no one was watching. Melinda had said the camera was off, but a precise red-lettered sign on each wall stated, "You are being recorded." I didn't know whether to trust Melinda or the sign.

He looked up, blinking through the swelling. "Thanks for coming to see me." His voice was tight with the hoarseness of exhaustion. "It's not easy in here sometimes."

"They don't make it easy for a reason." I kept my own tone dry and reasonable, but the harshness had crept back.

"I could use a little help," he said. "I think I'm in over my head."

Was it a con? The ones who were good at lies fooled you so completely you questioned reality in the aftermath.

"I don't know, Josh. You seem to be handling yourself pretty well. Making friends."

"What do you mean, friends?"

"Josh, they found enough cocaine in your cell to keep a range going for a week."

"You think I knew that was coming?"

"Oh, someone forced it on you?"

"Yeah, as a matter of fact." A genuine laugh. Then his face got heavy again, and he lifted a shaky hand to his forehead.

"What is it?" I asked, irritated at the joke I didn't understand.

"I need to get out of the infirmary and into population. I want to start my real time. I want to be on B-three. There's some people there who will look out for me."

I must have looked surprised.

"Crowley thought I was crazy to want out of the infirmary, too. He said I didn't know how good I had it. But they got me in there for a reason."

"Who's they?"

He said nothing. I waited.

"Keeper Wallace, for one. Roy."

"What are you talking about?" I wanted and didn't want to know about Wallace.

Josh showed a sullen hurt.

"Roy isn't sick. His ears bleed sometimes when he bangs his head. But he can do it whenever he wants, and the doctors can't figure out what's wrong, so they can't let him out. But he's really in there to put the squeeze on me. He's always asking about Crowley. About the comic book I showed you in the car. He wants me to remember what was in it. And whether I tell him or not, I'm afraid I'm going to end up like Crowley or Elgin."

"What do you mean like Elgin?"

Josh's face tightened, a flinch of anxiety or fear. He didn't answer.

"Josh, I don't understand any of this. What does that comic book have to do with anything? Why would Roy or anyone hurt you for it?"

"Roy says the comic book is a treasure map."

I sat back, the tired lines around my thirty-nine-year-old face a little heavier. I was flattened by the craziness of it, this silly boy's adventure.

"A treasure."

He nodded.

"Maybe that's why your friend Crowley wrote 'dig' on the door of the old segregation hole."

"He wrote dig?" His eyes widening.

"A treasure. Do you know how ridiculous you sound?"

"I don't care if you don't believe me," he said.

Could I just leave Josh? I wanted to go. I wanted to walk straight across the yard and out the front gate. Get the hell out of Dodge.

"How can I believe you?" I asked.

Another shrug.

"If you want me to make this happen, you have to tell me what's going on."

"How am I supposed to tell you what I don't understand?"

"Josh, you know more than you're saying. We both know that."

"Okay," he said. "Here's what I know. Roy isn't Roy."

I took a moment to answer.

"What do you mean by that?"

"You think Roy is this fat old man with one leg who smells bad and tells stupid jokes, but he's in on everything. He arranges deals. He makes things happen. I think Crowley did drawings for him as a way of passing messages."

"About what?"

"Money."

For the first time, I got a vibe of truth in my bones. Not Brother Mike's bullshit about a prophet in a prison, but that other profit.

"Money how?"

"I don't know."

"Christ," I said, weary again, wondering how to get more out of him in the time we had left. "Do you think you could draw a little bit of it from memory, show me how it worked?"

Josh looked up. "I gave it to you," he hissed. "If you'd believed me then, none of this would have happened."

All kinds of accusation in those eyes, and a little shine of fear. He was begging me. I thought of a shoe dangling from a barred window, the beggar's grate. I thought of hands outstretched and people in finery trying to avoid the touch. I had an insight then, a flash of understanding. The neediness for compassion was thicker than any need for money.

Something in me giving up, softening ever so slightly.

"Why do you want to transfer into B-three? That's Fenton's range. You really think he's going to look after you?"

Josh just peeled the gauze off his forehead and balled it up in his hand.

"Said he would."

"Who gave you the drugs, Josh? You have to give me a name."

"I can't," Josh said. "I can't rat on him."

"Was it Fenton?"

Nothing more than an eyeblink, but I knew I was right, except I couldn't do that to Fenton; my own complicity made it impossible.

"I understand," I said. "You're afraid. We'll say it was Roy Duckett. You've had lots of contact with him. It's plausible."

"Okay," Josh said. He winced, as if the reality of the compromise was painful to him. "That will work," he continued. "I'll make that work."

"You don't need to do anything," I warned him. "You need to keep yourself alive and out of trouble."

"I need to get into population," Josh said.

"I'll do what I can do."

"Soon," he said, and added, "Please."

33

Melinda poured us tall coffees and added the kind of cream that doesn't go bad even if it never sees the inside of a refrigerator. She swiveled back and forth on her chair, eager for information.

I was bone tired the moment I got out of the room with Josh. It wasn't healthy feeling this way, a plodding heaviness in my step, the ribs in my chest all sunken from the weight of lousy posture. My hearing wasn't right, as though my ears had popped without my noticing and had failed to recover.

"I'm not sure I understood everything he was trying to tell me." I stopped as though confused. "Can you even rely on an inmate informant?" I was trying to figure out what to say and how to blame Roy, and I needed some way to explain my reluctance. "They're born liars. They'll tell you whatever you want to hear."

"Sure, they will," Melinda said. "But how does the old saying go? Crimes committed in hell don't have angels as witnesses. The great big magical secret to all successful detective work is finding someone who will tell you what actually happened. Then you corroborate with evidence. But nobody trades information for free. They want leniency or special favors, and sometimes they want you to turn a blind eye to their own illegal activities. There's always a risk you can get played. But I get my best leads from inmates, or from people around the inmate with an ax to grind."

"What kind of ax?"

Melinda grinned. "Had a good example last week. I got a call from a woman telling me a shipment of drugs will be coming into Ditmarsh through a visit to a particular inmate. Sure enough, the inmate she mentioned has a PFV scheduled with a different woman that very afternoon. After it was over, we put the inmate in detention and waited, and retrieved a tube of pills once he dispelled."

I tried not to think about the condom of drugs in my pocket, wrapped in tissue like the dirty aftermath of illicit sex. Practically the same contents, as though it were a missed delivery rescheduled. "But what was the motive of the person who called the information in? Does that ever factor into how you handle it?"

Melinda hesitated, parsing her thoughts.

"You're asking me if I was doing someone's bidding, maybe hurting the competition on behalf of some rival distributor for example? Of course I question everyone's motivation. In the case I just mentioned, the motive was pretty clear. The caller was the inmate's wife. She ratted out her husband because of the girlfriend. But it comes down to basic principles. How can it be bad to stop a shipment of drugs, regardless of who is behind the information?"

Case closed. So black-and-white when viewed from Melinda's perspective. Such a tangled mess when viewed from Ruddik's.

"So what did Josh tell you?" Melinda asked. "Anything worth acting on?"

"He told me the drugs came from Roy Duckett." I was stuttering, hesitant, trying out my line in real time, obviously lying. But she kept listening. "He said Roy's been forcing a number of vulnerable inmates to bring stuff in, and he has people outside putting pressure on family members, too. Josh was an easy target."

Melinda said nothing for a moment, the information working its way through some algorithm inside her head.

"Roy Duckett. It's never who you expect, is it?" she said finally.

I nodded, worried that I'd strained credulity. I talked fast, pushing us forward. "I guess so. There's something more. Josh asked for a favor in return. I thought you'd be okay with it, so I said we'd make it happen. I should have asked first."

I could see the uptightness sneak into her expression.

"What is it?"

"In exchange for that information, he wants to be moved out of the infirmary and into general population, on B-three, where he has some friends."

She took it well.

"Not in protective? That doesn't sound very safe."

"He thinks the opposite. He thinks there will be less suspicion if he goes public."

"Maybe. Usually these guys want to run and hide."

"I guess he's tired of hiding."

"Okay. Let me make some calls. We'll get Josh out and lodge Duckett in dissociation while we start questioning him, figure out who else is involved. But Kali"—she gave me one of those locked-eye looks—"this is really helpful. This is the kind of teamwork we need between investigations and corrections. I've been pushing for better cooperation for three years, and you'd swear by the response I get that I'm trying to investigate COs. This is a start, Kali. You and I can make a difference. Spread some success around."

I shook her hand, wondering how hard you press a grip when you're betraying someone's trust.

By the time I was done with the Pen Squad, my shift was half over. Keeper Pollock asked me loudly, and in front of the others, if I'd be available for my duties now or whether I'd applied for a new job. I knew he didn't have the balls to ask much in the way of detail. But my status as a snitch among the COs had been announced.

When some of the longest hours of my life finally ended, I walked out into the parking lot, opened the truck, and sat inside. The engine groaned, and the heater jetted cold. The condom of drugs was still in the tissue in my pocket. I couldn't go to the library. They knew about the drop. I couldn't bring the drugs back inside. I'd have a fucking heart attack. I opened the glove compartment, wedged a map and a manual over top of them, and slammed it shut.

When Ruddik answered the phone, he could tell I was upset. He wanted to know what was going on. I told him about the Pen Squad calling me in. He waited for more. I told him that I'd carried the drugs inside, found out the library was under surveillance, and backed off. He told me not to panic. We'd come up with a plan. I didn't tell him about what I'd done to Roy Duckett. Instead, I told him what I'd learned from Josh about the comic book.

"He said it's about money. He said it was a way of sending messages."

"Well, I'll be damned," Ruddik said, respect in his voice. "That's interesting." And he stopped talking, as though lost in thought.

I got tired of waiting for Ruddik's contemplation to come to an end.

"What next?" I meant the drugs. I meant me extracting myself from the tangled web of my own lies.

He told me to go home and get some sleep. I wasn't sure I'd be able to pull that off.

34

A jack showed up at his drum and tossed him a canvas bag.

"Pack your shit up. You're moving."

He'd fantasized about the ways a transfer would solve all his problems. In the whirling part of his brain, the desire was part of a desperate calculation. Roy was trying to use him, and Roy knew too much about him. Seeing Roy with the drawings in his hand had spawned in Josh the worst kind of panic. But getting rid of Roy was only a partial solution to his problems. He needed to align himself with someone else. So he locked onto Fenton as an alternative protector. Fenton had sent Deanna. Fenton liked him. Fenton might be the only one who could stand up to Roy.

But now the reality of leaving the infirmary made his stomach sink. Could he make Fenton understand it hadn't been his fault the drugs were seized? He hadn't ratted Fenton out, thank God for that. Fenton might even appreciate that Roy was the one getting the blame. Josh wanted to deliver that news firsthand. He crammed clothes and letters and boots into the bag and prayed he was doing the right thing.

The jack avoided the yard and walked him through the tunnel. Josh had never been in the south tunnel before. The hallway was wider than he would have expected. Their footsteps echoed. He wondered why he felt so isolated and buried; then he realized there were no cameras. A jack could do whatever he wanted with an inmate down here. Josh kept his gaze dead forward but felt the jack's presence behind his right shoulder.

The gate sprung them into the main hub. The hub was empty of inmates. A group of jacks stood next to the bubble. He and his jack took the tunnel into B block. As they neared the entrance, the noise got worse. All the inmates were in their cells, but the block was a stadium of noise: music, singing, talking, whooping, swearing, clanking. Every sound thudded off the steel and concrete.

"Oh, you're not going to like this." The jack laughed softly to himself.

The third-level hallway was narrow, less than six feet across, marked down the middle by a peeling white line. On the right was the long row of cells. On the left was a railing separating the hall from the floor below. The floor above extended up and over, like a cliff ledge that could collapse. The smells. Body odor. Cooked food, rank dampness—all mixed into air that was bone cold. The doors were not covered, as they were in the infirmary. They were just bars. You could see into every house if you wanted to. Some of the men looked up and glanced at him. A few wolf whistled. Most ignored him, doing their thing, reading books, writing letters, playing paper chess with someone next door, fixing a shoe, taking a shit. He looked for Fenton but did not see him.

They stopped before an empty drum. Seeing it, Josh's heart dropped even further. Soiled sink and toilet. Peeling paint. Broken shelf leaning against the wall. The thin mattress was warped like a slice of dry toast and stained with shit or dark blood in the middle. He looked back at the jack, wondering if this was some kind of cruel hoax. But the jack pushed him in, then got his face into Josh's. Clean-shaven but ill-looking, black whiskers in his nostrils, lower jaw smaller than normal, an overbite.

"You little shit fucker. You make me waste my fucking time carrying your leash over here and now you don't want to run into your new home?"

He slammed the bars shut and keyed the lock.

"Don't choke on any cock."

Alone, Josh felt the weight of the bundle he carried a hundred times heavier than before. He put it down and leaned against the wall, staring at the bed. By the look of the dust bunnies and dead roaches, no one had swept the cell in months. The toilet was filled with a yellow-brown slurry that didn't stir when he pushed the handle. He lifted the mattress with the toe of his sneaker to investigate a big lump. There was a dead rat stretched lengthwise and wedged against the wall. He stared at it, unable to believe what had befallen him, and slunk down the wall into a crouch.

The grub buzzer sounded an hour later, and the bolts clanked back. A half step behind, Josh stumbled out and lined up with the rest of the men, hands dug into his pockets. He didn't know the routine, but his body followed. The jack shouted orders, and the line began to move. He'd never eaten in the mess hall before. The line stayed single file right up until the chow counter. He didn't see Fenton, an absence that was drawing him into panic. No one spoke to him, though he sensed looks. He grabbed an open seat at a table and regretted it immediately. A retarded man sat opposite him. A scared-looking man two seats over. A table for rejects and outcasts. Thirty-five minutes later, when the line got back to the block, there was free time. Some of the men sat in their cells with the doors open. Others hung out in the hallway or in the small rec room at the far end of the block. Josh flipped the mattress up and stared at the dead rat, wondering what the fuck to do about it. He found a piece of cardboard in the trash bin and used it to slide under the sodden, heavy body, fearful that it would roll into his hand and touch his skin.

He walked out of the cell with it and headed back to the trash bin in the middle of the range.

"Yo."

He looked over at the sound, the voice of a young man standing next to one of the cells in the middle of the range.

"Don't you put that fucking rat in my fucking garbage can. That belongs in your drum."

Josh stopped, sensing that everyone surrounding him was watching. He heard a few dark chuckles but knew it was no joke. Wordlessly, he turned and walked back to his cell, still carrying the rat.

"Yeah, just flush it down your toilet," someone else said.

That night he threw his arm over his eyes and told himself not one fucking tear. He knew if he started, he might never stop.

In the morning he wrapped the rat in his worst T-shirt. When he walked out with everyone, hands shoved into his pockets, bleary-eyed, stomach in pain, aching to use the bathroom, he carried the rat under his clothes. He hunched over slightly so that no one would notice the bulge in his gut, feeling the weight of the rat against his skin like a thing that could still shimmy and move. He ate breakfast with the rat resting under his sweater on his lap, trying not to retch. When he got out into the yard, he let it drop to the ground, and he walked away, swallowing the saliva that ran freely in his mouth.

35

I had two days off and nothing to do but think—about Fenton and the drugs, about Josh and Roy, about the comic book and the Ditmarsh Social Club. I tried the number of the couple in the BP who'd passed me the drugs. I wanted to explain, without providing any detail, why I hadn't gone through with it yet. But the number didn't work, like it had never existed. What made everything worse was the disconnect with Ruddik. Since my talk with Melinda he'd stopped answering my calls. Normally, I anticipated rejection as a natural matter of course. If I ever liked a guy and let myself ease up around him, I knew he'd back away from me soon after. But this wasn't some boyfriend-girlfriend bullshit. This was real commitment, based on my willingness to sacrifice my entire fucking career for his machinations. I got tired of ringing him from pay phones and started thumbing my cell phone at random spare moments, hoping to catch him. Going silent was the worst thing he could have pulled on me at this particular moment. I was sitting on a Baggie full of pills, waiting for my next shift, wondering what the hell to do. I called him three times the night before my day shift, then a dozen more times the next morning, from the moment I woke up at 5:00 until I pulled into the parking lot at 7:30, finally leaving him a message. I stuck to the anger and fought down the paranoia. It was probably something stupid, a lost phone or low battery. But why hadn't he contacted me?

I left the drugs in my truck, then walked into the north gate. Somehow that day I needed to make contact with Fenton and explain to him personally why I hadn't made the drop. I wanted the drugs out of my life. I worried that going to Fenton had been a serious mistake. I knew he played people. And once I did one job for Fenton, he'd compel me to do others. Julie Denly had probably moved stash for him, too. Julie would have done anything for Fenton.

At Keeper's Hall, I checked the board, hoping to see a little color-coded dot next to Fenton's name, a doctor's visit or a counseling session, some break from routine that would allow me to approach him more easily. Then I couldn't find Fenton's name at all. Keeper Pollack came around the corner and greeted me with his usual cheer, like all was forgiven between us.

"The coffee's for shit," he told me, shaking the pot. "I been waiting for Cutler to bring me my latte, but he ain't showed up yet this morning."

Then I saw Fenton's name. His tab had been pulled off B block and slapped onto dis.

"I see you had some action in dis," I said, as casual as I could manage. I needed to find out why Fenton had been transferred, but Pollock went on about Roy Duckett instead.

"Oh, you know," Pollock said. "That fucking Wobbles sure can complain."

"I thought he was in the infirmary," I said with all the false naïveté I could garner.

"The Pen Squad sent him to dis," Pollock confirmed. "Said they got enough drug-related suspicions on him to warrant a little isolation time. The warden okayed it personally. Called Wobbles an imminent threat to the security of the institution. I had to laugh. The only security Wobbles imminently threatens is his own fucking balance."

Pollock liked his joke enough for both of us.

"What about Billy Fenton?" I asked. My voice was fine, but my face had flushed up. The questions were above my pay grade. I had no official reason to care who was in dis. Wallace would have stared me down and told me to get out on my beat, but Pollock didn't mind talking.

"Fenton. Now there's a happy camper. Wobbles flew a kite on Fenton, and we found a whole shitload of contraband in the laundry cell on B-three, exactly where Wobbles said it would be. Don't think I'd want to piss off Billy like that. Bad move from a Darwin standpoint."

He grinned at his own morbid take. "That's not the real excitement around here, though, or haven't you heard?"

I had no interest in more gossip but forced myself to ask. Pollock showed me the city newspaper, tapping the local section with a thick finger, and let me read for myself. Another article by Bart Stone. A corrections officer, name withheld, currently working at Ditmarsh Penitentiary had once been arrested for downloading child pornography.

"Oh fuck," I said, not even knowing why I felt such unease. "Who's our diddler?"

Pollack just grinned. "You're going to love it."

And I waited, knowing I was not going to love it.

"Our own superspy, Michael Ruddik. He missed his shift yesterday, and I haven't seen him yet today. Doesn't have the balls to show his face."

I leaned against the counter, as if a cramp had hit me in the stomach.

"Another demonstration that informants of any stripe are a species not to be trusted," Pollock continued. He got on his high horse about sticking together, watching each other's backs. I withstood it until Cutler showed up with the Keeper's latte, taking an earful about being late.

I sat in the gym nest watching the inmates leap or loaf on the basketball court. The younger or smaller ones played all the time, energized and spunky, chasing the loose ball, clapping sweat-darkened backs. Every so often one of the hefty king shits would arise from his recline and muscle into the game, lumber for a few minutes, and swat a smaller player down with a move that would earn a suspension in college ball but was hardly worth protesting in the Ditmarsh gentlemen's league.

The news about Ruddik had left me sick, but I needed to deal with my own problems for the moment. A week after I ask Fenton for a job, I fail to come through on my end of the deal and he ends up in isolation. I needed to explain matters to him, immediately and without delay.

When the buzzer sounded, I stood and hollered, "Chow up!" The basketballs got released to the floor, scooped up, and loaded into the bin by a punk I pointed to. The inmates lined up and walked to the locked fence, waiting docilely for my God-given okay. I spoke the magic words to my radio, and the door unhinged. The gym emptied and became silent, except for the clank of weights behind me in the weight pit.

I knew Harrison would keep hauling and clanking. He was a plate-pumping fool who always ignored the buzzer to get in one or two more reps. It was the kind of behavior that could piss you off if you were a con-hating hard-ass. Otherwise it wavered on the shit scale somewhere between mildly annoying and almost endearing. The inmates who cared about some hobby or self-improvement strategy were always a little easier to empathize with. An interest in life beyond the next meal or the next minute made them seem almost human.

On a normal day I would have kept the rest of the inmates waiting until Harrison was ready, yelling down at him from the nest to join them. Today I decided to accidentally forget about Harrison until everyone else was gone. I unlocked the door of the nest and walked down the steps into the weight pit.

There were no cameras in the weight pit. It was dank and dark. The stench rose up at me—moldy rubber, metal, and sweat. Harrison lay on the bench pressing a metal bar upward, arched down by the weight of the giant disks on each end. "Almost there, Officer," he grunted, and I watched him heave the truck axle up and down another five times, breath hissing with each hoist, squeezing his elbows tight on the last one and flipping the bar off the back of his fingers to clatter on the rests. He sat up and twisted his head one way and then back. His neck, shoulders, and chest were ripped with muscles, his biceps like round shot puts below vein-ridged skin, his knuckles callused. He was blind in one eye and missing an ear, the eye punctured and the ear ripped off his head in a fight. I approached him from the blind side and sprayed his face.

With surprise and the right tools, it's easy to take down a big man. Harrison collapsed onto his hands and knees and tried to crawl away. I leaned over him and brought the baton down on his shoulder repeatedly, like I was walloping the dust out of a carpet roll, then kicked him in the ribs, the air grunting from his chest. I clamped my hand down on the radio and called hoarsely for help, the pepper spray getting to me. By the time Johnson and Tesco arrived, I had already zip-cuffed Harrison's hands behind his back and smeared pepper spray from the palm of my hand across my own eye. The welt came up immediately, a watery red furrow, as if I'd been clobbered or scratched bad. Johnson and Tesco were all business. Tesco kept his knee on Harrison's testicles while Johnson checked my condition. I was all right, I told him. "Big boy went apeshit on me when I told him to give it up." Harrison, slobbering, was barely coherent. "She jacked me," he protested. So Tesco raised himself up and fell back down, his knee blading into Harrison's balls, and Harrison rolled over, threw up, took a shot to the back, and collapsed in his own puke.

"He's mine," I choked. "I'm taking him to dis."

"Attaboy," Tesco said.

Johnson and Tesco lifted Harrison to his knees and told him to get up. Harrison didn't comply, so Johnson thwacked him in the kidneys with his baton. Harrison arched his back, struggled in the cuffs, and finally hauled himself to his feet. The boys loved the weight pit. It was the best no-camera room in the house.

I got a grip on Harrison's thumb, rather than the zip cuffs themselves, and twisted it on a hard angle to get him walking. Like a blind mule, he stumbled into the wall and up the stairs, hunched over, steps thudding. I tried not to listen to him sniff and moan.

Pushing Harrison before me, I entered the receiving zone of the dissociation range, an octagonal space with two other doors and a glassed-in cage on a platform. One hallway led to the standard isolation cells, one to the internal evidence rooms.

Two COs looked down from inside the glass nest. I recognized Droune, but not the other, and hoped my relationship with Droune would allow me to skip the procedural route and get inside alone.

"Got a parking space?" I asked.

Droune leaned down into the microphone. "That's a ten-four, Officer Williams. You got number seventeen, clean and waiting."

The door before me clicked.

"But not too clean," Droune added.

I pushed Harrison forward, and the hall became noise, as if a stereo volume knob had been spun to the right. I could discern protests at bad treatment, lack of food, demands for shower or yard time, lawyers, and mail. I directed Harrison along, counting off cells, feeling vulnerable even though the door slots were shut. Each door had three slots, one at eye level for communication, one at waist level for cuffing hands, and one at the ground for shackling ankles.

Cell seventeen was waiting for us, the door cracked ever so slightly. I prodded Harrison, a soggy wall of flesh, with the end of my baton. There was a narrow metal bench inside, barely wide enough for his girth, and a chrome sink and toilet unit built into the wall. Nothing else. It was a shit existence. An isolated, mind-numbing, life-sucking waiting room. And it would be Harrison's home for the next six to ten days for striking a CO and failure to comply with a direct. He turned around, expecting it to continue, this psychotic bitch in a uniform who'd taken him down on his blind side. His lips and cheek were swollen, his skin crusty with puke and rubbed raw from the spray, a bright purple lump rising from the top of his forehead. I hadn't done my case against Hadley any good. One more testimony to add to the witness list, if Hadley's lawyer ever heard the rumor. For the first time in my CO career I wished I could utter the word sorry. Any trust between us annihilated, Harrison waited for me to step forward and continue the ass kicking I'd started at the gym. I stepped out and closed the door instead, opened the waist slot, and told Harrison to stick his hands through the opening. A few seconds later I heard his back thud against the door, and his hands groped with the opening and popped through. I disengaged the zip-cuffs and released him, then walked away, listening to his denials and protests spray after me like an unlocked hydrant.

Four cells back down the hall, I stopped and listened at the door. The cameras were on the hall, and the COs in the glass nest would be watching me, deflated and then perplexed to see me walking out so promptly from Harrison's cube, no blood on my stick, no wet strands of hair in my eyes. I didn't have time to worry. I opened the face slot and saw Fenton lying on the bench, one knee raised, watching me.

"Even in here I recognize those catlike steps," he said.

The words wouldn't come at first, and then I forced them out.

"I had nothing to do with this, and I don't know why you're in here."

He did not nod or blink or indicate in any way that he believed me or cared.

"The library was blown. I couldn't go."

"Those pills. Have yourself a party. I don't even want to look at you."

"Give me another chance," I whispered. How far I had fallen, begging an inmate to deliver his drugs.

"Aren't you sweet," he said. "I almost wish I could give you a hug."

He didn't move, didn't smile. I closed the eye slot and walked down the hallway as fast as possible. Some of the voices hissed at me. They'd figured out a female was on deck. They talked about how bad they were spanking it that very second. I'd heard it all before, but the Greek chorus of loathing was as menacing to my ears on this occasion as it had been on my first day on the job.

"Officer Williams!"

The voice spiked out above the others, more unwanted attention. But I knew who it was, and I judged through the cacophony where the sound was coming from. The voice seemed to know I had slowed.

"You need someone to steer you right!"

I was at the slot, and I shot it aside.

Roy stood at the back of his cell, good leg and peg leg splayed.

"All right, then you tell me!" I yelled, but I could barely hear my own voice.

Roy tilted his head back and bellowed at the moon, "Shut the fuck up, you goddamn fucknuts!" so suddenly and with such volume that the command drove my face back inches from the door.

But then, behold, with a few protests and grumbles, the shouting lulled like the release of crashed glass. No keeper, no warden, no cocked shotgun amplified over a megaphone had that kind of imperial authority.

I think Roy read the startled blink on my face, because he tried to shrug it off. "What do you know? They listen!" Pleased as punch, his smile back, as if we were the oldest of friends and this the most coincidental of meetings.

"You get us a room with a little privacy, and I'll fill you in," he said.

"Fill me in on what?"

"Now, that would spoil my surprise."

I had no stomach for such shit. I threw the slot back across and strode away, the chorus of degradation rising again.

"You're going to love it!" he yelled after me.

At the nest, they had the paperwork for Harrison's intake ready. Nobody joked or smiled. I'd managed to arrouse the suspicions of inmates and COs alike.

In the parking lot, sitting in the Land Rover, I leaned back in the seat and closed my eyes. The stress pounded in every vulnerable region, the insides of my elbows and the backs of my knees. I flipped the cell phone and dialed Ruddik's number yet again, my habit for the past three days, like fingering prayer beads. It shocked me hard when I heard his quiet voice.

I asked him where the fuck he'd been. He told me to calm down.

"Why haven't you answered my calls?"

"I've had company." And he told me where to meet him.

36

The Mexican restaurant was one of those pink adobe haciendas at the end of a strip mall. I arrived as bidden, despite feeling sick, something heavy pressing me down, a cold, the flu coming on. The temperature had dropped, and I was chilled walking across the parking lot and into the restaurant. Busier inside than I could handle. I barely saw the hostess, just pushed past her. Ruddik occupied a booth opposite the bar. He told me I didn't look good, as if me looking good was important. He was drinking a lime margarita on the rocks. Virgin, he assured me. I ordered a tomato juice, craving vitamin C.

When the waitress left, he slid back to the corner of the booth and stretched out to get comfortable.

"Sorry I wasn't in touch before. They're monitoring my e-mail and my phone calls."

"Who's they?"

He didn't bother to answer.

"Is it true about the pornography?"

"Of course it's not true." There was anger in the abrupt reply. "Two years ago I was investigating an Internet child porn ring based out of a penitentiary in Tennessee."

The waitress returned with my drink and a basket of nacho chips. She asked what we wanted to eat. I had no stomach for anything and declined. Ruddik put in an order. Something chicken.

"A porn ring inside a penitentiary?" I asked.

"A private enterprise operated a call center inside the penitentiary and used inmates as workers. We suspected credit card theft based on a spike in inmate bank accounts, but it turned out they were using the call center Internet connection to distribute pornographic images and videos. Anyway, I surfed a few sites back then to research what was going on, set up a couple transactions to see where the trail would lead, and, just my luck, got caught up in a sting by a different agency. They cleared the charges right away, but the word got out to my brother COs. Now someone back there must have told someone here. Whoever leaked that information to the newspaper is trying to impede us. This is what happens when you get close. It's never clean. It's always messy. But I've been through it before, so I'm not panicking, and neither should you. Things will get worse, and then they'll get better. Trust me on this."

"I don't know if I can handle any worse. I have a bag of drugs in my truck, and Fenton thinks I put him away."

"They want the shipment. You'll get a call about the new drop. The drugs will take us somewhere interesting. You don't have to do any heavy lifting anymore. Just stay in position and handle the light stuff. I'm exposed. I'm in the open now. I'll do the rest."

He opened his briefcase and took out a file. Always a goddamn file.

"What you said about the comic book, the idea of money, passing messages. That really gelled for me."

"How so?"

"What is money but a kind of message? In the old days, before the U.S. had a government-issued currency, any note could serve as money. Sometimes it was just an IOU between two people, but in mining towns, for example, it might be company-issued. They called it scrip. But the problem with scrip and any currency has always been, how do you make it counterfeit-proof? You need a stamp of authenticity, some kind of marking that's difficult to copy. Otherwise it's just worthless paper."

"You think Crowley was drawing scrip?"

"A possibility worth considering. Inside a prison, you would need to disguise the fact that scrip is currency, because of the illegal activity it symbolizes."

The waitress interrupted with a hot plate, whatever food Ruddik had ordered sizzling and spitting on the metal griddle. Some sides to go with it and a little basket of tortillas. The way he dug in made me wonder how often he took the time to eat.

"But that's just speculation. You're going to love what I found out about Hammond."

He folded a tortilla, overfilled it with chicken and peppers, and stuffed it into his mouth. He chewed and swallowed.

"I've talked to my contacts and learned some very interesting things. About twenty some years ago the FBI began investigating the possibility that conventional gang business operations in several regional centers of the country were being directed by gang leaders already residing within state and federal penitentiaries. Business hadn't ended when the leaders got put away. Business got better."

"What do you mean?"

"Once the leaders were locked inside, the organizations got more sophisticated and effective. They developed reporting and financial recording mechanisms and assumed vertical layers of control and supervision. They got better at using prison employees."

"COs?"

"And secretaries, nurses, maintenance workers. In a few instances, senior people on the warden's staff. Everyone getting their little taste. When Hammond was in extreme isolation here, for instance, the gang activity in Ditmarsh—and, incidentally, in several other state prisons connected with Ditmarsh—continued unabated. He just ran things the same way he ran them up top, maybe better."

"But he was completely isolated. MacKay told me his mind was a mess."

Ruddik shook his head. "Not true. He used COs to do his business for him. The FBI figured this out too late. From the group of COs that looked after Hammond exclusively, about a quarter of them were later charged with corruption. They did his work for him while he was locked up below. The Ditmarsh Social Club was rotten."

"A few of them committed suicide."

"The FBI would have arrested more if they hadn't. But once COs started killing themselves, the prosecutor got cold feet. Some people felt it was not guilt, but the pressure of the investigation that drove them to suicide. So the order came to back off."

"So what happened to Hammond?"

"The extreme isolation tactic, if faulty in practice, seemed like a good idea. So the FBI tried removing top gang leaders from their natural habitats and dispersing them to various prisons throughout the country. They were handled only by special guards and administrators. Family visitations were cut off and contact with lawyers restricted. Effectively, those inmates were made to disappear."

"Sounds good to me." I did not mind the idea of the worst inmates getting treated as such.

"Hammond entered that program voluntarily. He was one of the flagship members. That's how he got out of Ditmarsh."

"And Hammond turned," I said. "He became an informant and started making antigang speeches."

"Some of the agents behind the program predicted that would happen. Once gang leaders were separated from their gangs, they would be out of danger and free to leave the code of the lifestyle. Maybe they'd start trading information for privileges. In fact, that's the story we started to tell."

"What do you mean story?"

"We wanted to discredit or stain the reputations of the leaders who'd been dispersed, so we spread the rumor that they'd become witnesses of the state and been given new lives even outside of prison, that their cooperation had paid off big-time."

"And that didn't actually happen?"

Ruddik shook his head. "No one except Hammond."

He passed me a poor photocopy of a newspaper article. The *Contra Costa Times*. March 8, 1992. In the picture, a man who was obviously an inmate stood at a microphone, answering questions on a crowded stage. His arm was extended outward, cutting through the air. The same bearing and posture as the picture of Hammond I'd seen in the *Time* article, except the face was not blocked by a black line. Still, despite a close look, I did not recognize him from the current inmate population at Ditmarsh.

"Hammond was different. He didn't want to disappear, and he convinced someone high up he could do more good if he went public and spoke out against the gangs. He gave speeches to new inmates, telling them about the choices they had available to them during their time in detention. He had a very effective message of personal development and avoiding gang activity or drugs, very self-help oriented. A four-step process: Shed your past. Change your thinking. Adopt new behaviors. Make a better future happen. Administrators and counselors ate it up. And what wasn't to love? A high-profile murderer and gang leader was expounding personal growth and a rejection of drug use, criminal acts, and self-destructive behavior. He started doing a monthly series on tape cassette, and they distributed it to penitentiaries around the country in the hope that his message would have a major impact."

"Brother Mike said they were compelling. They made a difference on the prison population."

Ruddik nodded. "They sure did. A non-gang movement began to grow. And Hammond was heralded as a kind of revolutionary of reform. They put him in *Time* magazine." Ruddik pulled out a photocopy, and I leaned in to see the close-up with the blacked-out eyes again. "Then they discovered that Hammond's tapes contained coded statements."

"What do you mean?"

"Some researcher in a criminology program started noticing key phrases and repeated words. Then a snitch came forward to dish that Hammond's group had undergone a power struggle or a coup prior to Hammond's disavowing gang life. From a number of isolated pieces of intelligence it was possible to start stitching together the whole cloth. Hammond had been undermined by his lieutenants. Once he lost that power, he looked to improve his own life first; then he set forward on an audacious objective. Through the taped messages of salvation, reconciliation, and personal responsibility he was undermining his old gang by sending out orders to a newly established criminal organization. He recruited, gave orders, developed new business lines."

"He started a second gang in California?"

Ruddik smiled. "No. Far better than that. He franchised nationwide. He generated dozens of small gangs all over the country. Wherever three or more men met to discuss his teachings, when we thought they were talking about Hammond's bullshit self-help message, they were actually focused on illegal entrepreneurial activities. With the small numbers and the lack of gang signs or credos or ethnic affiliation, it was all too micro level for us to pay attention to, and so they mostly operated below the radar screen, as isolated cells. When the FBI figured that out, they stopped fucking around and took Hammond off the grid for good. No one's seen him since the fall of 1995. You don't even hear his name anymore. He's nowhere to be found."

"But you must know where he is?"

"Are you kidding me? They don't design those domestic rendition programs with traceable addresses. They've got prisons inside prisons inside prisons. Files and cross-files and double-blind files."

"But you think Crowley was helping to spread Hammond's message? Is that what the comic book is all about?"

"I don't know, but there's someone out there who knows more than he's admitting."

"Who?"

Ruddik pushed the newspaper photograph in front of me again.

"All the network modeling I showed you before, all those lines and nodes didn't lie. Look closely. Recognize anyone?"

I leaned forward, scanning the faces, randomly at first, then one by one. When I saw what Ruddik wanted me to see, I couldn't believe it. I felt that hard pit in my chest, the exact spot where betrayal goes when it gets stuck, and a little groan escaped my throat. Younger. No beard. Wearing a dress shirt, the sleeves rolled up, leaning into Hammond's shoulder. Described in the inscription as his spiritual adviser.

Brother Mike.

STAGE IV

37

He fixed the toilet by thrusting his hand into the bowl, past the turds and floating paper, pulling out a sock wedged deep in the pipe. Nothing. He retched until he saw little bursts of sparkles. Then, miraculously, the bowl cleared itself out with an air-sucking gasp.

At breakfast, they were out of milk, so he put the cereal bowl down and opted for greasy fried eggs and potatoes. He still hadn't got used to the color of the eggs, a radioactive orange yolk surrounded by a slippery gleaming white. Farm-raised, a kitchen worker said. On what fucking farm, Josh thought, taking them just the same.

No milk for coffee either. He took a mug of watery Tang. Then he looked back up and around, wondering with the usual dread where he would sit. The only table available to him was the one for those too afraid to sit anywhere else.

It was near the door, no different to the eye from any other table in the room, but everyone who sat there was disdained. Carriers, diddlers, snitches, and skinners, a former gym teacher everyone called professor, a businessman with sores on his face. The whole rotating crew smelled of fear.

He took a seat next to an old man with an Eastern European accent and no teeth. The sound of the soft eggs slurped and then gummed up. Josh stared down at the plate and set to spooning his own food, avoiding eyes.

Two men sat down on either side of him, and he pretended not to notice. Then he saw a large hand reach across his plate and scoop up a fingerful of potatoes.

"Now, that's fucking good," the man said, licking the food off his fingers.

Back straightening, Josh fought the urge to push his plate away.

"Look at me, boy."

Josh looked. He recognized the face right away. Cooper Lewis from his new range. The one with the cut who'd visited him in the infirmary. Orange goatee hairs streaked with gray, broad and yellow teeth. Lewis was the kind of inmate who enjoyed making a spectacle.

"Fenton gone, and you show up. That doesn't sit right with me."

The fact that Lewis needed to explain his bad treatment gave Josh the feeling of small victory. He kept his gaze steady. "Fenton told me to transfer in, and I did. He said I was the kind of guy he'd like to have around."

"Oh, he's fucking modest, isn't he," the other man said.

"God as my witness," Lewis said. He stuck his finger into Josh's egg yolk and brought it up to Josh's mouth. Josh's jaw clenched hard as the finger felt around his lips and gums. He jerked his head to the side, and the finger traced across his cheek. The jack could see it all, but looked away.

"You got very smooth skin," Lewis said. Then the two men rose up and left.

Josh wiped his face and drank a mouthful of Tang to get the awful feeling away from his lips.

In the infirmary he could move around almost at will, and even leave the ward whenever he asked. Here he was confined to the drum or the narrow range for much of each day. They all were, but when the drum doors opened, the other men could hang out at the rail and talk, or take showers, or gather in the rec area with its three bolted tables and small plastic chairs, card games, puzzles, and a few paperback books. You hung a sign outside your drum if you wanted a special trip to the library or the gym or yard, but Josh's sign never got answered. There was an area the size of a double cell with six showers inside, but Josh was not allowed into the room with his towel. The first time he tried, an inmate told him they were all reserved, though only two showerheads were in use. The next morning, he saw a chance before chow lineup but got pulled back by a jack and told the showers were off-limits until midday. He didn't bother to try again. He couldn't even get his laundry washed. You put your laundry in a little bag outside your door in the morning and the range cleaner got it back to you folded the next day, but Josh's laundry got kicked across the hall, and when he tried to bring it to the laundry himself, the range cleaner told him to leave his fucking machines alone.

The only inmate who spoke to him was Screen Door. They knew each other from Brother Mike's art class. She pouted with sympathy, whispered to ask whether he was getting along all right, even appeared at his drum door one time and told him what happened to Fenton.

"They were all in shields and helmets, come busting into the range and drug Fenton out of his cell like he was an animal. He took it chill as can be, reminded them to put everything back the way they found it, but those COs found enough here and there to bust him down to dis. It was a shock, you know, and everyone wondering why he got knocked, figuring someone must have had something against him or known something they shouldn't, and the next thing, you show up. And someone said you were special treatment in the infirmary, with not even a cough or a sniffle, and that's why they fingered you."

He asked Screen Door to leave him alone. He wanted isolation. He would have stayed in his drum twenty-four hours a day if it wasn't for hunger. It forced him into bravery, made him drop into line with the others and put up with the shoves and words and even the time someone stomped on his foot so hard he thought it was broken. The smell of food emanated from the other men's drums. You weren't supposed to cook, but everyone had hot plates, rigged up with live wires stuck into sockets. Breakfast and coffee in the morning, late-night snacks, strange ethnic food. He swore he smelled pancakes and bacon one day, steak and onions one night. It almost killed him. In the evening, before lights-out, he could only lie in his cell and listen to the noise, the tremendous noise, of music and shouts and conversation and televisions, as though a traffic jam and an orchestra and a political rally and a football game were happening at once, every sound picking up speed as it bounced off concrete and steel, whirling around like particles in an accelerator, becoming some other form of matter. And then silence, utter silence in the middle of the night, and nothing to do but think.

On the walk back from the cafeteria the next day, his third on the range, Screen Door told him to be prepared.

He asked why. He wondered what could be worse than now.

"They're hoarding," Screen Door said. "I seen guys bringing back extra food in their pockets. Making heavy brew. Not getting high so much, saving their stash. All their laundry done. Push-ups and sit-ups like they in training. Writing long letters home. Some guys even praying. That means there's a shit tornado spinning this way. I got my eyes open."

They mounted the stairs.

"If you want, I'll sneak you food back from the cafeteria. You can lay low. Avoid the surprises."

They entered the range and stopped at Josh's drum. It was free time. The drum gates were open.

It was kind advice. A month ago he would have slunk away gratefully and hidden in his drum in embarrassment and fear. "I can't do it anymore, Screen Door. It's now or never."

And he walked to the back of the range.

He saw eyes looking up at him as he passed each drum. He felt a few men dislodge themselves from the rail or their bunks and stare after. In the rec space, he saw Jacko, Lewis, and two other men sitting at the center table playing cards. He hoped Jacko would put in a good word for him, some connection from their time together on New Year's Eve. The men looked up, amused and astonished to see him standing before them. Lewis's smile was pure joy, and Josh noticed he was missing the teeth on the left side of his mouth. He'd never seen such men before Ditmarsh, and now he could smell their onion breath and body odor, see their bare feet in sandals, their hairy backs and knuckled hands, their gold caps and earrings.

"I just came here to tell you I had nothing to do with Fenton getting shelved." He spoke loud, as if to the room. "There seems to be a general misunderstanding about that, and it's fucking wrong." He could hear music still, and a few televisions, but no one said a word, bemused grins all around, the best soap opera they'd seen in weeks. "I'm doing my stretch here like anyone else, and I sure as fuck don't need any trouble."

He had nothing left to say. His hands were empty, his chest rose up and down with the difficulty of breathing.

The four men at the table stared at him as if they'd never been so flabbergasted in their lives. Then Josh got a subtle, respectful nod from Jacko, and the thread of a smile. There was generosity in his eyes, an appreciation for balls and character.

Getting no other signal, Josh took Jacko's nod as acceptance, turned around, and walked away. He'd let them know he was a stand-up guy.

The great force blew him forward and to the ground. His ears popped, and all sound came to him through a depth of ocean. Pain stamped him everywhere, a hundred blows to his head and back. Wild eyes above him, fists flailing down. The bridge of his nose became an ax splitting his brain in half. Then he was jerked upright and dragged down the hall. His legs scrambling to keep up but getting no purchase, his eyes squinting away blood. He wondered why the walls around him were leaning in and heaving out.

He didn't remember who got him to the hospital or how. He rested on a gurney, staring at the high brick ceiling. He thought of Stephanie and started to cry.

"Stop it," someone said.

He tried to sit up and pull a piece of tape or cloth away from his face. It was impossible to breathe. A hand on his chest pressed him back, and he realized they were trying to kill him. Would it be a release? Only after his strength was gone and the silence became a frozen landscape in his head could he hear the voice telling him to calm himself, that everything would be okay. The gently pressing lie.

He found his steady shallow breath, as though rising up through deep water. Officer Williams's face. Her presence confused him, and then he felt the compassion in her hand, the gently pressing palm, and began to discern the words.

"Your jaw is fine, but they had to stitch your mouth and tongue. You've lost four teeth. Your nose is broken. They packed your nasal cavity with a half mile of cotton. You have to calm down and breathe through your mouth. Take slow, even breaths."

He did as he was told. He wanted the reassurance of that voice above him forever, but then it disappeared into the darkness. When he opened his eyes, he saw her above him again, standing with two other jacks. He watched them until they realized he could hear, and they moved away.

In the morning he was able to sit up and allow soup to dribble into the corners of his mouth around his huge tongue. After lunch he was able to stand. By afternoon he could walk. He made it out of the sickroom and walked around the infirmary down the hallway. He passed the man with no face, and then his old drum, and Crowley's. He walked on, hearing rebukes and warnings, like a ghost's voice in his head.

Later, he stood in front of his mirror. His eyes were a raccoon's. His skin looked as though he'd fallen out of a car and skipped along the pavement. Three of his top teeth and one on the bottom were missing, an old man's bloody gums. His tongue was too thick to feel the space.

That evening Roy showed up at his bedside.

"I just got out of dis."

Josh stared, ready for the accusations, knowing he had no explanation to give.

But something in Roy's sober expression reassured Josh that it was all good.

"I'm sick of this in-between shit," Roy said. "I'm ready to get back to the block, are you?"

Afterward, he wasn't sure Roy had been there at all.

38

I think it was heartache that led me back to Brother Mike's house. The bundling of anger and pain reminded me of those times, three or four in number, when I'd been cast aside unexpectedly in a relationship. Of course, I could not help but think of the collapse of my own marriage, but that pain was different. With Brother Mike I wanted explanations, I wanted to know what had been true and what had been lies. This betrayal was elemental and threatening, touching the taproot of familial insecurity, like the suspicion that your father didn't really love you.

When I visited his office, I learned from one of the weak sisters that he'd been suspended from work for his contact with Crowley. That hit me hard. When I tried his home phone, it rang and rang, not even an answering machine to leave a message. And so I took up the one privilege left to me, established by his facade of friendship, and drove to his home, prepared to knock until he answered, to yell until he calmed me down. I wanted to be the child and hold him at fault for all the cruel failings of the world.

But when I turned off the highway onto his bumpy, snow-chopped lane, another irrational thought came over me. The ruts in the lane looked deeper, more trafficked than I remembered, and I pictured other visitors and feared I would find him harmed. All the anger in me turned to worry. So I drove through that quiet forest a little too quickly for my own good, crashing through the branches in the Land Rover like a mechanical rhinocerous, and burst onto the lawn before his house.

His car was not there. The house looked sealed. I left my engine running, a lack of commitment to bravery, and stepped out of the cab of the truck. If I'd had my .357, I might have unholstered.

The porch was slanted beneath my feet, the railing tipped ever so slightly toward the yard. There were vases with small plants in his windowsill. A tabby cat moved out from behind a curtain and revealed itself on the top of the sofa within. Darkness inside, and no response to my banging. I hollered his name with disdain and frustration, as though I had come for the rent, even though I just wanted to see the sweatered shoulders and that white top of hair emerge from some back room, befuddled by concentration, and hear his stammered offering of tea.

No mailbox to check. I tried to remember whether there had been a box out by the highway. I peered in more windows along the side of the house, and when I got to the backyard, I saw the low mound of tarps that was his kiln. A little lump came to my throat. He'll be in there, I announced to myself, slumped against the wall, eyes closed. I don't know why I felt so certain about it. I approached. The warmth had ebbed, but there was still an aura of old fire, a smell of hide even in the cold winter sun. I held my hand out. I could not hear that whispering river sound of flame whooshing about. I started lifting tarps clumsily, searching for a door. Finally I found an entrance, low to the ground, like a tunnel into a snow cave or a sweat lodge, and I hunched over and snuck in.

The fire was gone, but the heat and the smell were still thick inside, a taste of ash and smoke. I couldn't see much at first, had no sense of the space inside. It could have been infinite. And then little cracks in the darkness appeared. Hair-line fractures of light. Slants of shelves showed up with small figures squatting on them like ghosts. I touched the baked clay and felt the warmth; the surfaces were not smooth like porcelain, but rough and gritty, deeply lined. Perhaps it was too soon to move the pieces, but it seemed wrong that they were still here, left behind. I swept my foot low along the floor to make sure no one was slumped unseen within.

I was sweating in my clothes, wet from the dense heat and stewed in betrayal, my bones the marrow for a murky soup. I felt exhausted suddenly, worn out by the untrustworthiness of other people, the litany of disappointment and lies. Wallace had been the first betrayer, but that was incremental, almost gentle in development. I'd idolized him, and he'd rebuffed me with his bureaucratic disdain, and then the corruptions had begun to acrue. MacKay's betrayal was more complicated. I could not even articulate the reasons why the difference between his act and his true feelings mattered, except that I'd been led along by the former and left wanting by his lack of strength. And now Brother Mike was gone, too, somehow the harshest loss of all.

My phone rang. I didn't want to answer in the dark, so I plunged through the low tunnel and out into the light again. I saw that it was Ditmarsh, and part of me thought, this is Brother Mike calling me. He knew I was looking for him. He wanted to explain.

But the voice on the other end was Melinda Reizner.

"I thought you should hear it from me," she said somberly.

I asked her what, and a dozen possibilities seemed likely, all of them bad, but it was none of those things.

"Our reasons for keeping Roy Duckett in dissociation"—she hesitated for the right word—"collapsed. I'm glad I didn't make more of the suspicion you told me about."

"What happened?" I asked.

"We asked Joshua Riff for a formal statement, and he recanted. Actually, worse than that, he claims he said no such things to you, that you're lying."

We were shackled together, it seemed, this little miscreant and me.

"He must have been put under pressure," I said, pulling myself together, talking my way back to rationality, arguing my own lie. "You saw him in the infirmary. They kicked the shit out of him."

"No doubt, but that doesn't help my case. It's my fault. I shouldn't have put you in the position. You need training and years of experience to make those kinds of professional assessments."

I could no longer listen to her superior put-downs. Outside in the cold, my lungs had opened up. I breathed freely, and thought, Melinda Reizner, Josh Riff, two more I couldn't trust.

39

Josh got delivered back to B-3 on the same day Fenton and Roy were returned as well. To Josh it seemed as if the range didn't know what to do. Roy and Fenton, Fenton and Roy. Fenton went inside his drum and stayed there, sulking. Roy limped the range hall talking to people here and there. He was loud. He made bad jokes. He complimented some of the boys and humiliated others. For a whole day he didn't visit Josh's drum, just walked right on by. Screen Door told Josh everything was going to be okay. He listened because Screen Door had such an earnest and concerned twist to her face. But Josh didn't trust anyone. Whenever he left his drum, he paused an extra second at the doorway to see what moved at him from outside. In the range hall, he maintained a distance from others, though he knew they could always jostle or swarm him on the stairs. He kept his hands in his pockets, like everyone else, but he gripped a two-inch piece of filed-down toothbrush in his left fist. Unlike metal, the plastic didn't go off whenever he walked through one of the detectors.

He pledged other new habits. He was determined to keep his drum spartan and tight, not a speck of dust, not a crease in the bedsheet, the blanket tucked, his boots lined up, his clothing folded precisely, his letters and the two books he'd managed to scrounge stacked spine out. He wanted to understand the exact condition of his drum at a glance before he entered it, to know if anyone had been inside, jack or con. Even when everything looked safe, he would still check under the cot before sitting down. He wouldn't shower. He would wash his clothes in the sink with a bar of soap and wash his body by hand. He would relax only when the big lock jammed across the door at key-up.

By the end of the next day Roy had them all cowed. He engaged in head-bowed conversations with hardened men. He clapped backs and moved on to others. He nodded sagely and burst out laughing. Josh started to relax when the laughter became more frequent. Fenton was invisible.

Fenton was sulking. Screen Door told him it wasn't over yet. Josh understood what she meant when he heard a great roar of noise that evening and stepped out of his drum to see what was happening at the rec tables.

Past the shoulders and heads he could see Roy bouncing, literally bouncing, like a spring-loaded thing. Then he saw a stick rise up in the air and swing around, and he heard a whoosh of appreciation from the crowd. Despite his anxiety in tight groups, Josh squeezed through until he reached the edge of the cleared circle. A thick-chested, long-haired inmate Josh had seen around but never talked to stood with his back against the railing, trapped and feral. Roy bounced. Josh had never seen such lightness in him, such energetic spring, and then Josh realized that Roy had detached his peg leg and held it in his fist like a sword. Rather than crippling Roy, it was as if detaching the false leg had freed him to shift forward and back with frightening leaps. The other inmate held a lightbulb, of all things, in his hand, and thrust it forward like a weapon. Roy swung the peg leg around again, thwacking the hand so hard the bulb smashed and the fragments flew through the air, spraying liquid in a quick burst and a smell of turpentine everywhere. Then Roy came around with another swing of the peg leg, a crack to the side of the head that brought the man down. He planted his peg leg in the man's back like a flag and spoke to the group.

"There ain't no reason for us to be so uptight. We're all men here, and we all need each other to get by. Doesn't matter whether you're friends with me or friends with the other fellow. Me and him get along fine, so it's about time you do, too."

Passive faces staring back at Roy, then some nodding, then more talking to one another in reasonable tones. Roy spotted Josh and gave him a big wink. When the crowd cleared, Josh remained. The only thing he could think to ask was why there was water in the lightbulb. "Homemade napalm." Roy laughed. "A gasoline and dish soap cocktail. Explodes when you turn on your light, and those flames stick to your skin. I caught Gabe there trying to fix it in my drum when I wasn't looking. Fuckers don't know when to give in." Roy snapped his peg leg back on, a kind of hook or wedge underneath the stump.

Screen Door dropped Josh a note that night and said the big talk between Roy and Fenton was on, kites flying between drums like mayflies.

The next morning after chow Roy appeared in front of Josh's drum door. It could have been an echo of that other time, so long ago, but everything had changed since then. Josh's face was a mass of lumps and ridges, sore spots and gaps. Roy was less a clown then a king revealed. Roy gave Josh's drum a long look, then nodded almost solemnly.

"Shitty digs," Roy said. "They used to use this drum for bugs and junkies. You been rolled."

"It's all right," Josh said. It was a hell of a lot better-looking than when he'd found it, and he sort of resented Roy looking down his nose.

"You need to spruce it up a little," Roy insisted. "I'll get one of the boys to come by with a can of paint and give these walls a coat. Get you some cardboard furniture, too. You'd be amazed what Sykes can make out of cardboard."

After lunch Fenton stood there with a small television set in his arms. Josh waited for the hammer to hit. But Fenton just nodded politely and stuck the TV up on the shelf. It was an old model, the kind that had a black casing. The newer TVs were slightly larger and had clear casings so that an inmate could not hide something inside the box.

"Wobbles mentioned you didn't have a pot to piss in," Fenton said. "One of the boys moved on and left this behind."

Josh didn't flinch, didn't move. Fenton was not his old self. His edge was less sharp. Then he met Josh's eyes.

"Don't take it personal," Fenton said. "I know you got rolled and I know you were stand-up about it. The other guys just jumped to assumptions. We're all good now."

Josh nodded. The beating, the con job that had suckered him in. All good now. When Fenton left, he allowed himself to stare at the TV. He'd wanted one for a long time, and the longing surged in his heart. He eased himself up off the bed and moved toward it, then turned around rapidly when he saw Fenton at his door again, knowing it had been a trick.

"Forgot the cable hookup," Fenton said, tossing Josh a snake.

Before evening jug Jacko arrived with an armful. "I took up a collection," he said, unloading the belongings on Josh's bed. A blanket, a homemade hot plate, a porn magazine, a book of matches, a half bag of beef jerky, a metal coffee cup, a bottle of shampoo, a pair of socks. "Since I'm one quarter Indian, Wobbles says I ought to know all about welfare."

The chow bell rang, and all drum rats still walking and breathing lined up for the forward march. Josh felt like a new man, reprieved, bewildered, visited upon by angels, like Job restored, but also wary, still waiting for the hammer. Screen Door must have hung back in her cell until Josh passed, because she fell in behind him. "You can take your hand off your prick now. Nobody's going to sneak up on you anymore," she whispered cheerily in his ear. Josh, holding the sharpened toothbrush tight in his left pocket, reduced his grip and wondered whether he had been that obvious all along.

40 ||||||||||||||

I worked the eight-to-four and got through the routine fortified by stoic bitterness. In any emotional sense, I was no longer of the COs, but among them, sharing a range of similar duties. The conversation in Keeper's Hall tightened up when I entered. There was no open mockery as with Ruddik, but the vibe was real, as though they were afraid of being turned to stone by the snake-haired Medusa walking by.

In the parking lot, a little more sunlight to the end of the day, maybe winter finally creeping off. I noticed my door was unlocked. Had I forgotten? Nothing seemed missing. I sat in the cab, turned the motor over and the defrost on high, listening to the radio. Bad weather coming, according to the talk on the radio. I watched the fog on the windshield transform into streaks and the streaks become words.

It dawned on me as my heart knocked around my chest that you tell yourself to be careful, but you can't sustain the vigilance. Eventually you relax. You stop paying attention, and that's when they show up behind you, their breath in your ear.

I dialed Ruddik's number on my cell automatically, hardly taking my eyes off the windshield. I didn't want to be alone.

We met in the parking lot of a Home Depot after the store closed that night. Ruddik parked beside me, walked over, and climbed into my truck.

I pointed at the windshield. The words and the upside-down fallout shelter symbol were gone. I'd washed it all off with the side of my hand and a bit of spit.

"It said, 'Home Delivery, Tues Night, 9.' I think they want me to deliver the drugs to Fenton's cell tomorrow night. I was waiting for a phone call."

The weather had gone colder again. Brisk particles of ice hung in front of the headlights. I was exhausted, and barely hanging together. I longed for a drop off in tempo, a return to lull, a day when I did not dread an unexpected happening.

Ruddik agreed with my interpretation, but he seemed more interested in the means of transmission.

"Someone painted the words into the windshield with water," he said. "You couldn't see it until the defrost went on. Primitive invisible ink, like lemon juice on paper, something a kid would do."

"They wrote it from the inside," I said. Did he not understand why this rattled me so badly? "It was a CO. It had to be. Who else would break into my truck in the middle of the day right in front of Ditmarsh?"

"Probably," he said. "I've got some more unpleasant news, unfortunately."

"I already know about Roy and Fenton back on the block." I did not need his calm.

But Ruddik shook his head. "Not that. It's Hadley's lawyer. He's gone missing, but they found his car in a ravine half covered in snow."

My throat went all tight, and I stared out the window. "You think that's got something to do with me?"

"You asked Fenton for help with Hadley. Maybe he put something into motion."

"Jesus," I whispered. I wanted to lower my face to my shaky hands and stay hidden there, never look up again.

"I don't think I can do this anymore," I said.

His hand came up to my shoulder, a little human warmth to the grip, not just an awkward squeeze of consolation, but something else. Did men ever realize how bad their timing could be?

"Are you working tomorrow night?" he asked.

I nodded. "In the bubble."

"I said you didn't need to do any more heavy lifting. I'll take the drugs to Fenton. He won't care where they come from, as long as he gets them. Then the pressure will be off you. No more rough stuff."

"He'll want me to do it again," I said. And again, I thought.

Ruddik laughed. "I'm not sure about that. Don't you think he'd rather work with someone who can deliver them right the first time?"

I snorted, betraying the fact that my nose was running and my eyes were teary from the stress.

"I'm going to turn Fenton," Ruddik said, ignoring my emotion. "This will be my introduction to him. And over the next few weeks I'm going to let him know everything I know already, enough to keep him in prison for another lifetime unless he works with me, and then he's going to help me go after the keepers and COs. We'll learn who's real and who's wrong. And it will be thanks to you, Kali, that we got there."

Thanks to me. Maybe I'd get a gold watch.

"Where are the drugs?" he asked.

"I was scared of leaving them in my truck, so I hid them in my house." In my underwear drawer.

"So bring them tomorrow. Bring them in one last time and pass them over to me once you're inside."

I shook my head like a stubborn five-year-old.

"I want to get rid of them now. Not tomorrow. Right now."

"Okay," he said. "We'll do it now."

In separate vehicles we drove back to my place. He followed me into my room when I went to retrieve the pills. I passed them over, and we stood there facing each other, not knowing what to do next. I felt sordid and small, and I think he understood that. His arms came around me. My need for him was helpless and juvenile. But when we fucked, it was much rougher and harder than that, and the urgency of it, the violence in it, came from me.

41

During rec, Fenton made Josh join him in chess. The board was missing five pieces, replaced by squares of paper. Josh understood the rules and the basic strategy, but he knew Fenton was going to wax his ass. A few men stood by and watched, adding to his bad nerves. Josh picked out his early moves, and Fenton got his own pieces rolling forward. Fenton talked to his pieces as he moved them, told his pawns to do their work. Told his horse to fly like the wind. Told his bishop to fuck Josh up. Five minutes into the game, Josh realized with a cold sweat that Fenton was an awful chess player. Moves that appeared to be puzzling sacrifices were actually blunders that made Fenton swear and slam his hand down when Josh took advantage, and caused the other men to shake their heads in amazement. "Dawg, that's some unlucky shit." "Oh, you really going to fuck him up now." Yet with each move Fenton got himself deeper into trouble. He told everyone to get the fuck away from him, stop breaking his concentration, and in the space that got made, Josh started losing as quickly as he could, making his own stupid sacrifices, trying not to be surprised when Fenton missed the obvious takes or, worse, mocked Josh for a bad move when he finally spotted one. They played three heart-pounding games, and Fenton won all three in dramatic comebacks, Josh worming around in a hunt for defeat. Fenton pushed back his chair after the third game and told Josh he was good, but it would be a while before he took the master.

Then Fenton suggested a drink, and Josh rose, wondering what bar they were going to hit.

Fenton walked to his cell, and Josh followed. Fenton nodded at or knocked fists with some of the men he passed. He spotted Jacko from a ten-foot distance at the laundry cell and gave him a hand signal, a fluid gesture that impressed Josh as both gangster cool and over the top. There was loose mail on the ground at the entrance to his cell. Fenton bent over and scooped it up as he went in. Josh hesitated. You weren't supposed to gather in drums. But

Fenton was already down on his knees beneath the sink on the far wall, working the scoop end of a broken-off spoon at the screws to the vent. When the last screw fell to the floor, Fenton pulled the metal grate from the wall and said, "Give me a hand." Josh stepped in and crouched down. Fenton slid the grate out, wider and deeper than Josh would have expected, and hefted it over. Josh strained to keep his hands in a good grip on the sharp edges, and Fenton told Josh to put it down next to the bed. Then Fenton reached deep into the duct and pulled out a large plastic bag filled with an orange liquid. There was a long tube extending from the top. Fenton snapped off the cap, and a sickly sweet smell of orange juice and yeast filled the room.

"How's it looking?" Roy asked, standing in the doorway with a tin cup in his hand.

"I'd say it's well cooked," Fenton said.

"Twenty-odd days got to be some kind of record," Roy noted.

Fenton agreed, as if they were best buddies. "I been hanging sheets of Bounce here the last few days, shit so pungent I was getting drunk in my sleep."

"They didn't find this when they tossed your drum?" Josh put in.

"I guess they forgot to look or something," Fenton said. "I better go tell them they missed a spot."

Roy laughed. "Go rouse some men of quality," he told Jacko, who'd appeared behind him.

Fenton sat on the bed and squirted out a mug for himself and another mugful for Roy. Josh settled on the floor and held a paper cup out. Fenton filled it. Screen Door appeared in the door.

"You boys invite me to a party?"

Roy sneered. "Smell of brew brings them out like flies."

Fenton was busy with the kit, but he said, "No offense, Screen Door, you can drink, but careful you don't HIV anything."

Screen Door got down on her knees, held her hands out to the side, and said, "Bless me father for I have sucked," then opened her mouth and received a jet of brew from an inch away.

Roy laughed and lowered himself onto the one chair.

"Secret to running a good range," Roy said to Josh, "keep the queens happy. You'd be surprised."

Jacko returned. "Lewis is bringing his strings." Lewis, Josh thought. Jacko wedged himself in front of Josh and Screen Door and planted his ample rear on the chrome toilet bowl. He held out a tobacco can for Fenton. The brew gurgled out of the tube like siphoned gasoline.

"It smells like open ass around here," Jacko said.

"No shit," Roy said.

Lewis entered, a wooden guitar, beat up like an old suitcase, tucked under his wing. Josh didn't see Lewis as the musical kind, and imagined he played guitar as well as Fenton played chess. Behind Lewis stood an inmate Josh had seen recently on the range but never connected with the crew.

"This here's Jim Lucky Bones," Jacko told Josh as the two men settled. "Sailed with Lewis back in the world. Where's Tyson?"

"Got a visit," Lucky Bones said. "Old lady wanting his money."

"I'd be having a tummy ache for sure," Jacko said.

It hardly seemed possible they could all fit within one drum. The voices hit the walls as if there were a hundred people inside. After the mugs and cans had been refilled with brew, Roy raised his cup and a silence fell.

"You're as nasty a bunch of devils as I've ever known. Here's a taste before we blow the house down."

After the clinks and the solemn nods and grunts, they threw their drinks back. Only Screen Door was lacking a receptacle, but she sat with a smile on her face, the mascot happy to be in the company of men. Jacko belched loud and long. Fenton accused him of having no respect.

"You see, respect," Fenton told Josh, "is a core principle."

A debate arose over principles, Roy arguing against Fenton and Lewis. Fenton said that without principles a man would suck pole, take it up the ass, waste himself on needles, turn animal.

"The only thing I respect is the length of my God-given penis," Roy countered.

"It's true," Jacko said. "Wobbles has an enormous wang." He picked up the tube and squirted another mouthful for Screen Door.

"Started growing again after my leg got chopped off," Roy said. "Someday I'm hoping it will reach the floor."

"Without principles," Fenton went on, "you're lost. Nothing but a beggar."

"Now, now," Roy said. "Let's not be divisive. Don't criticize what you don't understand."

But Fenton's words nudged Josh. He stared hard, so Fenton began to talk to him.

"This is what Roy overlooks. This is the important stuff that makes a drum rat a man. You keep your business to yourself. And don't tell anyone about anyone else's business. Share your spoils. Study your surroundings. Keep your friends first and your family second. Be willing to sacrifice anything except your own honor. Don't apologize, no matter what the bastards do to you."

"And lie every chance you get," Roy added.

A jack appeared at the door. Josh almost had a heart attack at the sight, but none of the others flinched. "I bet you boys are hungry," the jack said. An inmate carrying two boxes of pizza stepped in and laid the cardboard at the foot of the bed, then backed out.

Jacko leaned over, flipped open the box, and detached a slice. "It's cold," he said.

"Cold night," the jack said. "We're hearing a lot of noise outside," he added. "Think you could turn it down?"

"The fuck you say!" Fenton roared. The jack left, and everyone howled.

Lewis started playing the guitar. The sound was delicious and unexpected. Josh couldn't believe how well he played. Each musical note was a distinct entity in fluid space. Fenton gestured for Josh to join him on the bed. Clumsy, off balance, Josh pulled himself away from Screen Door and sat beside Fenton. "My mother's boyfriend beat me all the fucking time," he started, and he told a tale of woe with a sharp, evil laugh.

Josh tuned out, nodding at the appropriate stops, grinning Fenton's grin, but the brew had altered his sense of time and place. Lewis bent over the guitar, stroking the strings, muttering words, no one else paying attention. Was he really in prison sitting in Fenton's drum? He had become someone he didn't recognize. Was there a shred of him worth saving? He thought of Brother Mike's arms around him. Screen Door looked up, as though wondering what was wrong. "Nothing," Josh said, answering an unasked question.

"We get it, and then what?" Fenton said, and suddenly Josh realized that Lewis's music had stopped and everyone was looking to Roy.

"We get the comic book," Roy agreed. "We figure out what it's telling us. We keep the knowledge safe, between you and me, Billy. No offense, boys. We give up nice and gentle after that, pretend it was all a big misunderstanding, and we bide our time. A month from now. A year from now, we go after it and make ourselves very fucking rich. All of us."

"You think they'll really give it over?" Jacko asked.

"No, I don't think they'll really give anything over," Roy answered. "That's why we've got to have the big bang."

"The big bang," Lewis said. He stood up, lifted his guitar by the neck like a baseball bat, and swung it against the wall. Everyone ducked as it splintered. Lewis swung again and again, crumpling the body of the guitar into fragments.

"Holy fuck," Jacko said. "That was spontaneous."

Lewis grinned, but there was a sheen of sweat on his face. "Always wanted to do that. Just like the Who. The big fucking bang."

"I got splinters in my mouth," Screen Door said.

"You been sucking my leg by accident?" Roy asked.

"Roy's right," Fenton said. "We need the big bang. No other way."

"I generally am," Roy said. "About time you fellows figured that out."

"When?" Lucky Bones asked, standing as though antsy, as though he could charge off at a moment's notice.

"Soon enough," Roy said. He tried to hold a calmness in his voice after Lewis's outburst, but Josh could see he was barely keeping it steady. He lifted his mug.

"Drink up and be merry, for tomorrow or the next day or the tomorrow after that you may get your fucking head blown off."

The tins were raised in toast.

42

Driving the next evening, I couldn't have been tighter. The weather had turned harsh with a thick, snowy freeze, making the route to Ditmarsh nearly impossible. I willed Ruddik to make it in, too. I wanted to be there when he passed over the drugs. I didn't want to put Fenton off again, even because of an ice storm. I had that hunched-over posture, leaning up against the steering wheel and muttering, "Fuck fuck fuck," as I drove, like it was a prayer to Saint Christopher. I turned off the radio because I needed every brain cell on high alert. The highway was awful, squeezed down to a single furrow grooved through the snow. I counted three cars off to the side of the road in angles of abandonment, one almost mounded by ice and snow, the others freshly deposited. The slush on my windshield kept piling on and thickening up, congealing to cut off my view. The wipers worked harder and harder with each sweep, sticking at times and then unsticking, as though exhausted by the heavy push. When I spotted Ditmarsh, I felt relief as well as the usual dread. At least the end was near.

Inside, I stomped the snow off my boots and warmth back into my legs. The tile floor was a mulch of dirty slush, but the ammonia smell was as strong as ever. Brian Chester watched me from behind the high counter. I expected the usual banter, about how few of the dumbshits had managed to make it in and how fucked the boys stuck on shift were, but instead Chester told me Wallace wanted to see me immediately. Jesus Christ, I thought, again. Had Wallace caught Ruddik? I told myself, turn around, get in your truck, and keep driving. But after a second's pause I felt the momentum of routine pull me like gravity. I passed around the metal detector and beyond the point of no return.

When I knocked on the Keeper's door, I braced myself to meet a man I'd been trying to bury. But instead of encountering Wallace's dour vengeance, I found him smiling up at me from his desk as if he'd been awaiting my arrival with enthusiasm. Across from him sat a stranger, sober but languid in his chair. I knew he was a civilian, because he looked like he was on a *GQ* safari shoot, wearing khaki pants, a multi-pocketed hunting vest that was all fashion and no hunt, and a denim shirt open at the collar, the kind of goofiness that a prison visit brought out in some. Wallace asked me to sit in the third chair, as though GQ and I were students running for class president and Wallace our proud principal.

"Kali, this is Bart Stone, a journalist with the *Press-Times*."

If he'd introduced the man as Santa Claus, I couldn't have been more surprised. Bart Stone himself.

He looked different from what I'd expected, less wonky, more war correspondent tough, sandy-haired, tan-skinned, a nose that bent right a little at the end as if it had been broken in a bar fight. I'd obsessed about what I'd say to the prick in response to his article, and now I was inexplicably shaking his hand. Next I heard Wallace describing me to Stone as a top performer. He wanted Stone to get the full picture of me, to understand the facts, that I was a role model for the modern-day corrections officer—college-educated, military-trained, articulate, savvy to the psychological and cultural nuances of a varied prison population, thorough and disciplined, yet flexible enough for dynamic security, physically fit, and unintimidated by hard-core inmates. It was over-the-top praise I would have melted to hear a few short months ago, but now I sat numb and unmoved. Wallace crescendoed his description with the comment that I had been recently selected for the elite URF team, only the third female corrections officer in the institution to wear the riot gear as an urgent responder. He didn't mention that entry to the unit had been predicated on my filing a discrimination grievance with his name on it.

Stone, with the gruff voice of a country music–loving cigarette smoker, said he was pleased to meet me. "I appreciate your help in seeing me around."

Seeing him around? I looked at Wallace. "Sorry, I'm a little lost." Pleasant and baffled as can be.

"I've been in touch with Mr. Stone for the past few weeks, ever since he wrote his first article about us. I've been trying to give him a more fair and balanced perspective on the work we do and the dangers and difficulties involved. To get a better feel for the institution, Mr. Stone has asked that he receive a guided tour, but one that gets off the beaten path and onto the ranges. I can't think of anyone I'd rather have lead that tour, Officer Williams, and I thought it would be a good opportunity for Mr. Stone to meet you firsthand."

Wallace talking to Stone for weeks about me, about us, about what we do. I had the sense that he'd left me out there as bait while he figured out where Stone was willing to go with his reporting, and now he was offering me up. Maybe because he thought I was so pliant and lost.

Wallace looked to Stone to explain my confusion. "I didn't tell Officer Williams about your visit. I wanted her to show up for a normal shift and have you accompany her on rounds without any preparation. That way you'll see exactly how we function." Then Wallace was back to me. "Mr. Stone is going to shadow you on your rounds, just like a probationary CO on first shift. You're going to perform those duties like you always would, except with Mr. Stone at your side. This will give him an opportunity to see what we really do, how we work with inmates, and what challenges we face on a regular basis." Then Wallace gave one of his grim shrugs. "Unfortunately, it's not a good night. The weather throws inmates off, believe it or not. But since Mr. Stone made it in, we'll make an adjustment to our plans and begin after key-up, which takes place in forty minutes. I don't want to expose you to any inmate traffic, Mr. Stone. It's a safety precaution, but I think you'll get an honest view of routine penitentiary life, one that few civilians experience. I need to warn you, however, that your presence on the ranges will likely provoke some hostility or outspoken behavior. Officer Williams is at her discretion in assessing what is or is not safe in any situation, and her word is final."

Stone opened his mouth, some point he felt it necessary to make. "That's the way it goes with this job. When a reporter shows up, everything changes."

The world revolves around you, asshole. All the pleasantries were being tied up too neatly before my eyes. Naturally, I couldn't resist blowing it up, and I asked for a moment to speak with the Keeper privately. This provoked a bit of awkward silence until Stone clapped his knees and mentioned a profound need to use the bathroom before we toured the cellblocks.

Alone, I didn't know what to say. How do you speak to the boss you're trying to get indicted? But my sensitivity to personal injustice provided the push I needed.

"This is a bad idea. I'm scheduled in the bubble. Not a walk-around."

I needed to be in the bubble. I wanted to be there when Ruddik made the drop. I wanted to watch from a safe distance and know the deal had been closed.

"And you can't ask me to play tour guide with a reporter who has written lies about me."

Wallace nodded as though in full agreement, and I realized, to my astonishment, that I was listening to an apology. "I know, I know. This is way beyond the pale. I tried to cancel tonight because of the weather, but I couldn't reach Stone. Frankly, I think he ignored my call because he wanted to get inside so badly. Droune was going to show him around, but he's stuck in snow."

"But my shift is in the bubble."

"You'll take Droune's shift. Cutler can handle the bubble by himself until Droune arrives."

I laughed. "So you never intended me to be the tour guide? I'm just second-string."

The dour face was back. I'd provoked its return.

"I wish you could understand something, Kali. You are not second-string. You are excellent at your job in almost every aspect. If I had a CO staff that included ten Kali Williamses, I'd have a lot less to worry about."

"I don't believe you actually feel that way," I said. "You've kept me back, and you let me dangle for a month with this Hadley bullshit when I did nothing wrong."

The bitterness was all frothy in me now, and I could not help but spill.

Wallace spoke slowly. "When I've kept you back, it was with your best interests in mind. When I let you dangle, it was because we needed to."

"Explain it to me so I get it. I mean really get it." I had never spoken to Wallace more disrespectfully.

"You were accused of brutalizing an inmate. I was fifty feet away and saw nothing, and I knew it was unlikely. And I also know you. But what if I got this institution behind you one hundred percent and we turned out to be wrong? An old friend of mine in Arizona was a chief in a city police service. One of his officers shot and killed a fleeing suspect who had a gun. The family of the victim claimed the gun was planted. It seemed absurd. The victim was a seventeen-year-old gang member with several weapons charges and time served in juvenile facilities. So my friend got behind his officer and backed him to the hilt. Well, six months and a nasty state-run investigation later, it turns out that the gun *was* planted, that the victim was dealing for the officer, that the officer had a network of young dealers he coerced through imprisonment in the juvenile facility where his brother, also indicted, was a counselor. There will never be trust between the community and that department again. Not for generations. I think we can afford to suffer a little ambiguity and stress to avoid that kind of thing happening here, even if our community of inmates is very different from a community of citizens. In fact, I think it's part of the job of being a corrections officer. We don't get patted on the back all the time, and we learn to accept that."

I chose not to speak. Somewhere, I remembered seeing and talking to this Keeper Wallace and thinking that his moral view of the world was correct and that I would like to make it mine, too.

"I also believe, and hope," Wallace continued, "that we can turn this encounter with Stone into an opportunity. You have a career worth accelerating, Kali. Some good press for you, some admiring public words will be viewed extremely favorably by the warden's team. You wouldn't believe how much they scrutinize PR. I'm not sure what kind of leader you can be. I've seen a lot recently to make me wonder if I misjudged that capacity in you. But I also suspect that you are feeling disgruntled and stressed by the recent events here, and I'm willing to give you another chance. I'm wondering if you're willing to give me another chance in exchange?"

I didn't say anything. I couldn't speak

Wallace sagged a little. "Maybe I'm being selfish. At heart, I'm tired of us not getting the appreciation we deserve. There's something fundamentally wrong when every time COs get a mention in the media, it's because of some scandal or wrong done to an inmate rather than the hard, dangerous work we do. But I think we have a small opportunity here to put out a more positive story line on our own terms, using Stone. And when I think about that, I think about you. What have you got to lose?"

What did I have to lose? I didn't know whether to laugh or confess.
"I'd be happy to," I said.
We even shook hands.

I sat with Stone in the CO room, drinking coffee and killing time until key-up. We were not alone. There were other COs, and I announced loudly and with enthusiasm that our local reporter was doing an embed, following me around for the night, hoping to see the real Ditmarsh. I felt reckless and self-destructive, a little drunk on some suicidal release. Somehow that vibe hit my fellow COs just right. They were my comrades in arms before our watchful guest, in a groove together, amped up. They wanted to impress the shit out of him with their machismo and brutal knowledge. If Stone wanted to write a tell-all, he needed only to turn on his recorder and wait. Fagan gave Stone a demonstration on how to use zip cuffs, how to wedge a baton under a chin, where to rinse your eyes after a cocktail splash. Cutler went into detail about what ingredients actually comprised the average cocktail. Baumard called us all girls, in our eagerness to win over a reporter. This seemed to inspire Stone to ask me some provocative questions in front of the men. How did the inmates treat me as a woman? What was my first priority in the event of an emergency? Why did the COs not carry any weapons other than their batons? I gave short, sarcastic answers, and my colleagues appreciated the bemused bitchiness with which I delivered them. They were proud of me for once. I was a hard jack, too.

Then Ruddik entered the room. He was still wearing his dark-hooded parka and heavy boots, and he looked more tense than I had ever seen him. Fagan, still festive with hospitality, told him heartily to stop hanging on the doorframe and join the crowd. But no one else seconded the invitation. Ruddik put his parka and boots into his locker and got his equipment on while we watched. Even me, someone who'd lain naked with him the night before.

When Ruddik left the room, I told Stone I'd be back in a minute and followed after. As innocently as I tried to play my exit, I knew it would not go over well.

It took only a moment to communicate with Ruddik in the hallway. We spoke quickly, as colleagues might. He mentioned the weather and the difficulty of getting in. I told him that I'd been assigned a visitor tour with a reporter. "The asshole who wrote about me and Shawn Hadley." Discreetly, I touched the back of his hand, hooked my finger into his palm. He nodded, told me to have a good shift, and headed out for his own.

When I returned to the CO room, I recognized in the silence and the glances that my timing with Ruddik had spiked their suspicions of me. The festive mood was gone. Sour, I pulled Stone away from his new friends.

"Come on. Some of us do more than drink coffee. You might as well see what."

We walked into the main hub, and I explained the way the branches worked and how the other buildings connected. I pointed out the education wing, and the blocks. I waved my hand to the tunnel that went to the infimary and the dissociation unit, as well as the exit to the yard. I put my hand on the bubble, smacked its side, and elaborated on its benefits as a control center and a defense position in the event of a catastrophic breakdown of security. Then I stopped.

"Explain to me how this works," I said.

He asked me what I was talking about.

"If I say the magic words off the record, that means you can't report anything we discuss, am I right?"

Stone smiled at me like a man in a bar. "Just say the magic words."

"Okay, then, this is off the record."

He shrugged. "Go ahead. You make the rules. But whatever I see when we're walking around, that's straight-up dirt."

"Just now. What I'm going to say here to clear the air. That's the part I want off the record."

"Sure thing," he agreed, without humor or anxiety.

"You wrote about my so-called encounter with Hadley. Who told you about it?"

"Reporters go to prison to avoid revealing their sources, right?"

"You're in prison already," I pointed out.

He laughed. "Hadley's lawyer hooked me up. He gave me a letter from Hadley."

"A well-rounded version," I said. "Aren't you supposed to do any fact-checking?"

He stood tall, and I sensed his narcissistic side, a wannabe tough guy, a jock sniffer. He couldn't have been less interested in my concerns.

"I had another source."

A fucking CO.

"You know someone in here?" I asked. "Got a brother or a cousin or a golf buddy working inside?"

"I don't play golf."

"What you wrote was weak. You have no idea what really happened, so you painted a dramatic version based on a lying inmate's personal gripe."

"Put yourself in my shoes." Calm, dismissive. "Everything in here happens behind big walls. Without someone telling me what's going on, how would I know?"

"And you trust that their version is right?"

"I don't trust anyone. Anybody telling you something they shouldn't has got a reason for it. Doesn't mean they don't know what's going on. You can't dig up shit without smelling some sewer."

I thought of Melinda Reizner and her justifications for working with informants.

"I got a feeling it's not going to matter what I show you or how I act. You'll just write what you want anyway."

He told me to cut the tour guide shit and do my rounds, and we could work on the mutual understanding later. I laughed. It was better than telling him to fuck off.

I took him into dis, where all good inmates were snug in their drums, but they'd been roused by something, every third or fourth man at his face slot. I didn't like it. A voice yelled out, "You want to really know what's going on in here, ask me!" It was as if they knew Stone was a reporter. How? Porous walls, psychic talents, a CO letting the information slide to an inmate? "You want to know the whole truth?" another voice shouted. Four cells ahead, a splash of something liquid shot through the slot and hit the floor, startling me.

"All right, this is no good." I pulled Stone back by his thick and ungiving arm, nudging him reluctantly around and walking us hard for the exit.

You weren't supposed to show fear, and I was showing it now by abandoning dis, but I had responsibility for a civilian. I needed to keep his *GQ* duds dry and stain-free.

I spoke into my radio and buzzed for exit, but got no response. Fuck me, I thought as the hoots and jeers got louder. One Mississippi, two Mississippi . . . I buzzed again. Then the click, and I pushed the door forward and hustled Stone out. How heavy and solid the steel felt under my shove.

"Nice show," Stone said, as if I'd arranged it. "You let them out during the day?"

"Special caged playground, three at a time max, one hour give or take. We're not cruel. You want to see where we watch them take a crap?"

I showed Stone the evidence rooms and the floppy spaceman gloves tubed into the glass buckets by the inmate crapper.

"You really get your hands dirty here, don't you?" he asked.

"Somebody's got to," I said. "You want people to understand, you write about this. I'll give you a detailed description of the typical encounter."

I thought of taking him to the infirmary, showing him the bugs and the howlers and the ones wasting away like plants that never got watered, but I didn't want to stray too far from the bubble. I wanted to be in there, if possible, when the exchange between Fenton and Ruddik took place, just to make sure. So we walked back down the long tunnel to the hub.

"You want to know what I'd be doing right now if you weren't here?"

He nodded, the patronizing shit, and gave me his blessing to proceed.

"Officially, if I was on walk-around, that means I do timed checks of all the ranges on one of the blocks. I walk down each tier five times over the course of the night, counting heads. Brilliant, huh? Think you could do a mile in my shoes?"

"Sounds rough," he said.

"It's not," I said, "unless something happens."

"And what could happen?"

My turn to shrug. "A wind chime. An OD or other medical condition. A splasher. You'd love those. Did you know it burns the eyes? Maybe a group disturbance. A bad count. A hot shot. A gasher. Maybe you spend half your shift talking someone down from some drug they took. Maybe an incident on another range stirs up your range. Who knows how the news gets passed along. The boys get pretty good at hand signals and flying kites. But if you catch a kite, you probably can't read it. And you sure as hell can't read a hand signal. You just know it means something's about to happen. On a good night, it's mundane as hell, and you're grateful. But if you walk the shift believing it will be like every other, that's the night you'll get shot by a zip gun tipped with HIV or you'll miss a stringer even though you swear the dead man was sound asleep in his cot when you went by."

"Doesn't sound like you guards are actually running the show."

"'Dynamic security minimally manned' is supposed to give us the empowerment to handle an environment that's inherently unstable, but it brings up ratio issues. What it really means is we don't have enough COs to maintain total control. You can write it down and call me your unidentified source. The government's too cheap to let us do the job right, and people are endangered as a result. Not just COs—inmates, too." I couldn't wait to see that in print.

"Total control," he said. "You sound paranoid."

"Inmates are trying to subvert control all the time. To injure, con, overpower, manipulate, dominate, and corrupt COs and other inmates on a more or less constant basis. Would you say paranoia is the right or wrong response in that circumstance?"

"That's what I'm trying to find out."

The hub was empty, and the lights around the gallery were dim.

"You think we could go in there?" Stone asked.

I didn't answer, but led us to the bubble. I was able to see nothing inside from my low angle, but I stood before the door and signaled my desire to enter. Was Cutler alone or had Droune arrived?

No response from the barred door, as though someone inside was wondering what the fuck I was doing.

"What's next?" Stone asked. He hadn't noticed the delay, or he was too jacked up to feel anything subtle.

Then the door unlocked.

"We sit for a while," I answered. "You think we work this hard without a break?"

I swung the heavy door shut behind me and followed Stone up the five steps onto the raised platform of the bubble.

Cutler swiveled around at the console, a big man, fat and cheerful. Droune, a bit sulky I thought, made himself look busy, checking buttons before one of the monitors. He probably resented that a snowstorm got him knocked off the glory duty.

"What's going on?" I said.

"You here to show our writer friend who really runs this institution?" Cutler asked.

Stone, on cue, began to ask questions, and the boys obliged.

"This is your central command," Cutler said. He loved the attention. "We've got cameras on all access points and hallways, same system as there is in the Keeper's Hall and the front gate."

I made my way to the console board in order to watch the monitors, as if curious myself. The third floor of B block was empty and dark.

"So what makes it central command if there are two other setups just like it?"

"Attitude." Cutler laughed. "Isn't that right, Droune?"

Droune gave no response, just kept his hands on the control deck, locked into one of those dark and solitary moods that can hit a CO once in a while, usually just before he hits his wife. I watched the boards.

Cutler kept talking. "Basically, we're first in line when it comes to movement and response. And even though we're inside the security perimeter, we've got a shitload of ammunition in here with us."

"And where's that?" Stone asked. "I don't see any weapons."

"Down below," Cutler answered, and pointed to the hatch. The upside-down fallout shelter sign above the stairs. "Everything's in the gun lockers down the hatch. But the inmates know it's all within reach. They sense our power. You get that?"

"I'm not sure I do," Stone said.

"Well, let me give you a subtle demonstration."

I looked over, slightly alarmed, and wondered what Cutler had in mind.

He picked up a bottle of household cleaner from the floor at his feet, the kind with the spray nozzle, lifted it up, then turned on the microphone switch on B block. Leaning in, he put his mouth close to the microphone, spun the dial to maximum, and intoned, "Good night, boys. Pleasant dreams."

Then he raised the bottle of Fantastic and shook it hard next to the microphone, sloshing the contents repeatedly.

I saw a shadow on the second tier of B—the dim figure of a CO climbing the stairs—jerk around violently at the sound. Cutler's voice must have boomed in there like the word of God, and the sloshing would have sounded like storm waves crashing against hard rocks. It had to be Ruddik, I thought, making his way to Fenton's drum.

Cutler, laughing, flicked the microphone off.

"This is filled with CA," he explained. "CA means chemical agent. We mix it ourselves, the proportions diluted depending on the individual CO's mood and personal preference. You can scare an inmate with the sound the way you scare a cat. If you've ever been sprayed once, you never want to be sprayed again. Works better than the old-fashioned method of pumping a round into your shotgun in front of the microphone. Much more subtle, right? And less paperwork."

He looked to Droune and then to me for confirmation. Neither one of us was in the mood.

"That's cool," Stone said. "Can you show me how you hold your baton? You guys really call it a fuckstick?"

Cutler laughed and handed his over. "Never in female company."

Without trying to draw more attention to myself, I watched Ruddik reach the third range on B and walk along the tier, staying the obligatory two feet away from the cells, across the white line. He passed Fenton's cell, and I saw the flash as he tossed the package in through the bars. I felt a physical easing in my shoulders. It's over. I willed Ruddik to get out quickly.

Cutler swung his chair around against my thigh and turned back to the monitor. Had he caught Ruddik's gesture out of the corner of his eye? Most COs would watch and say nothing. But a guy could have a beef with the resident snitch.

"Who's doing the count?" he asked, and peered closer at the screen.

"I don't know," I answered. "Maybe whoever is in the nest."

The nest was empty, I knew that much. It shouldn't have been, but often was on a night shift, when the CO manning it decided to stretch his or her legs.

"Garcia's supposed to be there tonight," Cutler said. "But he's got a bad stomach and went back to Keeper's Hall for a shit break. I didn't see anyone go in, did you, Droune?"

"Uh-uh," Droune said.

"It's Ruddik," Cutler said, a little extra spite in there for our audience.

Ruddik reached the end of the tier and walked quickly down the stairs, too quickly I thought, and then stood before the gate.

"He's signaling out," I said.

"He can wait," Cutler said. "Let him talk his way through Garcia."

Ruddik's voice came across the radio. "Exiting B."

"Fuck a duck," Cutler said. "We still having trouble on B?" he asked Droune innocently, then spoke into the microphone. "We're going to have to wait for a manual there, Officer Ruddik. Our apologies."

"Jesus, Cutler," I said, and I reached forward and hit the gate button releasing him into the tunnel.

I'd crossed a line doing so. No matter what kind of an asshole a CO was being, you didn't circumvent the control of someone manning the bubble. It just wasn't done. Cutler jerked back at the brush of my side, and then his arms flew up in the air and he flopped out of his chair as though zapped by a Taser.

I didn't understand. It was as though an earthquake had suddenly tossed him. I saw Stone leaning over Cutler, swinging down with a long, blurry arm-stroke. It wasn't until the second blow that I realized a baton was in Stone's fist.

I looked to Droune, someone to share my shock, and veered away from Stone. But I fell in that same instant, my feet tripped up, and splayed across the floor, my left wrist driving hard into the concrete, my chin clocking it next.

I lay there for one or two seconds, stunned by my fall, stunned by whatever was happening. Then a hand helped me, grabbing roughly at the shoulder of my uniform, hauling me up like I was a doll. In the next instant, in an entirely unnecessary enticement to get me to my feet, I felt a baton pull up against my throat under my chin. When I squirmed and twisted, the baton came in tight on my neck, strangling the sounds I was trying to make, perching me up onto the balls of my feet, straining to see what was in front of me. Droune at the console, Cutler on the floor in a sloped lean against the console deck, a tipped-over chair resting crossways along his lap. "Jesus, you'll kill her," Droune said, and then the voice behind me said, "I fucking will kill her if you don't get on with it," and the baton pulled tighter.

When the baton relaxed slightly, the air poured in. Coughing, blinking specks, feeling gulps of spit in my mouth, I saw Droune at the controls, face withered with anxiety, muttering, "You never said this. You never said any of this." Behind me, reporter Bart Stone pulled a little tighter on the baton and told Droune to get on with it. I looked to Cutler, saw that his eyes were open but unblinking, and the urge to be brave got swallowed whole. Droune flipped switch after switch, the winch turning over, the big gears revolving, every cell door in every block opening. In one monitor I saw Ruddik running down the long tunnel for the main hub, and in other monitors I saw inmates pouring forth like ants, chasing him down. I willed him to make it. I willed him to get through to the hub, but when he reached the last door, it didn't give. With a sick, empty plummet in my stomach, I watched him turn to face them. Taking out his baton, he started swinging, wide sweeps cutting through the air before he was caught in the slithering tangle of bodies and pulled into their midst. He was gone.

My legs gave out, and Stone allowed me to slump into the chair, the baton tucked under my chin, pulling me back so that my feet splayed, toes stretching akimbo. When I reached up to pull the baton down for relief, it bit harder and my hands fell away.

"What are you doing, Droune?" I choked through my damaged air passage at one of the moments I could breathe. I'd never liked the man. I'd always despised this ass-kissing bully. But I couldn't hold back the startled question. At my words, as though released from a spell, Droune stood, gave me a frightened look, then ran by us both. Stone was just as surprised as I was, but he didn't reach out—as though not realizing he could release the ends of the baton wedged into my neck. Droune stumbled at the door and fell, splattering onto the floor of the hub. Stone jerked me around with the baton, nearly tearing my head off. He yelled to Droune to stop, but Droune kept going until he broke through the hub doors and disappeared into Keeper's Hall.

The abandonment was primal, every worst nightmare come true. I had been left alone with a monster, a beast in safari clothes kicking at the console desk.

"All right, we deal with it." Respite over, he tucked the baton under my chin again and lifted up. "You'll have to do it, you cunt."

Do what?

We walked like a shambling four-legged beast to the console.

"Open everything, every goddamn thing!"

And when I didn't reach out or obey, I felt one of his hands release the baton while the other kept it tight, and his fingers reach under my vest and through my shirt as though it were a flimsy curtain. His breath was hot on my neck. So this was the rape arriving. He scooped in past my bra and grabbed my breast, and I shut my eyes, expecting the hands on my belt next, the downward tug of my pants. Instead, a charge of electricity shot through my chest as he twisted my nipple with his thumb and finger like he was turning a dial hard. Then he slammed my face against the console, hissing in my ear to open everything. I couldn't move, and he threw me down. Released and stunned, I collapsed to the ground.

He pounded the console deck, furious that he didn't know how to operate it. He wanted to open the gates into the hub, but those switches were located off the deck, in a special panel below the central monitor. I tried to squirm away, to follow the path Droune had taken out the bubble door and into the hub, but that seemed to raise his anger again.

"Open it up, you fucking skank."

He walked over the stone floor and kicked me in the face. I realized, as my head bounced back, that the kick wasn't that hard, more shocking than injurious. Twisted away, I lay on my back, my forearm over my eyes. His viciousness had peaked. Then his boot stepped onto my crotch—softly at first, as though testing the thickness of lake ice—before pressing down with all his weight, drawing the breath out of my body in a single whoosh.

"Don't you fall asleep on me."

When he released the pressure, all the agony surged skyward at once and I rolled into a ball, hands wedged tight between my thighs. He kicked me again, in the ass this time, my tailbone exploding in a rosy bloom of pain that shot up my spine and spread to every hair follicle. "Open it!" he said. All resistance was over, and I mumbled through snot, and told him where the switches could be found, and heard him flick them rapidly, then the winching screech of the iron gates.

He was back in the next second, stepping past me, showing utter indifference. The disdain was gone, only arrogance left. I did not want to draw his wrath, to remind him that I was alive or that I had even a scrap of defiance within me. But the shock kept walloping my grasp of what was happening. He had knowledge of this place. He knew what he was doing, and he moved urgently and economically, part of something larger, something coordinated. Not a reporter. Not a guided tour. But an invasion. A tight crew. A suicidal urge came, and I grabbed the bottle of cleaner on the floor, rolled onto my side, and aimed the nozzle up toward him.

I saw him smile, looking at the stupid bitch with a bottle of Fantastic. Maybe he didn't believe it would hurt. I squeezed the trigger and kept pumping.

Little aspirating canisters of pepper were no good when you faced more than one man, or when you just wanted to douse a room and stick some wet cloths under the door to keep the bad air in. But the pump action of a bottle of household cleaner had the close-range velocity and volume of a Super Soaker. The sharp spray hit him directly in the face.

Never before had I been in an enclosed space with so much spray. The air around us became acid, but it must have felt like hellfire to him, ruining his eyes, wrecking his throat. The overpowering instinct was to claw your face and run from the vapor, but our training made you grind yourself low and restrain the gasping. Stone collapsed to the floor, helpless in his choking. I crawled toward the door, coughing hard, wanting out of the bubble. I got up on one knee, ready to sprint for it, when I saw the inmates running toward me.

A single inmate in bare feet and sweatpants with no shirt reached the outside of the door as I reached the inside. We stared at each other. He looked as startled as a teenager who had crept into an abandoned house and found a uniformed policeman waiting in the kitchen. I must have looked horrible to him, all red-eyed and leaking mucus, some lurching zombie come back to life, because he turned his back on me and fled. I hauled the gaping door closed and cranked the locks over. Then I scrambled under the desk below the windows.

Outside, an avalanche of noise. I heard the din at first like an echo of fireworks mixed with screams, maybe bombs exploding over the distant part of some city, the voices of people fleeing wrath from the sky. Then I felt the first rock or brick hit the wire caging and shatterproof glass of the bubble, and the pounding began on the door. The noise was deafening, the world caving in on top of me. The air was still acid with chemicals, as though we were sealed in an industrial vat. I wanted to hide below the deck like a child, but then I saw Stone rise to his knees and start to crawl away. It seemed impossible that he could still breathe, impossible that he was still alive. I lurched toward him with my fuckstick and slammed it down on his back with all my force. I clubbed him again and again, out of murderous fear. Then, to be sure, I wrenched his heavy, lifeless arms behind his back and zipped his wrists and his ankles before scrambling back to my hiding place.

I dragged the handset down below the level of the console to make radio contact. I got no reply for a minute, and repeated myself. When a response finally came, I felt as though I'd appeared suddenly before a roomful of startled people, some party or meeting called without me. The voice demanded I repeat, that I cite my position and provide my status.

I told them my name. I told them my status was very fucking bad. "I am in the bubble. I'm injured and alone."

A silence, a hesitation, then a different voice, one I didn't recognize.

"What's going on in there? Where's your shift partner?"

I struggled to get out the words.

"He's dead, I think." I looked over at Cutler's slumped body, the red puffiness on his head like the plumage of some exotic bird. "Alvin Cutler is dead. We have an intruder. We were compromised." I didn't know the words.

Another voice came on. I heard a tone of recrimination in the follow-up questions and could not seem to make myself understood.

"What happened to Cutler?" the voice asked me.

"Cutler was hit with his own baton. The reporter. Stone. I killed him, I think."

I knew I wasn't making sense, but the absence of any response drove my frustration higher.

"Droune did it! Droune opened the goddamn gates!"

No response again.

"Maintain your control."

It came as a disjointed command, something I wasn't sure I heard properly, and the radio went dead.

I gave up, and peeked above the deck to look at the consoles and through the glass. A torrent of freedom all around. Each monitor told a different story. Men running along the tiers in the cellblocks, crawling down fences, ripping away railings, ramming, wrenching, pounding at the walls and gates. A maelstrom of violence. This was not reparable. This was the book of Revelation. I felt numb with shock and helplessness. I could not put the genie back in the bottle. None of the gate switches worked. None of the doors would respond. They'd blocked and jammed everything, securing their exits and entrances. There was no battle out there, no shots being fired, the war already won. The COs had fallen back to the perimeters. Maybe there were pockets of them trapped in the blocks, the infirmary, or dis, but I was alone in the bubble. Then the monitors started to go blank, the cameras out on the blocks and in the tunnels covered up or knocked violently from their perches. I gripped the baton in my hand and squeezed my eyes shut.

43

When the others ran from their cells, Josh stayed inside. Screen Door appeared, arms braced on both sides of Josh's suddenly opened entranceway, and told him the block was inmate land now. "What do you think?" she asked, with a hand sweeping along her front, and Josh realized that Screen Door had fashioned a prison jumpsuit into some kind of evening dress, low on her smooth caramel-skinned chest, tight around the hips, trailing at the ankles. Then Screen Door waved and tottered off, and Josh was alone.

He thought he'd known the level of noise that could be generated by the men within the block, but he'd underestimated the depth of human arousal, the furious glee of sudden freedom, the expansiveness of its rage and joy. There was the bellow of many voices shouting and whooping, the pounding of running feet, the crash of steel toilet units smashed into warped fragments on the concrete floor below, the wrenching away of metal railings set in concrete and stone like dinosaur fossils. He braced within his cave and thought about how he might rip his own cot from the wall, set it up as a barricade, even as he wondered if that would provoke or protect. Then, after too many men running by slowed to look at him suspiciously, he lunged up from his squatted stance and stepped out.

He spotted Roy at the end of the tier, whooping to the men above and below, shouting commands. Whether anyone could hear or was bothering to listen didn't seem to matter. Roy acted like a maestro conducting an orchestra, coaxing some rage here, dampening some anger there, engorged by the hysteria. He saw Josh watching from afar and waved him forward. "Come on, Joshy! You're needed!" It was impossible to disobey such a direct command, so Josh made his way down the range, squeezing tight as others ran by, stepping over chunks of concrete and twisted pipes, careful not to edge too close to the gaps, the railings dangling like fragments of broken bridge over open space.

Roy slapped a heavy arm over Josh's shoulder and squeezed him close to his side. "Now you'll know what human beings can do when the lid's off, Joshy. You may never witness anything like it again for as long as you live."

They watched. Then water suddenly poured down from the railings above and curtained across the tier. Josh fought a sense of vertigo, as though he stood on the lower deck of a ship that had just rolled in a great swell and got swamped. The men yelled their surprise first, then their questions, and then their hearty appreciation. Toilets and sinks had been plugged, he supposed, and the water allowed to overflow until it made an impressive waterfall. The flood ended after several minutes, and someone yelled that the water was cut off.

"Beautiful." Roy smiled. "There goes the water. As if we wouldn't need to have a drink over the next few days. They'd burn their own clothes just to see a bonfire, and then complain that it was cold."

The television signal was next, all the small TV screens in cells lost in a sudden blink. In their place, boom boxes with batteries fought for audio room, the thumping rap rhythms and heavy rock colliding in a pileup of noise with the shouts and the bangs and the crashes and cries.

He was in on it but not part of it, hanging near Roy's shoulder, only occasionally noticed. The men played their parts so earnestly it almost seemed like a game, a fantasy gone delusional and bloody. Roy was the only one who seemed even remotely self-aware. He did and said everything, even the most violent things, with a mocking tone, terrifying and humorous at once.

"Let's review the troops," Roy announced, and they left their perch and walked the tiers together.

Wherever they went, Roy was the locus of a moving storm. He answered questions and received adulations and expressions of support. He made decisions like Napoleon, though they seemed random and sometimes contradictory to Josh. He cast words of encouragement or scorned and mocked men who were doing stupid or self-destructive things. He told the men to set up the barricades. Count and secure the hostages. Police the tiers to protect the helpless from the wolves and assassins. Establish communication. Build the traps, find the food, and have bloody fun. On several of the tiers the men were knocking holes in the drum walls, connecting drum to drum, creating a crooked tunnel you could walk from end to end, the concrete chunks piled up in front of the gate and along the tier fence like a construction site. It looked as though an earthquake had twisted the entire building in its powerful hands.

A few of the men acted like wannabe lieutenants and community leaders. They asked for permission to set up food search committees, radio transmission committees, dome watch committees, so many committees that it became comical, a bizarre play at democracy. Roy blessed them as though he'd been waiting for exactly such virtuous knights to step forward and do his bidding. Men told him about the stores of pipes they'd collected, the spears and machetes they'd fashioned, the flashlights, radios, cans of coffee, notepads, and coils of rope they'd squirreled away. The industriousness was impressive. Roy stirred their flames with one breath and muttered his contempt as soon as they'd hustled off. "You'll all be in chains by morning, you idiots. Jump and holler and let your worst out. Leave no urge or want behind."

As per another of Roy's commands, the hostages were secured in the drums at the back of B-4, despite the ease—some argued—with which a single group could be rescued in an assault. The diddlers and skinners were crammed like a freezer truck full of illegal immigrants in the two last drums, eyes wide in fear. Eight jacks were spaced across the next three drums, their uniforms torn, their arms pinned back by their own zip cuffs. Brute men stood guard at the drum entrances, their orders from Roy clear and precise: keep the men alive and safe, no matter how much verbal sport got made. Those with a curiosity or an urge for wanton cruelty sauntered by and peeked in, mocked and challenged, sometimes tried to squeeze through, and got thrust back. Roy encouraged them all, the attackers and the defenders, and he assured the captives that they were safe and their every need would be taken care of. The COs, Josh thought, looked weary and defiant but very very afraid. An inmate whispered in Roy's ear, and he nodded sagely and announced a new command. The hostages would have their uniforms stripped and be changed into green inmate garb. What's more, the homemade napalm bombs (a stack of capped soda bottles in the corridor) would be transferred to the drums containing the COs. That way, when the assault teams came or the snipers fired, they'd be picking off their own kind or blowing them up, and they could think about that when the counting of dead bodies was going on later.

"Make a flag," Roy told Josh. "Give us something we can rally around."

So Josh and Screen Door got to work on a white sheet, found some black paint and outlined a skull on it, and duct-taped it to a broomstick. When Josh brought it out to the gallery railing, Roy told him to hold it up high and wave it back and forth. The men loved it, cheering, whooping, and Roy barked harshly through a bullhorn stolen out of the block nest.

"In all my years I've never seen the jacks run so fast. You're excellent soldiers, even if no army in the world would ever take you." He roared with laughter and caused the others to laugh, too.

Then to Josh in a low, casual voice with the bullhorn lowered, "Look how scared they are."

"They don't look scared to me." He'd seen too much madness in the past few hours to think of them as scared.

"It's plain as mud," Roy said. "In any riot there's five or six men who got the will, and the rest follow like a herd of mad horses."

Josh saw Jacko make his way down the tier toward them. He'd been wondering where Fenton, Cooper Lewis, and the others were and what they were doing. Jacko looked determined, busy, like an office manager with a to-do list.

"We've got a visitor," Jacko announced when he stood with them.

"Already?" Roy said. "Tell me the warden is here, please."

"It's Keeper Wallace," Jacko answered.

Roy shrugged. "No surprise there. And not much fun either. Oh well, let sourpuss come in."

A single CO was led out of the tunnel and onto the block by two inmates. Everyone hushed, seeing the Keeper below, awed by the audacity of his presence, the calm poise he showed. Then the shouting started again. They scorned him. They wanted to tear the Keeper to pieces.

"Wave the flag, Josh!" Roy urged him. "Wave it with all you've got. We need a truce!"

From the third tier Roy shouted through the bullhorn until the men finally calmed themselves.

Keeper Wallace looked very alone, and Josh was tight with guilt at the sight of him. How brave did you have to be to walk into a cellblock full of loosened inmates? There was an obstinacy to it, a declaration of the Keeper's rightful place in a stolen kingdom. This was Wallace's domain, his presence said, no matter how overturned the world had become, and he was there to serve justice to the despoilers.

The inmates crowded the tiers like spectators in a Roman gallery. With Josh at his side, Roy lifted the bullhorn again and made his speech, a show for the Keeper's benefit and the inmates' reassurance.

"This uprising is a call for justice and better conditions."

The announcement roused a tremendous thunder among the men.

"It was inspired by the systematic mistreatment of our brothers."

He made a sweeping gesture with his arm, and Josh saw many of the men nodding.

"No one feels safe with all the brutality, oppression, and revenge that permeates this institution. We want to investigate the outlaw guard criminals among your ranks—"

The noise became impossible to withstand. Josh cringed and looked for the roof to fall, the walls to cave in.

"To end the practice of turning inmates into snitches! We want better living conditions and more free time outside the ranges! We want an inmate justice committee with the authority to investigate abusive and corrupt guards and staff. All the way to the top! We want immunity for all the crimes committed in the launching of this justified revolt."

And who, with concrete dust in their hair and wrenched pipes in their hands, could deny the virtue in that?

"In return," speaking to the lonely figure below, "I give you my solemn promise that for as long as I am the voice of these men, none of the hostages will be harmed."

The enthusiasm petered out, and there was a discordant confusion of banging and shouts. Josh could even hear some men protesting Roy's list, adding bullet points of their own, questioning his authority.

"And now," Roy said, still into the bullhorn but in a quieter voice, "I will meet you in the tunnel to present you with a written list of our terms—" And he gave up, lowering the bullhorn and looking to Josh. "Maybe I should have spoke from the higher level, do you think?" Josh didn't know what to say. "Fuck it, let's get down there and get this over with."

Josh left the flag leaning against the railing and walked alongside Roy to the stairs. His pulse flickered wildly with the dread he felt facing the Keeper.

When they reached him, Roy nodded thanks to the inmates who'd handed the Keeper over, and gestured to Wallace to follow him back into the tunnel.

"Join us in the shadows if you don't mind, Keeper."

Wallace stepped closer. He glanced at Josh, disdain in that pinched mouth. "Keeper," Roy said, passing a folded piece of paper over. "I've always respected you for the way you run a fair shift. I only wish the majority of COs in this shithole did the same, or we might not be in this position."

Wallace said nothing, just waited him out with grim disdain, and the tactic drove Roy to be hasty and anxious in his words.

"You know how the boys are," Roy confided. "Their blood's boiling, and God knows what they're capable of doing. It's a struggle to keep the lid on, and I'd appreciate some help. The better you make me look in meeting some of our more reasonable demands—for food, TV, etcetera—the more cred I get. Otherwise, there's ten guys waiting to take my place, each motherfucking one of them less reasonable than yours truly. If you could start with some sandwiches and coffee for the boys, that would go over well. We're starving already, and I don't put cannibalism past half of them."

He laughed at his own joke, but Wallace didn't smile.

"Here are my terms, Roy," Wallace said. "This ends now. Every inmate returns to his cell until we secure the hub and the blocks. Then we will assess what happened and who instigated it, and charge and prosecute each and every man for his part. No discussion."

Roy scratched his chest and gazed past Wallace down the tunnel beyond, as if checking for the arrival of some delayed train. When he looked back, he seemed disappointed and grim.

"Why, that's hardly the kind of response I can bring to the boys without causing upset. Keeper, you want me in this position, believe me. Every minute goes by, old Roy's power diminishes just a little bit more. That's the way the game gets played. But as you can imagine, I'm going to go back and sell them on some bullshit story, same as you will on your end, and all of this is going to be a bloody mess no matter what we say to each other." He tapped his wooden leg on the stone floor. "There are a couple paltry things you could do for me, though, if you want to avoid a hostage being executed before the night is out."

Josh had heard nothing of an execution, but there was a harsh honesty in Roy's tone that led him to believe it was truly in the plans.

"We want the comic book Crowley drew in Brother Mike's art class."

Wallace blinked. Josh could tell he was surprised. "What comic book? What are you talking about?"

"We know you have it. That Brother Mike gave it to you."

"That's not true. I don't know what you mean."

Roy laughed. "Then Brother Mike must still have it. And he says I have a lying problem. What a scoundrel. Here's the deal, then. Tell him we want it. And make sure he delivers it, personally and alone."

The Keeper's dark eyes opened wide. "Are you out of your mind? I can't ask a civilian to walk in here."

"Chief, you and I both know Brother Mike would be willing to exchange himself for a couple of tired, hungry, scared COs. If he brings it, we'll release a hostage or two in his place. Be thankful I'm not asking for an airplane to Cuba. Just take care of my urgent needs, and I'll take care of your hostages and inmates. On that, I'm not fucking with you even a little. There are some among us eager to slit a throat."

"All right, Roy. With what little authority I have left, I'll make your case." He looked to Josh. "Let him come with me now. We'll walk out, and you walk back. I'll get your damn comic book. And I'll see you in a cell by this time tomorrow."

"Sorry, Keeper, I'll need our friend here to keep an eye on my back. But I promise I'll do what I can to keep him out of the worst of harm's way. You know I'm fond of him. Think about the ones like Josh when you're telling your snipers where to line up. You'll be killing people who don't deserve killing, and you know it."

The Keeper pulled a cell phone out of his pocket and handed it to Roy.

"You can reach me on this when it's necessary to talk. There's only one number programmed into it. Just hit send."

Roy slipped the cell phone into his pocket. "You mean I can't order a pizza?"

He put his arm across Josh's shoulder and nudged him around. Josh could sense the Keeper watching him leave. If Josh wanted to, he probably could have broken away, raced down the tunnel, crying and running like hell. But it was easier to return to the madness than make a spectacle of his own fear.

44

I longed for fresh air and sleep. I wanted to drink. I needed to urinate badly.

Cutler was all death, and I didn't go near. He lay in a half slump against the wall, his face slacker than it had been when muscular impulses toned the flesh, his hair clumpy with red, his chin tilted downward, his eyes gone opaque and dull.

Stone was not dead. He'd rolled over and lay, like a twisted sandbag, on his side. His face was swollen as though it had been boiled in the sun, and it was caked everywhere with a hard crust of mucus. It was a wonder to me that he could breathe. A blubbering sound came from him occasionally, as though he were trying to cough up phlegm.

Outside, the battering lost its intensity. The inmates did not walk the hub freely, but seemed to be hanging out in the entrances to the tunnels, sometimes running from one tunnel to the other, low to the ground, zig-zagging, as if to avoid a sniper shot. The hub was in darkness, and I'd turned off the lights in the bubble, too. Searchlights swept by, altering the world around me in a passing instance, illuminating furniture, the wall. Now and then I peered up and out the windows to survey the hub. I hoped each time to find it empty, and imagined running wildly across the open space and flinging myself through one of the doors to the perimeter of safety. The radio stayed silent. Had the inmates somehow cut the signal? That didn't make sense. I wanted someone to talk to me. I wanted to hear a voice explaining the details of what was going on, and the strategy for how and when they were going to retake the hub and the blocks. I wondered if they'd switched channels. Was there a protocol for that? I couldn't get my brain to focus.

Instead, crouched below the console deck, I remembered a nighttime rocket attack in Iraq. I was living on the base. Those of us who thought of it had grabbed our rifles. The rest waited for the lull before making the embarrassing retrieval. Outside, the air was exhilarating, the stray whiff of burning powder. Some of us shot off rounds, little sparks and snaps sent spinning off into the darkness. When we moved, we did so in coordinated jumps and stops. Training that seemed so fake and macho had worked its way into our brains somehow. The best part was the elation once we knew the attack had been choked off and that it was random rather than the big assault everyone secretly feared. We shared the intensity of the experience. We grinned easily for a change. That feeling faded hard in the grime of daily life afterward, but I never forgot the glory of that night.

This time it was different. This time I felt only loneliness and fear. It didn't help that I was beaten up. Every breath was like a scaling knife grating my lungs. There were sore spots all over my face. Whenever I touched a cut or accidentally wiped my face with my forearm, I blinked more pain into my eyes with the rub of chemical agent. More than anything, I longed to stand beneath a shower and let cold water run over me for hours.

Stone spoke to me, his eyes cracking open into red slits, his swollen lips moving. "It's going to be fun," he mumbled, "when they get in. You're going to love it." Then he stopped talking and closed his eyes again.

When they get in. Stone was right. It was only a matter of time before they got determined about that. I had no idea whether they could force their way into the bubble or not, but if they did, they would have access to the armaments room and the Remingtons and flash grenades. Whatever else happened, I didn't want to see them get those weapons. The escalation of the riot would be unthinkable. A siege. An occupied city. But what could I do?

I was sluggish in my thinking, a reaction perhaps to the stress or trauma, or an injury from Stone's beating I did not want to acknowledge. It took me an hour to work through it, the idea forming slowly, and then I understood what I wanted to do. Stone was unconscious. I crept away from the console deck and over him, fearful that he could reach up even though his swollen arms were zipped behind his back. I opened up the hatch and went down into the darkness.

I did not dare turn a light on down below, worried that it would burst brightness into the room above. I let my eyes adjust to the blackness. Could I hide out down here, armed to the fucking teeth? It would not, I decided, prevent the inmates from getting the weapons. I could kill three or five as they came down the hatch stairs before the others got me, and the end result would be the same.

The weapons were stored in the armory lockers. I typed the code into the electronic keypad and opened the doors, then listened for more noise up top. Reassured, I took a moment to squat with my pants down and let the urine drizzle down onto the floor. Then I got busy.

There were six Remington pump-actions in the rack and twelve boxes of cartridges, plus a box of six flashbangs or stun grenades, along with four flashlights, two full sets of riot clothes, and one shield. I clipped a heavy flashlight and two flashbangs to my belt, and then I unhooked one of the Remingtons from the rack, bottom loaded it with two cartridges, and shoved four more cartridges into my pocket. I put the remaining boxes of cartridges into a tool bag and slung the heavy load over my shoulder.

The entrance to the City was taped over with yellow, but at the bottom of the stairs the door was still unlocked. I stepped down, guided by the beam from the flashlight at my waist, and pushed the door open with my foot. The cold, damp air came up at me. I breathed hard in spite of myself, remembering Crowley. There are no ghosts, I told myself, but even so, I did not like the taste of that air in my mouth. Inside, I leaned the Remington against the wall and hauled the bag of shell cartridges into one of the cryptlike cells. In the corner of the floor was a small but open drain. With shaking fingers I poured a box of shells into the hole. Then I opened another box and did the same until I'd gotten rid of each spare shell, except for the two in the Remington and the two in my pocket. Guns don't kill people. Bullets do.

I breathed better as I climbed the stairs out of the City and emerged in the armaments room. I started for the flashbangs, but heard a noise in the bubble above and realized the hatch door had been closed. I'd left it open when I came down, and now I felt the sickness a small animal must feel hiding in a dark cave when a larger animal has returned.

Were they above me? I tried to get my breathing back and listened intensely for mumbled conversation, a footstep, any kind of tell. I heard a thump and a bang, but nothing coherent to give me a picture of the situation. With the loaded Remington I crept skyward, step by step, until I reached the hatch door; then I propped it open a sliver with my hand and tried to see out, but could glimpse nothing. I flung it back, ran the next two steps, and saw Stone, seated in a chair, raking the side of his face against the console deck.

His hands were still zipped. He was trying to operate the switches, randomly I supposed, with insectlike determination. I took two strides to him and yanked him back hard, then kicked the chair away and sent it spinning toward the hatch.

Standing in the bubble, I looked around to get my bearings, see what had changed in my absence. That's when I saw Brother Mike walking through the hub. He wore a flak jacket and a helmet, and in his hands he had a manila envelope. He moved unsurely, like a tourist in a town square. I could imagine him wondering, had human beings done this damage unaided by machine? I waited for him to look my way, to wave or glance—my rescuer. But then two men appeared, picking their way fast through the rubble, dressed literally in loincloths. He did not move until they arrived, and for his patience, they grabbed him roughly, tore the envelope from his hand, put a sack over his head, tied his hands behind his back with strips of cloth, and pushed him forward. He immediately stumbled. One of the men tugged him up, and Brother Mike limped painfully as they hustled him away. Together they disappeared within the tunnel to B block.

I watched him dragged into hell, yet what hurt most was the lack of comfort for me.

45

Roy was unflappable, Josh thought. But whenever Fenton showed up, the two strong-willed men fought like an old married couple, and it didn't matter who could hear. Fenton confronted Roy with issues he'd neglected, called him out publicly on the matter of getting a prompt response to their demands, berated him for the fucked-up situation they found themselves in. Roy made up the most audacious lies on the spot, told Fenton and everyone within earshot that he had already achieved several key concessions, that the warden had been relieved of his duties and the president himself had been told of their demands. He claimed that the media, in trucks and helicopters, had converged on the parking lot and that CNN, Fox, *Entertainment Tonight*, and Geraldo Rivera himself were fighting for the best vantage point.

"You're full of shit, Wobbles, and you know it," Fenton seethed. "You're going to get us all killed and accomplish nothing. We can't get the guns. We don't have the comic book. Nothing you planned is working."

"Is it my fault your handpicked fuckup locked himself in there?" Roy sneered, then built up wind and mocked Fenton as a fear-mongering, nay-saying, cock-sucking do-nothing who could only criticize and never offer a single effective command.

Roy went too far, Josh figured. But Fenton didn't act on his anger, just left. The night getting late, Roy built a little fire outside an abandoned and disassembled drum, as though they were camping, and told him a story about a fishing trip he'd taken with his grandfather as a boy. Josh fell asleep on a mattress thrown over a pile of rubble. He woke up knowing something was wrong. The fire had turned to ashes, barely glowing. He was lying half inside, half outside of one of the ground tier cells. He sensed rather than heard the commotion and started walking, then running to the end of the tier, where Fenton had set up his headquarters, an expanded area of three cells. When he was halfway there, Screen Door met him coming the other way. Her Tammy Faye Baker eyes stared deeply into his own, all dazzled with tears. How many hours had gone by? He swallowed hard and asked Screen Door what was wrong.

"You need to come," she said. "Brother Mike brought the comic book. But Roy's in trouble now. Fenton's too angry to think straight. Maybe you can talk him out of it."

She led him along, holding his hand. Jim Lucky Bones and two other inmates huddled in the hall around their own larger fire and stood to block their way. Screen Door wilted at their menace, but Josh said he'd been called to join Fenton and Roy. Roy's voice bellowed from behind and ordered Josh through.

Jacko met him at the door to Fenton's cell. Over his shoulder Josh saw Brother Mike sitting against the wall, his pant leg rolled up and a long, watery smear of blood on his shin. The cell was full. Fenton, Jacko, and Cooper Lewis. Roy stood next to Brother Mike, and there was something wrong in that. Too close to him, a position of shared accusation.

"Joshy," Roy said, his good humor out of sorts with the situation. "Just in time for the unveiling. It's only right that you should be here."

Cooper Lewis pulled Josh in. There was something wrong with Lewis. His face was streaked with ash, his hair dust-covered, and there was a sluggish thickness in his eyes that made him look pill-heavy and cruel. A shard of metal with a taped-up handle was caught in the waist of his pants, a homemade machete that looked like a scimitar on his belt.

"Is everything okay?" Josh asked. He looked to Fenton for some kind of reassurance, but Fenton ignored him completely.

Roy kept talking. "Brother Mike's been kind enough to bring us Crowley's comic book, Josh, just like we asked. But Billy here hasn't got a drop of gratitude in him. And he doesn't appreciate yours truly much either. He probably thinks he could have gotten the comic book on his own, just by asking. Maybe we didn't need a riot. Maybe we just needed to be more polite."

"Every word that pisses me off, Roy," Fenton said, "I'll remember later. Tell us where it is."

Where what is?

Roy opened the envelope and slid Crowley's comic book out. Not again, Josh thought. The thing he'd tried to get rid that kept coming back. And still, it was with a held breath that he saw it opened. Crowley's work and his lines sharing the same pages. What seemed like many years ago.

"What we have here," Roy began, holding it up, "is a record of the work of Earl Hammond."

"What are you talking about, Roy?" Brother Mike said, an irritable old man, intolerant of fools.

Roy flipped pages for them all to view. Josh thought he knew every image by heart, but he saw it differently now, all of it more detailed and ornate. The convoluted walls of the city folded inward like a rose and became street walls, building walls, chamber walls. Roy stopped in the middle, where a battle raged, the city overrun. An army of men in masks, some with long beaks, some with large frog's eyes, swarmed the cobbled streets riding black horses with dogs' heads and lizards' tails, the men and women below them begging for mercy, everything on fire, as though the world were being consumed by hatred—a conflagration of murder, lust, violence, and disease.

"Hammond wanted records of everything, Brother Mike," Roy said. "Every transaction, every deal. You see, he thought we should run things like a real business. Record revenues. Tally costs and expenses. Reconcile it all annually, pay dividends out to shareholders, and keep lots and lots for himself. But in his genius, he put all the details in code. He got someone, probably someone like Crowley or Josh here, to draw pictures that would symbolize the activities of his organization and the amounts that were earned. That way, no one but the parties involved understood the details."

"Read it, Wobbles," Fenton said. "Get to the point."

"You don't read it so much as decipher it. A horse isn't just a horse, Billy, it's a delivery of heroin. A dismembered woman is a punk sold off for sex. Each page in this book is a quarter of a year. Every step, brick, window, sword, spear, and decapitated head stands for services that got bought and traded, and how much was dealt and how much got earned by it. This is a spreadsheet of every operation Hammond was ever involved in."

"You're insane," Brother Mike hissed. "How could Crowley know those details? He wasn't here then."

"We found the files, Brother Mike. I figured out your stupid code, and Crowley got everything you had in there from Hammond, all the old drawings and numbers. Then he recorded it all here, in a single book."

The anger surged in Brother Mike, and Josh barely recognized him.

"I told Jon about Hammond's life, not his criminal dealings. This book is the story of a brave man who tried to change other men's hearts. And you've turned that hope into violence. You evil man. You're making it all up. You lie and you lie."

Roy looked offended. "Why is it just because I hate to tell the truth, everyone thinks I lie? You're so naive it's a laugh. You think Crowley wanted your spiritual guidance? You think Hammond did?"

"Where's the money, Roy?" Fenton asked. "I'm not even kidding. You tell me where it is, and at this point I may even let you live to see the morning."

"Patience, Billy. Crowley figured it out, that rascal, and he wrote it down here, on the last page, the one page he wouldn't let me see, just out of spite. So let's take a look."

Roy turned the comic book over to the back and flipped it open. They all crowded in, fighting for a glimpse.

On the last page Josh saw the drawing of the Beggar in a room at the top of a tower, sitting naked like a Buddha, his misshapen bald head finally revealed, the skull tattooed with some bizarre spiderweb that spread with little order, like cracks in a window. What Josh liked about the drawing was the sense that the confined space had opened up. The roof of the tower was broken, and above were sky and birds and the sun and a snowcapped mountain—and a hint that confinement was an impossibility. It was a peaceful image to Josh, in a story that was otherwise wrinkled and torn with violence, a cliché of escape, like something you'd see painted on the side of an old van, but the image had been raw and poignant to him as Crowley described what he wanted. Trapped in Ditmarsh, the drawing was Josh's own wish, too, that he could travel to other worlds via his very brain.

"You remember this, Josh?" Roy asked.

"I remember it."

He remembered every line on the page, and how Crowley had, for once, given him the freedom to expand on it how he liked, without limits. It had come from his imagination.

"What are we looking for?" Jacko asked.

"A bank account number," Roy said. "The money is in a bank account, Crowley told me. All we need is the account number and pass code, and it's ours. Crowley put it here on the last page. But I can't read these images. It's not the code we used to use."

"I don't think he was trying to say anything about numbers, Roy," Josh said quietly, and then wished he hadn't.

Faster than Josh would have thought possible, Cooper Lewis pushed past him and stretched out with his machete, tucking it into Roy's neck, tilting back his head.

"Stop him!" Brother Mike said.

"Easy, Cooper," Roy said, as if his mouth were full. "Don't be rash."

"Not yet," Fenton said, and Cooper kept his hand steady, white spots showing up on his knuckles. "Where's the fucking account number, Roy?"

"Well, it's not in my neck," Roy said. "And if you give me a few more minutes to think, we'll puzzle this out."

A few more minutes. Roy had kept up his patronizing tone when he spoke to Fenton, but he looked pale to Josh, the desperation tainting the color of his skin, as though poison were working its way through his system. At Fenton's nod, Cooper Lewis pulled the machete back, and Josh wondered if he could turn and run for the tunnel, chase after Keeper Wallace. He didn't belong here with these men. But could he leave Brother Mike behind?

"These words, Josh," Roy said. "Did Crowley tell you anything about them?"

Josh was startled because he remembered no words. He leaned in awkwardly, the thought of running so strong that half his molecules were leaning in the other direction already. Then he forgot himself and tried to understand. The words were written in small print along the bottom of the page, two lines, like the beginning or the end of a poem.

"What does it say?" Fenton asked.

Jacko read, "'Humpty Dumpty stuffed in a cave. Humpty Dumpty dug his own grave.' That's it. What the hell does Humpty Dumpty have to do with anything?"

"Shut up and let me think," Roy said.

Twenty seconds went by, and Roy said nothing. The quiet tightened and strained in Josh's throat.

"Crowley used to sing a Humpty Dumpty song all the time," Josh said, unable to let another second go by. "The first day I met him, he was singing, '*Humpty Dumpty sat on a wall, Humpty Dumpty had a fuck of a fall. All the king's horses and all the king's men, couldn't put Humpty Dumpty together again.*'"

"Why was he singing that?" Jacko asked.

"I thought he was talking about himself because his arm was broken and it was like he'd fallen and couldn't be put back together."

"Fell a few times," Cooper Lewis said. "Sure as fuck."

"Humpty Dumpty is Hammond," Roy said. "You just count the letters in Humpty and add the D. Take away the umpty, which is empty. We coded him that way."

Josh couldn't tell if Roy was telling the truth or making up lies on the spot.

"So this message means what?" Jacko said. "Hammond's dead?"

"How does that help us?" Fenton asked.

"He's telling us to look somewhere," Roy said. "The account number must be written on another page."

And he began turning.

"Maybe there's a picture of a grave inside," Jacko suggested, and he took the book from Roy's hands and flipped faster, but found nothing.

Cooper Lewis laughed. "Look all you want. Wobbles has been playing us." And he turned the homemade machete again with an easy twist of his wrist.

Josh breathed out and knew he needed to begin talking. He wanted to tell them about the caverns and tunnels underneath Ditmarsh and all the demons that lived there. He wanted to tell them the stories Crowley had told him about the Beggar. He felt that if he could tell a story that was long enough and convincing enough, the sun might come up and turn these trolls to stone. But he had no such story in him.

"Crowley wrote 'dig' on the door when he was locked down in the old hole. I think that's Hammond's grave," Josh said.

They all stared at him, even Brother Mike.

"Bullshit," Cooper Lewis said.

"How do you know that?" Fenton asked.

"A guard told me. It's the truth. He wrote 'dig' before he died. That must be what he's telling us. We need to look down there."

It caught them. The idea of Crowley writing 'dig' was just strange enough and distracting enough to be worthy of pursuit. He could sense that they were on the edge between believing him and dismissing him, and that they needed a push. But he had nothing left in his mouth.

"Hammond was down there a long time," Roy said. "That's where he dug his grave. I bet he scratched the account number into the rocks. That's what Crowley's telling us to do, right here on this page. Go down there and dig and find it for ourselves. I bet that's why the jacks put him down there. Crowley told them it's where Hammond put the account number, only Crowley never gave it up, and that's why they let him rot."

It still seemed possible for the story to go one way or the other. Then Jacko moved it to the place where they all believed in it and needed to do something.

"How are we going to get in there?" Jacko said. "We can't break in. We've been trying to get those weapons."

"Breaking in is not a problem," Fenton said. "I just need to turn my attention to that obstacle."

He pulled Brother Mike up from the floor.

46

My leg was numb. My mouth was pasty and my head heavy for lack of water. I kept nodding off and pinching my cheeks to remain awake. I suppose I lost that battle. How else to explain the dreamy shock, the slippage in my attention when it happened? A bang came from above. I looked toward the ceiling of the bubble.

"This is it," Stone mumbled. "Finally."

I knelt, the Remington in my arms, facing the door in order to brace myself from the kick of the gun when I shot. Peering out, I saw three inmates standing around the entrance to the bubble. They were lifting concrete chunks and heaving them at the shatterproof glass. They swung pipes that landed against the cage in heavy clangs. It seemed pathetic and useless, a choreography meant to intimidate and antagonize rather than accomplish anything, but the noise got me deep in that place where fear puddles and turns you a little helpless.

"They're not getting in here, Stone." I argued with myself as much as him. "You can hope all you want. They're never getting in."

But I gripped the Remington tighter just the same and wished I'd saved more shells.

One of the men outside raised his arms to hail me and yelled. I couldn't hear a word over the clanging. He gestured for the others to stop and yelled again, holding the business end of a CO shoulder radio up to his mouth this time.

I stood in plain sight to see him better, safe enough in the bubble. I didn't understand. The inmate couldn't contact me by radio with just the mouthpiece. The CO who owned it had probably destroyed the walkie-talkie receiver before he was taken. We were supposed to do that. It was the fourth or fifth most important thing to do in a riot, just before you got taken hostage.

I heard a *fitz* in my own console then, and lifted the console radio. Outside, the inmate waved as if I'd finally understood, and scampered away.

"Told you," Stone said. "They're fucking coming."

I had a fantasy of turning the Remington on Stone and shooting him on the floor like a car-struck deer on the side of the road.

Once again the radio snapped and sparked, and this time I heard a voice.

"Officer Williams, are those your catlike steps?"

I knew then who it was, but I didn't answer or acknowledge any connection between us.

"Hey now, Officer Williams, you got to listen better than that. We want in to the bubble. We'll be there in five minutes, and you're going to put down all weapons, open the door, and step aside. If you do that, I give you my word, you won't be hurt."

"Why would I do that?" I asked.

"You will do it," he said. "I'll show you why you're going to do it."

He stopped talking. I waited for more. Was he trying to sweet-talk me into complying? Was he as deranged as that? Then I heard a voice again, a direction that sounded as clipped as something an air-traffic control tower worker might say to a pilot. "Watch your monitor."

My instinct was to resist any command, but my eye was drawn over to the console deck. One of the screens had come to life. They must have taken off the blanket, I thought, and then I felt a cold hand on my throat.

A hostage knelt on the floor of the range, back straight, blindfolded. At first I thought he was an inmate, because he wore inmate clothes, but I recognized the jawline, the uptightness of his posture, the slope of his shoulders. Ruddik.

Three inmates stood around him. They wore sacks with eyeholes over their heads.

One of them pulled Ruddik's blindfold away.

"What are you doing?" I said.

A second hooded figure held the radio to Ruddik's lips. He stumbled over the script, trying to remember.

"For the last eighteen months," Ruddik began, "I've been a federal investigator in this prison, posing as a corrections officer."

It was impossible not to listen. I felt sucked in by his confession.

"I have propagated a network of informants. I have entrapped inmates with drug buys. I've traced a large-size payment to the Keeper. I've shown that the warden and the assistant warden profit from companies that provide the institution with supplies and facility maintenance. All of these business dealings must be investigated further. I have. . . . The contraband problem in this prison—the root—the real criminals are the corrections officers."

A hard kick to the back and a flinch of pain as he hesitated or forgot his lines. My stomach flipped over at the way his body jerked forward and reset itself.

"I have entrapped inmates unjustly. I have relied on false evidence. I have built up a dossier of false information about the criminal activities of innocent inmates. Because of this, I am directly responsible for the violence that has happened today."

A change came over Ruddik's demeanor. For the first time, I saw fear smear across his face, and his voice began to warble. The last sentences he spoke were unintelligible. "I have—" he said, and tried again, and again.

"What's going on?" Stone called out.

"Good enough," a voice on the radio said.

One of the hooded inmates stood directly behind Ruddik and held his shoulders tight. A second grabbed his head and tilted it back by the hair. Ruddik began to twist and buck. I saw a metal sword in the third inmate's hand rise up to Ruddik's throat.

"Oh, Jesus, no," I said, and then yelled into the microphone, "Don't!"

My limbs had gone all tingly. I pleaded for it to stop, for the event to reverse itself. Ruddik thrashed harder at the touch of the long curved blade, thrusting his body violently to the sides, but the man behind him held him upright with a knee pressed into his back, and the third man grabbed his hair and tilted his head back, exposing his throat.

I looked. I watched. It was all I could give him. I wanted him to know that my eyes were on him and that he was not alone with those animals. Stone screamed that I was next, sounding like a hyena shackled to the floor, a rabid, frothing beast. When the sword moved, I flinched, but it was just a graceful slide across Ruddik's throat. The relief drained through me as I realized they'd spared him. They'd made the cutting gesture but faked the awful act. Then, most horribly, his neck opened up, the skin peeled away like a sudden manic smile, and a soft gray spray shot forth, gentle as a dolphin aspirating a puff of water into the air. The blood seemed to activate the hooded man's fury. He began to saw across Ruddik's throat with vigor, back and forth, while Ruddik's torso twitched and fought for balance. The cut wedged its way beyond a balance point so that a great yawn suddenly opened and the weight of Ruddik's head tipped backward. Then something soft happened, and the body fell forward, gracefully, like a tumbled tree, Ruddik's head held up by the inmate's fist.

"If you don't let us in," a voice said into the radio, breathing hard, "we do it again."

One of the hooded men stepped on Ruddik's back and forced the blood to roll out in a last great gush.

I threw up. I couldn't stop the shaking, and I couldn't stop myself from glancing up to Ruddik's body on the ground, alone now, his head resting on his own back like a balanced stone.

I couldn't ask God. I couldn't ask Ruddik. I couldn't ask Brother Mike. I had only one source for answers, and I paced the room, screaming at him, walking circles. Every time my revolution brought me close to him, I got into his face. "Why are they doing this!"

Stone's lungs, full of fluid, sputtered as he laughed.

So I smashed the butt of the Remington down on his knee.

"Who are you?" I asked. "Who the fuck are you?"

"Fuck you!" he said through snot and pain.

So I smashed the other kneecap like I was breaking rock.

He howled and moaned and twisted and tried to bring his knees up to his hands and roll around to grip them, but the zip cuffs just tightened. I found the CA bottle on the floor and shook it.

"Why is this happening?"

"I don't know!" he said.

I sprayed it straight into my hand, cupping the liquid in my palm, and reached down for his face. He squirmed and twisted away. I held my hand next to his mouth and nose.

"Money," he answered. "Hammond's money."

The liquid dripped through my fingers, little acid splotches. Hammond's money?

"What do you mean?" I yelled. "Tell me everything."

"You're going to die," he told me.

So I drove my finger into his eye slit and rubbed the eyeball hard.

I heard the banging outside and stood up, my breath heaving in my throat. I'd forgotten they were coming, as if days had passed since they'd spoken. I was more animal than human, some wild thing found in the forest who couldn't understand language or even gestures.

A dozen men outside, four of them hooded, visitors calling, waiting for me.

When I didn't move or answer, one of the inmates lurched a hooded man forward and twisted him down to his knees. The hood came off, and I saw that it was Brother Mike, dignified, tousle-haired. The blade rose and settled in on his neck.

I thought for one second about lifting the Remington up and roaring out, firing away, killing a few. Instead, I flung the shotgun against the wall and pulled back the iron slide and gave them entry. They tore the door away from my hands and poured in.

47

The sack was putrid, and Josh could barely breathe. Nothing but darkness. He stumbled at a step, not knowing it was there, and got shoved forward. He fell, expecting stairs and landing on floor. A minute later someone ripped the hood from his head and he looked up and around. Jacko stepped away and ripped the hood off Roy. It was a ruse, Fenton had assured them, a way of increasing the number of apparent hostages and holding off any violent attack. A jack slumped against the wall, his chin on his chest, the side of his head cracked like rotten fruit. A man in civilian clothes sat on the floor, his hands behind his back, his face a melted mess, like candle wax. Officer Williams lay on the ground propped on one elbow, one knee up, staring, wild with hate. Cooper Lewis aimed a shotgun at her, paused in that fierce moment before firing, the aim of the barrels pinning her in place.

"It's about fucking time," the man on the floor said. "Cut me loose."

"What happened to you, Boyd?" Fenton asked. "Where are all those guns you were supposed to get?"

"Ask this bitch before I choke her to death."

Fenton smiled. "You're the bitch." He pulled the machete from Cooper Lewis's belt, stepped toward the man, and drew the blade along his throat. Once again Josh wished he could have squeezed his eyes faster and kept them shut. The man fell back, coughing a pink spray, and his neck opened up to show the meat inside. Then his feet and knees started jumping and bobbing while his shoulders made twitchy shrugs and the blood that spurted out of his neck alternated between a fanning stream and abrupt, pulsing splashes. It took a long minute, all of them watching, before the dancing stuttered to a few final twitches.

Her face had been sprayed by the pink mist. Her mouth was twisted up with puckered disgust.

Fenton dropped the machete to the ground. "Let's get on with it," he said, and he hauled Officer Williams up, then led her by the scruff of the neck, like a child or an errant dog.

"That's the way down, Fenton," Roy said, nodding toward the back of the room.

Jacko flung open a large metal flap set into the floor. Fenton forced Officer Williams ahead of him, and when they neared the open hatch, he heaved her forward, flinging her headfirst into the hole, and she disappeared into the dark pit. "What are you doing!" Brother Mike yelled. In answer, Cooper Lewis swung the barrel of the shotgun across the old man's jaw, hurtling Brother Mike backward, clocking his head hard against the floor.

Fenton pounded down the stairs after her. Roy looked back for a moment and then followed, hobbling on his peg leg. Jacko waited, eyeing Lewis, eyeing Brother Mike. Josh breathed in and out, numbed by the quickness of it all. He'd misread Fenton's soul. He'd thought Fenton killed Boyd as a way of protecting her, but nothing could have prepared Josh for the disdain that came next, the way Fenton threw her down the stairs. A bag of garbage to him, a lifeless manequin.

"Help me carry him down," Jacko said. He meant Brother Mike, and he gave Josh a meaningful look. Do this with me. Don't hesitate. Don't get either of us in trouble. And so Josh, with all the cowardice in his heart, slung his arms through Brother Mike's arms, clasping him to his chest, and eased his weight up while Jacko got the legs. Brother Mike was awake, but his head rolled and his eyes looked glassy. They reached the stairs, and Josh backed down first, fearful of slipping and tumbling down. Jacko's help gave way. Josh stumbled with the sudden shift in weight, but reset his feet, cradled Brother Mike better, and pulled him down as gently as he could, legs dragging down each step. Gasping hard now, Josh hauled him to the side of the room and propped him against a wall.

Turning, he got a better look at her condition. She lay facedown on the floor, her torso twisted sideways, one leg bent, the other stretched long, the foot twisting slowly. She spit bloody drool from the corner of her mouth.

Fenton and Roy disappeared down the next set of stairs. There was no indication that anyone should follow. Josh looked around the room. A dark arched ceiling, an open cabinet with shotguns vertical inside, like a row of hockey sticks. Jacko stood before the cabinet, pumping each shotgun in turn, then dropping it with a clatter, bending over and tossing through empty shell boxes, increasingly desperate in his search for something. He muttered about bullets, and Lewis screamed at him to find them, and then Lewis screamed at Officer Williams. He called her a fucking bitch and stuck the barrels of the shotgun into the back of her head. Her arms rose up the way you do when you're arrested, and her fists clenched into tight balls. Josh strode toward Lewis, reaching for the gun, and told him to stop. He heard Jacko yell, and Lewis turned. The shotgun snarled and bit the air, and a wind flipped Josh over.

His heart was pounding. It wasn't that bad, he told himself, as soon as his breathing came back. On one knee, both hands on the floor, he looked down and saw cloth and bloody skin hanging from his shin, and tried to hobble up. But when he put weight on the foot of his injured leg, he dropped over as though he'd been kicked, all numbness and fire from his hip down. It calmed him to lie on his back and look up at the ceiling. His hand was pressed into the shin, and when he pulled it away, something came with it, heavy and wet, like a piece of liver.

Jacko put a hand on Josh's chest and told him to stay still. Lewis came into his vision, the shotgun still in his arms, and asked him if he was all right, then screamed at Jacko for startling him.

Suddenly Roy stood over him, returned from wherever he'd been. There was a sneer of disgust on his face. It was anger, Josh thought. He's pissed at me.

"What's going on up here, you goddamn fools?" Roy asked, not taking his eyes from Josh.

"He shot him," Brother Mike said.

"Shut up!" Lewis screamed, and thrust the gun at Brother Mike this time.

Take the gun from him, Josh said, but he wasn't sure the words came out.

"How you feeling, kid?" Roy asked him.

Every nerve in his body felt seared by the shock of what had been done to him, but he felt surprisingly okay. He was going to be fine.

"I'm all right," he said. "It fucking stings like hell."

Jacko laughed. Roy looked to Lewis.

"You're smart. Fenton loves this kid, and you shoot him in the fucking leg. You figure what happened to Boyd up there was an accident?"

"I know it wasn't no fucking accident," Lewis said.

"Great, your IQ must have jumped fifty points. It's a thrill to be working with a crew of such fucking geniuses. Maybe you want to tie Josh's leg off and make sure he doesn't bleed for the next few hours." Roy waited for Jacko to come into action, shook his head in dismay at Lewis again, and descended once more down the second stairs.

"I'm okay," Josh said.

Jacko told him, "Hold still. We'll get this tight."

Josh couldn't feel where his knee or foot was, all of it asleep and numb. He propped himself up on his elbows and watched Jacko work the stretch of cloth around his thigh.

"I think I got it," Jacko said.

"It's seeping," Officer Williams said. "Tie it tighter."

He looked over, surprised by her voice, pleased that she seemed stronger. She was sitting up. Her face was scraped, but her eyes were clear. He felt very calm staring at her.

"You shut the fuck up!" Lewis said.

Her mouth opened and closed. Then she stared at the floor, about halfway to Josh, and said nothing.

A silence came over them all. The only noise was the scuff of Cooper Lewis's shoes as he walked around and around the room.

Minutes went by. Lewis stopped pacing and stood facing the wall, his forehead touching it, like a chastised student. A long while. At least twenty breaths. Then he muttered, "Bitch," and started pacing again.

Josh felt an old hate surge up in him. He remembered, out of nowhere, the sensation of Lewis's finger pushing in past his lips and rubbing his teeth. Would that memory ever go away? Something flinched inside him, and he gasped, a piercing sound like a kettle whistle in his throat. He looked down at his leg and pulled himself back on his bottom, away from the source of the sudden pain, the leg trailing after him.

"Kid's not even twenty, Cooper," Jacko said. "And you fuck him up like that."

"Fuck, fuck, fuck," Lewis said, and paced the room faster.

"You need to calm yourself down, Cooper," Brother Mike said.

Lewis stopped, turned on them again, and screamed, "I'm fucking sorry, all right! I didn't mean to fucking do it!"

And he began to pace again. Officer Williams kept her eyes averted from him. No matter how close he came, she didn't look up, only flinched when he screamed bitch in her face and walked away again.

Josh wanted to keep the animal away from her. Then he clenched up again, some throb that pulsed through his thigh and shot up into his chest. It felt as though his leg were stretched out over a hot, roaring flame and the rest of him lay on the floor in front of the fireplace.

A calmness came back when the pain subsided again, and he tried to think it through. He'd end up in the infirmary, maybe in his old cell. Cell number 3. Crowley had been in DI-2. And then he remembered, all over again, that Crowley was gone. Somewhere below them, Roy and Fenton were digging in the place Crowley had spent his last few days. A wind chime. He looked up at Officer Williams. The soft line of her chin and nose. Your friend's a wind chime. He remembered her in the car, sitting beside him, how free he'd felt and how useless that freedom had been. Crowley died in a dark cave. Humpty Dumpty dug his own grave. He kept thinking about that final command, the call to dig.

"She's going to make it up to you," Lewis said. He stopped his pacing so suddenly everyone looked up. "Yes, sir. She's going to make it up to you."

"Don't make it worse," Brother Mike said.

Lewis plunged his hand down as if into water and grabbed her by the back of the hair, twisting her head up, forcing a gasp out of her.

"You say one more word, one more word, and I pull this trigger."

He stared Brother Mike down until he was sure the old man complied; then he turned his attention to her.

"Make it up to Josh," he told her. "He's only twenty, right, Jacko? You remember what that was like." A laugh, then serious again. He leaned over and hissed something into her ear, her face pulling away from his breath.

"Do it," he said.

"You do it yourself," she answered. He twisted her hair in his fist and pushed her toward Josh.

"Do it," he repeated.

She didn't move, as if hoping he would go away.

"I will pull this trigger right now unless you do it. Five, four." And he pressed the gun barrels against the back of her head again.

Something in her changed, a collapse in the sternness of her face, and she was crying as she started across the floor on her hands and knees toward Josh. Lewis thrust her forward with his shoe on her rear, forcing her to crawl faster.

No one spoke. They all watched silently, fearful of their own lives and sick with the shame. But there was nothing they could do in the face of that insanity.

She reached Josh where he lay, frozen and confused, and Lewis said, "Three," and she moved again, just her hands this time, trembling as she unbuttoned his pants and pulled them down over his hips.

"You see?" Lewis said, a smile come over him. "Now you know he's only twenty. Look at the fucking boner rising up. Good to go even when shot. Do it! Two, one."

Josh couldn't help the erection. He wanted to tell her that. It was not in his power to stop it. And suddenly he was thinking of Stephanie, and his drawings of her, and the night when he'd arrived at her house with his father's gun and demanded that she be with him again, that she kiss him, make love to him. It was his punishment to relive that awful moment, to have his erection surge upward in spite of all the shame he felt and even the injury to his leg, with the others watching, with Brother Mike watching, a gun at her head, and her trembling hands touching him as she wept.

And then the fumbling stopped and her hands fell away.

"I can't," she said.

He shut his eyes. He did not want to see her life end in a spray of blood and brains.

"What in the hell are you doing?"

Roy stood at the top of the stairs, very still, watching Lewis.

No one had the courage to speak up.

"You sick skinner bastard," Roy said. "Did someone fuck your mommy and make you watch when you were a snot-nosed kid?"

Lewis's gun lifted to Roy. "She's going to make it up to him. She's going to suck him off. Or she's going to suck on this gun."

"Oh, she is, huh?" And he waited, as if daring Cooper Lewis to act.

"Did you find it, Roy?" Jacko said. "Can we get the fuck out of here now?"

Josh wanted to hear yes, but Roy shook his head instead, eyes still on Lewis. "It says dig all right. But I guess we need to dig deeper. I never seen Fenton so mad."

Josh knew what he had to do. He struggled to pull his pants back up, embarrassed and angry, and he called out for their attention.

"I know where he is, Roy," Josh said. "You get Lewis away from us. You tell Fenton to let her go, and I'll tell you where Hammond is."

He wondered if they understood what he was offering them. Roy only stared.

"What do you mean where Hammond is?" Roy asked. There was no mockery in his tone, no dismissal.

"He's here," Josh said. "In Ditmarsh. I figured out what Crowley was telling us. You'll never find him unless I tell you."

"He's here?" Roy asked again.

"I'll tell you where when you let her go."

Roy tipped his head back and laughed. "In Ditmarsh all along." He bellowed down the stairs into the darkness for Fenton to come up.

"They'll kill him," Brother Mike said. "He's helpless."

"What do you want from me?" Josh asked.

Brother Mike didn't answer.

48 ||||||||||||||

Fenton looked as though he'd been digging for coal, his hands and face black, his eyes buggy. Josh wouldn't tell them what they wanted to know until I was free of them, and Fenton said I'd be free enough, locked in down there. Josh agreed and let them toss me down into the darkness.

It hurt bad. I lay at the bottom of the dark stair, and I couldn't see a thing, not even a crack of light where the door must have been. It was so black I wondered if I were unconscious or floating through space. I winced when I pushed myself up. Pain is weakness leaving the body, the recruitment poster said, but I knew that pain was gravity attaching you to the here and now. I crawled into the first narrow cell, out of the hallway, out of the line of sight, and sat up against the wall.

A minute later, maybe ten minutes, I heard the door open. I wondered if it was my rescue or my end. The light did not fill the dark passage outside but splashed through like a passing current. I heard a heavy thud, a groan, and a cry. I knew it had to be another body tumbling down.

"Brother Mike?" I called. I listened but heard nothing. Then the scraping sound of someone crawling. I should have gone out and found him, but I waited instead, still paralyzed with my own fear and the failure that smothered any desire to help.

"It's me," the voice said, and the creature slithered in to join me.

Josh, my rescuer, leaned up against the other wall. I heard him pant and groan.

"They're gone now," he said. "There's no reason for them to come back."

I nodded and closed my eyes.

Hours went by, I presume, or only seconds. I woke up in the same absolute darkness and wondered if he was still present or if the arrival had been a dream. I nudged his foot with my own and heard him cry out and start to cough. I wanted to know he was still with me.

A little strength had come over me. I felt a touch of the old me creeping back in. Resilience is the last thing to go. It keeps surging back like a forgotten tide, even when you think it has been banished for good. It was followed by anger. Disdain. Maybe loneliness, the great force beneath everything that keeps mashing us together.

"You told them that Hammond is here?" I asked him. "Why did they believe you?"

"Because it's true," he said. "He's been here all along. Crowley knew. That's what he was telling us."

My brain moved slowly, muffled by the darkness, the gears in it cranked and turned.

"Is Hammond Roy?" I asked. All along.

He coughed. The sound didn't go anywhere, just flapped from his chest and stopped in the air.

"No," he said. "It was dig."

I waited.

"The *G* was a six. Ditmarsh infirmary six," Josh said. "I was in Ditmarsh infirmary three. Crowley was in DI-two. Hammond in DI-six. I figured it out."

I tried to think it through and understand. DI-6? I counted down the cells in my mind and came to the one where the man with no fingers or toes, no face, sat on the edge of his cot and waited for the world outside to go by.

"That's Hammond?"

There were prisons within prisons, Ruddik had said. I was stunned by the thought that Hammond had been returned to Ditmarsh. Maybe Hammond shot himself. Maybe someone shot him. And when he was helpless and harmless and they had no other place to put him, they brought him back and abandoned him to a mute and solitary existence, his identity obliterated.

"I didn't know it was Hammond. I had no idea until now. But Crowley spent a lot of time with him," Josh said. "I didn't like to go near. Roy knew I was right. As soon as I told them."

The darkness around us. We were two voices and no physical bodies. We might have been talking on the telephone.

"What about Brother Mike?" I asked. "What did they do with him?"

I heard Josh shift, and then his voice came from lower than before, closer to the ground.

"They took him," he said, almost a whisper. "I asked them not to. I should have made a better deal."

"Why did they put you down here?"

He didn't answer, and I got used to the silence again.

"I'm cold," he complained, and the voice came from far away.

I'd like to say that my response was immediate, that I slid over to my rescuer with the little strength I could still summon and lay down beside him, that I put my arms around him and shared my warmth. I'd like to say that the impulse was natural and human and immediate, but it wasn't. I let him lay there alone for a long, long time.

His breathing became my stumbling metronome. When the metronome faltered, I waited for it to begin again, and I started to cry. I willed myself away from the wall and over to him. I found his form on the ground, lying on his back, and I stretched out beside him on the hard, damp stone. At first I put my hand on his chest; then I touched his forehead and his face, and rested my hand on his forearm, my mouth next to his ear. When he twitched, I slid my hand down further and grasped his hand in mine and imagined a little clench.

"I feel very close to him now," he said.

The words startled me. Did he mean Crowley, or did he mean his father? Someone on the other side. I had the feeling that there were explanations lingering inside him. You could call them confessions, or you could call them ghosts. Thoughts, hopes, regrets, things he wanted to release by telling me but couldn't any longer because he had slipped off. So instead of listening to those things, I told him it was going to be okay.

What was it like to die? Were you alone with your infinite thoughts and memories, a sense of greater existence, or did you feel the presence of others close to you? Was it enough to feel that presence, or did the overwhelming desire to reach someone cause you pain? Was that what eternal peace meant—an untethering, a drifting away from the pain of love, an understanding of its boundless power?

I heard the footsteps and the voice calling out, and I wondered, with a terrified tensing up of my stiff body, who it could be.

"Kali?" the voice called. "Kali, are you in here?"

The footsteps came closer. Keeper Wallace was calling my name. My eyes had become used to the darkness. When the door moved, I saw him standing there, filling its opening. He had a rifle in his hands and he was alone. The rifle clattered to the stones. He bent, his arms came under my back, and I felt myself rising up.

"Put your arms around my neck."

I hung my arms around his neck.

We climbed the stairs, my body rising up into the blinding light.

"Josh," I said. "We need to bring Josh."

"It's okay," Wallace said. "We'll get him later."

It took me seconds to blink my vision back. I saw Stone lying on the floor, a tangle of pink laundry on his chest. I saw Cutler sitting against the wall. The brightness of morning outside, but more dazzling than that. Flooded by fire hoses, Ditmarsh had become a castle made of ice. The floor of the hub covered in a translucent lava. Some of the beams and bars and railings dripping with the same opaque, stiffened candle wax, and all of it glittered in the first sunlight. I'd never seen it so brilliant.

I saw soldiers moving toward us slowly, spread out in formation, rifles in that familiar angled point, carefully walking the ice.

49

The same country road, the same rutted turnoff into the woods. Though most of the snow was gone, the trees and bushes were still skeletal. I tried to imagine a verdant burst of spring, the tangle of green choking the path, hiding the way. I wanted to see Brother Mike's house in the woods turn into something from a fairy tale, a place to dwell forever.

There was nothing but stillness when I pulled into the yard. I got out of the Land Rover and climbed the steps of the porch. I did not like the quiet, and I felt anxious rapping on the door. There was no answer. I turned the knob and pushed. The door stuck on the floor and then pried free. I called out and heard his voice answer weakly from within.

I had hoped for tea, even for one of those cookies, but he was in no condition for hosting. He'd described it on the phone as his "bad state" when I'd called to check on him. I saw the evidence now. The air in the room was slightly sour. He looked sallow, unhealthy. I guessed that he'd eaten very little. I said hello and sat down across from him.

"How are you?" he finally asked.

"Better," I said. And though it was a lie, I knew by now that the lie was going to become true. Eventually I would be better, maybe even whole. I still felt shame and grief and anger and fear, but the emotions were no longer as corrosive. I did not wake up every night and stare at the ceiling with my heart thudding in my chest. It stopped happening when I realized that Josh was with me. I felt very close to him now that he was dead. That still bothered me. It wasn't an easy or a comforting thought, to know I was linked to him forever, but it had become my reality.

"I'm very glad," he said, and added, "I'm still struggling."

There were many questions I wanted to ask him, but I did not know how to begin. Would the answers cause him more pain? I knew that whatever was eroding him had something to do with his basic beliefs. My own beliefs were flimsy and flexible. They could be reshaped. I was already molding them to make sense of things I would never have believed months before. But the impact on him was heavier than that, more structural. Some fundamental aspect of his universe had collapsed, and life in the aftermath was a difficult adjustment.

"I have a task," he said, "that I've been putting off for some time. I'm wondering, since you're here, if you would help me take care of it?"

The way he said it, it could have been a drain that needed snaking or a will that needed a witness's signature.

"Of course," I said.

That seemed to liven him slightly. He stood up stiffly, as though bothered by chronic pain, and walked into the kitchen. I followed. At the back porch, he found a large hammer and asked me to carry it.

We put on boots and crossed the backyard to the kiln.

"I'm having some difficulty bending over," he said. "So I was wondering if you would crawl in there for me and retrieve the pieces of pottery that are inside. It will be dirty work, I'm afraid."

"Sure," I said.

I lifted the tarp that covered the entrance. Still dark in there, but no longer as warm.

"Do you have a flashlight back at the house?" I asked. "I might trip and break something."

"Don't worry about it," he answered.

There was no arguing. I hunched over and made my way inside.

My eyesight adjusted to the darkness. I did not realize until I was standing inside that a closed dark space would bring back the anxieties. I felt a little bite of fear on the back of my neck, and my heart rate became more rapid. But that was then, and this was different. I saw the bowls and vases and cups along the shelves. They were cold to the touch. I took a vase in each hand and headed back down the tunnel. At this rate it would take me a very long time indeed to retrieve each precious item.

I handed the large vase carefully to Brother Mike when I was outside. It was beautiful, I decided. I was not normally one for precious objects, but this warped clay, formed by fire, moved me.

Brother Mike took it from my hands and tossed it away. It landed with a heavy thud on the hard ground.

"What are you doing?" I asked.

"It's ruined," he said. "I should have retrieved them at most two days after the firing. It's been six weeks. The humidity got to them."

He picked up the hammer and swung it down, obliterating the vase with one smash.

I did not pass over the other vase.

"But it's beautiful," I said. It was slightly shrunken perhaps, but exquisite. "Didn't you tell me that the unpredictable results of the firing were all part of the process?"

"Kali," he said patiently. "I have pieces in collections all over the world. Trust me. I know what needs to be done."

He took the vase from my grip and tossed it down. "And besides, it's therapeutic."

I did not share his view, but despite my reluctance, I went back for more. With each trip I handed him another couple of precious items, and he tossed, swung, and smashed. I gave up on the niceties and began rolling them down the tunnel ahead of me, until I could no longer stand the bad air and needed a break. I felt like a coal miner working a seam.

Outside, sweating from the latent heat and the exertion, I ran my hand across my forehead. Brother Mike started to laugh.

"What is it?" I asked, self-conscious.

"If you could see yourself covered in soot and sweat. You finally look like your namesake. Kali, the destroyer of worlds."

"I've been waiting for the right moment to reveal myself."

It was good to see his smile.

By the late afternoon we were inside again and drinking that tea I'd wanted.

"I'm sorry you were left down there," he said.

I did not want to think about that place and those things, and I did not blame him for them. I only wished there were pockets of time that could be utterly forgotten.

"Was it Hammond," I asked, "in the infirmary?"

He did not answer for a minute. I knew that Fenton and Roy had led Brother Mike back to DI-6 and that Fenton had butchered the man within. But there was no official confirmation about the identity, no trail to anyone named Hammond, only my insistence, and no one had paid my claims any attention.

"I don't know," Brother Mike said finally. "Jon Crowley had convinced me that it was Hammond. I'm sorry I lied to you about that, but I couldn't tell you the truth. I feared what would happen to Hammond if anyone learned he was there. I was only able to visit the infirmary once, and I didn't recognize anything about him. It was awful what Fenton did to him. Like a cow being slaughtered."

I wanted to ask if they'd found an answer on the man, a tattoo or some indication of the bank account number they were looking for, but I didn't have the heart to press for details.

"I suppose it was the comic book Roy wanted all along," I said. "If they ever catch him, that's the one thing I'd like to ask."

He had escaped from the window of the examination room of a city hospital, a place they'd sent the inmates with the worst injuries. I was still struck by the absurdity of a one-legged man climbing a drainpipe from four stories up, catching a taxi, and getting away.

Brother Mike did not seem to hear me.

"I think I feel most betrayed by Jon," he said. "To know that the comic book wasn't an artistic retelling of Hammond's life. To find out there were symbols and messages encoded in the drawings. And to realize that he'd used me to get the details, that he'd gone through my files for those reasons and not the reasons I thought. I was a fool to believe him."

I stopped him.

"You don't know what Crowley was thinking, why he did what he did. Maybe it wasn't clear-cut either way. Some of it might have been about the money. Some of it might have been about Hammond. Crowley may not have been completely free to act or feel as he would have liked. Roy might have forced him. Or maybe you were conned. That's a very plausible explanation, and the simplest one now. But it's also possible that Crowley was more complicated. I'm not sure anymore that you can ever know another human being."

I was speaking from the residue of my own bitterness, and I was thinking about Ruddik and Wallace and the others, and the different prices that had been paid. The inquiry into the riot had begun with great intensity. There were questions about accounting irregularities at the prison, a whiff of corruption among some of the COs, rumors of a secretive group called the Ditmarsh Social Club, and an imperative to turn over every rock no matter what might be found. But with Droune's suicide and Wallace's resignation, the mood had changed, and the investigation petered out. Instead, the media attention focused on the ex-con who'd impersonated a local journalist to gain entry to Ditmarsh; on me, the brave ex-soldier who'd held off the rioting inmates until the troops arrived; and on Ruddik—the man no federal agency claimed. His former employers, a prison in Kentucky and another in Tennessee, both acknowledged that he'd quit before they'd finished enough paperwork to fire him. Another mystery, and more pain for my heart. I was as disoriented by the attention on my so-called heroics as I was of the scornful way they talked about Ruddik.

"There is something I need to tell you, Kali," Brother Mike said, interrupting my downward spiral. "It's about Keeper Wallace and Josh."

I waited. I did not want to talk about Josh. The connection I would never shake.

"About eight months ago I was approached by a lawyer who'd made a donation to my restorative justice fund. The lawyer wanted to know who, inside Ditmarsh, could do the most to help an inmate, named Josh Riff, about to be remanded to the prison."

It was all very distant to me. I listened and wondered what fork in the path of my life had been decided without my knowledge eight months earlier.

"When I found out the inmate in question was such a young man, sentenced for such a long time, I introduced the lawyer to Keeper Wallace, and that's where I left it. Last week Keeper Wallace called me and confessed. He told me that he'd agreed to provide special protection for Josh in exchange for money."

With the words, a tightness formed inside me.

"They knew the Keeper's daughter was in trouble, that she had no money, a criminal record, and three children. They offered to build her a house if the Keeper looked after Joshua."

Brother Mike stared into my eyes.

"The Keeper told me it was the first time he'd ever been tempted to take a dime. He'd believed no one would be hurt and his daughter and three grandchildren would be taken care of. He had a lot of guilt around his daughter. The only sacrifice would be to his own integrity, and Keeper Wallace, because of various personal failings in her upbringing, believed he owed her that. In particular, the middle grandson was starting to get into trouble and needed an improved environment."

I nodded. "So he housed Josh away from gen pop."

"He thought he could keep everything under control. Obviously he couldn't. When he found out that Josh's father was dying of cancer, the Keeper realized he'd made a terrible mistake. Not because he might get caught, but because he'd taken advantage. He asked me to tell you what really happened and why."

It was difficult for me to hear. I no longer wanted to learn the details of the way Keeper Wallace had compromised himself, even if I could understand the human need behind it. Maybe, when I felt on more solid ground, I would be grateful to know that mere money had not been the basis for it all. But another pain slipped in as I sat there in Brother Mike's room. The pain that Josh had felt over his own father, and the distance between them.

"He did it out of love," I said.

Brother Mike nodded. But I don't think he understood. I meant that Josh's father loved him, and had known he was going to die, and that was why he'd bribed the Keeper. He wanted to do what he could to look out for Josh on the long road ahead of him. Out of all the mysteries that still lapped at me, that was the only certain thing I understood. He did it out of love.

"The Keeper is sorry," Brother Mike said, "that whatever he did to get you involved in this led to everything that happened to you. He wanted you to know that you deserved better."

It was my turn to stare. "You can tell him I'm going to be okay."

All the time, however, I was thinking about love. Distorted, complicated, even misguided love. I thought about the thin, tepid love I felt for my father. And the guilt-ridden love Wallace had for his daughter. And the mute and inexplicable way Josh's father had shown his love for his son. Was there any other force in the universe so strong? The absence of love. The hurt from love. The insecurity of love. The making up for love that had been imperfectly expressed. I had this insight, tickling the edges of my mind, that love caused all the pain in the world, was the source of all the hurt. I was in awe of the mystery of human compassion and the inability of love to make the distance between us any more bearable.

Brother Mike nodded as if I'd said the words aloud, and we sat quietly, drinking our tea.

ACKNOWLEDGMENTS |||||

This novel could not have been written without Chris Richardson, whose insights and experiences were essential to "getting it right" and whose instinct for story and character was only matched by his willingness to read every line many times. Beth Hollihan was also invaluable for relaying the perspective of a female law enforcement officer, and for opening important doors. A number of other law enforcement professionals involved in corrections work and criminal investigations were generous with their time, stories, and answers, as well as in the trust they showed me despite the natural caution engendered by a dangerous workplace. I'd also like to thank the friends and strangers who offered suggestions, access, and support. In particular, I am grateful to Mike Lambrecht, Robert Syliboy, Jeff McCann, Henry Tenny, Kory Beaton, Bix Skahill, Reema Abdo, Clea Felien, Janna Rademacher, Charlie Williams, David Richardson, James Ellroy, and Bruce Tapola. Karen Stephenson's network theory was applied in an unusual setting, and Siegfried Janzen's work in restorative justice hopefully echoes within. Two others were vital in making the book a reality. My agent, Helen Heller, was instrumental with her unconditional confidence and expert guidance, and knew when a vigorous baseball conversation was exactly the right thing. Peter Joseph at St. Martin's/Thomas Dunne Books championed the book and made it better with his creativity, enthusiasm, and commitment. Finally, my wife, Rosemary Williams, has been my creative partner every step of the way.